Anonymous

A Typical American

Or, incidents in the life of Dr. John Swinburne, of Albany, the eminent patriot, surgeon, and philanthropist

Anonymous

A Typical American
Or, incidents in the life of Dr. John Swinburne, of Albany, the eminent patriot, surgeon, and philanthropist

ISBN/EAN: 9783337304249

Printed in Europe, USA, Canada, Australia, Japan

Cover: Foto ©Raphael Reischuk / pixelio.de

More available books at **www.hansebooks.com**

A TYPICAL AMERICAN;

OR,

INCIDENTS IN THE LIFE OF DR. JOHN SWINBURNE

OF ALBANY,

THE EMINENT PATRIOT, SURGEON, AND PHILANTHROPIST.

COMPILED AND PUBLISHED BY

THE CITIZENS' ASSOCIATION.

———————

ALBANY, N.Y.:

ISSUED FROM THE CITIZEN OFFICE.

1888.

INTRODUCTION.

In presenting this sketch of the life of one of the most remarkable men of the period, — one in whom the people of Albany take the deepest interest; who is esteemed by all classes, particularly by the men who were found at the front during the Rebellion; and who, by his many kind acts to the poor, has endeared himself to them beyond all other men, — the citizens have no further apology than a desire to have the people at large know him as they know him.

To him is given the strange title of " The Fighting Doctor," because of his many contests with error in every walk of life. These conflicts have all been in the interests of the people, — as a volunteer during the Rebellion; in professional struggles to overcome malpractice and deformity in treating the sick and maimed; and in private and political life to secure better government, and overcome corrupt political cabals.

Aggressive yet tender and kind, he possesses all the characteristics of a true man, combined with a skill that places him at the head of his profession; self-made, he thoroughly understands the wants of the people; and possessed of a spirit of fearless independence, he has been by nature and circumstances well fitted to espouse the cause of the people at large without distinction of class.

From the days of boyhood, when deprived of a paternal guide and director, up to the present time, his life has been a remarkable one, full of thrilling adventures and unprecedented achievements. Rising by his own efforts from obscurity to eminence, and from poverty to plenty, his life has been eminently that of a typical American.

Every chapter in this life is a history of itself, and will be read with interest. In compiling it, the work has been somewhat difficult, because the doctor has never kept any scrapbook, either of the contributions he has made to science, or of the many good things others have said of him. We have therefore been compelled to resort to public documents on file in the State and other public departments; to the libraries; to the press, as far as these could be reached conveniently; and to correspondence with those who knew him in the various walks of life. The doctor having but little to say of himself with reference to his life and doings, we have been enabled to learn comparatively little from him to assist in the work.

In accordance with a resolution of the association, this work is respectfully presented to the public, believing that it will entertain and inspire a desire in others to emulate his example, however humble their position in life may be, as well as to make the people at large better acquainted with our brave, skilful, and humane fellow-citizen.

CONTENTS.

 CONTENTS.

CHAPTER X.

CHAPTER XI.

CHAPTER XII.

CHAPTER XIII.

CHAPTER XIV.

CHAPTER XV.

CHAPTER XVI.

CHAPTER XVII.

CHAPTER XVIII.

CHAPTER XIX.

CHAPTER XX.

CHAPTER XXI.

A TYPICAL AMERICAN.

CHAPTER I.

ONE OF NATURE'S NOBLEMEN.

Envious Rivals. — Brave and Philanthropic. — Sacrificing Comfort for Patriotism. — A Busy Life. — Thrilling Adventures. — Self-made.

" To be as busy as a Wallach woman, and do as little," was an old saying among the German settlers of Roumania; and the excuse given by the males for having wives was " to comb and keep them clean," as the men were a dirty, indolent, and cowardly set, except in the commission of such crimes as plundering, horse-stealing, and smuggling. For every neglect to live and act as human beings, they had an excuse. When the month of May arrived, — the proper season for planting, — they wasted an entire week in unmitigated idleness, under the supposition that their fruits would thereby be protected from the late frosts. These laggard husbands, however, were anxious that their wives should be always busy, and often frightened them into greater diligence by pretending that a fairy visits every house early on the morning of Holy Thursday, and inflicts on them some dreadful affliction if all be not found in order. Among more civilized people, and particularly with this nation, there are those who possess the same characteristics as the Wallachs, always ready with an excuse for not answering promptly the calls of duty as patriots, citizens, or humanitarians. Such men are the most anxious to disparage the works of others, and would, if they could, bury far from the sight of the world every record of heroism of their day, and blot from the pages of history those ennobling acts in the lives of fellow-beings that will live in memory long after their cowardly and selfish lives have been forgotten. Yet, to the credit of this comparatively young nation, this class of envious persons is small, compared to the great whole, and of a much smaller ratio than might be looked for among the heterogeneous mass from all nationalities, who make up the great American nation, and constitute a people whose bravery and humanity outstrips any records of ancient or modern times. It is the acts of individuals that make history for the future, as their deeds operate for good or evil in their day and generation; and truly the history of this nation is brilliant. as it is being written, with national acts of greatness, and individual deeds of daring and philanthropy, that obscure the most brilliant doings of the more ancient Spartan, or the chivalric deeds of the historian.

In the bustle and excitement of our progressive life in America, we are too prone to overlook the deeds of men while they are living, and await, because of ambitious jealousy for place and preferment, to render just tribute to the deserving, until the hand of death has laid cold the man the people should honor. When they have passed where earthly honors and mortal eulogies are as empty sounds to the departed, over their biers are pronounced the praises that should have been sounded in their ears while the senses were yet quickened to receive the grateful tributes. Not a month passes but history is repeating itself in giving to the world the sad tidings that some truly great man has passed away; and for a time the poisoned pen of partisanship is laid aside, and, the better nature prevailing in the presence of the dark spectre, a meed of praise is bestowed. But, alas! the just tribute to a worthy name is often too late, and only inspires the thought that merit has no rewards for the living to compensate for the sacrifices made.

When another century has passed away in the life of the American Republic, what an array of valiant men will be found to have lived and acted prominent parts in the great free government on this continent! Every page of history will sparkle with the names of men whose brilliant acts will shine out as startling constellations in the darkness of the struggles through which the country passed. Ever since the Indian war in 1675, that devastated New England, when Capt. Church of Massachusetts, and Capt. Dennison of Connecticut, became celebrated for their heroic ardor and fortitude, the list has constantly increased; and the acts of daring and self-denial have become grander as civilization has progressed, until in every emergency, in war and in peace, even the humblest citizens are performing acts that in other days would have caused them to be crowned with wreaths of glory.

The peculiar and striking bravery of the truly American is inspired only by that intelligence which assures him he is right, and to the commission of deeds which his conscience directs and approves, as the love of freedom animated to deeds of heroism the band of men under Gen. Putnam at Long Island, who fought with such bravery, with Gen. Clinton attacking them in the rear, and the Hessians in the front, when they believed neither valor nor skill could save them from defeat.

With us we have still living in active life, in the State of New York, one whose name will be in the future familiar among the votaries of science and the lovers of patriotism, and whose discoveries in the profession of his choice have already almost revolutionized the practice of surgery, and whose genius and skill will be honored by his profession for ages. His acts of intrepid bravery on the field of battle, his sympathy and care for the sick and wounded, his deeds of charity and benevolence among the poor, will be as familiar in the future as Ethan Allen's demand for the surrender of Ticonderoga is now, and his philanthropy will be as immortal as the poet has made Paul Revere's ride to Lexington from Boston.

Brave as a Wellington, yet tender as a woman; eminent as a surgeon and physician, yet plain as a man; polished and learned as a gentleman, yet humble as a peasant; a hater of fraud, chicanery, and dishonesty, yet jealous of no man; constantly moving about among the people, looking only to their interests, sacrificing time and money to make the condition of the masses better; supplying with a liberal

hand the wants of the poor, caring for their sick and unfortunate; fighting error and corruption wherever he finds them,
either in his profession or in government; and sacrificing
all personal comfort for the good of others, — is the man
to whom we would lead public thought, knowing that the
American people love the brave and humane, and only require to be reminded, to awaken to the according of deserved
honors.

The truly American, Dr. John Swinburne, has a life which
has no parallel or precedent in the combining of so many
distinguished qualities in any one man, and is a prototype for
others to emulate. As a patriot, the relinquishing of a very
lucrative practice, second to no other physician in Albany
County, and going to the front during the Rebellion as a volunteer surgeon without pay, was a sublime act, and endeared
him to the hearts of his countrymen; and his acts of bravery
while there, have entered his name among the multitude of
heroes of that period. His constant care of the sick and
wounded on the fields of battle, and his never-ceasing efforts
to have them comfortable, has made him an object of honor,
and almost reverence, among the hundreds of his brave comrades who felt his tender touch, or heard his kind words of
sympathy, while they lay in pain and agony. His eminent
ability as a surgeon, and his constant endeavor to cure the
injured and save the parts wounded; his aversion to the common practice of cutting and amputating; and his firm opposition to having the noble fellows, wounded for their country,
made subjects for experiments in cutting and amputating, —
won for him the gratitude of thousands whose limbs were
not sacrificed, but saved to them, as well as the respect and
esteem of all humane and honest surgeons, and caused him
to be hated and envied by the ignorant charlatans who practised human butchery and malpractice.

There is something phenomenally grand in the active, self-
denying, and busy life of Dr. John Swinburne as a surgeon
in the field of battle; as a health-officer, contending with the
terrible diseases of cholera, small-pox, and yellow-fever,
saving the people from their destructive ravages for years,

and finding the means not only to check but to suppress these diseases; as a philanthropist, establishing sanitariums, hospitals, and dispensaries for the care and treatment of the poor; and the introduction of a conservative system of surgery that saved rather than destroyed, and the application and use of remedies that are comparatively costless, instead of the high-priced drugs and minerals usually prescribed in treating the sick. His quiet benevolence, and yet bold aggressiveness in fighting error and corruption in high places, both in professional and official stations, has given his life a charm unequalled in the past, and has won for him the unyielding love of the masses of the people. To these are added other events that render his career one of thrilling adventures and bold aggressiveness, that intensifies the charm, and holds the strongest admiration. As a medical expert on the stand, surprising the courts by his bold statements, arousing the opposition of almost the entire profession of the State, and finally satisfying the courts that he was right, proving his grounds as the only correct ones, and completely silencing his opponents, were remarkable victories, and have established him as the most reliable of medical experts, with whom others do not desire to cross professional swords. In a besieged city, where the shot and shell were falling fast, and riot was rampant on the streets, he was there cool, and, from the promptings of humanity, devoting his skill to the care of the wounded without money and without price, and winning in that foreign nation the highest position in his profession, — a place accredited him by all the nations of Europe.

Like the other eminent names which grace our history, starting to work out their destinies from the tailor and shoemaker's shop, from the tanyard and wood-chopping, and ending with the presidency and vice-presidency, this man, from sleeping on the floor and living on seventy-five cents a week while a student, who has attained the highest pinnacle in his profession, is an eminently typical American.

In his address to the jury in the celebrated murder-trial in Albany in 1853, of John Hendrickson, jun., for causing the death of his wife by the administering of tincture of aconite,

a vegetable poison, the Hon. L. S. Chatfield, attorney-general,
said of Dr. Swinburne : —

"Who is John Swinburne? John Swinburne, with that
frankness characteristic of the man, — sunny frankness that
knows no guile, — he comes here and tells you he is a native of
Lewis County. He was of humble parentage, and, like other
poor boys, I suppose he had to work to acquire the means to
further him in knowledge. He finally is found in the Lewis
Academy, thence he went to Fairfield, and from thence he
comes to this city. At the medical college here, he acts for
two years as demonstrator; since when he has had a private
dissecting-room, and has probably made more *post-mortem*
examinations than any man in the State.

" John Swinburne was not put on that stand because he
had a diploma in his pocket, nor because he had been born
with a silver spoon in his mouth, and been reared in the lap
of luxury. We placed him there because we knew him to
be an intelligent, scientific, and honest man ; because we knew
that he would give us truth, which we were seeking for.

" I have yet to learn that colleges, or college honors, make
the man. Wherever you find distinguished talent, in whatever profession you find mind leading in the race of popularity and distinction, in whatever walk of life you find
prominence and true superiority leading to honor and respect,
you will find that zeal, courage, virtue, industry, indomitable
will, and untiring perseverance, underlie it all. These men,
cast in Nature's noblest mould, are learned and intelligent
in spite of colleges; and in our land nineteen out of every
twenty of the men who have deservedly received honors
from the hands of their fellow-citizens have fought their way
to their exalted position from the humblest walks of life.
They have conquered disadvantages which would have appalled the softer-natured collegiate, and, thirsting after true
and useful knowledge, have attained it because it was attain-
able to the intelligent, the industrious, and the good.

" If I were to look for the intelligence of the land, I would
look to what is termed the middling classes : for it is there we
find sound, practical sense; it is there we find incorruptibility;
and it is there we find those qualities of head and heart
which endear man to his fellows. It is there, also, that we find
that patriotism which protects the interests and institutions
of our country. It is to that class John Swinburne belongs.
He does not come here resting on a diploma, but he comes
here with a pure heart, a clear head, and a richly stored mind.

"The community will cherish such men as he; and I here tell the gentleman that the name of John Swinburne will live long after his bones have mouldered in the dust. Confident in his integrity, his intelligence, I am willing to bring John Swinburne here, and I am willing to rest this case on his credibility; and I wish we had more men of as clear heads and pure hearts as he, instead of the scores of charlatans and quacks who can use muriatic acid for a tooth-wash."

CHAPTER II.

A Volunteer Surgeon. — A Turkish Tradition. — Among the Wounded in the
Rebellion. — A Carnival of Death. — Medical Superintendent of Wounded
New-York Troops in Full Command. — A Hard Road to Travel. — Official
and Press Eulogies.

DURING the trying days of 1861, when the arsenals and
factories were busy moulding the weapons of death; when
the steady tramp of armies of valiant men in blue were
marching from every section of the North, East, and West,
to the sound of martial music, with a tread that shook the
nation from centre to circumference; when loved ones were
taking their farewells, perhaps forever, and the nation was
in the throes of a terrible and wicked revolution that
threatened the destruction of the grand republic of the
free, so much patriotic blood had been spilt and hardships
endured to establish and perpetuate, — Dr. Swinburne was
living in Albany, enjoying the largest professional practice in
the city. When the first struggles took place between the
loyal and rebel forces, he entertained the hope thousands of
others in the North indulged, — that the conflict, though it
might be a sanguinary one, would be of but short duration,
and that the foolish leaders of the Rebellion would recover
from their delusion, and, renouncing treason, return to loyalty
and peace. As the months wore on, and the spirit of rebellion intensified, he realized that the end was not yet, and gradually arranged his business that he might go where he could
do the most service to his God, humanity, and his country,
and to this end tendered his services, without pecuniary compensation, to Gov. Morgan, as a volunteer surgeon. The
governor, knowing the abilities of the surgeon and physician,

and the pressing need there was at the front for one so skilled, promptly accepted the voluntary offering for his State and country; and, despite the earnest solicitations of the doctor's friends and patients, he was duly commissioned on April 7, 1862, a volunteer surgeon to care for the sick and wounded troops belonging to New-York State, and immediately left for the peninsula. Since that time, up to the present, the life of this remarkable man has been a continuous chapter of surprising personal achievements in military, scientific, and civil life, affording realities stranger than fiction in the active performances of a man impelled to exercise the gifts that God had endowed him with for the good of others.

From the breaking-out of the Rebellion, up to the date of his commission, he had not been a passive looker-on in the first stages of the terribly wicked and cruel drama, nor a drone in the hive of loyalty's busy defenders. At the very opening of the first tragic scene in the conflict, he was made chief medical officer on the staff by Gen. John F. Rathbone, and placed in charge of the sick in the Albany (N.Y.) depot for recruits, where, according to the report transmitted to Gov. Morgan by the then State surgeon-general, Dr. S. Oakley Vanderpoel, the result showed the wisdom of the appointment. The surgeon-general stated in that report, " Dr. Swinburne not only gave the sick soldiers his whole time and attention when needful, but, when it became necessary to put some seventy patients in another building, the same care and supervision were exercised." He further added, " The abstract accompanying this report is the best commentary of the fidelity and skill exercised by himself and his assistants," and then announced that up to that date, Dec. 13, 1861, " about three months, the whole number of cases treated by Dr. Swinburne during the period of his administration was fourteen hundred and twenty-seven, and the deaths only twelve."

It will seem scarcely reasonable that one who, because of his prominence in his profession, held such a position as surgeon-general of the State of New York, would, after inditing such an official commendation, and others equally laudatory, to which further reference will be made, because of professional jealousy, plot to undermine and destroy the reputation of the man he so praised. Yet it is true that in the hours of peace the mask of friendship was thrown off, and Dr. Vanderpoel became one of the chief actors in an ignoble and bitter but futile effort to destroy the fame of the eminent physician and surgeon, because he would not aid and abet error, nor cover up the professional and public shortcomings and lack of integrity, of this man and some of his associates.

The reader will pardon this digression, but will, by events that follow, see the connection in what occurred after Dr. Swinburne's military career, his success for years in fighting disease, and establishing as health-officer of the port of New York the best system of quarantine in the world, and winning a fame abroad such as was never bestowed on an American surgeon. These successes aroused the envy and hatred of some professional men who stood at the bottom of the ladder of fame, without any ability to mount it, much less to reach the eminence Dr. Swinburne had succeeded in reaching, and recalls the Turkish tradition of Moses and the Israelites. The story goes, "that while the Israelites were marching to the conquest of the Promised Land, Moses, desirous of contemplating the wondrous works of God, set out to travel. He voyaged for thirty years in the east and west, in the north and south. After many wanderings in distant countries, the patriarch returned to his tribe; but, instead of being received as the wisest man and the first of legislators, he saw his fame as a prophet and a traveller eclipsed by the gold of a banker. During his absence, there had risen up a man among the Israelites, — a man who had never ventured near the flames of Sinai, and had not the least admiration for the wonderful works of creation, but who had spent his days in ingenious speculation among the money-changers of the wandering children of Israel. Despising in his wealth the poor man, who returned from his travels, he would not recognize him as the lawgiver of Israel. In order to make him contemptible in the opinion of those who still retained feelings of respect and gratitude for the ancient leader, he instituted a process of law against him, and suborned false witnesses. But these witnesses were stung in their consciences before the tribunal, and proclaimed the truth, and Moses triumphed. The people again received him for their leader, while the earth opened and swallowed up the banker with all his wealth." The tradition is in many points analogous with the treatment of Dr. Swinburne by the "tribe" (one of whom had acquired wealth by what was considered questionable means) who controlled the Albany Medical College and some of the hospitals at that time, in that most, if not all, of them are without honorable fame or preferment now, while he is the most popular man in the State, as proven in the overwhelming majority with which the county of Albany has made him its "lawgiver" in the National Congress, and in having twice elected him mayor of the capital city of the Empire State.

But to return to the story of his achievements in the fields of carnage and war. The commission given him by Gov. Morgan as a volunteer surgeon was applied for that he might have a broader field in which to exercise his universally conceded superior skill, and transferred him to a point where these qualities were eminently and urgently needed; and afforded opportunities to gratify his ambition to do much for his country, and won for him plaudits and honor few men acquired during his term of service. As an auxiliary volunteer surgeon, he reached the headquarters of Dr. Tripler, medical director of the Army of the Potomac, at the White House, on the Pamunkey River, Virginia, on the 18th of May, 1862, and was by that officer assigned to the establishment of a hospital at that point.

A letter in the "Albany Evening Times," dated White House, June 10, 1862, will give some idea of what the surgeons had to contend with at that place, and the inadequate provisions made to care for the sick and wounded, — an emergency almost entirely neglected. Dr. Swinburne, with Drs. Willard and Lansing of New York, and Hall and Page of Boston, were assigned to the establishing of a hospital there, where they succeeded, after one week, in erecting wall-tents sufficient to hold from twelve hundred to fifteen hundred patients. When they commenced their work, there were only a few tents up, while patients were pouring in at the rate of from one hundred to one hundred and fifty a day. Indeed, there were nearly three hundred sick and wounded under the trees at the time, awaiting admission to a hospital, and a severe rain-storm approaching. Shelter was soon provided. The next consideration was something to keep them from the ground, in the form of beds. Straw arrived, but it was found to be wet from the insufficient housing, like all Virginia economy; but by means of India-rubber and boards they succeeded very well in keeping dry. The next day Dr. Baxter, brigade surgeon, sent in his private stock of hay (about four thousand pounds), and distributed it through the tents, in lieu of wet straw; and thereby the patients were made very comfortable. The next thing to be attended to was food for these hundreds of sick. Now came the rub. It was not intended to make this point a hospital of any size, and hence no provision had been made for such an influx of patients; but the unhealthiness of the peninsula about York-town, Williamsburg, West Point, and other places, added to the almost constant exposure which our men endured, rendered them victims to malarious disease. What was to be done? No fresh meat; no kettles to cook it in if they had it; and no water, except what was brought in pails from springs a half-mile off.

"I firmly believe [Dr. Swinburne wrote at that time] that more men will die who go home in this condition (remittent and typhoid fevers), from the insufficient knowledge of the physicians to whose care they are intrusted, of the character of this disease and the requisite for its removal, on the one hand, and, on the other, from the injury accruing from moving them in their feeble state, coupled with the closeness of the vessels in which they are transferred. Besides, during the stages of convalescence, the habit of lounging and drinking, to which they are inclined, adds very materially to the danger of collapse. On the contrary, if they are kept in open hospitals, like storehouses or wall-tents, and are supplied with proper nourishment, stimulants, medicines, etc., the mortality of those received before the stage of complete cerebral exhaustion would be very small,—not more than one or two per cent,—while many of them who had arrived at this stage of exhaustion could be saved. Nearly all the latter die (if moved to hospital ships) from syncope. I think the removal in this enfeebled condition is all wrong; and, under any circumstances, it would be far better, both for the troops and the government, to build large storehouses, sufficiently wide for two rows of beds and a spacious walk in the centre of the room for the nurses and surgeons; the rooms to be at least twelve feet between joints, the roof built after the old Dutch peak style. This structure could be built a few feet from the ground, and grating made in the floor all along the line of the middle of the building and between the beds. The expense of this class of buildings would be very small where fine pine is so cheap. In this kind of hospital, with proper sanitary arrangements, medical attendance, etc., the mortality would be very small, while to the government millions of dollars would be saved. Out of three thousand sick I have seen, more than one-half are simply exhausted from sudden changes of heat and cold, long marches, wet, etc., and only require rest and appropriate food."

The hospitals established at White House were in readiness none too soon. Hardly had the last peg been driven, and the anxiety of the surgeons been set at rest as to shelter and food, when the terrible battle of Fair Oaks sent them plenty of employment to occupy their minds and hands. On Saturday night the brave boys began to come in in greater numbers, weary and wounded in every conceivable manner, shattered by shot and shell as only brave men could be, and bearing their terrible pains with a sublime heroism which cowards know not of. By those who were on the ground, it is reported that Dr. Swinburne worked from four o'clock in the morning until midnight, and was again at work the next morning at daylight.

Into this carnival of death and destruction he had voluntarily entered; and those who were so unfortunate as to be wounded, and yet so fortunate as to fall under his care, say his pleasant words of greeting and encouragement, with no dismal forebodings and no sign of discouragement on his countenance, encouraged many a brave fellow to struggle through who would otherwise have given up and died. He believed, and infused the feeling into others, "that he who laughed most was surest to recover." With a heart as sympathetic as a child, and with a nerve only an approving conscience could insure, he moved from one to another in his humane work, encouraging all, and deceiving none.

After the completion of his work at White House, he returned to Albany on the 12th of June, 1862, the city papers announcing his arrival; the "Albany Evening Journal" adding "that he was anxious to return to the hospitals, but urgent calls at home might prevent his return." How little even his journalistic friends had divined the nature of this noble man, was apparent when they thought that there was any business of so important a nature that he could consider it of more importance than the demands of his country and its brave defenders, as was shown in an announcement in the same journal only two days afterwards.

Again he was commissioned by Gov. Morgan, not as an auxiliary surgeon, as before, but as medical superintendent of the wounded New-York troops; and on the 14th of June, two days after announcing his arrival, the "Journal" said,—

"Dr. Swinburne left this city last evening for Yorktown, to assist in attending upon the sick and wounded soldiers. The doctor came home much displeased at the manner in which our disabled soldiers were treated, and, obtaining letters here to the heads of departments such as he desired, started off immediately, hoping to remedy the existing evils. That the doctor will succeed, is beyond a question; and that he will ultimately carry out his plans, there can be no doubt."

These letters referred to were the commission as medical superintendent of the wounded New-York troops, and a letter of recommendation and indorsement from Gov. Morgan to Secretary of War Stanton. Equipped with these, he started for Washington, where the secretary indorsed the letter to United-States Surgeon-Gen. Hammond. That official promptly entered into an agreement with Dr. Swinburne for "medical and surgical services to be rendered in connection with the Army of the Potomac."

In the letter to the secretary of war, Gov. Morgan said, —

" No surgeon in the State enjoys a more deserved reputation than he ; and, from his urbanity and uniform courtesy, I am sure that no misunderstanding can occur between the United-States authorities and himself."

On his arrival at Fortress Monroe, he was requested by the medical director to take charge of the hospital at Newport News, — a proposition he declined on the ground that lively times were soon to take place on the peninsula, as the army drew nearer to the rebel capital, and that his desire was to be as near the front and the heat of battle as possible, where he would be able to effect the most good for the greatest number of sick and wounded; that the demands and dangers were the incentives to make him the more anxious to be with the advance, as there was where his services would be in greatest demand.

Dr. Swinburne had scarcely entered upon his duties, when he received a signal mark of distinction from the commander-in-chief, Gen. McClellan, who ordered him to repair to Savage Station, which was to be an important point in the approaching conflicts, and to establish there a depot for the wounded, giving him full powers for the carrying-on of his department, and full command over all the forces in that section so far as pertained to a surgeon in charge of the sick and wounded.   He also issued the following order : —

HEADQUARTERS ARMY OF THE POTOMAC,
CAMP LINCOLN, VA., June 20, 1862.

SPECIAL ORDER No. 186.

Thirteen men of the Second Army Corps, ten from the Fourth Army Corps, and fourteen from the provisional army corps, will be detailed by the corps commanders to report to Acting Assistant Surgeon John Swinburne for duty at the hospital at Savage Station.

On the requisition of Acting Assistant Surgeon John Swinburne, in charge of the hospital at Savage Station, the subsistence department will issue such rations, and the quartermaster's department will furnish such transportation, as may be required for that hospital.

By command

Major-Gen McCLELLAN.

S. Williams, *Assistant Adjutant-General.*

In connection with the establishing of the hospital at this point, one of the incidents illustrating his foresight was shown. In company with Gen. McClellan and Medical Director Tripler, he was at Savage Station, and said to the general, "You must have a depot here for the wounded." — "How do you know?" asked the general. "Well," said the doctor, "you cannot go to Richmond without a battle here; if you are victorious you will want a hospital here, and if you are defeated you must leave your wounded behind." The general answered, "You are not supposed to know any thing about such matters." — "Perhaps not," said the doctor, "in military parlance; but I know, nevertheless." Soon after this conversation, the general carried out the suggestion. and issued the order.

At the time this order was given, it was believed the year would be pregnant with the fate of the Republic, as the premonitions were that events were approaching a decisive termination. McClellan's preparations around Yorktown, and for the advance on Richmond, were about completed; and the imagination started back appalled, at the vision of slaughtered heaps, and garments rolled in blood, that rose in the future. The government, the officers in command on the field, the army, and the people, believed that in the few coming weeks the Army of the Potomac would pass through a terrible ordeal of war, and that the entire peninsula from Yorktown to Richmond would be a succession of desperate struggles, carnage and death. Both armies were in excellent condition, and anxious for the hoped-for final struggle, which the whole North and the army believed was to end in the fall of the rebel capital, the overthrow of treason, and the hasty and permanent suppression of the Rebellion, — a consummation every royal heart prayed the God of battles would hasten, and which every traitor in the North feared, but hoped would not come about.

No man in the army or in civil life realized more keenly the terrible tide of fire through which all the actors in this field were to pass, than did Dr. Swinburne, unless it may have been the commanding general, George B. McClellan, himself. That in no arm of the service was true patriotism, bravery, and courage more requisite than in the medical and surgical department, was well understood by the general. If the army was victorious, the wounded must often be left with the surgeons in the rear, subject to be harassed and besieged by enemies and adventurers. If it met with defeat, they would, in all probability, fall into the hands of the enemy. As near to the front and the field of battle as possible, the surgeon was wanted. In selecting for the supervision of this important duty on that anticipated and inevitable field of slaughter, the general had reason to place in Dr. John Swinburne the utmost confidence as to his patriotism, bravery, and skill. The doctor knew the dangers and duties of the position; but he was there from his love of country and humanity, and like many of his comrades, while realizing the dangers, never thought of shirking duty, but determined to offer his life as a sacrifice, if it were requisite. Events that followed proved his devotion and bravery, when to be brave was to ignore self for others, and demonstrated the wisdom of the general in his selection.

From the evacuation, by the rebels, of Yorktown on May 3, to the retreat of the Union forces from Savage Station on June 29, the army had passed through a baptism of blood, brilliant victories, and shattered hopes. During so brief a period the annals of history show no record of greater achievements and personal acts of heroism than were there performed by our brave fellows, and none greater in self-denial and fearlessness of danger than that exhibited by the noble surgeon whose profession, and part in the conflict, was not to destroy life or limb, and make widows, but to save the one, and prevent the other. The order was, "On to Richmond," and, as the Union chain was being drawn closer and closer around the Rebel capital, the times became more trying. Flushed with victory at Yorktown, and the rout of the enemy at Hanover Court-House, our gallant army swept onward. These were as a prelude to one of the most desperate battles so far fought on the peninsula, that of Fair Oaks, when the Rebel army, led by Hill and Longstreet, dashed down on our lines, determined, apparently, to annihilate our whole army. The mantle of darkness fell that Saturday night, as a funeral shroud, on a ghastly spectacle of the slain, who lay in heaps; and, as a requiem over these dead, the breezes were laden with the moans of wounded on their gory bed, presenting a scene of which those who were not there, or remained in the quietude where war did not rage, can never dream, much less realize. The following Sunday, June 1, presented a spectacle over which angels might weep, when over ten thousand men lay, by the cruel fates of war, among the dead and wounded, but over which the heart of the army bounded with joy, as these sad tokens were the proofs of a terrible conflict, and a glorious victory for our forces. There was no rest for the doctor that Sunday.

The New-York troops who were in the brigades of Heintzelman, Kearney, Sickles, Meagher, Meade, Hooker, Sumner, Franklin, and French, through these days of fire on the Chickahominy up to the seven-days' fight and battle of Savage Station, — where Dr. Swinburne, in the heroic discharge of his duty, became a voluntary prisoner of war rather than desert the wounded patriots in his charge, — will never forget their comrades, or withhold from them the honor and praise they have earned.

They owe to posterity and to the memory of the brave dead, that they should not take council from the "Albany Argus," — a journal which, at the very time they were sleeping in the swamps and miasma around Richmond, declared the "war a failure," — and disband their Grand Army posts, but ever keep alive, and kindle anew, the memories of the heroism of the days of the '60's; and, in bearing their scars as a proud heritage to their offspring, many of them will remember the surgeon who volunteered first his services, and then his liberty, and at the time possibly his life, for the benefit of the sick, wounded, and dying boys in blue.

Testimonials of appreciation of his services in military life were showered on him not only by the press of the city of Albany, which took a natural local pride in his eminent services, but by the press of the country, the officials at the head of the National Government, and from those high in authority in the State Government.

Soon after his arrival at Savage Station, he received the following official letter from headquarters •in the State of New York: —

STATE OF NEW YORK, SURGEON-GENERAL'S OFFICE,
ALBANY, June 25, 1862.

DEAR DOCTOR, — Your letters from Washington and Savage Station were both duly received, and read to the governor. He is very much gratified with the success you have met, and feels assured great good will result from your mission. I really wish you God speed and success. I assure you, your great labors are appreciated by your friends, and we all feel you are in a field where the greatest good will be accomplished.

Truly yours,

S. OAKLEY VANDERPOEL,
JOHN SWINBURNE.   *Surgeon-General.*

This, coming from the head of the medical department in the State of New York, was a grateful tribute, well earned, and but faintly reflected the feelings of the hearts of the people who knew the recipient. It was, however, but a snow-flake in the shower of compliments bestowed on him by press correspondents, historians, medical men, and others, who were eye-witnesses of his devotion and bravery before and after he was taken prisoner.

A correspondent of the " New-York Tribune," writing from Mechanicsville under date of June 23, said, —

" Dr. John Swinburne of Albany has recently been appointed acting assistant surgeon-general, and has been assigned to take charge of the hospital for wounded soldiers at Savage Station. Since yesterday he has caused to be put up tents to accommodate six hundred patients. Every thing necessary for the wounded has been provided. During the week, additional accommodations for over two thousand men will be provided; so that the wounded will not be compelled to be out under the scorching sun by day, and the cold and heavy dew by night, as was the case at the recent battle of Seven Pines or Fair Oaks."

The Rev. James J. Marks, a volunteer chaplain to a Pennsylvania regiment, who, true to his mission, remained with Dr. Swinburne at Savage Station, caring for the sick and wounded, and was taken prisoner, said in the preface to his work entitled "The Peninsular Campaign, or Incidents and Scenes on the Battle-Fields and in Richmond," —

"This work is given to the public with many misgivings; for it has been prepared by camp-fires, in the midst of hospital labors, and on marches on the Rappahannock, in the mountains of Virginia, and under the pressure of exhausting hospital duties. In the haste of such compilation, I may have made criticisms too sweeping and seemingly too severe, as is intimated by my excellent friend, Dr. Swinburne; but let it be remembered that no man's vices in the army are pushed into such an odious and unendurable prominence as those of a self-indulgent, intemperate, and heartless surgeon. No one endures more and perils more than the faithful surgeon."

In giving an account of the scenes of the seven-days' battles, or the second battle of Fair Oaks, which commenced on the 25th of June by the advance of Gen. Heintzelman's brigade, he says, —

"The picture of the friendly interchange of papers and tobacco between the men of the two armies was changed to one of hatred, blood, and carnage. The opening of the slaughter was made by the advance of Gen. Hooker; the attacking column consisting of Grover's, Sickle's, and Robinson's brigades, with Gen. Kearney protecting the left, and Col. Hicks, with the Nineteenth Massachusetts, on the right. Slowly and steadily the brigades advanced, the occasional shots of the advancing skirmishers changing to an incessant fusilade of infantry and the booming of cannon; and shortly after, the clouds hung heavy with smoke, and streams of fire, and the whole line was engaged in the struggle of war."

In speaking of a number of surgeons who at the battle of Fair Oaks had distinguished themselves by surgical operations, among whom were Drs. Page and Hall of Boston, Bliss of Michigan, and Swinburne of Albany, Dr. Marks said, —

"The latter gentleman had been sent to the army by Gov. Morgan of New York to minister relief to the wounded soldiers of that State, and to give them the benefit of his eminent surgical abilities. To a most unflinching hand he added the gentlest heart, always sparing when there was the least hope for a shattered limb, and by a thousand acts of kindness endearing himself to a multitude of sufferers."

All correspondents at the front agree in their testimony that this volunteer surgeon from New York, who was there without any pecuniary compensation, and who has never solicited or received one dollar for his eminent services, was not satisfied with the simple dressing of wounds, but, over the unfortunate sick and disabled, exercised a mother's watchfulness and care, always aiming to secure for them all the comforts of life it was possible to secure. Unlike too many of the paid and heartless surgeons, he did not wait for the arrival of the unfortunate to provide them shelter, but labored for these before they were in demand; and, as a result, the wounded were unusually fortunate who came to his department.

CHAPTER III.

A PRISONER OF WAR.

Retreat of the Army from Savage Station. — A Shocking Scene. — In the Hands of the Rebels a Volunteer Prisoner. — Eating from the Operating-Table. — The Surgeon and the Picket. — Loyal to the Core. — Return Home, and Cordial Reception. — Honored by the Enemy. — An Heroic and Daring Act. — A Ludicrous Sight. — Notices of the Press.

THE "American Medical Times," in an article during the war, said, —

"To be in the medical service of the army is now a patriot's privilege, and we predict that it will soon become a higher honor than ever before to be a member of the medical staff of the American army."

A war correspondent of the "New-York World," in writing from the front, in referring to the provisions of a bill to abolish the office of brigade surgeons, said, —

"It might seem a matter of regret that the surgical corps of the army should be reduced instead of being re-enforced; and yet, on the other hand, it must be confessed, that, if brigade surgeons generally are on a par with those in the majority in the department of the South, the office may be abolished with little diminution in the professional acquirements and efficiency of the surgical corps. Some of them are unfit to hold any position demanding either soundness of judgment or rectitude of character."

The criticism of the " World's " correspondent would apply with equal force to many of the surgeons in the department of the peninsula where it was found necessary to discharge from the service more than one or a dozen surgeons for incompetency, and want of character, still leaving a large number who would have made better butchers than surgeons. Of the class to whom the " Medical Times " refers, Dr. Swinburne belonged, although it is a question whether the service was

not more honored by his being in it than its honoring him.
No intimation of incompetency or immorality was ever
breathed against him ; and it is doubtful whether any other
gentleman attached to the medical and surgical corps ever
received such honorable mention as he did.

On Sunday, the 29th of June, the Army of the Potomac
retreated from Savage Station. It was found impossible to
take with it all the wounded, and consequently thousands of
these were to be left to fall into the hands of the enemy, to be
treated by them as only prisoners in Rebeldom understood.
There were no military orders to compel Dr. Swinburne to
remain ; and it was purely a question whether he would at
the last moment look to his own safety, and do as others did,
— leave these men to their fate, — or acting on the impulses
of humanity, and love for the brave fellows, remain, and share
their unfortunate lot. The people of the loyal States, and the
army, had learned too truly to realize that to be taken prisoner
was equivalent to an almost certain slow, torturing death ; yet
the doctor promptly responded to the impulses of his noble
nature, and decided to remain with those in the hospitals.
The announcement that this noble volunteer had risked his
all, and was a prisoner, was received with sorrow as a great
public loss. The press universally recited his many acts of
bravery, and printed eulogies on his humanity.

Of the place where he voluntarily elected to remain, the
" Richmond Examiner " gave this description : —

" The battle-field, surveyed through the cold rain of
Wednesday morning, presented a scene too shocking to be
dwelt on without anguish. The woods and the fields on the
western side were covered with our dead in all the degrees
of violent mutilation ; while, in the woods on the west of the
field, lay in about equal numbers the blue uniforms of the
enemy."

It was a busy time for the surgeons, such as remained, for
some time ; and one correspondent wrote that the brave Dr.
Swinburne was untiring in his work, making in one day
twenty-six exsections of the shoulder and elbow-joints, a
number of amputations, and extracting a double handful of

bullets. He had a barn and two sheds assigned him, and never left the operating-room while the wounded were being brought in. During the lulls, he ate his hard-bread and hominy, and drank his coffee, from off the operating-table.

In a letter to Gov. Morgan from the medical director of the army, officially announcing the capture of Dr. Swinburne, the director said, —

"Dr. Swinburne was left with the wounded at Savage Station. The courage and devotion exhibited by Dr. Swinburne will secure to him the deepest gratitude of those of the sick and wounded under his charge, and the unqualified esteem of the public at large."

The fortitude, heroism, and self-sacrificing spirit of Dr. Swinburne and some of his associates have been described by a writer, and incorporated in the "History of the Struggles at, and Retreat from, Savage Station." He says, —

"By order of Gen. McClellan, Dr. Swinburne had been placed in charge of this station. And, while the army was near that point, there was an abundance of help to be had from the surgeons of the army; but, after the defeat of our army at that point, most all the surgeons and nurses had been ordered to their regiments or to other points. As the army was preparing to leave, and the rebels were preparing to cross the Chickahominy, most of the wounded had been removed. There were still one hundred and fifty of the most severely wounded remaining at the hospitals. To every officer on the ground it was well known that to remain there would place them, in a few short hours, in the very centre of a field of carnage, cut off from all means of escape; and that becoming prisoners of war, with all the honors and privations such a fate was well sure to bring, was inevitable. Under these circumstances, a number availed themselves of the last opportunity, and left with the army.

"On Sunday morning, June 29, every thing was ready, and the march of the army in the direction of the James River was commenced. The enemy was then crossing the river. On the bluffs overlooking the river was Meagher's Irish brigade. The general saw the situation, and the fate that must so soon overtake those in charge of the hospital, and sent Col. Burke of the Sixty-third New-York to urge the removal of all the inmates as speedily as possible, as the probabilities were now almost certain that in a few moments the enemy would rush up and plant their batteries in the fields, and the house and barns would be seized in the coming conflict, alternately by both sides, as places of rallying and defence.

"He was told that they were without ambulances, that every one had been ordered away, that there was not a wagon or horses, and not more than six men well enough to help the others away, and that for these to remove one hundred and fifty sick was simply impossible, and the only alternative was to remain and trust to God, as they had done before.

"The general and colonel both realized the desperate condition, but could render no assistance. Every man in the brigade was needed at his post, and, if they could be spared, the place to which they might carry the sick might prove to be the spot of the severest carnage.

"At the earnest urging of Col. Burke, a volunteer chaplain from Pennsylvania rode to Gen. Heintzelman's headquarters to make known the state of affairs. The general listened to the story of the devoted chaplain, and replied that nothing could be done, that all the wounded at Savage Station would have to be left behind, and that it was a matter of stern necessity to leave the wounded in the hands of the enemy. The chaplain then asked what the general deemed was his (the chaplain's) duty under the circumstances, to which Gen. Heintzelman replied, —

"'I cannot advise you. If you remain, you will become a prisoner; no man can tell what you will have to endure; you will lose all. You have no commands holding you here, and, if you please to go with the army, no one ought to blame you.'"

To leave the sick and wounded under such circumstances, as some did, would have been dishonorable; but Dr. Swinburne, the chaplain, and a few others, remained, and resolved to die, rather than cruelly desert the men who now, more than ever, demanded their care. That evening the conflict began, the shot and shell falling among the sick and wounded; and at night they were prisoners of war. These voluntary prisoners, prompted by love of country, and sympathy for the sick, elected capture and all its hardships by a cruel and heartless foe, rather than freedom and all its comforts. What they feared in the event of capture was fully realized. They were subjected to privations and hardships under which many succumbed and died; while others were so shaken and shattered physically, that soon after, "beneath the starry flag where they breathed the air of freedom in their own beloved land," they were numbered among the army in eternity. And it is safe to say that no man who fell into the enemy's hands as a prisoner of war ever recovered his former vigor and wonted health again. The nation owes a debt of gratitude to these men for their heroism and devotion, and the expenditure of their individual means to make the sick and wounded comfortable in captivity, which no pecuniary compensation can extirpate.

The surgeon too often, like the picket, has been passed over with a simple announcement, "He was shot on picket," or, "Our pickets were driven in," or, "The enemy's pickets were put to flight;" and occasionally the poet told us in song that "the picket is off duty forever." Of the surgeon we were told, "He was killed by a bursting shell," or, "He fell in the discharge of his duty." Yet these are positions eminently demanding, in their discharge of duty, courage, caution, patience, vigilance, and often a nerve of iron. If the pickets were timid, cowardly, negligent, or faithless, the thousands and tens of thousands depending on them were in danger. The success and safety of the army always depended on the pickets' faithfulness, and through them some of its most brilliant victories were won. Equal responsibility in the prompt care of the sick and wounded depended on the presence, honesty, and skill of the surgeon. Of the latter class was Dr. John Swinburne, whose never flinching from the discharge of duty in any of the walks of life, has won for him the gratitude of the soldiers, the people, and of the State; all of whom have repeatedly honored him, the latter through its officials of both parties in elevating him to positions of official trust, and the former in repeatedly electing him to some of the highest positions in government within their power to bestow. In every instance he has proven worthy the preferment bestowed; and he still grows warmer in the hearts of the people, whose appreciation will manifest itself still further while he is living, and will cause his name to be held in grateful and honored memory long after he has ceased to take an active part in the duties of life.

From among the hundreds of notices of his life in the army, published in the papers of this State, we collate a few from the journals of both parties who united in paying tribute to this eminent gentleman.

The Fortress-Monroe correspondent of the "New-York Times" gives this account of the characteristic fearlessness, and devotion to his noble calling, on the occasion of the advance of the rebels on Savage Station : —

"I am glad to say that all those who were at Savage Station on Friday, June 27, were safely removed, except one hundred and fifty. Three thousand were safely transferred on board five steamers at White House, and conveyed to Fortress Monroe. Drs. Rogers of New York, Swinburne of Albany, Charles R. Greenleaf and J. Allen of New York, were the parties who conveyed them to the White House, Dr. Allen proceeding with them to Fortress Monroe. Dr. Swinburne was taken prisoner at Savage Station, and all concur in testimony of his great bravery and loyal devotion. The published statements that the rebels fired upon the hospitals are quite true. Dr. Allen assured me that they continued shelling the building, full of the wounded and dying men, until Dr. Swinburne boldly sallied forth with a flag of truce, when they desisted."

The correspondent of the "New-York World," writing from Savage Station under date June 28, said, —

"Every available spot of tent-room, or shaded greensward, or outbuilding, is crowded thick with the wounded from yesterday's conflict. Besides, the train loaded this morning is still filled with the men, most of whom can walk, and who long to reach some spot where they can receive care."

On the 29th he wrote, —

"I find myself suddenly almost alone, — no companions save the sick and wounded, and the faithful surgeons (under Dr. Swinburne) in attendance upon them. All the wounded who could walk have been started down the road towards the river. I learn that all the ambulances and wagons that can be used for the purpose have been filled with the severely wounded, and started toward the river. The balance, nearly eight hundred, have been provided with tents and hospital stores, and are to be kept here for the present, in care of the surgeons, who have volunteered to stay and minister to their wants, and trust to the clemency of the enemy."

In a correspondence published in the " World " on July 5, the writer said, —

" This is not the time to pay tribute to the living heroes. Hereafter I shall name them, and do them full justice. Dr. Swinburne had the general supervision of the hospitals necessarily abandoned by Gen. Porter. As many of the wounded as could, retired with the army ; but large numbers remained, and Dr. Swinburne with others remained with them. The country and the world will honor them for their heroic self-devotion."

The war correspondent of the " New-York Herald " on July 1 paid this compliment to Dr. Swinburne : —

" The best possible care is being taken of our gallant wounded. Commanding. generals occupying the dwellings on the field in the earlier part of the day as headquarters, have all yielded them to be used as temporary hospitals. For hours, as fast as ambulances can convey them, they have been taken to Savage Station, where accommodations for their care exist on a scale of magnitude somewhat proportionate to the necessities of an army of our size. I am told that already over four hundred have been taken to the latter place. A large and efficient corps of surgeons has been detailed to give prompt and proper attention to them, the whole under charge of Dr. Swinburne."

Under date of July 7, the correspondent of the " Herald " said, —

" By Sunday, however, the general movement of the army towards the James River was so far advanced that it became necessary to abandon Savage Station. Heintzelman's whole corps fell slowly back from Savage Station towards the White-Oak Swamps. There being no means of transporting them, twenty-five hundred sick and wounded soldiers were left behind at Savage Station, in charge of Dr. Swinburne of Albany."

The correspondent also details the firing on the hospital, when Dr. Swinburne exposed himself to the fire by advancing with a flag of truce, and having the cruelty stopped.

The " Herald " editorially, on July 10, said, —

" The recent retreat of our army from the Chickahominy to the banks of the James River, conducted as it was with order and steadiness, was yet marked with one deplorable feature : we were compelled to leave behind, and at the mercy of an infuriated enemy, a large number of our wounded. This fact is attributed entirely to the known inefficiency of our ambulance system. In the French and Prussian armies an occurrence of this kind would be almost impossible, and, at all events, could not fail to bring down the severest censure on the department responsible for it."

While the war correspondents were a unit in commending the management, skill, and bravery of Dr. Swinburne, they were all led into the same error as to the reasons why so many wounded were left behind. They saw there were a great many, even thousands, but, in the excitement of the hour, did not learn the real cause. And this unintentional error on the part of the correspondents misled the editors at home. Dr. Swinburne had provided amply for the transportation of all who were in condition to be removed, and they were taken to a place of safety. There were numbers of ambulances sent away without any wounded from the hospitals at that point, simply laden with food ; and all who were left were in such a condition, many of them in delirium, that to have attempted a removal, even for a short distance, would have proven fatal. When the doctor realized that the position was more than probable to fall into the hands of the enemy, he began sending forward such as could be removed, and, by his words of encouragement, induced hundreds to walk away themselves, many of them wounded in the upper extremities, some of them with wounds in the head and body.

On the 15th the " Herald " correspondent said, —

" Since the battle, most of the wounded have had a hard time. Many have been obliged to lay on the ground. Nearly all the medicines were stolen by the rebels, and every bottle of liquor taken away. Every case of surgical instruments was taken. In addition to the depriving of these invaluable accessions in taking care of the wounded, the only food furnished was maggoty bacon and musty flour. I was told there were still about nine hundred wounded there, and that Dr. Swinburne, who was in charge when the enemy came in possession, had still the supervision, aided by a corps of surgeons."

Another correspondent of the "Herald," in describing the arrival of the sick and wounded at Harrison's Landing on July 28, most of them being brought from Savage Station, where Dr. Swinburne still had full charge, said, —

"Among those with whom I had the longest conversation was Dr. Churchill of the Fourteenth New-York, who stated, that, while remaining behind to aid in taking care of the wounded at Gaines's Mills, he was taken prisoner. He was sent from there to Savage Station, where he was given, by Dr. Swinburne, charge of about five hundred wounded. He remained there three days, when he was sent to Richmond in care of about six hundred sick. He said the sufferings of our men at Savage Station from want of medicine, surgical instruments, and shelter, and the privations and hardships undergone by the surgeons, have been too frequently described to render a repetition necessary. They paid from fourteen to sixteen dollars apiece for lambs to make soup for the men, and some died of actual starvation, including two surgeons, notwithstanding all the care bestowed."

The "New-York Tribune," in describing the battles of the 26th and 27th of June, 1862, said, —

"During the afternoon and night the ambulance trains were engaged in bringing the wounded to Savage Station, where extensive arrangements had been made for their care by Dr. Swinburne. Tents and other arrangements had been made for the accommodation of about six hundred persons, and long before daylight (28th) it was necessary to lay the poor uncomplaining soldiers on hay in the open air. They received the kindest and most prompt care from Dr. Swinburne, who asked seventy-five hospital tents and received sixteen, but, with the 'flies,' made thirty-two of them."

These few out of the many notices of Dr. Swinburne's work at the front, from two representative journals of each of the two political parties, published at the metropolis, speak loudly of the faithfulness of the volunteer surgeon, and will command the esteem of all. The adage that "a prophet is not without praise save in his own country," did not apply to the eminent physician in the days when he was at the front,

any more than it does now. The press of both parties in the
capital city, the home of the doctor, were agreed in commending his ability and patriotism, and, on his release from
prison, gladly made the announcement as one of great joy,
and united in giving him a hearty and cheerful greeting on
his return.

The "Albany Times" of July 28, 1862, has this excellent
tribute to Dr. Swinburne: —

"The following extract from a private letter to one of the
editors of this paper, and the accompanying statement of a
released chaplain, will be read with interest by Dr. Swinburne's numerous friends, and by our citizens generally, who
remember that he became a voluntary captive rather than
abandon his sick and wounded, and who are therefore interested in his fate. It is the first authentic tidings received
from him since his captivity.

PAYMASTER-GENERAL'S OFFICE,
WASHINGTON, JULY, 24.

I returned this morning from Harrison's Landing on the James River,
having finished paying Gen. Gorman's brigade for March and April.
On my passage down the James River yesterday morning, I met on board
the boat Chaplain James Marks of the Sixty-third Pennsylvania Regiment, who was with Dr. Swinburne at Savage Station, and was taken
prisoner, but since released. I obtained the following particulars in
regard to Dr. Swinburne from him: —

"Chaplain James Marks of the Sixty-third Pennsylvania Regiment remained at Savage Station with Dr. Swinburne. There were fifteen hundred wounded and sick there from the battles of Thursday, Friday, and
Saturday, June 26, 27, and 28. On Sunday night, the 29th, the enemy
surrounded the place; but Sumner's division drove them back, and they
retired towards James River. On Monday morning, about seven o'clock,
the rebels came in and took prisoners all of the wounded and sick, and also
all our surgeons and nurses, leaving Dr. Swinburne in full charge, as before. About twenty surgeons, of whom four or five were sick, remained
to assist Dr. Swinburne in taking care of the wounded and sick. During
this day, and on Tuesday, five hundred more wounded were brought in.
Dr. Swinburne's labors at this time were constant, presiding over all
departments, directing all amputations, and securing the confidence and
esteem of all the surgeons and the officers. After the battle of Tuesday
evening on Malvern Hill, information was brought to Dr. Swinburne that
his presence was immediately demanded in various hospitals on the battle-
field. The doctor immediately left, and, after going through various

divisions of the rebel army, found his way to the hospitals on Nelson's Farm, the scene of the battle on Monday evening, and assisted in all of the amputations.   Thence he found his way to the battle-field on Malvern Hill, and assisted and gave counsel to the surgeons.   He then returned to Savage Station, and told his story to Chaplain Marks, who assisted him, obtaining such supplies as were needed, which were sent in rebel ambulances to the hospitals.   Dr. Swinburne directed the return of the chaplain several times, passed through the lines and divisions of the rebel army without molestation, and visited the hospitals beyond the White-Oak Swamps, carrying food and medicines.   He remained in full charge at Savage Station as late as the 13th inst.   Chaplain Marks was sent by Dr. Swinburne, in charge of seven hundred wounded men, to Richmond, on Sunday, the 13th inst.   Subsequent to this, he did not see the doctor, but heard of his continued health, activity, and benevolence.   He speaks in the highest terms of Dr. Swinburne's talents, and skill as a surgeon. His ear was ever open to the complaint of the poorest soldier, and he was untiring in his exertions to promote the welfare of the sick and wounded. Among the rebels, he was looked upon as one of the noblest and best of men."

R. H. KING, Jun.

On the 28th of July the " Times " said that the conduct of Dr. Swinburne was the theme of universal praise, and on the 30th said, —

" Our citizens will be pleased to learn that by a telegram received last evening by Dr. Vanderpoel, Dr. John Swinburne, who was taken a prisoner at Savage Station while attending to our sick and wounded, has arrived at Fortress Monroe, *en route* for this city, with Capt. McRoberts, Capt. Vanderlip, and Lieut. Becker, all of the Ellsworth Brigade."

On the 2d of August the " Albany Evening Journal " announced his arrival in Albany in these words : —

"Dr. John Swinburne of this city, who has for several weeks been discharging the responsible duties of medical superintendent of New-York troops with so much devotion, came home this morning.   All will recollect that Dr. Swinburne was in charge of the hospital at Savage Station, nine miles from Richmond, when that station was taken by the Rebels, and that he voluntarily remained in charge.   He, of course, became a prisoner of war ; but, under an arrangement previously entered, physicians were permitted to leave without restraint.   He could therefore have returned to the Union army ; but he preferred to continue with our sick and

wounded, who, more than ever, required his supervising care.
It is proper to add that they are now all, or nearly all, away.
We have spoken repeatedly of the humanity, skill, and bravery evinced by Dr. Swinburne in the performance of the
service assigned him, — so honorable to his profession and
the man. His opportunities and experiences have been of
the most varied character. He will be warmly welcomed
back by our citizens."

A few days after his arrival home on sick leave, having
been greatly reduced physically because of his incessant
labors and the hardships endured while a prisoner of war, he
received the following official letter: —

STATE OF NEW YORK, SURGEON-GENERAL'S OFFICE,
ALBANY, Aug. 5, 1862.

SIR, — I am requested by his Excellency Gov. Morgan to
express his high appreciation of the services rendered by you
while serving with the Army of the Potomac as medical
superintendent of the forces from this State, and acting assistant surgeon of the United-States Army, and to return you
thanks for the same.

An expression thus officially made is not intended as in-
vidious to the noble corps of volunteer surgeons who so
promptly and faithfully gave their time, their energies, their
professional abilities, and in some instances their lives, to
ameliorate the sufferings of the wounded; but that the position in which you were placed by the authorities of the
State, the peculiar circumstances which resulted therefrom,
and the manner in which you conducted yourself, both professionally and as the representative, for the time, of your
government, call for, as it is most cheerfully bestowed, the
commendations and approval not only of the constituted
authorities, but of a whole community, who have watched
with vivid interest the responsibilities, privations, and labors
to which you were subjected.

As the head of the State Medical Bureau, I cannot forego
the opportunity of thanking you for the bright example your
labors have furnished of conservative surgery upon the field
of battle.

Had you merely, in the performance of your labors, done all
which humanity demands, you would have merited the compliment proffered, but to that you have added the exercise
of high professional skill. When in a hospital of two thousand sick and wounded you amputated less than half a dozen
limbs, but strove, rather, to save by exsection, you illustrated

and carried out the views of the most intelligent of the profession.

Wishing you, in your safe return to your family and friends, the enjoyment of a well-merited confidence,

I am, with respect, your obedient servant,

S. OAKLEY VANDERPOEL,
Surgeon-General.

JOHN SWINBURNE, M.D.

Within the rebel lines Dr. Swinburne maintained the same deportment as within our lines, and treated the rebel officials, in his intercourse with them, with the same politeness as he did his own, refusing on all occasions to enter into any discussion on political or other questions that might engender any feeling that would work to the injury of those under his care, and was at times austere in enforcing the same course in those under him. On one occasion, in passing through one of the hospitals, he overheard one of the nurses discussing the situation with a rebel captain, the nurse expressing sentiments such as a loyal soldier ought never to utter. The doctor stopped, and, turning to the nurse, said, " You are not here as a diplomat, to discuss questions you know nothing about; neither are you a general with any military knowledge; and, as for your ability to talk politics, you never had any. You are a nurse here, and to that business you are to attend strictly, or I will send you to your friends in Richmond, with whom you seem to sympathize."

Among the rebel authorities he won the utmost esteem, and paid the same attention to their wounded as he did to our own. He had many of the rebel sick to look after, among them Col. Lamar of Georgia. Standing in front of the hospital one day, Gens. Orr and Jameson, and a number of other rebel officers, came up, and, saluting him, entered into conversation, the discussion turning on the war and probable results. After they were through, the doctor answered, " Gentlemen, I am here to take care of the unfortunate, not to discuss these questions. I came here because the North is right, and you are wrong. I know your movement is wicked, although many of you may be misled. You will have to yield, and it is only a question of time. For your sake and ours, the North will never let you succeed, if it should take twenty years to conquer you. Now, I am a volunteer prisoner, holding the order of Gen. Jackson to command of you safe protection into our lines whenever I desire to go; and I have but one request to make of you, — as gentlemen, that you will not introduce this subject again, and that you will use your interests to have our wounded sent into our lines as rapidly as they become fit to travel. My views cannot be changed, and I do not think yours can be until you are thoroughly flogged." From that time out, he had a warm friend in Gen. Orr, who had learned to honor the brave man in what he had only known before as a skilful surgeon.

This feeling of Gen. Orr was demonstrated afterwards, when want and necessity were killing the disabled much more rapidly than their wounds. In the hospital as a nurse was a Rev. Mr. R., who had formerly lived in Richmond. He insisted on going to that city, and placing the situation before the authorities, alleging he knew the people, and knew he could induce them to alleviate matters. The doctor endeavored to dissuade him, assuring him they would surely arrest and hang him as a spy. He, however, was obdurate, and persisted in going. After his departure, Gen. Orr rode up: the doctor detailed the circumstance to him, and asked the general to ride into Richmond and save the poor ——, saying he was only a harmless fanatic, and did not know enough to be a spy. The general did so, and, on returning, assured the doctor they had arrested the preacher, and were about to hang him when he (the general) arrived; that he told the authorities the doctor's story, and the fellow's life was saved.

Before the capture of Savage Station, and when the hospitals were being shelled, the doctor sallied out with a flag of truce. For this he was summoned before Gen. Sumner, who denounced the act as in violation of military discipline, and said that the surgeon had no right to presume to go out with the flag without first receiving orders to do so, adding, "I shall have you cashiered." — "All right, general," said the doctor, "you can have me cashiered now, if you want to. I don't know any thing about military law, but I know enough to take care of my rights. You may kill me, just what the rebels were going to do, and that is all there is about it. I was looking out for my rights, as you will pretty soon for yours." He was not cashiered.

There was not a military officer around Savage Station who was not always ready to afford the doctor all the protection and assistance within his power; and when he applied to Gen. Stonewall Jackson for a pass to visit the various hospitals in the vicinity where our men were confined, the general, in granting him the pass to go wherever he pleased, in a very complimentary note referred to the doctor's skill and humanity, and informed him that he was not to be considered a prisoner of war, and that the pass would carry him safely through the lines, and into his own, whenever he desired to go.

The doctor himself, in reporting from Savage Station to our government, at a time when feeling was the most intense and bitter, with reference to the treatment of the sick and wounded under his care, said, —

"I feel assured that all the deficiencies and difficulties which we experienced were not the fault of Gen Lee, his officers, or his medical staff, since all the generals and medical officers with whom we were brought in contact were unusually attentive to the necessities of the wounded and sick. But that there was a fault somewhere, there is no question ; and that fault I attribute to the inhumanity of the authorities at Richmond, which has been fatal to many of our wounded soldiers."

His eminent skill and acknowledged ability made his services sought in every hospital in that section. On the morning of July 12, while passing Gen. McGruder's headquarters, he was handed a letter directed to the general from Assistant Surgeon C.S.A., C. B. White, and dated Malvern Hill, in which the writer said he had several cases which needed capital operations. He added, "If Dr. Swinburne can come (I hear he is in the vicinity), I would like it." The doctor responded, and going to Malvern Hill, with Drs. White, Chamberlain, and Jewett, performed all the operations.

During his term in Rebeldom, the volunteer surgeon's career was marked by many incidents of daring. On one occasion his services were in demand at Malvern Hill, whither he repaired. On his arrival there, he found the men were suffering for provisions. Without awaiting to send for these, he commenced a foraging expedition, and in the upper portion of a deserted house near by he found a large quantity of beans. Without waiting for any orders, or asking permission, he confiscated the " Yankee favorite berry; " and in four hours the six hundred men were all at work regaling themselves on bean-soup. On the completion of his work at this hospital, he started back for Savage Station on foot about sundown, walking a distance of twelve miles without a guide, passing through the rebel lines several times without molestation, and arriving safely, — a feat to others seemingly impossible, and demonstrating that some unseen protector was always with the surgeon.

Perhaps the only laughable part of the doctor's military career was during one of his trips back to Albany, when he boarded the steamer at New York, penniless and ragged, to beat his way to Albany. With an old slouched hat; boots out at the toes, and run over at the heels ; pants of the latest cut (as they were all cut to pieces) ; and an old blanket thrown over his shoulders, — this was the ludicrous condition he was in when recognized by a member of a Broadway firm as he lay stretched on the deck, and fast asleep. The regular surgeon of the army had pay and stores to draw from to prevent such a condition ; but the faithful volunteer was without resources, and yet returned again to the front to undergo the same hardships.

CHAPTER IV.

FIGHTING FOR THE WOUNDED.

Bold Words to the Rebels. — Defects in the Medical Department. — Controversy with the Sanitary Commission. — Strange Anomaly. — Observations on Surgery. — A Brave Colonel killed by Malpractice. — Red Tape in the Army. — A Fearless Man.

THE treatment our sick and wounded were receiving was an all-absorbing thought with this unselfish physician, and incited him to make every effort for their relief. Under this feeling, he attacked the very highest in authority in the Confederacy, always using polite but plain Anglo-Saxon English, that could not be misunderstood, and appealed to all the better feelings of manhood. To the Confederate general, Winder, he wrote from Savage Station, July 24, 1862, —

"Now, if you judge this the kind of food furnished your sick and wounded prisoners North, or as in accordance with the usages of war among civilized nations, you are mistaken. I have had to buy fresh meat for soups, and bread to supply the deficiency, since we have no means of cooking flour suitable to the sick. Now, I submit that flour and poor bacon are entirely unfit for the sick and wounded, since many have died from sheer exhaustion or starvation ; and many more will die unless better fed. Many of those taken to Richmond, and detained so long in the depot without proper attention, have also died. Now, sir, all I ask is to have the sick and wounded who have become the recipients of my care receive the attention due them as prisoners of war, agreeably to the usages of civilized people ; and that the surgeons to whose care they are intrusted be treated, not as felons, but in accordance with the precedents which have been established, and which you publish in all your papers, as the laws of the land. If we cannot be fed in accordance with the common usages of war, — in other words, if you have not the material with which to feed us, so as to keep us from starvation, — I feel assured that your elevated sense of humanity will assist us to reach our own lines, where we can be attended to. I have seen and attended your sick and wounded at New York, Philadelphia, Fortress Monroe, and in this hospital, and have never seen any distinction made between them and our men. Now, with the insufficient nourishment supplied us, our funds failing, what are we to do? I leave the answer to your impulses of humanity, and ask you, in the name of the common obligations due from man to man, that you interpose your dictum, and change the status of our condition."

And to S. Guild, M.D., surgeon and medical director department of Northern Virginia, he wrote,—

"Sir,—I regret exceedingly to again trouble you, but, under the circumstances, I must call your attention to a fact which I have before stated to you, that some of our surgeons are sick. One of them breathed his last yesterday afternoon. Some others are still sick, and all are more or less unwell. Lieut. Johnson, the commandant of this place, is now very sick, as is also several of his men. Lieut. Lacey Stewart has recovered, and has gone to Richmond to-day to procure rations for the patients. I feel as if I could not resist much longer the combined influences of this pus-generating place and the insufficiency of flour and bacon as food. It is not, however, for myself that I am so anxious. I have in my keeping many valuable lives, and I feel that every exertion on my part is due to them, to the end that they may be spared to their families.

"In view of these facts, I have purchased two sheep daily from my own funds, and have converted them into soup for the patients, hoping that it might contribute somewhat to their physical force during this trying ordeal. I trust, therefore, you will continue to exert your benign influence in behalf of suffering nature, so long as our necessities remain in the present status, or until we can all be removed to our own homes. I have to thank you for many kind attentions which I can never repay, or which, at least, I never expect to repay in the same way. So, also, Gen. Lee's attentions have surprised me, since he is burdened with a thousand cares incident to a life like his. I can only attribute it to his sympathy with those in distress, whether friend or foe. Now, sir, will it be possible for me, or some one of us, to go with these sick surgeons, who are delicate, and place them on board our transports, and to superintend the removal of sick and wounded? I hope you will excuse this constant interruption in affairs, since my whole heart is set on getting proper food for the sick and wounded. For myself, it matters little, but please don't allow us to remain in Richmond over night."

To all his communications to those in authority in the military or medical departments of the Confederacy in the field, he received the most courteous replies, in which, while those addressed regretted their inability to grant the relief he sought, they assured him of their sympathy, and the exercise of their influence in securing such relief from the government at Richmond as was possible.

While in active service in the army at the front, Dr. Swinburne saw many glaring defects in the management of the medical department which might be remedied, and thus tend greatly to the comfort of the sick and wounded. In the interest of the soldiers and humanity, he conceived many plans that would add to the comfort of the sick, and tend to the preservation of many valuable lives, — a subject in which his thoughts seemed to be absolutely absorbed. On his arrival home from prison, he placed these views, with a statement of the facts as he found them, with his deductions from these observations and the results to which his experience enabled him to arrive, before the New-York State Medical Society. This body of scientific men, after fully discussing the matter, and hearing his recommendations, gave them their hearty indorsement, and appointed Drs. Swinburne and S. D. Willard a committee from that society, to confer with the governor, and to secure, if possible, an appropriation to carry out the design of obtaining more ample means for the relief of the sick and wounded New-York troops. Gov. Seymour, who then occupied the executive chair, feeling as he did a deep interest in the troops at the front, and knowing the eminent skill of the committee, gave them frequent and early hearings; and, as a result, a bill was draughted appropriating two hundred thousand dollars to carry out the views suggested by the volunteer surgeon.

As soon as it became known among a certain element, who professed to be especially working for the wounded soldier, that such a bill had been draughted, and the objects for which it was intended, there broke out a strong opposition in the ranks of a selfish volunteer organization, whose desire to gain notoriety exceeded their love for the soldier. This spirit of jealousy might have been expected, to a certain degree, from the regular medical department of the army, because of their training, and the assumption that in war every thing connected with the regular army was perfection, and, the greatest of all, that whatever they did was right, and that interference with their assumed superiority was to be regarded as an innovation not to be tolerated. But it was not from this source the opposition came, but rather from the executive committee of the United-States Sanitary Commission, — a volunteer organization supposed to enjoy only the same privileges accorded to other volunteer organizations, or societies of individuals, presumed to be working on the same humanitarian impulses.

In their opposition, this executive committee pathetically invoked the aid of the then surgeon-general of the State, Dr. Quackenbush, to defeat the measure, alleging that "the National Government is the national soldier's best friend," and "that whatever has hitherto been effectually done to benefit the cause of the sick and wounded soldier, has been done by increasing the force, improving the regulations, elevating the rank, or selecting more efficient presiding officers of the United-States Medical Department."

This executive committee of a society claiming to be composed of volunteers who desired to help the government, and benefit the wounded soldier, and who were still anxious to obtain broader fields and an exclusive monopoly, made the strange and irreconcilable assertion in opposition to the bill, "that already the great beneficent general system of the government in its medical department has been constantly embarrassed by the well-meant efforts of benevolent associations, either representing States or communities, who have insisted in pursuing their humane work." They further advanced the absurd proposition, "that the National Government is making provision at this very moment to do for the New-York troops, and every other soldier, precisely what the bill proposed, but could not do so if the bill were passed." The appeal to the surgeon-general, in closing, exposed the motives underlying the opposition, — that of jealousy, lest the States, in assuming to do their duty to their sick troops, might find a more certain and efficient channel than through the sanitary commission. They stated that "it [the commission] collects money on the largest scale ever known to volunteer benevolence, and gathers supplies in an equal scale of vastness."

The reply of the committee, Drs. Swinburne and Willard, was prompt, cutting, and to the point. It said, among other things, —

" The State clings to her citizen soldiers in the army. Her care for them is not lessened by their absence over the State line, and it is right it should not be. If committees from the city common councils and the village board of trustees visit them, and give them courage and hope, and help and good cheer; if the State sends committees to attend to their allotments; if the Legislature provides that they may vote; and if the State looks well to their pay, and secures it or advances it early, — if all these acts of kindness and care are manifested for the well soldier, how eminently proper and just, nay, how much more it is demanded by every consideration of humanity and good faith, that the thousands of feeble, maimed, and dying should be cared for, or at least inquired after, and their misfortunes alleviated in as kind and affectionate a manner as possible! And yet, when this latter course is suggested by the benevolent and philanthropic of the State, whose means of information as to the actual necessities are unquestioned; when a measure of relief is initiated, — the executive committee of the sanitary commission, under whose administration these neglects occur, as was admitted by their own confessions in leaving every thing they had to be destroyed, or fall into the hands of the enemy at Gettysburg, proclaim that "voluntary associations, State societies, and local committees have constantly embarrassed the medical department of the government."

To this strange anomaly of the sanitary commission, the committee from the New-York Medical Society very pertly replied, —

"If this be true, well may the people of this State suspend efforts, and by so doing send comfort and joy to the soldiers, the sanitary commission, and the medical department of the Army."

To the cynical opposition of the commission, the committee make this cutting satire : —

"After the seven-days' battles before Richmond, not a single agent of the sanitary commission remained to care for the sick and wounded, and not one of them was taken prisoner. Their hospital supplies, deserted by their agents, were destroyed. The agents left at that time some five thousand sick and wounded to be cared for by the charities of the enemy, who had nothing to supply their wants."

This was a stinging rebuke, coming from a man like Dr. Swinburne, who had no honor to gain, and yet remained true to his mission, and was himself, while at his post of duty, taken a prisoner. There were no members of the sanitary commission taken prisoners at Savage Station, but there were several volunteers: among them, Felix R. Brunot of Pittsburgh, Penn., since an Indian peace commissioner under President Grant, with twenty-four nurses from that city; the Rev. Mr. Marks of Pennsylvania; the Rev. Mr. Reed of Washington, D.C.; and a Mr. Howell of Chicago, and several surgeons. Two of the latter, Drs. Milnor and Sutton, exhausted from their labors among the sick and wounded at that station, finally perished from starvation in the hands of the enemy.

The protest against the passage of the bill was made on March 11, 1864; and on the 30th, Gov. Seymour, in a communication to the Senate, recommended that an ample appropriation be made by the State for its sick and wounded troops. On April 24 the bill was unanimously passed by the Senate, and sent to the Assembly on the same day, and there passed without a dissenting voice, and before the sun went down was signed by the governor.

During the controversy over the passage of this bill, Surgeon-Gen. Hammond used his official position in an attempt to frustrate the measure, and wrote to J. V. P. Quackenbush, M.D., surgeon-general of New York, —

Surgeon-General's Office,
Washington, D.C., March 2, 1863.

Sir,—I have the honor to acknowledge the receipt of your communication of the 25th ult., enclosing the copy of a bill proposed to be enacted by the Legislature of the State of New York, and asking my views upon the same.

I have read the bill very carefully, and, whilst admitting the correctness of the motive by which its framers have been actuated, I am satisfied, from much experience, that its chief effects will be to create trouble and confusion, to cause ill feeling between the representatives of the United States and the State, and to injure those whom it is intended to benefit. I am satisfied that no military commander who has the good of the troops at heart would allow any agent of any State to interfere in the manner proposed in this bill. It would be found in practice wholly inoperative, and lead to the results indicated above, without any corresponding advantages being received. Doubtless there are deficiencies in the medical administration of the army, as there are in all other departments. Perfection is impossible of attainment; but if I, with all my efforts, with the assistance of medical inspectors, medical directors, and over five thousand surgeons and assistant surgeons, together with the support of commanding officers, and all branches of the Federal Government, and the control of over ten millions (dollars, doubtless) per annum, cannot reach it, I am certain the agents of the State of New York will not be able to do better. I therefore hope you will use your efforts to defeat this bill.

I am not alone in my opinion in regard to it; as all to whom I have mentioned it, including several officers of rank, agree with me that its passage would be most unwise.

I hope you will excuse me for the freedom with which I have written.

I am, sir, very respectfully, your obedient servant,

WILLIAM A. HAMMOND,
Surgeon-General.

J. V. P. Quackenbush,

   Surgeon-General of New York, Albany, N.Y.

The criticism, severe as it was, on the conduct of those who deserted the helpless brave in those trying days, had its effect, and was justifiable in Dr. Swinburne, as he, having remained and become a prisoner, had clearly won the right to condemn the cowardice of those who, acting on the motto that "self-preservation was the first law of nature," left the twelve hundred brave men at Savage Station.

In the Transactions of the New-York State Medical Society, submitted to the Legislature in 1863, is a full report from Dr. Swinburne during his imprisonment, with the communications that passed between himself and the Confederate authorities with reference to the exchange of prisoners, and his efforts for their comfort, as well as some severe strictures on the management of the medical department of the army. It also contains some able articles on resection of joints, and conservative surgery, on amputation when necessary, and the treatment of gunshot wounds.

His observations at the front confirmed the opinion, previously entertained, that there were by far too many amputations performed in the treatment of those wounded in battle; and that by the introduction of conservative surgery, if practised throughout the army, two great ends would be secured, — the saving to the government of large amounts of money; and, what was of pre-eminently greater moment, the saving to the wounded of their limbs, and thus preserving them as their Maker would have them, and not having them crippled for life. He believed, if one limb was saved to a man who would live ten years, the government would be benefited to the amount of $2,050; and that if one surgeon would save, during a great battle, ten limbs from mutilation, he would save to the government, on the basis of ten years as the media of life after wounding, $20,500. While this was a pecuniary consideration, he felt more keenly, from humanitarian principles, a stronger desire to see the principles of conservation practised, feeling, that, if he could accomplish this, a great blessing would be achieved, and that he had been instrumental in doing some good to his fellow-beings. In this his ambition has been in a large degree gratified in seeing this system very largely adopted, both in military and private practice, although he was strongly opposed at the outset by many leading surgeons who have since acquiesced in the humane practice.

That he was eminently successful, has been demonstrated

by the strongest arguments, — results. To show the wisdom of conservation, and the brutality or ignorance of the old system, a few cases are cited from this State. Lieut. Felix Angus of Duryea's Zouaves, while making a charge at Gaines's Mills, was wounded in the right shoulder by a minie-ball. Several surgeons insisted on an amputation; but he objected, saying he would rather die than lose his arm. Dr. Swinburne performed an operation of excision rather than amputation, and "four weeks later, I was in New York, riding in Central Park, and enjoying life as well as ever," he afterwards wrote to Dr. Swinburne. He also wrote to the doctor, " I consider myself under a lasting debt of gratitude to you for the benefit you have done me; for you saved my arm, if not my life. As it was, you remember you took out my right-shoulder joint, and during the operation I felt no pain whatever." He afterwards raised and commanded Company I. One Hundred and Sixty-fifth New-York (Duryea's second) Regiment. Dr. Julius A. Skilton, who was present at the operation, and afterwards dressed the shoulder at White-Oak Swamps, in writing to Dr. Swinburne, said, " I am sure it would have done you good to see the satisfaction with which he expresses his gratitude for the preservation of his limb, and the manner in which he handles his sword with it now."

Lieut. Henry A. Wynkoop of Rochester was so severely wounded as to require the removal of the head and three inches of the shaft of the humerus; and still, at the end of four weeks, he had so far recovered the use of the arm as to be serviceable, and to give a tolerably warm shake of the hand. Less than a year afterwards he wrote to Dr. Swinburne from Rochester, —

" I must thank you again for saving my arm; and no money could make me feel as happy as this disabled arm does, thanks to your skill and kindness. The arm you operated upon was my right arm, and tnis letter is written with the same. After you left me at Fortress Monroe, my arm improved rapidly, and in four weeks not only was entirely healed up, but I was able to walk without in any way supporting myself. The wound never opened after it once healed up. I can use my hand as well as ever."

The young gentleman is still engaged in a banking-house near Rochester, and continues to write letters of gratitude to the surgeon who saved his arm.

In a volume of reminiscences of the war, a paper by Dr. Swinburne, dated July 23, 1863, in speaking of the losses of life occurring, as they did, not alone by the ravages of grim-visaged war in their usual phases, but in numerous instances from the want of care, disease, pestilence, and almost famine in camp and hospital, said: —

"This awful destruction of life outside the usual course of war has been attributed by friends and supporters of the different parties in the country, and by the followers of different officers, to as many different causes as there have been parties or officers interested or implicated in the matter. Many of the alleged causes are truthful to a certain extent; but all of them are overdrawn, and very many more are entirely unfounded, disgraceful to those charging them, and only arise out of the evident desire of their supporters to heap unwarranted contumely upon the government, or the officers by them arraigned; and that, too, with a design thereby to further the still more evident and grossly treasonable intent to hinder the government in the speedy and successful prosecution of the war, and thus give aid and comfort to the enemy in such a covert manner as to shield the authors from the penalty of open treason.

"Foremost among these assigned causes has been the alleged inefficiency in the conduct of the medical department of the service during this campaign. It will be recollected that the celebrated Dr. Tripler, an old army surgeon, whose most valuable works on military surgery have justly attained a fame as world-wide as the subject itself, was medical director of the Army of the Potomac at that time. It has been charged, that, by reason of his neglect, the Army of the Peninsula was left without many things which were absolutely requisite for the proper administration of the medical department of that army; and that thus the soldiers, worn out by the fatigues of the march, weakened by exposure to severe storms and the dangerous miasmas of the swamps, and brought down to the hospitals by disease, were literally allowed to die from want of these necessaries, when they could have been promptly obtained at any time, it is said, upon proper call. This charge, it has occurred to me, is grossly unjust to one whose highest aim in life has been to serve his country faithfully, and make himself a useful and shining ornament to the glorious profession he has adopted, and a lasting benefit to the human race. The office and duties of a faithful surgeon, even in civil life, is no sinecure; and when a surgeon of noblest mind and purest purpose, impelled by love of country, has chosen to abandon even the emoluments to be derived from the practice of his profession as a civilian, and is willing, for the paltry pittance allowed by government, to assume the responsibilities, and devote his utmost energies to the duties, of medical director of an army so large as that over which Dr. Tripler had charge, it seems to me that even the pardonable anxiety of the friends of those dying under his charge is not excusable for a violation towards him of the ordinary rules of charity which are, in the Book of books, laid down for our conduct towards all men.

"In my own experience in the peninsular campaign, I found it at times difficult to obtain a sufficient supply of many materials which were absolutely necessary for the proper care and cure of the sick and wounded, and, in fact, I was many times utterly unable to obtain articles most needed; and yet I have had the most convincing proof that the medical director cannot be justly held responsible for this. The fault, I am convinced, lay nearer the government at Washington. To my mind, the surgeon-general (superior officer to the medical director) — having the means at hand at Washington for ascertaining, if he did not know, the proportions of war the campaign was assuming; and knowing, as he must have known, the size of the army, the dangers by which that army was beset from the effects of the climate, the character of the country, and the probabilities of battle — was in duty bound to see that all necessary material was provided for the medical department of the service; and it would be but a sickly compliment (as it is an illy-consoling excuse) for that officer to say that perhaps he did not realize all the necessities of the case. And yet the fact is patent that there was, during the whole of the campaign, a lack of supplies for the medical and hospital departments, which, without doubt, was the cause of more deaths than occurred by the other and more direct casualties of war.

"After the removal of Dr. Tripler as medical director, the same lamentable state of affairs existed, and the same defects in the medical service, to a greater or less extent: as in the location of, and supplies for, the hospital at Windmill Point, where days are said to have elapsed before necessary food and medical supplies were obtained, and where a great number of our men actually died from lack of them; the medical history of the battle of Antietam, at which it is charged by Dr. Agnew that at least five hundred men died from the want of medical supplies; the battle of Chancellorsville, where thousands were, it seems to me, needlessly left in the hands of the enemy, when they might and should have been transferred to the other side of the river, and there received proper care and surgical attendance. It is said, that, after this battle, our brave wounded soldiers in many instances lay for days without proper food (and in some cases without any), and with no medical relief, many of them left to the tender mercies of the enemy, a large number of them dying from sheer neglect, and many others buried alive in fires occasioned by the contending armies in shelling the woods, and burning the Chancellor house."

As medical superintendent of the wounded New-York troops, he was not only ever anxious and vigilant in caring for them, but, wherever he saw bad management, was prompt and fearless to call attention to it.

In a letter to his Excellency Gov. Morgan, dated Falmouth, Va., Dec. 21, 1862, Dr. Swinburne again strikes some pretty hard blows at the head of the medical department of the army. He said, —

"It may seem presumptuous in me to offer any suggestions to men of such eminent ability as are to be found directing the medical department of our armies. I shall, however, offer to you, as the executive of the Empire State, such suggestions as shall seem to me appropriate and just in the present emergency, and particularly as you have seen fit to honor me as the accredited medical representative of the State of New York, to look to the interests of our troops now in the field. I should therefore prove recreant to my duty were I not to make all the suggestions which I deem pertinent to their welfare.

"In my judgment, there is something radically wrong in the manner in which surgeons are selected to fill certain positions. Merit or competency is in many instances entirely ignored, and seniority takes its place. . . . As it is now, many of the more useful, intelligent, conservative, and handy operative surgeons are acting in a purely executive capacity, as superintendents of hospitals, directors of brigades, corps, and divisions, instead of which they should be employed in selecting and deciding upon the operations to be performed, if any were requisite, and, if need be, to perform the operations in a manner most likely to give the patients the best chances of recovery. I know full well that there is a prevalent idea that the army is a good school for surgery. Now, while this is true in a certain sense, it is not so in another."

As an instance of the misplacing of surgeons in the field, the doctor wrote, —

"Take, for instance, our own Frank H. Hamilton, who consented to leave an elegant home, lucrative practice, and temporarily relinquished his position as teacher of surgery in Bellevue Hospital, to go out with a regiment of volunteers. What was the result? He was soon misplaced by being made a medical director of a corps; and that, too, where he was mainly useful as an executive officer, and where his peculiar talents could not be made available at the time of a great battle, when his genius would have relieved and saved many valuable lives. I mention this simply as one among the many instances in which talent is being constantly misplaced in this grand army, where there are thousands of the best men in the country, who command and obtain at home the best medical talent. Now, if these officers and men are willing to offer their bodies as a sacrifice to assist in saving our country from *villanous treachery* and *rebellion*, I think they have a right to *demand of our government* the services of the most experienced surgeons, at any cost. In this respect our government has displayed the most sordid penuriousness."

During the three days in June, 1862, while the wounded were being brought into Savage Station, the doctor performed twenty-two excisions of the shoulder and elbow. Of these, six resulted in good limbs; two which would have resulted well, were afterwards amputated by others without cause: the others, being removed to the pest-houses or "tobacco warehouses" in Richmond, were lost sight of.

In striking contrast to this humane system of conservative surgery, is a case given in the "Medical and Surgical Reporter" of 1863. On Sunday, May 3, Col. Newman, of the Thirty-first New-York, was wounded in the left foot by a grape-shot; the ball passing obliquely upward from the left side of the foot, crushing the anterior part of the tarsus, and lodging just under the skin, but not involving the ankle-joint. From twelve to fifteen hours after the injury was received, the ball was extracted, and the colonel sent, after the wound was dressed, to the National Hotel at Washington; the surgeons at the front deciding the foot could be saved. On invitation of a nephew of Senator Wilkinson, Minnesota, Dr. Swinburne called on the colonel, and, coinciding with the opinion of the surgeons at the front that the foot could be saved, washed out the wound, and dressed the foot. In the evening the doctor called again, and was told by the colonel that an army surgeon had been in and said that the foot must be amputated. As a friend, the doctor advised against amputation, and continued to wash and dress the wound twice a day. On the fourth day the inflammation had very considerably abated, and suppuration had commenced; the wound in the skin and soft tissue had begun to granulate; the whole appeared healthy; and the constitutional symptoms had subsided. His appetite was good. He slept well, and experienced little or no pain except when the limb was moved. Dr. Spencer of Watertown, Dr. Green of New York, and five army surgeons of good standing, who saw the colonel, agreed with Dr. Swinburne. On the 11th, however, he was told by Surgeon-Gen. Hammond, upon whom he called on business, that he (Hammond) objected to Swinburne visiting Col. Newman in any capacity, even as a friend; that the National Hotel, at which he was stopping, was located in a certain district in Washington, and that an army surgeon had charge of the district; that the patient belonged to such surgeon, and that he (Swinburne) had no business to call in any capacity. At the special request of Col. Newman, Dr. Swinburne called again, in company with Dr. Spencer, and advised the colonel to get permission to go to New York, Dr. Spencer offering to accompany him. But the army surgeons decided against this course, and said he must have the foot amputated, or they would not attend him; and that, if he did not submit to their decision in regard to him, he would be reported to the surgeon-general for contumely, and dismissed from the service, the colonel assuring the doctor a friend of his had been thus treated. The surgeon informed the colonel, he said, "that, if he did not submit, they would have to leave him, and that he should have neither pay nor medical attendance, but that they would strike him from the roll, and that they had the authority of the surgeon-general for saying this." The surgeon also added to the colonel's friend, "If I find a citizen surgeon in the room looking at any of my patients, I'll kick him down stairs." These remarks were made by Dr. Clymer. The amputation, after much dallying, was finally made by Dr. Clymer, assisted by Surgeons De White, Swasey, Farrel, and Allen, notwithstanding the patient was rapidly improving; and the colonel died. A friend of the colonel, writing to Dr. Swinburne after the butchery of this brave soldier, said, " This noble soldier often expressed his thanks for your kindness, and could not convince himself, that, in handling and dressing his wound, any hands were as soft and delicate in their touch as yours."

In reviewing the case in that fearless manner always characterizing the doctor's course when attacking malpractice on the soldier or private citizen, he raised these important points : —

First, The surgeons on the field decided upon the propriety of not amputating the foot of Col. Newman; that it could be saved without amputation.

Second, That the injury was inflicted on the 3d, and the surgeons on the field decided not to amputate. When he arrived in Washington on the 8th, while the whole limb was tumefied, and absolutely shining with inflammation, the surgeons in Washington wished to amputate. This was delayed from day to day, and still the foot improved, in spite of the depression of mind caused by the constant threats of amputation. On the 13th they demanded amputation, and it was delayed, the same condition of things existing, and I learn the surgeons decided upon waiting for a few days. On the 16th Col. Newman was troubled with little pain. Meanwhile his wounds freely suppurated; and, in fact, his condition had continued to improve, so that suppuration was free. On the 16th "the surgeons administered ether, and made a perfect examination"— of what? Why, a wound into which you could easily put your thumb and all your fingers. This examination resulted (as the surgeons stated) in finding a small bit of leather, and in wrenching by great force a piece of crushed bone, about one inch square, from its connection with the living tissues, besides doing other irreparable injury to the soft parts. All of these loose bones, leather, etc., would have dropped out of the wound whenever loosened by nature.

Third, The 17th (next day) he was attacked with tetanus. How significant! Cause and effect are sure to follow. The story of the apples over again : you need not knock them from the tree, since, if let alone, they will fall when ripe. And so the bone will surely follow the organic laws of nature : *ergo* the ignorant interference with the bone caused the irritation which resulted in tetanus, the amputation and hemorrhage followed, and the sequel, death, was the result.

Fourth, If amputation was to have been performed, why make the "examination" at all, in the manner it was made? since the eye could scan the entire wound, and the finger could easily pass through and into the wound, and ascertain its condition. Then why irritate the parts at all, before amputating? since it is the desire of all good surgeons to avoid it, in order to save the shock, — the pyæmia gangrene, or tetanus. That the latter followed so soon after this injudicious interference, there need be no wonder.

The review of this case by Dr. Swinburne, and the deductions he drew, created quite a *furore* among the surgical profession in the army and with the public. It but proved the assertion made two months later by the "Medical and Surgical Reporter : " " While on the whole there has been but little to complain of under the circumstances, regarding the employment of irregular practitioners by the government, instances have occurred, and still exist, where they have occupied prominent positions in the government service."

The " Reporter," in an article on " Tyranny in the Medical Department of the Army," referring to the case of Col. Newman, said, —

" On another page of this number we publish an article from a responsible source, detailing a case in which a cold, heartless, tyrannical exercise of power on the part of the highest medical officer under our government, and a subordinate who, if we mistake not, when the war broke out was engaged in mercantile pursuits, certainly not in the practice of medicine or surgery, seems to have cost a brave officer and worthy man his life. Let our readers peruse the article, and note the facts. Let them observe that at a public hotel a wounded man was denied the privilege of calling in the surgical aid of one of the first surgeons in the State from which he volunteered, who was then on official professional duty from the executive of his State, *and was compelled to submit to an amputation against his own wishes, and against the judgment of a number of able surgeons;* and that, too, when confessedly those who insisted on taking charge of the case *had not time to give it the attention needed* to save the limb. We had supposed, that, in the circumstances in which Col. Newman was placed, he had a right to choose his medical adviser, and that he also had a right to refuse to have his limb amputated. It seems, however, that he had no rights at all, that Brigadier-Gen. Hammond and his subordinates were bound to respect. The surgeon (Dr. Swinburne) of the patient's choice was one of high standing and acknowledged ability, and one who, in his capacity as surgeon, was officially connected with the government of the State to which the wounded man belonged."

In company with Senator Wilkinson and a governor of one of the Western States, Dr. Swinburne waited on Secretary of War Stanton, and indignantly denounced this piece of butchery, and other practices in the medical department of the army. The secretary, turning to the senator, asked, " Who is this man who so boldly makes these charges?" The senator replied, " He is a gentleman who knows of what he speaks, eminent as a surgeon, and successful beyond all others, terribly interested in the soldiers; and, if you don't know him now, you will soon know all about him."

The doctor wrote to the " Medical Times " a severe criticism on the management of the medical department for the care of the sick and wounded after the battle of Fredericksburg. This communication was suppressed; and in its place laudatory articles appeared, praising the surgeon-general, who was reputed to be one of the proprietors of that journal, and who was busily engaged in preparing a medical and surgical history of the war.

Of this official and his enterprise, the " Medical and Surgical Reporter " said, —

"The office of surgeon-general of the United States is one of great importance and dignity. Its occupant should have a better claim to it than any founded on mere personal or moneyed influence, or the advocacy of parties whose influence has tended to degrade the medical bureau. He should be · a man of experience, a practical man. The head of the medical department is collecting material for a surgical history of the war; and army surgeons have been discouraged from publishing cases that have occurred under their observation, lest it should detract from the freshness and originality of the contemplated work."

On May 4, 1863, Dr. Swinburne was again commissioned, this time by Gov. Seymour, and left for Washington with a letter from the governor to Secretary of War Stanton, in which the governor wrote, —

"Having had much experience in hospital practice, and also having seen much service with the army, I deem him eminently qualified for the duty to which I desire he may be assigned. Under letters from my predecessor, Gov. Morgan, Dr. Swinburne was placed in the position which I desire to have him occupy."

He also had with him a letter from Ex-Gov. Morgan to Secretary Stanton, in which the writer said, "I need not repeat to you that Dr. Swinburne is one of our most efficient surgeons, and has, by his skill and scientific treatment, saved many limbs and lives."

He had also a letter to the secretary from the late Thurlow Weed, in which he said, "You know how generously he has served the country, and the cause of humanity, and will, I doubt not, promptly pass him to the army."

On his arrival in Washington, he presented his credentials to Surgeon-Gen. Hammond, and was told "that it was the special request of Gen. Hooker and Medical Director Latterman, that no civilian surgeons be allowed to pass into the army lines at this time; that those who were there when the movement commenced were to remain, but additions were not desired." .

The doctor then, with the assistance of the late Senator Sumner and others, persisted in an effort to get a pass to the front as a citizen in search of a friend, but in every effort failed; Surgeon-Gen. Hammond declaring he would submit the application, with his disapproval, to the war department, showing the animus and jealousy that actuated that official. In one conversation the secretary, in a very excited manner, declared the fact of giving the information Dr. Swinburne did to Gov. Seymour was wrong, and that of itself was evidence the doctor was a "bad and dangerous man." The doctor replied, "If doing my duty faithfully, and reporting the result to Gov. Seymour, who had sent me, and who was entitled to know the result, made me in his (the secretary's) estimation what he had been pleased to term me, then I acknowledge you are right."

Notwithstanding the efforts already made in vain, yet at the request of Senator Sumner to renew the application, and on the receipt of the following telegram from Adjutant-Gen. John S. Sprague, — "Renew your application : it is the governor's desire that you go to the Army of the Potomac if possible," — the doctor made one more effort.

On this effort proving a failure, he telegraphed to that effect to Gov. Seymour, and received the following from Adjutant-Gen. Sprague : —

"The governor is gratified with your zeal, but thinks he cannot ask the government to violate its rules. He hopes and believes you can be of great service to those who come from the army at Washington and vicinity."

Notwithstanding, both the secretary of war and surgeon-general, in refusing to allow Dr. Swinburne to go to the front, had suggested this very course; yet, when the governor's telegram to this effect was presented, a refusal was again met with. Surgeon-Gen. Hammond, who had said, "You can be of great service to the sick and wounded," now said, that, after what had occurred, he did not desire Dr. Swinburne, or any other medical representative or agent of the State of New York, to visit the hospitals about Washington, or offices in Washington.

In consequence of these several refusals of the war department and Surgeon-Gen. Hammond to recognize Dr. Swinburne as medical agent from the State of New York, or to allow him to visit the army as a citizen, the doctor felt that his remaining in Washington longer would certainly call down further opposition from the war department, influenced as it was by Hammond, and perhaps involve the doctor's personal safety; and realizing he was debarred from carrying out the mission for which he was sent, or the prompting of his own heart to benefit the sick and wounded, he left Washington for home. The dwarfish system of the head could not bear criticism, and knew he was safe from any censure by those who adhered strictly to military red tape, and wore the insignia of a regular of the army.

In 1864, Surgeon-Gen. William A. Hammond was, after a trial by court-martial lasting four months, dismissed from the service, and forever disqualified from holding any office of honor, profit, or trust under the Government of the United States. Soon after his removal, he inaugurated, according to the "Reporter," the "Medical Monthly," of which enterprise the "Medical and Surgical Reporter" said, —

"It is reported in New York that the sanitary commission has subscribed to three thousand copies of this journal. We can scarcely believe that such a misappropriation of its funds has been made by that organization, certainly not to the extent reported, though it will be remembered that among the singular expenditures of the commission is a considerable amount for the publication of medical essays for the use of surgeons on the battle-field and in hospitals. It is possible that the commission has undertaken to *distribute* three thousand copies of the 'New-York Medical Journal' as a favor to its reputed principal proprietor and editor."

As in all other conflicts where the doctor espoused the cause of the suffering soldier or the people, results brought about by time proved he was always right, and, when right, earnest.

CHAPTER V.

FROM WAR TO PESTILENCE.

In 1864 the State of New York, and the large portion of the nation to which the port of New York was the key, were threatened with another enemy more subtle than that of war, which was at the time creating such cruel havoc among the people in the southern portion of the country. This subtle foe, in the nature of the pestilential yellow-fever, was then infecting a larger number of ports with which our commerce was carried on than during any other season for sixty-six years, excepting, perhaps, the year 1856. The anxiety of the residents of that city, of the State, and of the State Government, was naturally aroused at the impending danger threatened; and prompt measures were deemed essential to meet this foe that must inevitably come to our shores, and, if possible, check it before its ravages had reached the land. This could only be done by an efficient and effective quarantine at the port of New York. To meet this emergency, the Legislature, in 1863, had enacted a law for the establishing of a system of quarantine in the lower bay. The very thought that there was even a possible danger of the plague spreading over the State, and adding its horrors to what the people were already enduring, was a strain almost too great to bear, and alarmed them to a degree that even the excitement attending the news from the fields of battle could not eclipse. Of what avail, it was readily recognized, would be laws to establish a quarantine, however well framed. or the appropriation of millions of dollars to effect the desired end for the purpose of saving the people, unless the right man was in charge as health-officer at the port of New York? For that position an eminently qualified man must be chosen; and Gov. Seymour, having the appointing power, by that intuitiveness for which he was characterized, realized the dangers that threatened, and the kind of a man the emergencies of the times required.

Dr. Swinburne had returned from the army, where he had been working out his plans for the relief of the sick and wounded, and where he had, after meeting with great opposition because of professional jealousy, accomplished much of his undertaking. Having no other desire than to succor and benefit the soldiers, and having come to fully comprehend the obstacles that were being placed in his way as a volunteer surgeon, he believed further effort would be the cause of intensifying opposition from the head of the medical department of the army, and necessarily in a large degree prove futile, he resigned, and returned to Albany. Gov. Seymour had watched with deep interest and pride the work accomplished by this volunteer surgeon, his boldness in denouncing mismanagement by those in high places, as well as his intrepid fearlessness as to personal danger, combined with his acknowledged skill in fathoming the causes of sickness, and applying the remedies to eradicate disease, saw in him the official he wanted for the responsible position of the times, and promptly sent his name to the Senate for confirmation as health-officer of the port of New York.

When the nomination of Dr. John Swinburne as health-officer was sent to the Senate, the two branches of the State Government — the appointing and confirming powers — were politically opposed to each other, and the number of applicants for the position was numerous. Yet, to the credit of all parties concerned in making the appointment, the same loyal spirit which had so often manifested itself during the previous years, when vital questions affecting the safety of the nation or the peace and health of the people were agitated, triumphed. There were no political lines of demarcation drawn: Republicans and Democrats arose to the demands of the hour, and were Americans. The fame the doctor had already achieved was known to every member of the Senate, as it was to the governor; and, as a sequence, one of the grandest indorsements of any man ever given in public life was there recorded of this gentleman by his appointment, made by a Democratic governor, being unanimously confirmed by a Senate. a large majority of whom were Republicans, in less than half an hour from the time it was placed before them.

That the appointment was heartily indorsed by the press, is evidenced by the comments of the journals of both political faiths, but by none more warmly than by the press of New York, politically opposed to him.

The " New-York Herald " of March 20, 1864, said, —

" The public will be a little surprised to learn that the Senate confirmed the nomination of Dr. John Swinburne of Albany, for health-officer of the port of New York, in place of Dr. Gunn, who has held that position for several years past. This programme was agreed upon in the Republican caucus of senators the previous evening. There were facts presented to that caucus, in regard to the condition of affairs at quarantine, that justified, and, in fact, was considered by the Republican senators sufficient to demand, on their part, immediate action. The caucus decided to have the Senate go into executive session, and suspend the rules, and confirm the appointment of Dr. Swinburne, that he might immediately be commissioned. A messenger was sent to Dr. Swinburne, notifying him, that, if the governor would send his name into the Senate, it would be confirmed without delay. In accordance with this understanding, Gov. Seymour sent in his name. The Senate went into executive session, suspended the rules, — which require that the appointments by the governor shall be referred to a committee, and lay over for one week, — and unanimously confirmed the nomination."

On the following day the " Herald " said, —

" Dr. Swinburne, whose appointment as health-officer of the port of New York by Gov. Seymour was confirmed by the Senate on Friday last, is a resident of Albany, and enjoys a high reputation as a physician and surgeon. During Gen. McClellan's campaign on the peninsula, he, with other New-York surgeons, volunteered his services, and at Savage Station and elsewhere rendered much aid to our sick and wounded soldiers. He was in charge of the hospital at Savage Station when that point was captured by the enemy, and accompanied our wounded soldiers, where he remained with them, devoting all his time and surgical talent to their care. Again, immediately after the battle of Fredericksburg, he, with other surgeons from this State, offered his services to attend upon, and look after, the welfare of our wounded soldiers, but learned, on reaching Washington, that an order had been promulgated excluding all volunteer surgeons from the front. Although a Republican in politics, it is understood that Dr. Swinburne's claims upon the Senate rested mainly upon his conceded professional qualifications, and the valuable services he has voluntarily rendered to our troops."

The "New-York World," in announcing the appointment of Dr. Swinburne, said, —

"He is a bright, energetic, ambitious surgeon, who has in hospital and camp, in private practice and in a wide range of action, as in the army, and as in the prisons of the enemy, held bold and strong place, and made himself a name acceptable to Gov. Seymour, and accepted by the Senate. It is a remarkable step forward, as Dr. Swinburne is a lively man, and will make a good officer. It is a pleasant idea that in any thing there should be an *entente cordiale* between the governor and the Senate. It is an appointment that will be canvassed by the medical profession, who are somewhat distinguished for a sharp and severe criticism of each other; but the doctor is used to conflicts of this kind, and can smile at the storm. He finds himself suddenly, this sunshiny Saturday, health-officer of the great New-York harbor. It is waking up to find himself famous, and the surgeon will undergo the dissection of criticism. That the nomination met with unusual favor, is shown by the fact that the appointment, in its confirmation, was immediately sent to the governor. Of course, it is the event of the day."

The "New-York Times" said of the appointment, —

"He is an accomplished physician, and one of the ablest surgeons in the State, and devoted to his profession, and is among the foremost in developing its skill, and extending its usefulness. Personally, no man can possess more popular qualities, and no man is more deservedly popular. It was Dr. Swinburne who, volunteering, and leaving a lucrative practice, was sent by the governor to the peninsula, where his skill and fidelity were of the greatest value. During the seven-days' battles, refusing to leave the sick and wounded under his charge, he was taken prisoner; and it was due to his firm and

manly appeals to the rebel authorities that much of misery
and death were saved, and comforts secured to our suffering
soldiers. He will bring to the position of health-officer all
the ability necessary to fill it, and the will to do so faithfully
and valuably."

"That a prophet is not without praise save in his own
country," did not apply to the honored physician. The press
of Albany, his residence, where he was better known than
anywhere else, was decided in their comments of the wisdom
of Gov. Seymour in making this selection.

The "Albany Evening Times" said, "This is an excellent
appointment, and one well deserved."

The "Evening Journal," "In nominating Dr. Swinburne,
he selected a gentleman of high professional character."

The "Albany Express," "We think the fact that politicians
of both parties dislike the appointment is the most satisfactory argument that could be offered that the governor nominated, and the Senate confirmed, just the right man."

The "Albany Argus," whose editor was well acquainted
with the private and military career of the doctor, said editorially on March 21, "Dr. Swinburne was pressed by men of
all parties, and by the medical profession of the State generally, not only on account of his scientific position, but on account of the service he had personally rendered our soldiers
in the hospitals and on the battle-fields. These considerations
induced Gov. Seymour to make the appointment, and the Senate, without a moment's hesitation, to confirm it." And on
the 23d he again said editorially, "It was understood that a
political appointment in place of Dr. Gunn would not meet
the concurrence of the Senate. In nominating Dr. Swinburne,
he selected a gentleman of high professional character, and
one who devoted earnest and salutary labors to the soldiers
of New York."

This position he held for six consecutive years, until the
advent of the Tweed *régime*, and the inauguration of that era
of public plunder which followed, marking the most corrupt
epoch in the history of the State, ending at last in the ignominious death of the chieftain in a felon's cell, and the flee-

ing as outcasts, and fugitives from justice, of some of his most active princes and leaders. During that period, he established and built up one of the best, if not the best, quarantine systems in the world. The peculiar and fitting record of the esteem in which he was then held was greatly augmented in later years by his re-appointment as health-officer by Gov. Fenton (Republican) when he succeeded Seymour (Democrat), as did Seymour when he succeeded Morgan (Republican), in the re-appointment of Dr. Swinburne to a position in military service.

The appointment opened up a new field of professional activity and research to the inquiring mind, that had been restless for years in searching after greater truths in his profession, and the developing of more efficient means to suppress disease ; as he had labored for years before, in introducing a more conservative system of surgery for the saving of limbs, as well as lessening the tortures that had heretofore almost caused the blood to chill at the mere mention of a surgeon, whose profession and practice were thought to be synonymous with cruelty and amputated members. All the diseases humanity so revolts from, such as cholera, small-pox, and yellow and ship fevers, he met at the watery gate of the city, and successfully conquered, often fighting these loathsome and dire diseases at quarantine, while the residents of the metropolis slept in safety, not even knowing danger was so near. The work accomplished at that station was even greater than that accomplished by him on the field. Here he had no ignorant superior, or professional jealousy, to contend with, and hence pushed forward his work with such marvellous success that he received the congratulations of the Executive in an annual message ; and the Legislature, fully appreciating his work, by law enacted, after his retirement, that one of the artificial islands built by him in the bay should forever be known as Swinburne's Island Hospital.

No record of the living will ever reveal what was accomplished during the time Dr. John Swinburne held the position of health-officer ; and it is utterly beyond all human power to conceive what evil results his knowledge and science, and the system of prevention he adopted, were the means of averting. That he established a great quarantine, to prove a continuous safeguard, is a matter of history ; that he run the quarantine department when the duties of the health-officer were much greater, at seventy thousand dollars per year less than one of his successors, Dr. Vanderpoel, is a matter of record on the books of the comptroller; that he never gave occasion for a suspicion of dishonesty during his management, is a pleasant reminiscence in official life ; and that the results of his searching after the origin and nature of cholera and yellow-fever, as well as the most effective means to check and eradicate these diseases, have been accepted and dwelt upon as reliable authority ever since, must be gratifying to his professional pride, free as he is from vanity as a gentleman, and from professional jealousy — an outgrowth of the known and envied superiority of others — as a physician and surgeon.

A man filling such a position would be more than human, and nothing less than infallible, if he met with no opposition in the discharge of its duties. Dr. Swinburne was not exempt from complaints; but they came solely from persons who had pecuniary interests to serve, — from owners of vessels, who were more anxious their crafts should prove profitable investments than they were in the preventing of the spread of disease; from stevedores, who were willing to jeopardize the lives of their men in the holds of infected vessels, and in the handling of disease-poisoned merchandise; and from boarding-house runners and scalawags, who would risk any thing to satiate their desires to plunder the "green-horn," and bleed the open-hearted sailor. All these the health-officer met with a firmness that knew no yielding. He was there to prevent the spread of disease; and effectually he accomplished that end by the enforcement, rigidly, of the rules his experience taught him were essential, even though some of them, at times, appeared harsh and even oppressive.

When he assumed the control and management of the quarantine, there were absolutely no provisions made for the effectual carrying-out of the purposes of quarantine. There was but one floating hospital, and this vessel was in a leaky and decidedly bad condition. There were no proper residences for the health-officers, and no wharves for the discharging of cargoes, and no warehouses for the cargoes, if discharged, during fumigation. To wait for another session of the Legislature, before active operations, was not in the nature of Dr. Swinburne. He held as a motto, " To be fore-warned is to be fore-armed," and not only immediately commenced arranging for any emergency that might arise, but devoted himself to even a more searching diagnosis of the fever that threatened, as well as making the most minute and thorough analysis of its nature, growth, and the causes from which it emanated, so that, in the event of its arriving at quarantine, he would know on the moment what to do, and when and where to do it. His quarantine resources were less than limited and adequate, for in reality there were none. Yet when the season arrived, and the yellow-fever made its appearance at quarantine from the infected ports, with a larger number of vessels arriving from them than in any previous season, the health-officer was prepared to meet it so effectively that not a single case passed quarantine.

The commissioners, in their report to the governor that year, stated, that, on entering upon the discharge of their duties, they found that nothing had been done towards the establishing of the quarantine, contemplated by the act of 1863, and found the health-officer destitute of means. The floating hospital ship which had been provided, and in use for five years previous, for the reception of persons sick with yellow-fever, was found in a leaky condition, requiring extensive repairs. With their report, they submitted to the governor the report of the health-officer, asserting that it contained so much valuable information that it should be presented in full. His Excellency, in submitting the report to the Legislature, accompanied it with a memorandum, stating "that it was replete with information regarding the various diseases which came under the health-officer's observation and inquiry, and abounded with valuable suggestions affecting the sanitary and commercial interests of the city and State."

In that first report, Dr. Swinburne, as health-officer, presented a number of suggestions and recommendations with reference to the erection of hospitals, warehouses, wet docks, and floating hospitals, as well as the necessity for a . better system of police regulations, all of which were carried into effect during his administration. He treated the subject of yellow-fever in a manner that allayed much of the apprehension and fear entertained with reference to the disease, and afforded a feeling of safety such as had not been enjoyed before. Of the fever, he said, " The malignancy of this disease, which but a few years ago was regarded as an incurable plague, has at length been compelled to yield to the power of medical science. The origin, nature, habits, and peculiarities of this infection have at length become so thoroughly understood, that we are now enabled to guard against the extension of its poisonous effects with a certainty of results almost as definite and fixed as that attendant upon the care and cure of any other disease."

While during some of the previous years the infection had been carried on shore, and communicated to vessels in port, and in some instances had afterwards raged in a most fearful manner, not a single instance of this kind occurred during the season of 1864, the first that Dr. Swinburne was in charge of the quarantine as health-officer.

In 1865 there was no diminution in the danger of being infected with yellow-fever, still prevalent in many ports, with the means to check the disease at quarantine still in a crude condition, and far from what was deemed actually necessary in the discharge of the duty to which the health-officer was assigned. But again he was equal to the demands upon him, and exhibited that unconquerable spirit which he so often displayed in civil and military life ; and knowing that to delay was dangerous, and that procrastination is the thief of time, he was able to meet the disease at the opening of the season, and again successfully blockade it at quarantine. During that season two hundred and thirty vessels arrived from ports infected with yellow-fever. On board fifty-three of these vessels, there were two hundred and forty-six cases. All these were quarantined, inspected, cleansed, and fumigated, and the disease, so far as that year was concerned, as completely conquered as was the Rebellion the same year by the Union army in the front; with even grander results, for not a case, as in the previous year, had passed quarantine.

So universal had become the fame of this health-officer at this critical period, that it won for him plaudits almost as great as those his valor on the field had called from the press and public. Pleased with the work the health-officer had accomplished, and the praise that was being bestowed on him, Gov. Fenton, under date of Nov. 4 of that year, expressed his pleasure to the commissioners in these words: " I am glad to know that the health-officer, Dr. Swinburne, has attracted honorable mention in the discharge of the responsible duties of his position, and that he is unwearied in his efforts in connection with your board, and other authorities of the city of New York, relating to the sanitary condition of the city."

From Washington came also words of praise. S. K. Barnes, surgeon-general of the United-States army, in writing to Gov. Fenton, said, " In this connection, permit me to congratulate you upon the energy and efficiency displayed by your health-officer, Dr. John Swinburne, and to express the conviction, that, if sustained in the exercise of the necessary precautionary measures, he will be fully equal to any emergency that can now be anticipated."

Such words of approval, coming from the chief executive officer of the State, and from the head of the medical department of the United States, would have aroused no small degree of vanity in the majority of mortals. With this matter-of-fact but eminent physician, they elicited no further feeling than the satisfaction of knowing that his efforts to do his duty to the State and the people were appreciated by those qualified to know the magnitude of the work, and the results attained.

Again, the following year, the commissioners, in submitting their report, deviated from the established custom, among officials, of giving a mere synopsis of the health-officer's report, and transmitted it in full. They said, "The report of the health-officer contains much valuable information in regard to the principal quarantinable diseases which have visited our port, and shows a most gratifying result attending the administration of our quarantine system during the past season. It is replete with so many interesting statistics and practical suggestions, that, notwithstanding its extreme length, we have deemed it advisable to transmit it entire to the Legislature."

The health-officer, in his report, again presses the absolute necessity of a number of provisions for the hygienic treatment of the persons who arrive at quarantine sick with disease. This, like all other reports by him, is not confined to a formal statement of facts, of expenditures of the department, and the number of arrivals, sick, and deaths, but is accompanied with a minute statement of his observations of yellow-fever, and the conclusions scientifically arrived at after investigation, thus affording information of value in the present, and for time to come. In this connection Dr. Swinburne said, "While a climate may be generally unfavorable to the extension of disease, yet instances are not wanting where places, for years exempt from disease, have become infected: for instance, Newbern, N.C., for a long period of years considered one of the most healthful ports. During the year 1864 it became infected with yellow-fever, which prevailed in so malignant a form as to nearly depopulate the town. So with Key West, never infected until 1862; but the past season it has been the most malignant port, and no vessel could touch there without being poisoned." He cited the case of the ship "Tahama," which touched there on June 12, taking no cargo, only landing a gun; and yet in four weeks, while in a northern climate, yellow-fever was discovered, and within seven weeks twenty-six cases had occurred. "I may safely say," he adds, "with the exception, perhaps, of 1856, no period has been fraught with more danger to the port and harbor of New York from infection than was the past season." He was inclined to doubt the possibility of purifying vessels infected with disease, — whether by frost, fumigation, or otherwise, — without the absolute discharge of cargoes therefrom. He recommended proper facilities for the purification of poisoned goods, especially clothing, etc., as no such existed; and all kinds of expedients were resorted to, to accomplish this work.

It was not till this year that the first appropriation was made for the carrying-out of the system of quarantine islands and hospitals, as recommended in two previous reports.

CHAPTER VI.

A QUARTET OF PLAGUES.

Contending with Four Plagues. — Cholera, Small-Pox, and Yellow-Fever. — Best Quarantine in the World. — A Sleepless Official. — Criminal Consols.

In 1866 the trying ordeal began in earnest when we were threatened with four diseases, — the Russian plague, cholera, yellow-fever, and ship-fever. The officials at quarantine were then like a traveller in a mountainous region, standing on the edge of an abyss so deep and dark and fearful, that he shudders to look down into the chasm; and humanity recoiled at the bare thought of these visitations, so terrible were the devastations they would inevitably cause if once landed upon our shores. The times and circumstances demanded a peremptory policy. The threatened quartet of plagues created a necessity for immediate action, and admitted of no negotiations, postponements, or half-measures. It was then that the experienced scientist, surgeon, and physician proved that he was " forewarned and fore-armed," by assuming that " cholera was a communicable and controllable disease; that its causes are not in the atmosphere; that it accompanies human travel and human traffic; that it progresses at the rate of vessels across the ocean, and never precedes them; that it is transmitted by clothing and effects as well as passengers; that it never appears in a new locality without communication, directly or indirectly, with persons and places; and that it may be arrested, like the plague, by an absolute quarantine of a short duration : " and he recommended a uniform system of quarantine throughout the country as a safe and sure prevention. That his constant searching after knowledge had eminently fitted him for the suppression of the scourge, and that he had arrived at a perfect diagnosis of cholera, were manifested by the establishing in accordance with the principles laid down, and on the recommendation of Dr. Swinburne, of a quarantine, which the commissioners, eleven years afterwards, when Dr. Swinburne was engaged in another field, pronounced " the most extensive and complete quarantine establishment in the world, — an establishment which, perhaps, properly conducted, affords every guaranty against the inroads of pestilence which human experience and forethought can devise."

Under the act of 1863 there was contemplated provision but for one hospital; and this, between the 1st of April and the 1st of November, was to be appropriated *exclusively* to the care of persons sick with yellow-fever, and during the remainder of the year might be used for the care of typhus or ship fever. The only direction for the care of cholera patients was, that they " shall be provided for by the commissioners of quarantine in such manner as they may determine, and occasion demand, until permanent provision shall be otherwise made by law." This law gave the commissioners no jurisdiction over any land, and prevented them from **exercising** any over Staten Island, Long Island, or Coney Island, and over no land contiguous to the harbor except over New-York City. Neither had they money to provide any means for caring for the sick. The law further provided, " In no case shall persons sick with different diseases be put in the same hospital; " and yet there were none others than the one floating hospital, and that was reserved by law for the sick with yellow-fever. This was the condition of affairs at quarantine when " The Atlanta " arrived, Nov. 2, from London, with over five hundred passengers on board, with sixty cases of cholera during the passage, sixteen of which proved fatal. Twenty-two new cases were found on arrival, and twenty-one other cases afterwards. She was detained twenty-eight days at quarantine. Notwithstanding the prevalence of the disease upon the vessel during the passage and after arrival, in consequence of the precautions taken by the health-officer, no cases occurred beyond the limits of the vessel.

Under these circumstances, the health-officer, Dr. Swinburne, was similarly placed·to the Polish Gen. Bem in Transylvania during Kossuth's Hungarian war. In that country, Bem found not a single fortress in the hands of the Hungarians; but, the more he felt their importance, the more anxious he was to gain possession of them. Events proved, that, in Kossuth's selection of Bem to conquer Transylvania, he possessed the discernment to choose the most able man from among the multitude; as did Gov. Seymour, when he appointed Dr. Swinburne health-officer, prove that he understood equally the importance of the task to be undertaken, and who would be the proper man to successfully accomplish the desired end. The simile between these two eminent men —one of war, and the other of health and preservation, both patriots — is striking. Bem, like the health-officer Dr. Swinburne, was a thorough organizer and strict disciplinarian, making no distinction because of social standing among his troops; and hence it was that the young sprigs of nobility preferred service in other corps, where more consideration was paid to their pedigree. Bem was peculiarly attached to the artillery, and believed in meeting his enemy at as long range as possible, and dealing heavy blows before they came to close quarters. But when the hand-to-hand conflict came, he was ready, as was shown when, at Rothenthurn Pass, with his small army, of which the Polish corps and the German legion were the flower, he drove the Russians in the wildest flight, and routed the four Austrian generals, Puchner, Pfarsman, Graser, and Jovich. His conquering Transylvania justified the confidence of Kossuth, and confirmed the reputation he had won. With Dr. Swinburne, pedigree had no weight; and he, too, believed in meeting his enemies at as long range as possible, and exterminating them. His conquering the four pestilences, and saving the people from their ravages, justified Gov. Seymour's confidence, and confirmed the reputation he had won.

So grand was his success that year, that Gov. Fenton, in his message to the Legislature in 1876, in treating of the cholera epidemic of the previous year, said, —

"Six hundred and fifty-one persons have been treated under quarantine since the facilities were provided. The number of cases on vessels during the passage and after arrival here, is estimated at two thousand; and of this number, at least one thousand have died. It is believed that few if any cases of cholera have appeared on shore, the origin of which can be traced to the sick under quarantine. This is the highest testimony in favor of the vigilance of the health-officer."

This indorsement from the highest official in the State was a tribute of esteem a less eminent and capable gentleman than the then health-officer would have paraded with unlimited ostentation. It was not only an indorsement by the highest official, but implied the inestimable debt of gratitude every resident of the State, whether in the thickly populated cities or in the smallest hamlets in the extreme northern, western, and eastern sections of the State, was under to the vigilance of the health-officer.

In his report for that year as health-officer, Dr. Swinburne, without any suspicion of self-laudation, again presses the necessity of renewed watchfulness on the part of the people, and the urgent demands for proper quarantine facilities. He said, —

"Nearly all agree that cholera is contagious, and can be quarantined at a port of entry, providing the proper precaution as to non-intercourse, isolation, disinfection, cleansing, etc., be carried out. The fact, that, with the very inefficient quarantine facilities now afforded us, we have succeeded in preventing the spread of cholera upon our shores, furnishes no reason for supposing, that, with the same accommodation, we shall succeed as well in like endeavors during the next season. From our knowledge of the history of the migratory conduct of the disease, it is safe to infer that the visitations we received last season from the malady are premonitions sent out like heralds to warn us to prepare for its more severe and powerful approach. As the falling of the smaller stones and light bodies of snow from the mountain-side are but the forerunners of the avalanche which suddenly appears, prostrating wide-spread forests and populous villages in its course, and distributing devastation and death for miles around, so these instances of infected vessels approaching our harbors may be the precursors of such an extended increase of their class, during the coming season, as will require all the improvements which the State can furnish, and all the vigilance and skill which science can supply, to enable us to prevent the due infection from invading our shores, spreading through the land, and visiting every hearthstone with affliction and death. 'Forewarned is fore-armed,' should be an axiom for worthy action in every case. If, after observing it in this instance, the great Providence who is the dispenser alike of life and death should arrest the approach of this terrible destroyer, and turn it from our shores, we shall have yet the consolation of knowing that we have done our whole duty; and if, in his wisdom, he may yet permit it to come upon us, we shall be at least prepared to do all we can to weaken its attack, subdue its effects, and confine its march."

The report of the commissioners for 1863 gave the arrival of eighteen vessels in port infected with cholera. On these, six hundred and two persons were sick on arrival, at or during detention at quarantine, of whom two hundred and forty-two died, — a mortality much less than that which attended the disease in Europe, and greatly below that which occurred among the passengers of " The England " while under quarantine at Halifax. The commissioners, in speaking of Dr. Swinburne as health-officer in that trying state of affairs, said, —

" The floating hospitals owned by the State would accommodate less than eighty; yet at one time he had to have accommodation for upwards of one hundred and twenty, while over fourteen hundred persons who had been exposed to the disease on shipboard were to be provided for in some more suitable place of detention. In view of the means for the care and treatment of the sick, the commissioners regard the results as truly wonderful, and speak volumes in praise of the health-officer, Dr. Swinburne."

They added, —

" The health-officer, in his report, has paid a truthful and graceful tribute to the services rendered by those who were charged with the care and treatment of the sick, but modestly omitted to state the share which he bore in looking after and alleviating the sufferings of the sick, and affording aid and consolation to the friends of the dead. Charged by law with duties which oftentimes required him to be in attendance upon the Metropolitan Board of Health, or at the office of the commissioners, and at the same time to be at his post at the boarding-station, or among the sick in the lower bay, he seemed almost omnipresent. No duty, within his power to perform was neglected, and he looked after all under his care with a sleepless vigilance which seemed to know no fatigue, and experienced no relaxation while any thing remained to be done. What was said of him by a writer in describing the services rendered by Dr. Swinburne as a surgeon during the peninsular campaign in the late Rebellion, might be said of him in reference to his labors under quarantine."

They quoted : —

"Of this man I cannot speak in terms of too high praise. He was thoughtless of himself, forgetful even of the wants of nature, untiring in his labors, uniting to the highest courage of man the tenderness of a woman and the gentleness of a child. In that terrible hour when other surgeons were worn out and exhausted, no labor appeared to diminish his vigor. After days of toil, and nights of sleeplessness, he was as fresh and earnest as though he had just stepped forth from a night of quiet sleep. And while others became impatient, and had to escape from those scenes to seek repose, he, operating for hours at a time, found relaxation and refreshment in going from tent to tent, counselling the surgeons, advising the nurses, and speaking words of cheer to the wounded and the dying."

The latter portion of that part of the commissioners' report quoted is from a volume of reminiscences by the Rev. Dr. Marks of Pennsylvania, and, although quoted on a previous page, is repeated here simply to demonstrate the high esteem in which he was held by every honest man with whom he came in contact, whether strangers, or acquaintances of years, and because, if the commissioners deemed this tribute from one of another State worthy of incorporation in a necessarily limited report, it is valuable enough to incorporate here.

In 1867 yellow-fever was more destructive and wide-spread than at any previous period. That year two hundred and thirty-five vessels arrived in the port of New York from sixteen ports infected with the disease, and five hundred and seventy-three vessels from infected and doubtful ports were detained at quarantine for examination. During the year, one hundred and fifty-two vessels were quarantined for sickness, with one thousand and thirty cases on board, of which three hundred and eighty-four died. Twenty-eight of these vessels had small-pox on board, to which sixteen thousand six hundred and eighty persons had been exposed. Of these, twelve thousand nine hundred were vaccinated in quarantine; and only four cases of sickness of any kind in the metropolitan district could be traced to infection from this large number of arrivals.

Between the 18th of June and the 5th of November, 1869, two hundred and eleven vessels arrived from infected ports, twenty-seven of which had sickness on board. Nearly all had cargoes of a character calculated to carry and retain the seeds of infection. On board these twenty-seven vessels, ninety-two persons were sick with yellow-fever in the ports of departure, of whom forty-six died. Sixty other cases occurred during the passage, twenty-one of these proving fatal. The same vessels had twenty-five cases of other diseases on board. "These statistics," said the commissioners, "are scarcely without a parallel in the same brief time in the history of quarantine; and, in view of past experience, it seems hardly credible that all of the dangers attending the arrival of so many infected vessels could have been confined to the limits of quarantine. Yet the commissioners are not aware that a single case of yellow-fever occurred on shore during this season; and so little publicity was given to the fact of the arrival of so large a number of vessels from infected ports, that no uneasiness was at any time excited in the public mind."

In their report for 1870, the commissioners said, —

"Although that terrible disease which has become an annual visitor to our shores found a large number of victims among those engaged in our commerce with tropical parts during the past summer, our citizens, happily, escaped its ravages. The scourge of cholera, which made the years 1866 and 1867 memorable in the history of quarantine in the port of New York, sought its victims in other climes. The tide of emigration has continued without diminution, but has been unattended with the introduction of any foreign pestilence to excite the apprehensions of the public. Many who enjoy the quiet of their own firesides, and are exempt from the visitation of pestilence, care little to inquire to whom they are indebted for such exemption. Resting in fancied security amidst the luxuries of their own homes, they little dream that they are surrounded by perils which hourly threaten to bring foreign contagion to their doors, and they fail to appreciate the sleepless vigilance which protects them from the approaching danger."

The season of 1869 was the last that Dr. Swinburne was in charge as health-officer; but, during the period he held that position, he accomplished a work, and established a quarantine system, and facilities to suppress disease, which will remain as monuments to his scientific and executive abilities long after the present generation shall have ceased to be actors in the great drama of life, and the curtain been rung down on the last scene. Many who are prominent to-day will enjoy but a brief career of eminence, and be only as chimerical delusions, rapidly coming to the front, and as rapidly vanishing from memory; while the name of Dr. John Swinburne, because of his great achievements in this and other walks of life, will be ingrafted in the pages of history among those who, while living, made the world greater, and whose memory will sparkle for generations to come, throwing on the future a reflection and splendor of achievements as brilliant and far-reaching as the rays of a setting sun that bathe and beautify the western horizon.

One of the greatest obstacles with which he had to contend as health-officer, in his struggles with the plague of cholera, was the avarice and deceit of traders and other nations, and the culpable neglect of our consuls abroad. Most all the vessels arriving at the port of New York during the cholera epidemic, from the countries where it raged, had clean bills of health; and in but few instances did the consuls give any official intimation of its existence. During the prevalence of the disease in Paris, no official notice of its existence there was received; and in 1867, when whole villages in Germany were being depopulated by its ravages, vessels arrived from all the German ports with clean bills of health.

In contending with these diseases at quarantine, Dr. Swinburne, as health-officer, was enabled by his scientific ability and deep research, in addition to the construction of the artificial islands, to arrive at a clear and definite knowledge of the diseases with which he had to deal, and thus was enabled to transmit valuable information to the profession. He thoroughly demonstrated that neither the vessel nor the cargo carried the poison of either cholera, small-pox, or ship-fever, but that the personal effects of passengers did. In cholera the greatest amount of contagion came from excretions. The bulkhead of a vessel separating the second-class passengers from the steerage passengers, and between their respective water-closets, where, for instance, they were sick in the steerage with cholera, and free from it in the cabin, was sufficient to prevent the contagion from spreading. Of the nature of yellow-fever, he discovered that the hold of a vessel, with its bilge-water, induced the disease in persons, and that vessels lying at docks infected with yellow-fever poisoned the district and the inhabitants. An important discovery touching this disease was that persons with clean clothing might be sick with yellow-fever in any place, and those around them not be affected, and that their vomit and defections were not dangerous. In other words, he held that the well might sleep with the sick, under circumstances of cleanliness, without danger of infection. He further came to the conclusion that dead bodies did not infect or propagate the disease, and that the same was true regarding clean vessels and clean cargoes.

By the superseding of this gentleman, for partisan reasons, the State was the loser in a sanitary as well as financial point, as was proven afterwards. In 1870 and 1871 a number of ports with which our commerce was being carried on were suffering from an epidemic of small-pox; and from these ports the infection was brought to the city of New York, where in 1870, the first year after Dr. Swinburne left quarantine, there were two hundred and ninety-three deaths from this disease. The next year (1871) there were eight hundred and five deaths,— the largest record from small-pox in a century, the next largest being six hundred and eighty-one, in 1853.

Jackson S. Shultz, president of the Board of Health of New-York City, of which Dr. Swinburne was an *ex-officio* member, said in substance, at a dinner given on his (Shultz) retiring from that office, that the Metropolitan Board of Health had not accomplished as much in two years as he expected it would in one month, and that the quarantine under Dr. Swinburne had been the only successful branch connected with the board.

CHAPTER VII.

An Odious Comparison. — Artificial Islands. — Corruption in Quarantine. — A
Political Trick. — Bleeding the State.

COMPARISONS, while not always, are often odious, at least
to some of the parties brought into comparison; and while
there is no desire to resurrect the misdeeds of men who have
passed away, or who are long since no longer prominent, it
is seemingly necessary, that for a better appreciation of Dr.
John Swinburne's honesty, integrity, and ability as a health-
officer, his administration should be contrasted with that of
some of his successors; and it is to be regretted that in the
comparison the distinction is so marked as to make him appear a giant along side of a pygmy, to at least one of his
successors and traducers, scientifically as a physician, morally
as a man, and in integrity to the people and the State as an
official. The comparison is so odious that it must necessarily
create some ill will and anger, although it would be impossible to paint it in colors that would do justice, or describe it
in language in any way adequate to convey the great difference. Ill feeling, however, will only come from those who
dare not publicly deny, and have no defence.

In drawing this comparison, it is well to state that the
commissioners, a board under whom the doctor had never
served, six years after his retirement, in their report to the
Legislature in 1876, said, —

"Any apprehensions entertained at the beginning of the
year, that Asiatic cholera would again make a lodgment in
our bay, have not been realized: indeed, as one season after
another passes, and the ravages of the once deadly scourge
are averted, there is an increasing confidence in the ability
of the quarantine authorities to at all times arrest its prog-

ress at the gate of the metropolis. While it is uncertain what a year may bring forth, there are now seemingly some grounds for this growing confidence. We have unquestionably here, in the harbor of New York, the most extensive and complete quarantine establishment in the world, — an establishment which, properly conducted, affords every guaranty against the inroads of pestilence which human experience and forethought can devise. It is true that the artificial island system necessitated heavy expenditures, yet the since low rate of cholera mortality bears striking testimony to the wisdom of our predecessors."   .

Prior to the appointment of Dr. Swinburne, the quarantine facilities had been located on the mainland, to which the people were violently opposed, going to such extremes as to destroy the buildings used. When the health-officer proposed the erection of the two artificial islands in the bay for quarantine, the celebrated New-York engineer, Craven, declared the scheme eutopian, impracticable, and simply impossible of carrying out. He was consulting engineer to the health-officer, and was the projector of the Croton Waterworks, and chief engineer of the works up to the time of his death. When the work was well under way, and no longer a question of doubt, Mr. Craven declared it was the grandest piece of engineering skill of the age. The upper island was named Hoffman's Island by the commissioners, in honor of the governor under whose administration it was constructed; and, by act of the Legislature, the lower island was named Swinburne Island Hospital. These artificial islands, constructed in accordance with the recommendation of Dr. Swinburne, were the first of that nature ever undertaken.

In 1872, two years after Dr. Swinburne's time, what was known as West Bank Hospital was, by an act of the Legislature, "hereafter to be known and designated as Swinburne Island Hospital," in honor of the efficient officer who had established it. For two years after this enactment, Dr. Vanderpoel persisted in calling the island West Bank; and it was not until the Legislature, by a resolution twice adopted, unanimously insisted on the island being named as the Legislature had directed, — "Swinburne Island Hospital," — that the commissioners were able to compel the health-officer to comply with the law. Dr. Vanderpoel's attorney has since stated that that official had agreed with Gov. Dix, that, if he would re-appoint him health-officer, the island should be named Dix Island. The governor fulfilled his part of the agreement, but the health-officer was prevented by the Legislature from carrying out his part.

The islands, as shown in the illustration, are Swinburne Island, with Hoffman Island farther up the bay, and Staten Island in the background. The two islands are of the same size and construction, with the exception of the buildings. Swinburne Island is located on the lower bay, about two and a half miles south of Fort-Thompkins Lighthouse at the Narrows, and about two and a third miles from the Elm-Tree Lighthouse on Staten Island. The foundation is hexagon in form, two of the sides being two hundred and sixty feet in length, the other four one hundred and sixty-one feet. The exterior of the crib-work is thirty feet in width at the base, twenty feet at the top, and twenty feet in height, and is constructed of large timbers firmly fastened together and filled with small stones, the whole surrounded by a riprap of heavy stones. The superficial area of the structure is about two acres, while the area at the base of the riprap is over three acres; the extreme length at the top being five hundred and four feet, and two hundred and twenty-eight feet in width. To construct the island, nine thousand cubic feet of timber were required, and seventeen thousand cubic yards of stone in the riprap, five yards of stone to fill the crib, and fifty-six thousand four hundred yards of sand to fill the space enclosed by the crib-work.

On Swinburne Island there are eight hospitals, each eighty-nine feet long, twenty-four feet wide, and twelve feet three inches from floor to ceiling, and all connected by a covered corridor. To supply the island with fresh water, there are twenty-two cisterns, capable of holding forty-four thousand gallons of water; the whole of the buildings being lighted with gas manufactured on the island from gasolene.

The contract bid for the carrying-out of this experiment,

never before tried in any harbor, was $310,618, and no more than that amount was paid.

In Chapter 733, "Laws of the State of New York, 1872," it was enacted, "And the lower of the West Bank Islands, built under the direction of Dr. Swinburne, shall hereafter be known and designated as Swinburne Hospital Island."

One of Dr. Swinburne's successors, persisting in calling the island Dix Island, and publishing diagrams of the island with that name in his reports, and also in the first volume of the "Report and Papers of the American Health Association," published in 1873, the Hon. Mr. Vedder, on Jan. 23, 1874, offered the following in the Assembly: —

Whereas It is provided and declared in and by Chapter 733, Laws of 1872, that the lower of the West Bank Islands, built under the direction of Dr. Swinburne, shall hereafter be known and designated as Swinburne Island Hospital; and

Whereas The health-officer, in his report to the commissioners, in their report to the Legislature for said year, in disregard and defiance of said legislative provision and declaration, did refer to and designate said hospital otherwise than by its true name, thus tending to produce confusion in the records of the State; and

Whereas The Legislature at its last session, by joint resolution of the Senate and Assembly, did direct that the said report of the commissioners and health-officer should be so amended by striking out the name given by them to said hospital in said report, inserting in place thereof its correct statutory name, and also directed that in all reports and papers said island should be designated as Swinburne Island Hospital; and

Whereas The said health-officer and commissioners, in further disregard and defiance of said legislative provision and declaration, have, in their annual report for the year 1873, just submitted to the Legislature, again ignored said statutory name of said hospital, and have therein designated the same by a name of their own selection, not sanctioned by law: therefore

Resolved (if the Senate concur) That the said last-mentioned reports be forthwith returned by the clerks of the Senate and of the Assembly to the commissioners of quarantine and said health-officer, and that they cause the same to be amended by striking out said unauthorized name of said hospital in said reports wherever the same occurs, and inserting in place thereof the name given to said hospital in and by the law aforesaid, and that they return the same to the Senate, thus amended, within ten days from this date.

On Jan. 9, Mr. Prince, from the Committee on the Judiciary, to whom was referred the resolution, reported in favor of the passage of the same, which report was agreed to; and on Feb. 3 the resolution was reported as engrossed.

On March 18 the resolution was adopted by a vote of sixty-seven in favor, to seven against.

The cost of this island, with the hospital thereon, was four hundred and ten thousand dollars. The enacting by law, at this time, that in the great port of New York there should be a "Swinburne Island," was an unusual honor to bestow on a man who had never aspired to political fame or preferment, and was intended as a mark of esteem that should be enduring, and become world-wide in reputation. It was voluntarily bestowed on the man who had conceived and executed such a perfect safeguard to the State, because of his faithfulness and honesty in the discharge of a duty affording such opportunities to plunder the people at large, and the mercantile interests of the State of New York in particular. During his term in the office, every report of the commissioners contained eulogies of the most complimentary nature of the health-officer; and these but expressed the views of the officials of the State in high positions, who were the guardians of the mercantile and commercial interests of the city of New York, and of the interests of the people at large.

To peruse the reports during the period when Dr. Swinburne was health-officer, and then for a number of years after he retired, is like being suddenly transformed from the genial warmth of a balmy, invigorating day in June, into the cold, dismal, and chilly breezes of a dark December night, — the first abounding in praises of Dr. Swinburne: and the other charging others prominent afterwards in the same responsible position with defiance of law; trickery in plundering the State of large amounts of money; swindling the shipping interests of the city, and the commerce arriving in New-York harbor; using the State steamers for the collection of ship news in the interest of the associated press, making no return of the moneys received to the State, and recommending the attorney-general to institute an action for the recovery of the same; illegally collecting fees from merchants for "medical attendance, and transporting the sick;" the "diverting" of money appropriated by the Legislature; and the withholding of money due the employees of quarantine and others.

If the quarantine established by Dr. Swinburne, and the commissioners working in unison with him, saved the people from plague, some of their successors determined that they would be worse than seven plagues in plundering the State treasury, and all with whom they had dealings. The virtues of one man are better understood when placed in contrast with the disreputable acts of another, as the fragrance of the rose is enjoyed after the senses have been attacked with the odor of *Mephitis*. In 1880, when the people began to realize how they had been plundered during the last decade, it was a consolation to review the transactions at quarantine for the previous decade, and feel the assurance that all men intrusted with great public interests were not recreant to their duties, nor faithless to the people.

In their report in 1877, the commissioners said, —

"When the supply bill of 1870 was printed and made public, not a little surprise was caused by the discovery of a clause which transmitted the power of appointing, dismissing, selecting, and licensing to the health-officer. Thereupon followed the organized exactions down the bay, which became such a terror to our mercantile interests during the seasons of 1870 and 1871."

Under the general law of 1863, the commissioners had this power, and, as they were ignorant of the changes, the natural deductions are, that they were effected at the instance of the then health-officer, Dr. Carnochan, by means only those conversant with the manipulations of the lobby at Albany understand, whose "interests" in such affairs are always for those who have "designs," and are secured by "circumstances." By this change it is apparent "in what a hurry some persons were to become rich" as soon as an honest, fearless man was out of the way, Dr. Swinburne being then in Europe. The same report said, —

"When, in 1866, the law was passed providing for the building of the artificial islands, it associated the mayors of New York and Brooklyn with the commissioners of quarantine in their construction. In 1873 a five-line clause in the appropriation bill wiped out the commission, and transferred all its powers and funds to the then health-officer, Dr. Vanderpoel, making him the construction board."

To effect such an unprecedented and outrageous proceeding, there was unquestionably sinister motives to secure a collusion necessarily fraught with such dangers as this one was, and opening avenues to plunder. Such a power Dr. Swinburne never asked, and it is doubtful whether any honest man would covet it. By the statements of the commissioners themselves, who were in political sympathy with Dr. Vanderpoel, and not with Dr. Swinburne, the State had reason, as did the merchants of New-York City, and the owners and masters of vessels arriving in New York, to mourn the change that had been made from good to bad, and from bad to horrible.

The intention and purpose was to have no portion of the quarantine on the mainland except the burying-ground; and, to this end, buildings for the residence of the health and other officers were erected on Hoffman Island.

Of these islands and quarantine, the commissioners said, —

"The year which closes with the date of this report has witnessed the completion of the new hospital on West Bank (Swinburne Island). It may be justly regarded as one of the most important and successful undertakings ever entered upon by the State. The magnitude of the structure, and the obstacles which have been encountered in its erection, have been very little understood by the public; and but few know the extent of the provision which has been thereby made for the care of the unfortunate victims of disease who are brought to our shores."

When these were completed, the Legislature, in 1873, when

it centralized all power in the health-officer, appropriated a hundred and twenty thousand dollars for new grounds and residences for the health-officer and his assistants upon Staten Island; and Hoffman Island, with its three massive brick buildings, became solely a place of detention for well passengers; and thus property costing the State at least four hundred thousand dollars, and how much more is not known, became practically of no benefit. In 1876 and 1877 the commissioners suggested that the quarantine residence and connecting property on Staten Island, which had cost the State a hundred and seventy thousand dollars, be sold, and the headquarters of quarantine be transferred back to Hoffman Island, where the original intent was to establish them. Certain it was that to have every part of quarantine as far from populated districts as possible was a wise, humane, and judicious scheme; and no other motive than the supplying of jobs could have been the foundation for having a new residence erected on the mainland.

Dr. Swinburne's successor, Dr. J. M. Carnochan, in his report for 1870, said, —

" The completion of the new hospital at West Bank (Swinburne Island) has removed one of the greatest defects in the quarantine establishment at the port of New York. The old hospital ship, which had been in use since the destruction of the quarantine buildings on Staten Island, beside being ill suited to the care and treatment of the sick, had accommodations for a very limited number of patients, and, when overcrowded, was no doubt greatly detrimental to the lives and health of the patients, attendants, and nurses who were obliged to remain in the poisoned atmosphere of a crowded vessel. The value and importance of the new hospitals, and their adaptation to the necessities of quarantine, were fully apparent in the epidemic on Governor's Island, to which I have already referred. They afforded means for the prompt removal and isolation of the sick from the vicinity of the city to a place where they were surrounded with every comfort. While the new hospital at West Bank may be considered one of the most important additions that could have been made to the quarantine establishment, it is not less necessary that the other structures intended as a place of detention for those who have been exposed to contagious and infectious diseases should be completed without delay. . . . There is no doubt that in previous years many valuable lives have been sacrificed for the want of a place to which those who had been exposed to infection or contagion during the voyage could have been transformed immediately upon their arrival at quarantine."

And in his next report he adds, —

"The present quarantine hospital at West Bank has answered admirably the purpose for which it was intended, and may be justly regarded as the most important addition which could have been made to the quarantine establishment. The pure air of the lower bay, the perfect ventilation of the hospitals, as well as the care and attention bestowed upon the sick, have all combined to promote their recovery and convalescence; and it is not too much to say that during the year many lives have been saved which formerly would, no doubt, have been sacrificed."

This gentleman's term, which for reasons it was thought would be of benefit to the State, was limited to two years, and the appointment of Dr. S. Oakley Vanderpoel followed. Of this official, the commissioners, after five years' intercourse with him, said, —

"So long as the remuneration of the health-officer is left to exactions upon commerce in the shape of fees, just so long will he seek to retain as large a portion of the fees as possible for himself, and pay out as little as possible for the State; and if the keeping of the quarantine establishment in repair is to be thus left to his generosity, or to his biassed sense of its necessities, it will not be long before the State property will go to ruin."

During the three years following the administration of Dr. Swinburne, when first Dr. Carnochan and then Dr. Vanderpoel were the incumbents, there was an annual expenditure, amounting in the three years to $110,000, for the health-officer's residence, grounds, furniture, etc., — an amount exceeding the entire appropriation for quarantine for the two years of 1864 and 1865 under Dr. Swinburne.

In referring to the property at Clifton, Staten Island, — for the purchase of which, and the erection of buildings thereon, the Legislature in 1873 made the appropriation. — the commissioners intimate, that, after the amount appropriated was expended, the then health-officer's (Dr. Vanderpoel) interest in keeping his residence in good condition vanished, and his ardor cooled. They report in 1878, " Since then (1875) the commissioners have expended little or nothing upon these grounds ; and, inasmuch as the health-officer has devoted no portion of his revenues to keeping up the property, it is in a dilapidated condition." About two hundred feet of the sea-wall fronting the grounds had been undermined, and fell, owing to the removal by the health-officer of gravel between it and low-water mark, to cover the walks around his residence, at a loss to the State of over $2,000.

Twice during his term was Dr. Vanderpoel the subject of investigation by legislative committees, — in 1873 and 1876. And at these investigations it was developed, " that in 1873, while the duties of health-officer had greatly fallen off. the expenses of quarantine had nearly doubled, being over $70,000 a year; that the expense of furnishing the health-officer's house, and of paying the quarantine employees, had been laid on the State instead of on the health-officer : that the expenses had risen from $60 per patient in 1866, to $1,500 per patient in 1872; that the services rendered to vessels by the quarantine tugboats, the revenue from which should have been turned over to the State treasury instead of into the health-officer's pocket, was reduced by Dr. Vanderpoel one-half; that over $600,000 had been spent in partly finishing one of the islands in the lower bay, when $150,000 was ample to complete both islands; that the State was made to pay over $20,000 per year for steamboats used in examining vessels, which should have been paid out of the health-officer's own fees; and that the employees of the State were utilized in fumigating vessels (the fees of which amounted annually to a very handsome competency), making the State pay $20 per week for a fishing-yacht, 'Gertrude,' besides charging the commissioners of emigration $75 per month for allowing their agent to use a quarantine boat in going on board emigrant vessels as a boarding-officer." In the investigation of 1876 it was claimed that the health-officer, Dr. Vanderpoel, had by some means secured appropriations amounting to $702,000, of which $600,000 had in some way been spent for his benefit; and that $139,000, placed at his disposal for the construction of quarantine islands and buildings, had not been accounted for; that he had used the State tug "Fenton" to collect ship news from incoming vessels, receiving therefor $4,000 a year, which was pocketed, and by this speculation, five men, who formerly did this work, were thrown out of employment, and their families thus deprived of support; and that for the use of the yacht "Gertrude," worth but $2,500, the State was charged $5,000 per year; that the State wells, engines, and machinery in pumping water, which was sold at $20 per month, had been used without proper credit; that twenty-five tons of hay had been mowed in the burying-ground, and the money for which it was sold retained; and that also anchors, chains, etc., had been sold in the same way.

During the administration of Drs. Carnochan and Vanderpoel, it was reported that $750,000 had been expended to complete the buildings and facilities at quarantine; but all there was to show for the expenditure of this heavy amount, in further improvements than those completed by Dr. Swinburne, was a boarding-station on Staten Island, worth less than $20.000, and three brick buildings on Hoffman Island, which could have been constructed for less than $30,000, much of the $700,000 mysteriously disappearing under the administration of the "new construction board," or one-man management, — a natural result where a scrupulous scientific officer of executive ability was removed to make room for one lacking in these requisites as a public officer.

There was nothing of this nature ever intimated against Dr. Swinburne, who persistently refused, while health-officer, to handle one dollar of the State moneys, insisting that the commissioners of quarantine, and the construction board, were the proper parties to handle the funds; and therein lays the sequel why one health-officer possibly grew so rich in a short time, while the other, after many years of arduous duty in the same position, retired comparatively poor, he having expended over $90,000 of his own funds, at a time when gold was worth from two hundred to two hundred and eighty, in the work he accomplished, — a sum for which the State has never reimbursed him. The two artificial islands suggested by Dr. Swinburne were completed at the time he was superseded by Dr. Carnochan. On Swinburne, the lower island, all the buildings were erected, furnished, and completed with the exception of painting, and Hoffman Island made ready for the buildings, at an aggregate cost of $750,-000. When this scheme was proposed, it met with strong opposition from the press, some of them styling the proposition as "Swinburne's folly," and for a time from the Legislature, on the ground that the outlay would amount to over $3,000,000 for the construction of this stupendous undertaking. These two islands were built in about twenty feet of water, at low-water mark, with three thousand miles of ocean beating against them, and averaging over three acres of land each. Among the papers to oppose the undertaking was the "New-York Herald," which years afterwards, when the cholera was discovered among the troops on Governor's Island, assured the public that ample provision for the sick, and the safety of others, was provided in the "salubrious little Swinburne Island."

In their report dated Jan. 31, 1876, six years after Dr. Swinburne, the suggester and propagator of the scheme for the erection of artificial islands for quarantine, had been superseded, the commissioners said of Swinburne Island Hospital : —

" When this artificial structure, having a surface base of three acres, was undertaken below the Narrows, many were of the opinion that it would not withstand the action of the tides and currents, and vast bodies of ice which at certain seasons of the year are discharged through the Narrows. These fears have not been realized. With some repairs, the foundations of the island are as firm as when first laid."

To recapitulate briefly. During the six years that Dr. Swinburne held the position of health-officer of the port of New York, the appropriations aggregated $861,027.49, out of which was expended, on the islands and buildings, $750,000, and for which the State holds that amount of property, with the exception of certain furniture and other movable articles, valued at $25,000, supposed to have been spirited away by the rats since 1872. For the succeeding six years, under Carnochan and Vanderpoel, the appropriations aggregated $1,264,-478.16, or $403,450.67 in excess of the previous six years; and for this outlay the State has not exceeding fifty thousand dollars' worth of property.

During his term as health-officer, Dr. Swinburne was but once summoned before a legislative committee. In 1868 complaint was made against him, and a committee appointed and instructed to investigate the office of the health-officer of the port of New York relative to his duties. The report, after a thorough investigation, was submitted March 18, 1868, and not only exonerated Dr. Swinburne, but complimented him on his open frankness, and willingness to have his department investigated. The seven members of the committee signing the report said, " Dr. Swinburne promptly responded to the notice, expressing an entire willingness that his official acts should be subject to the fullest scrutiny and investigation. Your committee proposed such general inquiries as seemed to be necessary to elicit such information as would enable them to determine whether there were any abuses, with the administration of his duties, which might be proper subjects of legislation. That the answers submitted by the health-officer to these inquiries satisfied your committee that there were many burthens imposed upon commerce in the administration of quarantine in the port of New York which very justly form the subject of complaint on the part of those engaged in it, but for which your committee is satisfied the health-officer is not responsible."

The report of the commissioners for last year (1884) asked, in view of the threatened appearance of cholera on our shores, for an appropriation of $24,500 for quarantine ; and the New-York papers pertly remarked, " Give them the money, and call back the old officials," — a very natural request where the health of the people is in great danger, and one which illustrates that even political journalists believe at times in the doctrine of "the survival of the fittest" when the health of the people is in imminent danger. And one of the leading journals of New York, in commenting on the request, said, "Give them the appropriation, and then call back some of the old quarantine officials," — a very direct recommendation of Dr. Swinburne, and the commissioners with whom he acted when the country was before threatened with cholera. The health-officer, in his report last year, said, —

"There is a saying that 'like causes produce like effects.' If this adage is necessarily true, then cholera will certainly secure a lodgment at some place in our country in the near future. The same causes which have existed on other occasions of this dreaded disease's approach to our shores doubtless exist now. It is the same disease that has decimated our population in times past. We have held the same and greater commercial intercourse with the stricken people in many localities. An immigration has existed for the year past, and still continues, far in excess of that which obtained during any previous invasion of cholera.

"But, if like causes operate now to produce like results, those causes are better understood than formerly. The sanitation of ships is more intelligently conducted, at least, than in the earlier visitations of the diseases. The agents believed to act as germicides or disinfectants are better understood. The cleansing of ships, and the disinfection of cargoes and baggage, are more thorough and efficient, because the agents employed can be more easily manipulated, more readily controlled, and therefore successfully applied. Hence there is reason to hope that the disease, if not controlled where it has already developed, will be arrested at our maritime quarantines."

The condition of the quarantine of New York prior to the appointment of Dr. Swinburne and the removal of Dr. Gunn may be inferred from an editorial in the "American Medical Times" of Aug. 9, 1862: —

"It has been well said of the commissioners of health, that they 'perform the same relative service in regard to the public health as would a fifth wheel in the progression of a coach.' The principal duty assumed by the health commissioners is the supervision of the quarantine. There is here a wide field for useful labor. did they but apply themselves industriously and conscientiously to the interests committed to their charge. It is but too well known that gross abuses have always existed in the management of our quarantine. The confidence of the public in that board, never strong, has been greatly weakened by its recent action, which sent yellow-fever afloat in this community. If we accept the intimations of the ' Richmond-county Gazette,' this body is negligent of its duties, and allows the quarantine to be so managed as to render the occurrence of an epidemic of yellow-fever this summer not improbable. Vessels are allowed to come to the upper quarantine station with yellow-fever on board, and, immediately after the removal of the sick, the vessel has discharged its cargo at our wharves. The conviction is firm, and rooted in the popular mind, that all of these organizations are subservient, not to the public interest, but to the interests of individuals or of party. And this conviction is not based on any trivial circumstance, but has been the growth of years of observation of the grossest official malfeasance. They have seen a terrible epidemic approach the city with steady step; but no barrier was raised to stay its progress, because the proper authority did not care to call together the Board of Health, justly esteeming the latter more dangerous to the public health than the former. It will require something more than mere assertion to make it evident that the health commissioners do little else than give official sanction to the extortions of the health-officer."

In another article, the "Times," in an editorial on the prospect of health reform in New York, said, —

"Quarantine, managed for the pecuniary benefit of the few, is become a formidable obstruction to commerce. but a ready method of introducing epidemic diseases directly to the city. Disease of every form and variety stalks abroad unchecked and unrestrained by the ignorant and corrupt officials who disgrace the health department."

The "Richmond-county Gazette," in 1862, in commenting on the defeat of the New-York health bill by the Legislature, said, —

"We don't blame Dr. Gunn so much as Mr. Opdyke, if at all, seeing that he had a motive which, leaving supreme selfishness out of the question, might be called a candid one. His pocket was in interest to defeat the bill for at least another year, should his good luck in drawing the prize of rich office continue under the next governor, as it has for four years under the present. Dr. Gunn would have received. under the bill, about $10,000 for the year. By its defeat he is secured in $30,000 gross, and at least $20,000 or $25,000 net revenue."

" To put the right man in the right place would be a novelty in the history of quarantine," said the " American Medical Times." That was exactly what Govs. Seymour and Fenton did in appointing Dr. John Swinburne, as the history of quarantine before and after his term as health-officer undeniably demonstrates. That the right man was in the right place during Dr. Swinburne's term, was attested not only by the reports of commissioners years after his removal, but by the Board of Health in 1873, when, in their report for that year, in giving the death and sick rates of the metropolitan and police districts of New York for the year, they said that in 1867, 1868, and 1869 it fell to a minimum rarely if ever reached in that city; the mean ratio for these three years being equivalent to about 26 in 1,000 annually, in a total population of 935,100, while in 1873 it was 29, in a population of 1,000,000. During that period, Dr. Swinburne was, by virtue of his office as health-officer, a member of the Board of Health, and during 1867 had to meet small-pox, cholera, and yellow-fever arriving from a large number of infected ports. It was of 1869 that the commissioners said, " These statistics are without a parallel in the history of quarantine," and in 1870 said, " The scourge of cholera made 1866 and 1867 memorable in the history of quarantine."

A most remarkable instance in his term at quarantine, and illustrating how thoroughly he was qualified to be the " right man in the right place," was, that during the entire time there was not a death from any of the diseases he met at quarantine among the employees, and no cases of sickness that he had heard of coming from the diseases, notwithstanding it was their duty to care for the sick, bury the dead, and cleanse and fumigate the vessels on which sickness had existed.

CHAPTER VIII.

UNDER TWO FLAGS.

Winning Laurels in other Lands. — Siege of Paris. — American Ambulance.— Only Successful Surgeon. — A Touching Scene. — Always at the Front. — Distinguished Installation.

THE change of scenes in the great drama of life, in which men and women are the actors, and where only the angels are allowed to be lookers-on, passed so rapidly, and presented in such rapid succession this remarkable and eminent man in the leading *rôle*, that one is almost persuaded to believe that the presentation is the production, by the dramatist, of a mythical character drawn from the imagination. With a vast majority of human beings, the excitement, philanthropy, and danger attending the career of Dr. Swinburne, as recited in the chapters already given, would have been sufficient, in the life of any single individual of the most thoroughly patriotic, philanthropic, and American impulses, to afford material for a biography replete with thrilling incidents and eminent achievements. But the events following those already recited furnish a still more intensely notable period, eclipsing any previously enacted, and winning again for him a crown of glory in other lands, of which every American may feel justly proud.

Among the galaxy of names adorning the history of this nation in patriotism, science, the arts, and literature, a page is reserved and a niche provided to commemorate, as one of the most brilliant, the fame of Dr. John Swinburne.

Of a clear night, when one turns the eye heavenward, the vision beholds the whole arch above studded with stars, sparkling as so many diamonds, each reflecting a greater or lesser degree of brilliancy. They are all stars, and differ only in their magnitude, while the number is countless; but, of all these constellations and celestial bodies moving around each other, there are but comparatively few sufficiently grand to have specially called the attention of astronomers and the world. Occasionally, among these dwellers in ethereal space, there appears a comet, whose advent is a matter of wonderment, and whose luminous train presents a magnificent track over which it has passed, obscuring the others. More brilliant it grows as it approaches its zenith, and then passes away, leaving an enduring remembrance of its magnitude and beauty. So it is with the dwellers on this terrestrial globe: some reflect no beauty; others, but a scarcely perceptible twinkling; while others are like the swift-darting stars, moving from one point to another, steadfast as the sun, and whose lives on earth leave a course behind them as brilliant as the comet, and as clear as the Milky Way. This class is limited. Only to a very few is it given to attain permanent brilliancy, and to be noted almost simultaneously in many nations and on two continents. Among this class we believe unwritten history for ages to come, both in this nation and in Europe, will enter the name of the man of whose valor on the field of battle for the preservation of his nation, of whose eminence and skill as a physician and surgeon, and of whose scrupulous honesty, executive ability, and superior science in a great official public position, we have been reciting a few incidents taken from actual life, and not drawn from imagination.

Having been taken a prisoner of war, witnessed the misery there endured, and felt all the gnawings of privation and hunger, it would be but natural to suppose that an exercise of discretion, said to be the better part of valor, would prevent him from again placing himself where he would possibly have to re-endure the same hardships. Yet, strange and anomalous as it may appear, this skilled physician and surgeon, with the recollections of his last military campaign as a prisoner of war, from which he had not wholly recovered, and but recently relieved from official duties amidst pestilence and disease, voluntarily enters a city in another nation, whose walls were being surrounded by an enemy, to give by his skill aid to the sick and wounded, with no music but the tramp of armed hosts, the bellowing of cannon, the bursting of shell, and the shrieks of the wounded and dying.

When superseded as health-officer of the port of New York, at the opening of the reign of plunder under which New-York State suffered under Tweed, he returned to Albany, the city of his former residence, where he met with a reception and greeting such as is accorded only the eminent and great. Among the first to give him a cordial greeting was the Albany Medical Society, who, to reflect public sentiment, and to express the honest feeling of the profession of the county at an official meeting on Feb. 7, 1870, unanimously adopted the following preamble and resolution : —

" *Whereas* This society has been informed that Dr. John Swinburne has purchased his former dwelling-house for the purpose of removing his residence to this city : therefore

" *Resolved* That the Albany-county Medical Society has heard with pleasure of his intended return, and extends to him a cordial welcome, and that the president and secretary are requested to write him a letter expressive of these sentiments of this society."

At the time of the adoption of this resolution, none better understood the ability, character, and standing of Dr. John Swinburne than this society of medical men, holding all kinds of political views; and, when the letter was received by him, it bore the signature of almost every member of the society.

The active life of constant professional anxiety, of unremitting toil and excitement, which he had passed through during the previous decade, had necessarily strained his nervous system to more than an ordinary tension ; and, when the hour of relief arrived, it was natural, at the thought of responsibility being lifted from his mind, that, nature asserting its rights, he should desire relaxation and rest for a time; and, seeking a change of scenes, he left for a trip through Europe. But the fame of the great surgeon and physician had preceded him ; and, soon after his arrival in London, he was apprised of the fact that his skilful services in the cause of humanity were as anxiously sought in the Old World as they were in the New. A new theatre of action was opened, upon which he entered, that gave a change of scenes pre-eminently more exciting than he sought, if it did not afford the recreation and rest he crossed the Atlantic to secure.

At this period, war, with all the horrors the doctor so well understood, was spreading over the fruitful valleys and along the beautiful rivers of France; and two nationalities, for whom the great American physician and surgeon entertained a feeling almost akin to that he felt for his own countrymen, were slaying each other in bloody conflict. When the clouds of war were gathering, and the murmurs were portentous of what followed, a large meeting of American citizens residing in Paris was held in that city on July 18, 1870, when it was decided that they as non-combatants would organize a system of " Help for the Wounded of All Nations " on strictly humanitarian grounds, and elected as an executive committee Thomas W. Evans, M.D.(president), Edward A. Crane (secretary),Col. James McKaye, Albert Lee Ward, and Thomas Pratt, M.D. As late as the 26th of August neither the French minister of war nor the representatives of foreign governments would guarantee to recognize the proposed American ambulance at any headquarters, asserting no special passports could be accorded it, and adding that all movements made by the ambulance must be at its own risk and that of its *personnel.* Besides these obstacles, there was a feeling among the French soldiery that all foreigners not attached to some branch of the French army were Prussian spies. This was the condition of affairs when three members of the committee, indorsed by Minister Washburn, visited London, and solicited Dr. Swinburne to accompany them to Paris and voluntarily take charge of the American ambulance, and introduce, for the sake of humanity, his system of conservative surgery which had proven so great a boon during our civil war. It must, in this connection, be remembered, that every service to be rendered was to be voluntary, each person attached to the ambulance bearing all his individual expenses. Because of discouragements, the zeal in the movement had largely subsided; but on the appearance of the committee in Paris, accompanied by Dr. Swinburne, a new vigor was infused into the movement, and it was restored to its activity. The doctor, when appealed to, did not stop to consider the merits of the questions over which these nations were exercised, and which they were endeavoring to settle by the cruel arbitrament of war: he thought only of the sick and wounded, who would " no longer be soldiers, but men," and, accepting the call, repaired to the gay capital, a city of excitement and communism, to take charge of the American ambulance. From his arrival in Paris on Sept. 7, 1870, to March 18, 1871, during the Franco-Prussian war, he found an ample field for the exercise of his natural promptings of humanity, tenderness of feeling, and skilful abilities, all of which he exercised in such a manner as to win not only the praises of the French themselves, but of their enemies and all Europe, and to be honored with a rank such as few foreigners were ever accorded by the French Government.

During his stay there, times were unusually exciting, even for Paris: the empire was destroyed, and the republic established; the cry of " Vive l'empereur! " turned to bitter curses against the emperor and all his officers; and the air was made to resound with the cry, " Vive la république! À bas l'empereur! " "The gayest city in all the world" became transformed into one of the most extreme suffering, the residents being reduced to the eating of horse-flesh and similar food. In the winter season it was almost impossible to procure fuel, the inhabitants dying of cold and starvation. To these sufferings were added the prevalence of small-pox. No person within the walls of Paris, during that period of suffering, lived without enduring some, if not all, of these hardships, besides being constantly subject to slaughter by a communistic outbreak, or death from the bursting shells constantly falling in the city.

From the closing of the gates on the 18th of September, to the capitulation and surrender in January, the heroic doctor was ever alert and at work. The scenes of want were horrible and beyond description, with no meat or solid food to eat excep horse-flesh and fat, the disagreeable odor which it gave out, while cooking, haunting the whole city. Half the northern portion of the city had been transformed into ambulances, and places for the care of the sick and wounded, the Grand Hotel being turned into a huge hospital. The continuous fall of shells in the city, often bursting among the hospitals and ambulances, killing the sick and wounded and their attendants, was a trying ordeal for the non-combatant volunteer American surgeon. The condition of that city where "our" philanthropic surgeon was performing voluntary service such as to excite the wonder of the people, and the admiration of the profession, may be faintly surmised by the state of affairs when the years 1870 and 1871 came together. For the last week in 1870 there were 3,280 deaths in the city, not including those in the hospitals, which were crowded. From 400 to 500 deaths were caused by small-pox weekly, while typhoid-fever and bronchitis were causing an equally great mortality. At that time, for food, the butchers bought large dogs at from 200 to 300 francs each, smaller ones bringing proportionate prices; cats varied in price from 9 to 25 francs each; and a pair of camels sold, for food, for 4,000 francs.

Dr. Swinburne, in the carrying-on of his work of mercy, had the active co-operation of his countrymen residing in Paris, and for his assistants chose men who were wholly ignorant of medicine or surgery, but who were in financial circumstances such as to enable them to devote their entire time to the work, and bear their own expenses. His chosen assistants were Frank M. O'Connell; J. B. B. Cormack, son of the physician in charge of the English hospital, who desired that his son should be trained by the great American surgeon; Louis Winfield, a brother of Lord Powers of Powerscourt, Bray, Ireland; Gilead Peet, a literary student; Joseph K. Riggs, a brother of the then prominent Washington (D.C.) banker, and Frank Riggs, a nephew, and now banker in Washington, D.C.; and the two Bower brothers, proprietors of an establishment for the preparation and sale of chemicals used in laboratories. These gentlemen were absolutely ignorant of the methods to be used and the

services to be rendered by them in this new and voluntary
field, all of whom rapidly acquired a proficiency in the
treating of fractures and gunshot wounds, and the dressing
of wounds, thus practically illustrating the theory of Dr.
Swinburne in therapeutics, — that 'men whose minds were
free from the old established rules and ethics of ancient,
unenlightened, and traditional surgery, and who had not to
exhaust time in unlearning what they had studied, became
more easily better assistants. In a few days he had succeeded in making better assistants of these gentlemen than
many graduates of the Hôtel Dieu, the greatest and oldest
hospital in Paris, after years of training in the dressing of
wounds, — a fact conceded by the French surgeons and the
people. Of one of these assistants, Joseph K. Riggs, a writer
quoted by Dr. Evans in his "History of the American Ambulance in Paris," said, —

" I never shall forget the surprise I felt on the very day of
the affair at Chevilly, at seeing Mr. Riggs in the operating-
room, assisting Dr. Swinburne, then engaged in amputating
a thigh, and that with all the *sang-froid* of a veteran surgeon. Daily accompanying Dr. Swinburne in his visits, he
soon qualified himself to discharge all the duties of a surgeon's assistant, and became, perhaps, the most expert dresser
in the ambulances."

The work performed at the American ambulance was not
done in secret, and the eminent surgeon did not put his light
under a bushel. He was willing that all who were ready to
profit might see for themselves, being particularly willing,
the French journals said, to explain to the profession, and
those engaged in alleviating pain, this simple yet grandly
successful system of conservation in surgery. Among the
almost daily visitors to the American ambulance were
Minister Washburn, and the consul-general for the United
States, Gen. Reed. Gens. Burnside and Sheridan, while in
Paris, made frequent visits to the ambulance, expressing the
greatest pleasure at the successful work there being done.
Almost all the foreign notabilities who were admitted into
Paris during the siege, or arrived in the city after the sur-

render, heard of and visited this ambulance. Among other prominent personages who honored it with their presence was the Archbishop of Paris (Darboy), " who, after expressing his sincere thanks to the skilful surgeon Dr. Swinburne, who performed the operations, and to those who aided him, who brought as much of heart as of science to this generous work, left, after blessing all the tents, and the gentlemen connected with them," says " La Semaine Religieuse de Paris" of Nov. 26, 1870.

So universal had become the renown of the celebrated American surgeon, and the work of the American ambulance, that it seemed all Paris was desirous of paying homage to those engaged there ; and it was no uncommon sight to see thousands of people standing in the avenues, looking in wonderment at the row of tents, one eye-witness stating that the Avenue l'Impératrice, eight hundred feet wide and three miles long, was crowded from the Arc de Triomphe to near the Bois de Bologne for nearly two miles every pleasant day, to see what the Americans were doing. So loud were the praises bestowed, that the attention of the government was directed to it, and it became the object of many official visits, one by the military governor of Paris. Of this visit, says " Le Petit Moniteur" of Nov. 6, " Last Sunday Gen. Trochu visited the American ambulance, and expressed his complete satisfaction with the admirable installation of the different services, as well as with the care taken of the wounded."

After the close of the siege, and the declaration of peace between Germany and France, Dr. Swinburne, on March 18, 1871, took his departure from Paris ; but the ambulance, and the gentlemen he had trained, remained, and did noble service in the era of blood that followed and deluged that city. Soon after his departure the gates of the city were again closed, and a reign of terror and plunder inaugurated by the nationalists and communistic elements, that continued without cessation until the capture of the city by the government. Men were arrested, and shot in cold blood, as was the Archbishop of Paris, whose only crime was his exalted position ; churches were sacked, the services stolen, the images desecrated, and dressed in attire of the most diabolic and wickedly brutal nature; and priests and the best citizens were thrown into prison. Nothing was wanting but the guillotine to complete the horrors of this barbarous and hellish state of affairs. The city was reduced to a condition of abject terror in which no man was safe in life or property: the prisons were filled, the hospitals crowded with the sick and the wounded, the atmosphere heavy with the shouts of wild and maddened men and women, the streets red with human blood, and the highways and public buildings mined, and prepared for destruction; for the commune had declared its intention to blow up and set fire to Paris rather than surrender. All avenues of escape were closed. Provisions were again running short; and M. Theirs had declared he had shut up the insurgents to perish like rats in their holes, while they, in turn, had declared their resolution to die, if need be, amidst the remains of their beautiful city. One scene in this carnival of death between the forces in the streets of Paris, and the part the ambulance took in the affair, was given in the " London Times," and afterwards incorporated in McCabe's history. The writer said, " I waited in the entry of the ambulance for an hour. I saw for a quarter of an hour one wounded man carried into the one I was near every minute, for I timed the stretchers by the watch. Looking into others, I could see the courtyards littered with mattresses and groaning men."

Through all these scenes of blood and communism, the corps trained by Dr. Swinburne were true to their teachings to save, and continued their work of mercy. It was during this state of affairs that one of his assistants, Frank M. McConnell, at the personal risk of his own life, succeeded in enabling over thirty priests to escape from the city by attaching them to the ambulance, and attiring them as attendants in the ambulance costume; thus enabling them to escape from the city, and thereby saving these Christian men from horrible deaths at the hands of the bloodthirsty mob. He was constantly in attendance on the archbishop up to the time the good man was shot.

What a bright picture this conduct of Dr. Swinburne and his assistants, in working for humanity, presents, compared to the dark and bloody record to blot the fair escutcheon of American citzenship, as made by Cluseret and Whitton, the only two leaders among the insurgents claiming to be American citizens! The first were as that of angels from the regions of the blessed, on a mission of mercy; while the others were as emissaries of destruction, sent from the bottomless pits of Hades.

The history of the work of Dr. Swinburne in Paris was fraught with unprecedented success, causing a just pride among the American residents of Paris, and drew forth universal and honorable comment from those in official position, —from authors, the press, and scientific men, who heretofore indulged the idea that America, while a great nation, was still, in the developing of science and scientific men, as a "babe in swaddling-clothes." The citizens of the capital city of the great State of New York feel a natural pride in reading these comments of other nations on the achievements of one of their fellow-citizens who is eminently of the people. Believing their perusal will arouse a similar feeling of pride, not only among the members of the profession he has so honored, but in the hearts of every America-loving resident in Dr. Swinburne's native State of New York, we collate and condense a few from the many.

Dr. Evans, in his "History of the American Ambulance," says, —

"Every little *coterie* was ambitious to have its ambulance, which it could direct and talk about. Hospitals had their lady managers, whose sole qualifications were rank, wealth, and the unconquerable determination to keep at the head of fashion, through whatever singular paths it may lead. In these private establishments the doctor often played only an inconsiderable *rôle*. He did what he was told; he was obedient and submissive; he was necessary — and so was the scullion."

In speaking of the successful treatment in the American ambulance, Dr. Evans said, "Dr. Swinburne's highly successful

exemplification of the benefical action of conservatory surgery, and of the re-formation of bone, excited the greatest
interest among the medical men who visited the ambulance,
in which oakum was employed in preference to lint, on account of its antiseptic qualities, and compresses of hot water
were mainly employed for dressing, to the exclusion of many
of the usual applications. Of *seven* cases of amputation of the
thigh, only *four* resulted in death; while, at the ambulance
established in the Grand Hôtel, every case of amputation
terminated fatally, just as is always the case in one deadly
ward of the Hôtel Dieu (the largest and oldest hospital in
Paris), where scarcely a patient amputated has ever yet escaped death from gangrene or pyæmia. At the ambulance
of the Grand Hôtel the deaths have been said to have exceeded forty-five per cent of the number of cases treated.
However this may be, the administration up to the present
time (1873) has declined to make public its record. Now,
in the far more economically conducted American ambulance,
the proportion of deaths before the engagement at Bougert
was only three and a third per cent."

A comparison of the results obtained in the American
ambulance with those obtained in other ambulances and
hospitals show conclusively that the objects those in charge
of the American ambulance desired to accomplish were attained, — that of demonstrating the excellence of their system
of surgical conservation, and the superiority of tents over
solid buildings in the treatment of wounds, as well as the
importance of hygienic conditions as a means of preventing
disease and effecting cures, — essentials so tenaciously insisted
on by Dr. Swinburne during his service in our " unpleasant-
ness."

In paying tributes of praise to Dr. Swinburne and the
spirit which impelled him and his associates, and in de-
scriptions of the properties and facilities connected with the
American ambulance, the press of Paris, official, scientific,
religious, and secular, notwithstanding the exciting events
that pressed upon their columns, seemed to vie with each
other as to which should excel in complimentary notices of

the American institution, its surgeon, *personnel*, and installation, a few of which we incorporate.

In describing a visit to the ambulance, M. Picard, in an editorial in "Électeur Libre" of Oct. 3, 1870, said, —

"Yesterday we visited the American ambulance. Is it necessary that we should dwell upon the scrupulous cleanliness of this ambulance, or the assiduous care with which our wounded are there treated? It is truly touching to see these foreigners of wealth thus giving themselves up without reserve to this humane work. We have seen these gentlemen assisting the surgeons in their duties, holding the limbs of patients, and engaged in all the details of dressing wounds, and that, after having yesterday been under the fire of the enemy, to pick up these same wounded. These generous men would be unwilling to have us give their names to the public. All that we are able to say is, that their benevolent devotion and their indefatigable ardor assure to them the gratitude of France, whose friendship was long since gained by the States of the American nation."

The humanitarian work of Dr. Swinburne and his corps of assistants was gratefully appreciated by the French people; and in reflecting their opinions, " Le Reveil " of October, 1870, said, —

"Never was a sacred work of sacred humanity better conceived, or better put in practice, than by this band of generous and devoted men, who, able to find security everywhere else for themselves, their families, and their fortunes, have preferred to remain in our midst, to encourage us by their presence, and, with open hearts and open hands, to give us their sympathy, their aid, and their succor — fraternal and so practical — in the terrible crisis through which we are passing."

The " Journal Officiel de la République Française " (the official journal of the French Republic), on Nov. 27, 1870, said in an editorial article on the American ambulance, occupying two entire pages of the paper, among other things, —

"It is now understood how it is brought about that one may breathe under the tents only an air warm and healthful. And is there occasion for being astonished, that, as a consequence, where the American system is applied, everybody should be absolutely ignorant, or as much as it is necessary to be, not only of what purulent absorption (scientifically called pyæmia) and hospital gangrene may be, but even of the fever, which is not a necessary consequence of a wound?

"Every morning, Dr. Swinburne, a gentleman as modest as he is well informed, accompanied by his aids, attends to the dressing of wounds. Formerly port physician of the city of New York, he was travelling in Europe when the war broke out. His devotion has kept him here, to assume the noble task which he is fulfilling with such admirable skill. Aid Nature instead of affronting her, — such is their device; and such is henceforth, we know, that also of our greatest French practitioners. It is forever the admirable and simple expression of our own Ambrose Paré, 'I dress his wounds: God cures him.'

"We hardly need to add, after all this, that at the American ambulance every one is a declared partisan of conservative surgery, that delicate art which is happily also in honor among us.

"And now a word about those who extend these unremitting attentions to our wounded, who generously offer them these effective consolations. Shall they find us indifferent? No. How could we fail to recognize that which they are doing for us, if it was only by showing how singularly practical are the ideas of those excellent surgeons who have come from the other side of the Atlantic to place at our service, with so much generosity, their incontestable science and their indefatigable devotion?[1]

"We shall be excused for having passed over in silence many technical details to which we might have usefully referred; but we should not have accomplished, even now, half our task, had we stopped only to enumerate the new curative expedients, perhaps still unemployed in France, — in a word, the innovations of every sort for which hospital science is indebted to the Americans."

The "Union Medicale" of Feb. 4, 1871, said, —

"Let us hope this new experiment will not be fruitless, and that it may confirm the results already obtained. While the genius of destruction multiplies its ravages, and accumulates

---

[1] The writer is enthusiastic over the system of heating and ventilation. "The temperature," he says, "was uniform throughout the whole length of the pavilion, ranging from 15° to 18° (Centigrade). In fact, nothing could be simpler or altogether more ingenious than the system of heating and ventilation employed here, for *it is the system of heating which secures the ventilation.*"

ruins, it is a consolation to believe that the genius of conservation — less powerful, alas! — has been able at the same time to make a step forward. We shall be happy, if, in the midst of these bloody orgies of force, we have been able to save a few lives more than formerly."

This notice of the "Union Medicale," of the conservative surgery practised by Dr. Swinburne for six months in a city where are all the leading surgeons of Europe, is significant, coming as it does from a scientific journal which never draws conclusions, or advances a recommendation of any kind in medical ethics, until it has well tried the subject, and is positive of results.

Early in the siege, this at first called innovation introduced by the American surgeon, John Swinburne, began to draw attention as above the others of the numerous ambulances, and on Oct. 31 the "Paris Journal" said of it, —

" We soon, however, began to hear it admitted, not only that the Americans were laboring most earnestly in a humane manner, but that unusual successes were rewarding their efforts. The American ambulance established in the Avenue Uhrich is one of those which, up to the present time, has given the best results in the curing of wounds. After the battle of Chevilly, Dr. Swinburne and his assistants obtained from the Prussians the restitution of a number of wounded French, all severely wounded; and their care has saved them all."

One of the instructions to the ambulance attendants was to bring in the most severely wounded as quickly as possible. That this order was well carried out may be seen by an item in "L'Universe" of Nov. 1: —

" Upon the Flanders road, deserted and gloomy, obstructed at every step by trees which lay in the way, we met the American ambulance, always at the very front (*au premier post*) whenever it was a question of comforting courage in misfortune."

"La Semaine Religieuse de Paris" said, —

" Their ambulance may also be said to be a model of its kind. Setting out with the principle that hospital wards, where the sick are commonly heaped together, are, to use the expression of Cabanis, 'magazines of corrupt air,' the Americans have lodged our wounded under tents grouped together in picturesque disorder, yet separate one from the other. The whole medical apparatus is carefully concealed: it only appears when indispensable. There are no herb-teas: these are replaced by wine. The drugs are purchased of the butcher, and the apothecaries are left to advertise."

"Le Nationale" of Dec. 11, 1870, in an article, said, —

"Among all these ambulances, whether old or new, which exist in Paris, there is one distinguished by its organization, and particularly by its system of installation, — the American ambulance."

M. Lafarge, in a lengthy article on *l'ambulance Americaine*, published in "Le Figaro" on Jan. 26, 1871, said, —

"About halfway down the Avenue de l'Impératrice, on the right, you perceive a number of tents — not a large number, a veritable little city of canvas: it is the American ambulance. You are at first surprised that the wounded can be treated almost in the open air; but if you enter, you will very quickly change your first impression. . . . Let no one fear that bronchitis and other diseases of the respiratory organs have been occasioned by this practice. Facts have settled this question. . . . In the very coldest weather, a sufficient temperature can be maintained inside of the American tents. During the severe weather of December, when the cold was ten or twelve degrees below zero (Centigrade), the temperature was maintained within the tents at from $+ 12°$ to $+ 15°$, and that without forcing the fire. . . . Go and visit the American ambulance: not only will you meet there with the most gracious reception, but you will obtain from the lips of the wounded themselves the expression of their lively gratitude for the intelligent care they are receiving."

Comments like these quoted, all from leading journals and authorities, speak volumes of themselves, and breathe praises such as the French press, always jealous to maintain the highest positions for Frenchmen, never before bestowed on any foreign surgeon. To comment favorably was but natural, under the circumstances, and might be expected from the grateful feelings and naturally complimentary Frenchmen; but placing the American surgeon's system of conservative surgery as eminently above their own, and one they would adopt in the future, was only accorded on pure merit, particularly as the press had their own ambulance, of which they were extremely jealous and proud. These press notices are rendered the more valuable when such eminent literary men as M. Sayrce, and such scientists as M. Desault, go still further in according the palm of excellence to Dr. Swinburne, his corps and ambulance.

CHAPTER IX.

THE WONDER OF SCIENTISTS.

These People are our Masters. — Great Results with Small Means. — Conservative Surgery. — Remarkable Operations. — Surgeon *Par Excellence.* — Only Success. — The Field-Stretcher.

FRANCISQUE SARCEY, a distinguished literary gentleman, in "Le Temps" of Dec. 21, 1870, and in his work entitled "La Siège de Paris," a book that ran through twenty-four editions in six months, said, —

" I met, a few days since, one of the thousand acquaintances which every Parisian, a little known, has upon the Boulevard, — a physician by profession, distinguished, I might also say celebrated, in a surgical speciality, and who, like most of his *confrères*, is attached to one of our numerous ambulances. The conversation fell naturally upon the subject of ambulances. He was full of it; and it happened also that I was a little acquainted with it, being very intimate with one of those persons most occupied with the direction of the ambulance of the press. I had also studied with great care the remarkable work by Dr. Chenu, with the intention of making in my turn, and with his facts, a campaign against the organization of the medical service in our armies.

" ' You are interested in this?' said he. 'Very well. And you have very probably visited the American ambulance?'

" I confessed that I had not.

" ' Then I must take you there. Ah, my friend! those people there are our masters. How simple, ingenious, and practical is every thing connected with its organization! It is made of nothing, as we should say. Their installation has scarcely cost twenty thousand francs; and they have a hospital the most healthful, the most convenient, and the best furnished, — the model hospital, — the hospital of the future. Our most eminent physicians have visited this ambulance. I have met there Nélaton, Record, Jules Guerin, Démarquais, and others. They have pronounced it excellent. Every physician in Paris should go and see, and convince himself

112

with his own eyes of the superiority of the American installation. The public should come to the rescue, that adminis-
trative routine may be forced out of its absurd paths by a
vigorous and irresistible pressure of public opinion. The
medical journals are only read by a profession which it is
useless to convince. It is through the ignorant and the humble, through the crowd, that important reforms and great
revolutions are effected. What a distance there is between
theory and practice! There had been *twenty* amputations at
the Grand Hôtel, and out of these *twenty* cases there had been
twenty deaths. At the Hôtel Dieu never has an amputation
succeeded.'

"'Very well,' said I. 'Let them put the amputated somewhere else. Very simple! I see you are still an innocent,
my dear fellow. Nothing is simple in administration. A
sick man is brought in, and there is an empty bed. The sick
man is put in his bed, and he dies; but there is nothing to
be said. The number was in its place, good order is preserved,
and the register is correct. Every thing is for the best in
the best administrations. The hospitals are not for the sick
man, but for the doctor.'

"He said to me many other things besides, which I do not
remember. The next morning, however, he took me in his
carriage to the American ambulance. I had invited one of
my *confrères* to accompany me, M. Armand Gouvien, who
was the director of the ambulance of the press. I was very
desirous that he should see with me these pretended marvels,
and give me his opinion of them.

"We were received by the surgeon-in-chief, M. Swinburne,
and by M. M. Brewer (one of the Brewer brothers), who speak
our language with the greatest purity, and who gave us
answers to all our questions with the most perfect courtesy;
and it would be impossible to accuse them of having had in
view, by so doing, any publicity through the press. My name
(I confess it very humbly) seemed to suggest nothing to them,
and whatever special attentions were paid, were offered, as
was proper, to my two friends, who were of the party; and
they were in ecstasies over the admirable simplicity, according to them, of certain methods of placing the persons in bed,
and of dressing wounds, which Gouvien declared he would
have tried for certain cases of fracture in the ambulance of
the press. Not being learned in such matters, I must confess
that I only half appreciated the ingenuity of these inventions;
but that which struck me there was the evident fondness of
practical methods in the solution of the most complicated

problems of surgery, — methods which were at the same time convenient and elegant. To do much with little, without trouble and without expense ; to employ that which is at hand, modifying it ingeniously to suit the case presented, — this is the groundwork of their system: no outlay for the apparatus, none for the setting it up. They have no other vanity than that of curing their patients.

"The Americans have given the last blow to the prejudice. The hospital as it exists in France, as routine has constructed and maintains it, must be killed, and we shall reach our end."

The celebrated physician, Dr. Dusart, in "Le Rappel" of November, 1870, says, —

"Under these circumstances, we have been in no wise surprised to find all the wounded with fresh, rosy complexions and cheerful countenances, — signs of a well-being which all were earnest to announce. All the men whom I questioned affirmed that the only fever they had, occurred during the twenty-four hours immediately following the fight. . . . France will owe to the intelligent and devoted efforts of the American colony the privilege of seeing many of her soldiers returning to the army after a short treatment, while many of the wounded will have preserved their limbs, which anywhere else would certainly have been cut off."

Dr. de Rause, editor "Gazette Médicale de Paris," said, —

"American surgeons are accused generally of an over-fondness for operating: on the contrary, we have noted with pleasure the efforts — efforts crowned with success — of their conservative surgery. M. Swinburne is the only surgeon of the ambulance."

M. Gustave Mousnereau, in a thesis on the ambulances, said, "I have reserved for the last, as being the most important, the American ambulance," and after giving a detailed system of heating, etc., added, "I feel justified in affirming that the American ambulance is the best of all the ambulances established in Paris. This superiority of the American ambulance has been admitted by the most eminent surgeons of Paris; and an attempt has already been made by Dr. Depaul (clinical professor of midwifery) and Dr. Dubreuil (assistant professor and hospital surgeon) to apply the American system

AMERICAN AMBULANCE IN PARIS,

As shown in F. W. Evans, M.D., D.D.S., Ph.D.'s "History of the American Ambulance."

by establishing two similar tent hospitals. . . . At the American ambulance the deaths have been only five per cent; of seven amputations, only three have died; there has not been a single case of hospital gangrene, and not one case of purulent infection. These figures speak for themselves, and suffice to demonstrate the superiority of the American system."

M. Nélaton, one of the most illustrious representatives of French medical science, on a visit to the American ambulance, left on the visitors' book this significant indorsement: "You have here shown what great results may be obtained with small means."

Jules Guerin wrote that he was happy to echo the same sentiment, as did Démarquais; and Baron Larry, before the Academy of Sciences, declared that the American hospital system was most complete and favorable.

M. Nélaton was the celebrated French physician and surgeon called to examine the wound of Garibaldi, and who declared the bullet was still in the wound, indicated the time when it could probably be removed, and predicted a favorable result. This opinion was directly the reverse of that given by the English surgeon, Partridge, who, in his opinion, was supported by the Italian surgeons Porta and Barretti, and afterwards by Pirogoff, the celebrated Russian surgeon. Events proved Nélaton was correct, and his opinion triumphed. By following his views, the physicians attending Garibaldi happily succeeded in removing the projectile. Partridge's visit and blundering surgery cost three thousand dollars; while Nélaton, the true surgeon, went to Italy without fee or reward.

Among the appliances more directly concerned with surgical science, used at the American ambulance, and which found great favor among the surgeons of Paris in the treating of suppurating wounds, the merits of which were previously unknown in France, was the employment of oakum as a substitute for *charpie* ("lint").

"Indeed," Dr. Evans writes, "the interest taken by the medical profession of Paris in every thing which concerned the ambulance was very great. Scarcely a day passed in which some well-known name was not entered in the list of visitors. No sentiment of professional jealousy was ever exhibited; no exclusive feeling of nationality was ever manifested: there was but one sentiment, but one feeling, among all, — that inspired alike by an earnest desire that the history of the experiment might tend to the establishment of some new truth to the honor of science and the benefit of mankind from the first-fruits of a New World's experience, brought to the very shrines of venerated oracles, to there compete with the established principles of ancient tradition, and even with the practice of classic surgery."

That these honors and expressions of gratitude from a notably brave and proud people were justly earned, may be realized from the actual results of the surgical treatment by Dr. Swinburne. Most, if not all, of the eminent surgeons had discussed the theory of conservation in the treatment of the wounded, but had failed to enforce it in practice, it was so foreign to the old-school system to which they had been educated. When introduced by the great American physician and surgeon, it was absolutely regarded as an innovation rather than an advance in science. Yet these opinions and comments quoted prove how promptly the great scientific minds of that city availed themselves of the ideas and practices they witnessed, with their good results, and in the interest of science, and for the good of humanity, declared their purpose to adopt them. They believed their surgeons were equally scientific with the great American, and indeed insisted they were more proficient. Yet here were facts; and the truly honest searchers after knowledge knew that theory, when contrasted with facts, vanishes as rapidly as the sparkling dewdrop is kissed away by the rising sun. Here were results upon which these learned men were to decide as to the claims for pre-eminence for conservative surgery, and the simple means adopted in dressing wounds. The comparisons were conclusively convincing. At the American ambulance the most severely wounded were treated, because the corps of stretcher-bearers had specific orders, which were rigidly enforced, to look after these, as they were in need of the earliest possible attention; and the American ambulance corps, being always first to the front, picked up the most seriously wounded. And yet, of the *247 surgical cases treated, only 47 died, of all causes.* Of these wounded, *126* received compound fractures, some having two or more comminuted fractures. During the siege, there were but *9* amputations of long bones; *7* of these being of the thigh, *5* of the wounds being through the knee-joint.

The ambulance Rothschild, in charge of Dr. Job, situated on high ground, with all proper ventilation, and considered one of the very best in Paris, was provided with ample nourishment and food for the sick ; while in the other hospitals and ambulances it was about all those in charge could effect, when they secured sufficient nourishment to keep life in the patients, some of them failing even in this. Yet at this luxuriantly supplied hospital there were but *56* wounded men treated, *10* of them dying of their wounds. There were but *4 amputations performed, all proving fatal ;* and in every case but *2*, where the bones were involved in the wounds, all died.

At the ambulance of the press, under M. Démarquais, 281 wounded were treated prior to Feb. 1, 1871; and of these, 63 ended in death. Of *16 cases of wounds of the upper extremities, 13 proved fatal.*

At the Barracks Hospital at Passey, of the 1,486 wounded treated, 347 died.

To these results the medical profession of Paris, at least the learned, expert, and scientific portion, — and at that time it embraced eminent men from all portions of Europe,— would not allow prejudice to obscure their better judgment, and were not only willing, but anxious, to adopt this course, and re-learn how to treat the wounded.

Among the celebrated surgeons in Paris during the siege, from other portions of Europe, was Charles Alexander Gordon, M.D., C.B., who was sent to that city by the right honorable secretary of state for war of Great Britain. This celebrated English surgeon was the author of a number of works on military surgery and hygiene. In his work entitled

" Lessons on Hygiene and Surgery from the Franco-Prussian War," he quotes from M. Pirogoff, " that the extensive practice of primary amputation has been abandoned, because statistics prove, that, in gunshot wounds of the upper extremity, secondary amputation is as favorable as primary; that the attempt to save the limb is not, therefore, made at the risk of life; and that it is to the honor of modern surgery that but few amputations of the upper extremities were made."

" Such," says Dr. Gordon, " are the views expressed by this eminent surgeon, and they deserve every attention. Perhaps nowhere," he adds, " so much as in the American ambulance, was extensive simplicity of arrangements carried out in the treatment of gunshot fractures: certainly in none were the results more satisfactory. Dr. Swinburne brought to his aid vast experience gained in the war of secession; but the most simple and extemporized apparatus seemed always to have been adopted by him. The appliances made use of depended upon the extent and position of the wounds; but, as a rule, the more simple their construction, the better."

This acknowledged eminent scientific authority, in discussing the treatment in dressing the wounded, said, —

" Whether used as an independent application or not, water had to be used for the purpose of cleansing the surface of wounds. Perhaps it was so to a less extent than in the English hospitals; and, with every respect to our French compeers, there is some room for believing that a more extensive use by them of this simple element would have been to the advantage of the wounded. Moist and hot cloths applied, and covered with oiled silk, were much used in cases of wounds of the long bones or joints, and sometimes to the limbs after amputation. After excision of joints, these, placed along the whole extent of the limb, proved very grateful. Their employment was carried out to the greatest extent in the American ambulance. . . . The degree of ease that such simple means will give is remarkable in the case of a wounded limb."

In his summing-up of the results of treatments in the several hospitals and ambulances of Paris, he said, —

" We had in Paris, however, in the American tent ambulance, *undoubtedly the most favorable results of any*, taking into

The American Ambulance Tents,

With Improved System of Warming and Ventilation.

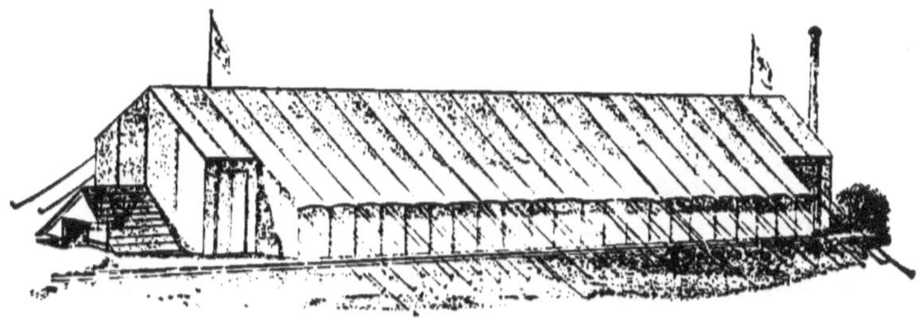

Fig. 1.—Elevation.

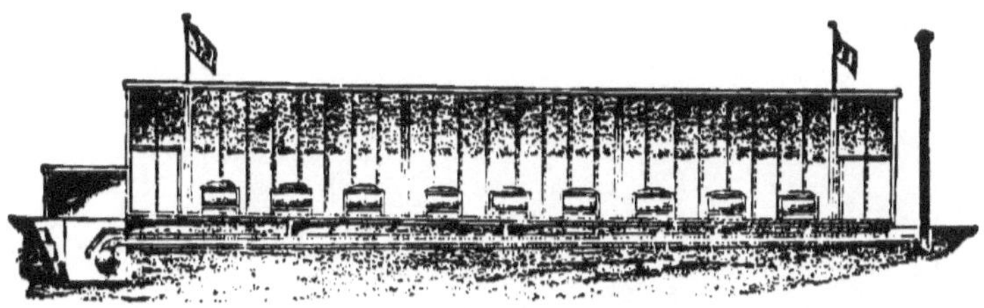

Fig. 2.—Longitudinal Section.

These cuts of Dr. Swinburne's Ambulance in Paris are taken from Charles Alexander Gordon's Work on "Lessons on Hygiene and Surgery from the Franco Prussian War." Dr. Gordon is the author of several important works on military hygiene, and was sent to Paris during the Franco-Prussian War by the Right Honorable Secretary of State for War of the British Government.

account the severity of the cases treated. Thus, out of 247 cases treated, there were 126 of compound fractures, these occurring in 114 individuals; yet the mortality among all was at the rate of *19* per cent."

In commenting on the treatment of gunshot wounds, Dr. Gordon said, —

" It is true that the method of treating gunshot wounds of the chest, as practised by Dr. Swinburne, is condemned by some surgeons. It is beyond question, however, that the results obtained from it in the ambulance (American) in the Avenue de l'Impératrice during the siege were very satisfactory, so far as they went, and of a kind to justify its further adoption. It seems to me, therefore, that in future wars the treatment indicated is this: provided the bullet passes completely through the chest, close the opening, as Dr. Swinburne did, and so treat the patient. In several cases where the missile had passed completely through the chest, and penetrated one lung, recovery took place with comparatively little constitutional disturbance, and with a rapidity that became matter of wonder. Some of the officers and men taken to that establishment (the American ambulance) with wounds of this nature, their respiration oppressed by blood-discharges from the pulmonary wound into the bronchiæ, and with blood and froth issuing from the openings in the chest during expiration, were treated in the simplest possible way, and successfully. The usual treatment adopted by Dr. Swinburne was to hermetically close the outer opening by means of adhesive silk.[1] Little if any medicine was subsequently administered. In cases thus treated from the early periods of the wound, suppuration into the pleural cavities seemed to be averted. The results seemed to indicate that the effused blood was not necessarily a source of danger; that its action was not like that of a foreign body; and that, as recovery progressed, it gradually became absorbed. In none of the cases thus treated were counter-openings made or required."

He then refers to other cases treated on different plans, in which puriform effusions and hectic followed the counter-

---

[1] The plaster referred to by Dr. Gordon was Husband's silk adhesive plaster, placed over the wound, adhering to the chest above the wound, and acting as a valve. The lower portion was kept moist by discharges, on expiration, allowing the blood and froth, pus, and other discharges, to be forced out, and then closing, allowing the air to come in through the mouth and windpipe, and not through the wound in inspiration; and to this extent alone was the wound hermetically sealed."

openings, and then death. In one, the bloody liquid with which the chest speedily became filled was pumped out, and the operation described as *brilliant*, but the patient died ; and in another, empyema occurred, the chest was punctured for the escape of fluid, and the patient also died.

During this period of which Dr. Gordon writes, there were in and around Paris six hundred and thirty-four ambulances, in addition to ten hospitals, and at least three thousand surgeons from all the nations of Europe, many of them holding the leading places among their professional brethren as physicians and surgeons. It is a remarkable feature in his work, that, out of this multitude of ambulances, he selected the American as the model one in its installation, on which to treat at length ; but a still more remarkable feature was his selection of numerous cases treated by Dr. Swinburne, out of the thousands, and the minutiæ with which he described their treatment and results as of the most vital interest to science. In his book he devotes more space to the work of the American surgeon, and cites more of the cases treated by him, than by any other individual, or, indeed, the whole of the other surgeons combined. So necessary does he consider it to be specific in the details of all the methods used by Dr. Swinburne, that he devotes much space to their description, and the appliances and methods used by Dr. Swinburne in placing the patient in bed, and introduces a plate of a common field-stretcher designed and used by the doctor for carrying the wounded from the field, and the treatment of fractures by extension, and upon which they can be treated until well. In describing this stretcher, he says, —

" By means of a common *brancard* ("stretcher ") ingeniously arranged by Dr. Swinburne, a soldier or officer with gunshot fracture of the femur can be carried with an advancing army over any extent of country. Upon one of the handles at each end, a bent iron arm, having an eye at one end, was fixed by means of a screw. It admitted of being moved along the handle, or from one end to the other, according to the seat or side of the injury, and, from those at the head and foot of the extension and counter-extension, could readily be used. A mattress adapted to the dimension of the *bran-*

PLAN FOR COUNTER EXTENSION WITHOUT SPLINTS.

In Simple, Compound and Comminuted Fractures of the Leg or Thigh.

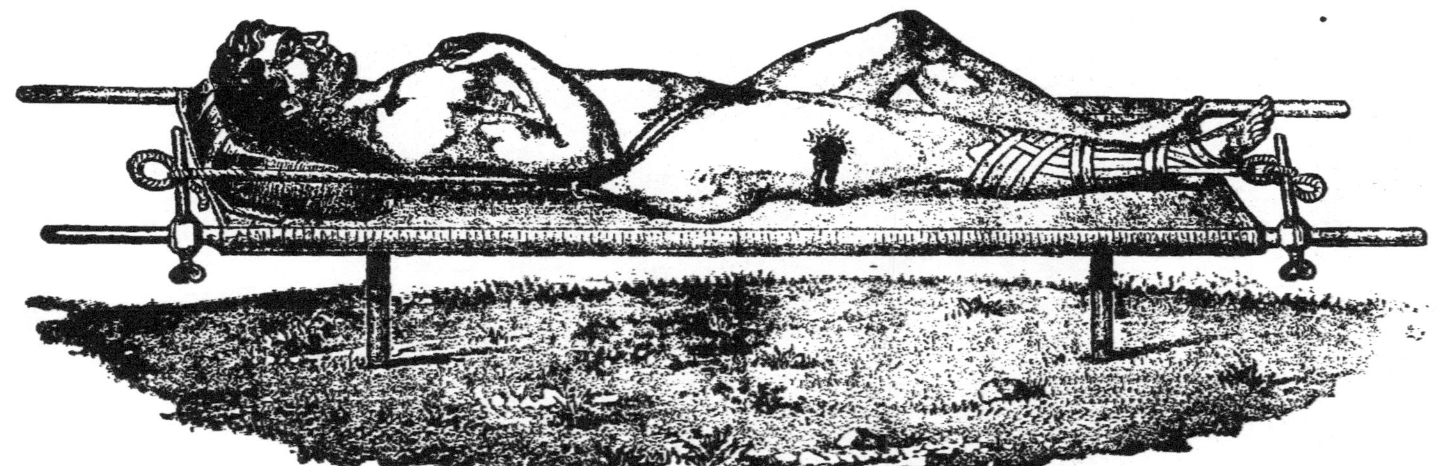

This design for a field stretcher was devised by Dr. Swinburne during the Rebellion, and submitted to the head of the medical department of the army, who refused to adopt it. The English and French governments have both adopted it. The perineal belt, where it comes in contact with the perineum, should be made of a large sheet, in order to equalize the pressure.—[See Gordon's Work on Military Hygiene and Evans' Report on the American Ambulance.]

card being provided, transport of a wounded man can be readily effected, either by means of two *brancardiers* (" carriers ") or by placing the litter upon a wheeled conveyance. The contrivance is further so suggestive in regard to a convenient method of securing patients with fractured thigh-bones on shipboard, that it is commended to the notice of surgeons at sea. By means of a staple eye secured in the bulkhead, at either end of a bed, immobility of the ends of a fractured femur would readily be insured."

This invention, when first conceived and designed by Dr. Swinburne, was submitted to the medical department of our Government during the Rebellion, and refused, for what reason those at the head of the department at that time only know. It was afterwards adopted and put in use by both the French and English Governments.

Dr. Gordon cites a case as a very remarkable piece of surgery, where a wound was received through the lower jaw, and effectively treated by Dr. Swinburne, showing how such an injury may be treated so as to avert a great deformity.

" A soldier was injured in the lower jaw, involving the front of the bone, by a bullet. The soft tissues were dissected back by Dr. Swinburne. The fragments of bone other than the very small ones, instead of being removed, were ingeniously secured to the existing teeth by means of wires; the ends of these being twisted off, and their ends protected by a case of wax. A frame was then fitted on to the chin, and moulded to its shape, oiled silk and bandages enveloping the whole. Recovery was progressive, and the deformity scarcely perceptible."

This was regarded by the author as an exceptional and extraordinary case, and one requiring unexceptional skill in its management, and hence was given to the scientific world as an illustration of what great achievements the delicate science of surgery *may* accomplish. With the surgeon who performed the operation, Dr. Swinburne, it was not new. A number of years before, the late Col. Jackson, formerly of the firm of Townsend & Jackson of Albany, fell from the window of the second story of his residence on State Street to the sidewalk (a distance of fifteen feet), and, striking on his head, crushed and fractured the entire jaw. By the use of the delicate wire, the shattered bone was brought to its place and healed, leaving no deformity. He was afterwards killed in battle.

"The eminent surgeons," said Dr. Gordon, "whom the writer had an opportunity of seeing operate, had several different methods of proceeding, and of performing the subsequent dressing. In amputating the lower third of the thigh, a cut was made from the surface upwards and backwards, through the muscles on the anterior aspect of the part; the posterior flap being afterwards made by transfixing, and cutting from within outwards. The flaps, both of which were equal in length, were retracted by means of a fillet, and the bone sawn across; the vessels were then secured by ligature, hand-pressure on the main vessels having been kept up during the operation. It was remarked, however, that a considerable mass of tissue around the vessel was included, and that the double ligatures were generally used, both ends being cut off. The surface of the flaps, after being sponged with cold water or alcoholized water, were brought close together by silver wire and sutures; *linge fénétré*, soaked in glycerine, was applied; a large, soft compress to each aspect of the limb supported the flaps; and a bandage applied from above downwards secured the whole. Other surgeons used the interrupted suture; and Dr. Swinburne, in one case of amputation of the thigh, left the anterior flap much longer than the posterior: the line of union was thus quite at the back of the limb, and the stump provided was a soft one."

In treating the merits of primary *versus* secondary amputation, Dr. Gordon said, —

"So far as the experience within Paris went, it simply confirmed that of former wars, — that these operations must be performed before suppuration has set in, to give them a chance of success. It is pointed out, however, that primary amputation cannot, under all circumstances, be performed. A wounded man may, as not infrequently was the case on the occasion of the great battles before Paris, be so benumbed by cold from protracted exposure upon the field as to put amputation of a wounded limb out of the question, until such times as the powers of the body are partly restored by stimulants and other means; and, by the time this has been attained, the period for primary amputation has passed. On the other hand, an amputation may, on some occasions, be performed with ultimate success upon a patient in a very great state of weakness."

To sustain this latter assertion, he again referred to an operation performed by Dr. Swinburne as an extreme typical case, and said, —

"A soldier was brought to the American ambulance in Paris, his leg carried away by a shot. Amputation below the knee was performed by Dr. Swinburne while the man was in a state of collapse, and pulseless. The man continued in this state for twenty-four hours after the operation; he then passed into delirium, which continued during four days, the stump being much disturbed in the mean time, the flaps gaping, and the bone projecting. Nevertheless, this man ultimately did well."

The doctor himself, soon after his arrival in Paris, wrote to Dr. Bailey of Albany, —

"Here I am, within a few rods of the inner fortifications of Paris. I had been in England, Ireland, and Scotland, visiting hospitals and other places of interest, until last week, when I received notice that I was wanted here. With Louis (my son), I immediately left for this place, where the Americans have established a hospital and ambulance corps out of American manufactures, including tents and about two hundred American patent beds, stretchers, etc. You would not blush for America, could you see these arrangements, and compare them with the English, or even the French. In truth, they are the admiration of the place. The soldiers say, if such accommodations were provided them, they would not mind being wounded. I have many things to say to you, on my return, in reference to surgery. Among them is the fact that the surgeons of Great Britain do not amputate for disease of any joint, but, on the contrary, resect. The result is, that more lives are saved, and less mischief results from the diseases, than from the old barbarous mode of amputation. Many a mutilated creature may bless the day that progress has its sway."

CHAPTER X.

LIVING ON HORSE-FLESH.

It used to be an old proverb that "Good Americans, when they died, went to Paris." It was true, a longing desire existed with a large portion of the American people to visit the gayest city of the world, and enjoy its frivolities and sights for a period. But, at the time our noble-hearted philanthropist was drawn to the French capital, the events were more exciting, and the gay colors of uniformed regiments more imposing, than the traveller usually witnessed. When the iron cordon of the Prussians was drawn around the city, belching forth its fire, and giving to the inhabitants a grand but undesired brilliant pyrotechnic display, the position was not comfortable. When provisions ran scarce, and all the beef had been consumed, and the *menu* consisted, in part, of horse and dog flesh, whose noxious exhalations, while being cooked, permeated the city, and when "pussy" was a delicate and delicious dish, it was hardly the place for realizing the celestial aspirations of our pious Americans. But here in this dreamed-of paradise, turned into a purgatory, our humanitarian, Dr. Swinburne, worked with his usual zeal for the good of mankind, without hope of pecuniary reward, as he did during our Rebellion, and by his great skill won a still greater name, even among those who were wont to believe nothing good could come out of the Western Nazareth.

The English press, science, and people were ably represented in Paris during the siege, and while always anxious to believe, and if possible make the world believe, that the best of men came from Britannia, they were at first inclined to underrate the "star" from the West, that had so suddenly appeared to the scientific world. As his works manifested themselves, they became dazzled by their brilliancy, and then charmed, and finally admitted the superior skill of Dr. Swinburne; one English writer asserting that he must be a descendant of the Swinburns of Swinburn Castle, after whom the townships of Great and Little Swinburn, near Hesham, in Northumberland County, were named.

The prompt and efficient work of the American ambulance made such an impression on the correspondent of the "London Daily News," that in writing to his paper in September, after referring to the others, he said, —

"The English ambulance is now prepared to fulfil requisitions made upon it from any quarter; and it may be of some use, provided the staff have not consumed, in the mean time, all the medical comforts in aiding the sick in the hospitals of the town and in the fortress. But I submit that it is not sufficient for a concern like the English ambulance to take its ease in its inn, and to intimate in a slipshod way, by casual journeys to the front, that it is in a condition to supply requisitions."

In a letter published in the "London Times" Sir J. T. Sinclair said, "Except the Anglo-American ambulance, under an American physician, which is only partially connected with the National Society for Aid to the Wounded, I believe little good has been done by the English surgeons." Capt. Henry Brackenbury in a letter to the same paper, in describing his visit to the English hospital, in charge of Dr. Frank, tells how Dr. May, attached to an American ambulance under Dr. J. Marion Sims, rode back with them in the dark to show to Dr. Frank a peculiar method of using some particular splint. This splint, and the methods of using it, were first introduced into practice by Dr. Swinburne.

. A correspondent of the "London News," under date of Nov. 15, said, —

"The ambulance in Paris which is considered the best is the American (under Dr. Swinburne). The wounded are under canvas; but the tents are not cold, and yet the ventilation is admirable. The American surgeons are far more skilful in their treatment of gunshot wounds than their French colleagues. Instead of amputation, they practise exsection of the bone. It is the desire of every French soldier, if he is wounded, to be taken to this ambulance. They seem to be under the impression, that, even if their legs are shot off, the skill of the Æsculapii of the United States will make them grow again. Be this as it may, a person might be worse off than stretched on a bed, with a slight wound, under the tents of the Far West."

He further adds in another issue, under date of Dec. 23, —

" At the central ambulance of the Société Internationale, the simplest operations are usually fatal. Four out of five of those who have an arm or leg amputated die of pyæmia. In the American tents four out of five recover."

This compliment to the skill and ability of Dr. Swinburne, the only American surgeon in Paris at the time, and a very flattering reference to the lady assistants and to the American women in general, were republished in the " Diary of a Besieged Resident in Paris."

A Paris clerk of Messrs. Bowles & Brothers, London, who had been one of the corps of the American ambulance, in a private letter to his firm under date of Jan. 10, 1871, said, —

" Of course you have heard of our success, — how the American ambulance is the model ambulance of Paris ; and how few our losses are, compared with others. ·Dr. Swinburne is really the only surgeon in the place. It is no easy work, especially after a battle like Champigny, where we had one hundred and thirty men come in in two days. I brought in the first wagon-load of six at four o'clock, and from that time until the next midnight we were bringing them in. Several were severely wounded, and died that night. Most of the men were severely wounded: we looked for that kind on the field. Dr. Swinburne seemed scarcely to sleep at all, and his aids and the ladies worked like Trojans. We had two Prussians: both were mortally wounded, and died soon after, though the last one struggled on three weeks. It was a wonderful case, for his pelvis was literally splintered. Splendid fellows, both of them, and it grieved us to have them die."

The most popular foreign representative in Paris during the siege was the American minister, Washburn, as was Dr. Swinburne the most popular surgeon. Wherever either appeared, they were cordially greeted. On the 27th of September, the "New-York Herald's" correspondent said, "The American ambulance corps and Minister Washburn were loudly cheered on the streets to-day. The crowd was so dense, that the new police appeared on the Champs Elysées, and opened a passage for the ambulance." The same correspondent on the 3d of October, in telegraphing with reference to the battle at Chevilly, said, "Dr. Swinburne describes the wounds of the needle-guns as terrible. The balls are of a larger size than any other used by contending armies. The ambulance went farther into the Prussian lines than into those of the French after the last battle. It was fortunate that the party fell into the hands of intelligent Prussian regiments, or they would not have escaped in safety."

A gentleman named Reed, who had charge of the branch house in Paris of Tiffany & Co. of New York, and who left Paris, with other Americans, on Oct. 25, said in a New-York paper, —

"The American Sanitary Commission is doing a noble work. Several large tents compose its hospitals, and on Oct. 25 they contained fifty-five wounded. The great superiority of the American over the French system in caring for and treating the wounded was clearly illustrated. They are regarded by the French as much better than their own. In case of a battle, the American ambulance men are always first in the field, and go to the front, and even into the lines of the Prussians."

The superiority of the American ambulance is testified to, said the "New-York Tribune" of Nov. 17, by a correspondent writing from Paris, who said, —

"A friend who went out with the American ambulance in the *sortie* of the 22d ult. says that the wagons came back laden with wounded, among whom were two soldiers belonging to what was not long since one of the finest regiments in the world, — the Third Zouaves, — but since dwindled down to seven, of whom three are lying at the American ambulance. One of the principal Paris papers is loud in its praises of this ambulance, and equally severe upon some of the others."

The condition of affairs in Paris was such as to ordinarily render the introduction of any system in the treatment of sick and wounded, different from what had been practised, very difficult of favorable results. Portions of the city, particularly where the American embassy had existed, became so hot from Prussian fire, that Mr. Washburn had to vacate, and retreat to more secure quarters. A most absorbing thought, with many of the correspondents, was something to eat, and the bill of fare of the besieged was at times the burden of their despatches. One of the first announcements in this respect was from a London correspondent, in a telegram to the " New-York Herald " of Oct. 12, which conveyed the intelligence that on the 7th inst. the residents began to slaughter and eat the animals in the menagerie, Jardin des Plantes. This was the forerunner to the famine that followed, and cleared the city of almost all the canine and feline hordes within its walls. The capricious epicurean, whether French or foreign, had to appease his whimsical palate with a dish a New-York street Arab would disdain. Some of the correspondents and ambulance corps, however, under the adverse circumstances, became used to the diet, and indeed became attached to it, declaring as *connoisseurs* that "kitty," under the manipulations of a French cook, was as tender and delicious as a rabbit.

There was a difference of opinion as to the success of Dr. Swinburne's system of conservative surgery as practised in Paris; but the implied question as to its success was generally given to the world by those who only arrived in Paris after the siege was raised. In no histories of other wars have the hospital treatment of the wounded, and the skill of the surgeons, been brought so prominently forward as during the Franco-Prussian. Scarcely a pamphlet has been issued regarding the war, that there was not a reference to the ambulances.

Archibald Forbes, who arrived in Paris after the raising of the siege, said in his "Experiences of the War between Germany and France," —

" Half Paris seemed converted into hospitals, if one might judge from the flags. So far as I could learn, the French surgeons in the early days of the siege, when the conditions were favorable, were earnest in the pursuit of conservative surgery. But as the siege progressed, times changed. Circumstances became unfavorable to the recovery of the wounded under any surgical conditions. True, it was possible still, in some favored lazarets, to pursue conservative surgery (a most favorable example was that of the American ambulance, under Dr. Swinburne); but all the receptacles for the wounded manifestly could not share this good fortune. There were crowded and long occupied wards, generating pyæmia, gangrene, and erysipelas; there were overworked orderlies; and there was food of a character inevitably tending to the impoverishment and vitiation of the blood. These conditions presented but a poor field for the successful practice of conservative surgery."

In referring to the excision of the knee and elbow joints, and the establishment of a juncture between the parts on either side of the excised joints, Mr. Forbes said, —

" The value of such an operation successfully consummated is immense; and under favorable conditions, with skill in the operator, a fair bodily condition in the patient, and sedulous after attention, such an operation is successful in most cases to a pitch which our ancestors did not dream of. The surgeon has to consider the practicability of diminishing the risk to the lowest possible minimum. The dressing is complicated, and the demand on the vital energies that stimulate the healing-power is probably larger. On the other hand, when he amputates, he exposes but one surface, and the other risks are smaller in every way. I fear the success of the operating surgeon has been in no case encouraging: it was hardly in the nature of things that it should have been so."

An historical fact connected with surgery in the French army during that war, and admitted by the scientific men of England and France, was that the greatest and only successful surgeons were Dr. Swinburne in Paris, and Dr. Marion Sims of the Anglo-American ambulance, outside of Paris, both Americans, and both following the same system of conservative surgery. Had this practice of conservation been followed in the other hospitals and other ambulances, and the operating surgeons understood their work, the eminent English surgeon would not have been called on to record, that, " in the American ambulance in Paris, we had *undoubtedly the most favorable results of any.*"

Three years after Dr. Swinburne left Paris, the following letter was received, dated the United-States Legation, Paris, Oct. 28, 1874, and signed by Minister Washburn : —

" I learn that the friends of Dr. John Swinburne are anxious to have him appointed professor of surgery. Dr. Swinburne remained in Paris during the siege as chief surgeon of the American ambulance, and acquired great distinction. I think he was regarded as without an equal in any of the military hospitals of Paris. Many of his operations were remarkable, and attracted great attention among the profession. In acknowledgment of his services, the French Government decorated him a chevalier of the Legion of Honor."

" In securing the services of Dr. John Swinburne as surgeon-in-chief of the ambulance," said Dr. Evans in his work, " the committee was particularly fortunate. Dr. Swinburne was a surgeon *par excellence*, an earnest advocate of conservative surgery, an enthusiast even as regards the conservative treatment of compound fractures, and a skilful operator when operations were required. He possessed a rare and highly valuable quality."

On the 17th of March, 1871, as he was about to leave Paris, " La Vérité," in an article, said, —

" We are happy to learn that Dr. Swinburne, the surgeon-in-chief of the American ambulance, and Dr. Johnson, physician-in-chief of the same ambulance, have just received the Cross of the Legion of Honor. The services rendered during the siege by the American ambulance are known. The devotion exhibited by the members of that ambulance is also known. In the accomplishment of their charitable work, they have recoiled before no effort, before no sacrifice. The distinctions which they may have received are the merited recompense of their zeal and their earnestness to aid those afflicted with the greatest misfortunes. We may add, that long experience and great skill secured to most of the wounded confided to their care cures often unexpected, and that the excellent system of tents, which had already been tested during the secession war, has offered at Paris, as well as in America, the most surprising results. The leaders of the American ambulance have nobly proved their sympathy for France, and they have gained, what is worth more even than honorary distinction, the esteem and the gratitude of all."

The age of chivalry was pre-eminently an age of individualism, and he who had power was ever eager to show the world he possessed it. A knight distinguished for his courage, strength, and skill, added to his honor by the splendor of his equipments. An ostentatious display was eagerly engaged in by them, and every gathering of these valiant knights became a scene of magnificent display. One of the greatest incentives to acts of heroism with them was to receive the smile of a lady, or kiss the hem of a garment woven by her fair hands. In this age of enlightenment and true chivalry, ostentation is ignored by the eminently great, and, like our honored countryman and distinguished physician, their ambition is to perform great acts for humanity, rather than to seek the plaudits of men. In the conviction that he has done his duty to his fellow-beings at home and abroad, Dr. Swinburne takes more pride than in all the official honors or decorations the heads of nations can bestow, although he appreciates these, because they were bestowed on him, not as marks of political favor, but as tokens of appreciation of his unselfish labors. Truly great is the man who in our own Rebellion, and in the French capital when besieged, labored for others so bravely without a dollar's remuneration from the government of either nation.

CHAPTER XI.

REVOLUTIONIZING SURGERY.

THE study of the history of that portion of science which treats of surgery or chirurgery, affords, even to the general reader, some very interesting incidents, and demonstrates an advance in that branch of science unprecedented, perhaps, in any other scientific research and improvement. All through its history, from the ages when it was enshrouded in ignorance, up to this time, when it ranks among the greatest scientific attainments, every step in its progress has been marked by the same professional jealousies that are manifested at the present time, and the same persecution of those who have led it step by step from its ignorant surroundings up to the high scientific plain it occupies. The reader of history will find much of interest in its perusal, and everywhere will notice the striking coincidence among the learned and the professional bigotry and persecution by those who, having settled into a traditional rut, are still desirous of remaining there, and who are opposed to any methods of treatment not in accord with the lessons taught them by those who lived in generations long since passed away. Formerly surgery was altogether and exclusively practised by the priesthood; and the ignorant masses believed the invocation by these of the help of spirits, good or bad, was the only effective remedy for the amelioration of the sick, maimed, and suffering, who are now treated on scientific and enlightened grounds, as far as possible with the knowledge of the present day. The Council of Paris even went so far, but a few centuries ago, as to pronounce the practice of surgery degrading to the dignity of the sacred office of the priesthood, and beneath the attention of men of learning. History says that Pythagoras was the first to raise it to the dignity of a science, by bringing philosophy to bear upon the practice, he believing that the physician, who had hitherto been considered as one gifted with divine knowledge, must, to be accomplished or successful, possess an intimate knowledge of the principles of surgery, if not with its practice, as it is conceded in this age that a perfect knowledge of anatomy and physics is absolutely essential in an accomplished surgeon.

In the beginning of the sixteenth century, when surgery was in that condition to which it had retrograded after the efforts of Celsus, Albucasis, Æsculapius, Paulus Ægineta, and Pythagoras to elevate it, and where it had remained for a couple of hundred years, when its practitioners were confined to barbers, farriers, cobblers, and tinkers, France produced the great Ambrose Paré, who did not think it any thing derogatory to have applied to him the title of " barber surgeon," even as our eminent surgeon, John Swinburne, does not feel humiliated at being called the " fighting doctor," because of his contests with professional malpractice and political corruption. Paré's experience in the treatment of gunshot and other wounds on the field of battle, in 1569, naturally directed his attention and investigation to the subject of hemorrhage; and to him was accorded the discovery of the method of arresting bleeding from arteries by ligature. Yet so averse, says a writer on surgery, are mankind to abandon their ancient customs, that the improvements of Paré met with strong and bitter opposition, and were not sanctioned until after much abuse and persecution directed against himself and his discoveries. Indeed, so bitter and unrelenting were his jealous brethren, that he was compelled, for his own safety, to adduce garbledand incorrect extracts from Galen and other ancients, in proof that to them, and not to him, the invention was to be referred. · He was, however, amply repaid by future fame for the opposition which he had at first sustained. He rose to an unparalleled height of popularity afterwards with the army, and was absolutely adored by the soldiers. So great was his influence over them, that on one occasion his presence in a beleaguered city, where the troops were about to surrender, infused among them a new vigor, and the besieging army perished under the walls. His has ever been an honored name in French history, and to him the "Journal Officiel de la République Française," in an editorial on Nov. 27, 1870, enthusiastically compared the American surgeon, M. John Swinburne. The seventeenth century gave to surgery in France Desault and Petit, — names ever proud in the annals of surgery. These men had to endure the same envious opposition which seems to have been the inevitable fate of nearly all those who have occupied, or now occupy, an advanced and prominent place in the profession. Desault, who improved on the apparatus for fractures, and invented a splint for fractures high in the femur, was, through jealousy, arrested while delivering one of his lectures in the theatre, and cast into prison ; where he remained, however, but a few days, when he was released, and he afterwards received many official honors. During the same century, when surgery had made but little advance in the British Empire, England produced Percival Pott, and Scotland, John Hunter, both eminent men. Hunter, who at the age of seventeen years was working at cabinet-making with his brother, became the very head of surgeons afterwards, and because of an outspoken charge against his colleagues in St. George's Hospital, that they neglected the proper instructions of the students under their care, brought out a very bitter controversy, which was frequently repeated. During one of these heated disputes he was taken with one of his old attacks of spasmodic heart-disease, and in a few moments expired. Because of a similar charge made by Dr. Swinburne when professor of clinical surgery, against some of his colleagues in the Albany Medical College, that faculty found it convenient to their own comfort not to remove him, for that they dared not do, but instead abolished the chair he filled. But the doctor did not die, physically or professionally, in the conflict, and has lived to be as a thorn in the sides of ignorant and unskilful surgeons, who are powerless to remove him from his high position, or silence him professionally because of his superior ability.

Pott's attention was more particularly directed to the treatment of fractures, of which he had some painful experience in his own person, having sustained a compound fracture of his leg. His own knowledge led him to believe there was a greater success, with less suffering to the patient, to be attained in this particular branch of surgery; and, as a result of his investigations, another step in advance was accomplished. He achieved a most important beneficial reform in the profession by employing the cutting instruments with greater caution and more reserve, and showing more regard to the laws of nature. As a straw indicates the direction of the wind, increasing from a gentle zephyr to a destructive hurricane, so the most trivial occurrences in life have given us the greatest results. Dr. Swinburne had not received any fractures; but those intimately acquainted with him may have noticed one of the fingers of one of his hands a little shorter than natural, because of having lost one joint; and it is probable that the maltreatment of that finger in his boyhood, trifling as it may seem, may have been one of the incentives to prompt him to devote his talents to surgery, which has given to America one of the greatest surgeons of the age. Of course, like his learned and eminent predecessors, he has been the object of bitter professional persecution, which at one time annoyed him, but now has no more force than a dog barking at the moon, and demonstrates that even the most idiotic prefer to throw stones at the tree which bears fruit, and which they cannot pull down.

The names of Paré, Desault, Petit, Pott, and Hunter all live in history, while those of their envious persecutors have been forgotten, just as John Swinburne's will live in history when the faculty who opposed and endeavored to injure him will be unheard of, as they are now unknown, except to a small and very limited circle, notwithstanding their herculean efforts to obtain newspaper notoriety. Dr. Swinburne, like the eminent men referred to, found time, in addition to the many other labors he performed, to prepare and contribute to medical literature a number of the most valuable papers of the century on surgery and the treating of diseases, many of these calling forth the highest indorsement from the medical journals; some of his views, like those advanced by his learned predecessors, arousing discussions among the profession, and calling forth captious criticism, which only proved the superior knowledge of the writer.

In the second volume of the "Surgical and Medical Reporter" is a detailed account by Dr. O. H. Young, house surgeon to the Albany City Hospital, of the "Exsection of the Middle Third of the Fibula," by Dr. Swinburne. On the 5th of June, John Kane, aged forty-five years, was admitted to the hospital. Five years previously he began to be annoyed by a deep-seated pain in the right leg, with exacerbations at night, and otherwise presenting the characteristics of acute periostitis. On June 8 he was rendered fully unconscious by chloroform; and Dr. Swinburne proceeded to operate by making an incision upon the bone about six inches in extent, and crossed above by another about three inches, in the form of a T. The peroneal muscles and inter-osseous ligament were then dissected off, and the trephine applied above and below the diseased portion, thus separating, with the aid of powerful bone forceps, a section of the fibula measuring four and a half inches in length, including the buttons removed by the trephine, three inches in circumference at one, and three and a quarter at the other extremity. This portion of the bone was entirely perforated in its centre, and greatly enlarged, roughened, and hardened by disease, rendering the use of the trephine a very laborious task. On Aug. 8 the leg was found to be entirely healed, with the exception of a portion about an inch in extent, which was not yet covered with skin. No fistula opening could be found in this ulcer. The patient at that time was hearty and strong, slept well, and had a good appetite; was entirely free from pain, and walked with much less halt than was to be anticipated so soon after the operation. A few months afterwards he was entirely restored, and has experienced no return of the pain since.

In the third volume of the "Medical and Surgical Reporter," he contributes an article on the dislocation of the radius (forwards and upwards on the humerus, so as to prevent flexion of the arm to any considerable extent), and fracture of the ulna, with mode of reduction and treatment, nine weeks after the injury. This was the case of a boy belonging in Denmark, Lewis County, N.Y., who fell, and, striking on the left hand, produced a fracture of the ulna at the junction of the second and lower third, accompanied by a distortion which was not reduced. Six weeks after the accident, several physicians and surgeons who were consulted advised non-interference. Two weeks afterwards Dr. Swinburne examined the arm at the seat of the fracture, when he found the ends of the ulna overlapped, and united at an angle of twenty-five degrees, the upper fragment projecting beyond the line of the bone, so as to produce an oblong tumor of an inch in length, and half an inch in width, almost protruding through the skin. With a view to reforming this deformity, and restoring the usefulness of the elbow, the patient was placed under the influence of chloroform, and the ulna seized above and below the fracture, and by steady efforts the union broken up, and the extremities rendered movable. For ultimate success, it was necessary to maintain permanent extension, both to prevent overlapping of the ends of the ulna, and also to reduce and retain the head of the radius in position, as well as by a constant and permanent reductive effort to restore the symmetry of the joint, the bones being constantly forced towards their proper places, the effusion being absorbed by the pressure. To effect these requirements, an apparatus was contrived. A full description of the apparatus is given, and the principle involved, which, he said, may be illustrated very easily by simply placing a bit of board on the fore-arm, from the fingers to the elbow, fixing it at the joint with the other hand, and then flexing, when it will be seen that the splint extends two inches or more beyond the fingers. This splint, or apparatus, was applied Oct. 24; and on the 29th the patient was able to bend the arm to an angle of seventy-five degrees, so that the hand could be carried up to the mouth, with the limb of full length, and the head of the radius in its normal position. When the patient first came to Dr. Swinburne for treatment, the head of the radius rested upon the anterior face of the humerus about one inch, and could not be dislodged till the ulna was broken and extended. Nine days after the splint was applied, the ends of the ulna were in perfect apposition, with perfect freedom of motion in flexion, extension, and rotation ; and the boy left for home. In that article he stated that extension could be obtained by two simple boards united by a hinge, and padded so as to be comfortable; so that in cases of emergency an extemporaneous appliance could be readily procured.

In July, 1859, he contributed an article to the "Medical and Surgical Reporter" on the reduction of the dislocation of the humerus (arm-bone) five months after the accident. This was an interesting case. On the 28th of June, Anson Ormsby of Lewis County came under the treatment of Dr. Swinburne, twenty-three weeks and three days after the accident, to be treated for a dislocation of the left humerus from the shoulder by falling. On the day of the accident a physician treated the dislocation who believed he had succeeded in restoring the head of the bone to its socket, and pronounced the joint perfect. Six weeks afterwards the same physician confirmed his former opinion, and volunteered to warrant a complete success. Nearly twelve weeks after the accident the same physician, on an examination, declared the shoulder had been re-dislocated, and labored three hours unsuccessfully to reduce it. Six weeks afterwards he went to Brownville and Watertown, Jefferson County, to seek surgical advice, and was recommended by all whom he consulted to have no more attempts made at reduction, inasmuch as it was considered irremediable after so long a period of time. He afterwards applied to Dr. Swinburne, and the reduction was effected in three-quarters of an hour. The remarkable feature in this case, as set forth in the article, was that the length of time between the date of dislocation and reduction was more than twenty weeks, when it was considered that dislocations are rarely considered reducible after three months, and that the deformity did not appear immediately after reduction, as is always the case in recent dislocations. The doctor, after detailing the methods adopted, asked, " Is it not possible that surgeons may be sometimes in error, in cases of long standing, from this circumstance, and that cases are sometimes abandoned as irremediable because of the impossibility of restoring immediate symmetry, whereas, by securing the parts as accurately and firmly as possible, the deformity may gradually pass away, as absorption of deposited matter progresses, and the head of the bone settles more and more accurately into its natural position?"

In the fourth volume of the same work is an interesting paper by Dr. Swinburne on the reduction of a dislocated humerus after eighteen weeks. On Oct. 13, 1859, William Sutliff of Brockett's Bridge, Herkimer County, was thrown from his wagon, and the arm near the shoulder-joint fractured. In two months after the fracture had been reduced he had gained the use of his arm, with the exception of utter inability to extend it from him, or raise it to a horizontal position. The attending physician, Dr. Walker, suspected the cause, and, on making a thorough examination on the 1st of January, discovered that the humerus was dislocated downwards and forwards. He was brought under the charge of Dr. Swinburne on the 18th of February, and on the 21st rendered insensible by means of chloroform. The relations of the morbid structures of the shoulder were accurately diagnosed; the head of the humerus lying in the axilla, as in ordinary dislocations, downwards and forwards. The head of the bone was considerably thickened, and there were indications of great deposits of fibrine in and about the axilla; so that the motion of the arm was greatly limited. Efforts were made to reduce precisely as in ordinary recent cases. But, undoubtedly from obliteration of the glenoid cavity deposits, the head of the bone would not remain *in situ* when the extension and other reductive efforts were relaxed. He then had recourse to permanent and constant means which he had made use of in similar cases with unexpected results. About the 15th of May, Mr. Sutliff returned home under general instructions, and placed himself under the care of Dr. Walker, who afterwards wrote Dr. Swinburne, —

"I continued the dressing you had applied, re-dressing about every other day, till the 9th of April. . . . I then discontinued all dressing, and advised him to use the arm moderately, which he has been doing; and he is now working some at his trade (boot and shoe making), chopping wood, planting, etc., and, on the whole, regards his case as a *providential cure.*"

This paper, like others by the doctor, gives a minute and comprehensive detail of the case and the treatment, and is of interest to the profession.

There are a number of cases similar to these to be found in the practice of Dr. Swinburne in the county of Albany, and other parts of the State, which would be termed remarkable if published in the books, but which have never been given to the public. As a sample, we give the case of Mr. William Doyle, a stove-manufacturer in the city of Albany, a gentleman weighing over two hundred pounds, as related to the writer by Mr. Doyle himself. In 1857 he was thrown on the Troy road, and the shoulder dislocated downwards, resting on the nerves. A professor in the Albany Medical College was called, and claimed that he had reduced the fracture. For several months afterwards Mr. Doyle suffered the most excruciating pain, with the flesh badly swollen and the skin colored. Unable to bear it longer, he called in Dr. Swinburne, who, on an examination, found that the dislocation had not been reduced; that the joint, instead of being in the socket, was off to one side; and that the bones had grown together in this unnatural position. By the use of rubber extension and counter-extension, Dr. Swinburne tore the parts apart again, and properly reduced the dislocation to its normal condition, Mr. Doyle saying it required the power of ten men to break it apart. Notwithstanding the pressure was thus removed from the nerves, it was several months before the nerve-power of the hand was restored, or the pain subdued. He considers his ever having the use of his arm still a matter of surprise to him; and although he has the use of his arm and fingers, and can lift with the arm as with the other, owing to the bone having so long rested while out of place on the nerves, he cannot put his hand to the back of his head, or hold it up for any length of time.

Another similar case was that of a Mrs. Jones, who was treated by a professor of the college and another physician for a dislocated shoulder. Months afterwards it was examined by Dr. Swinburne and another physician, and was found to be out of joint, and resting down on the nerve. The dislocation was then reduced; but, owing to the time it had been out of joint, the nerve-power of the hand was destroyed. An action for damages was brought by Isaac M. Lawson against one of the physicians, and a verdict of two thousand dollars recovered.

Another instance where the doctor was called to attend a similar professional error, as told to the writer, was that of a lady over seventy years of age, who had sustained a dislocation of the shoulder, and had been treated by another professor and an assisting physician, who dressed the shoulder in plaster of Paris. A month afterwards they removed the dressing, and declared it had been again dislocated. Six months after this, Dr. Swinburne was called by the lady's friends, and asked to remedy the wrong. Notwithstanding his desire to give comfort and ease to all, owing to the advanced age of the woman, and the length of time that had elapsed, he declined to make the effort.

These are but specimens that might be cited *ad infinitum*, notwithstanding Dr. Swinburne's assertion "that the reduction of dislocations has been made very simple:" and he suggests the adoption of one of two alternatives; i.e., that those who undertake the reduction of dislocations or fractures, or the treating of the sick or maimed in any manner, should either qualify themselves for the work, or refrain from in any emergency interfering with that most delicate creation of the Maker "so strange and wonderfully made."

In the "Reporter" of December, 1860, he had an article on entomology pins *versus* metallic and other sutures. In this paper he presented the use of the pin as a universal substitute for all other forms of suture when applied to the external surface of the body, not even eccepting the metallic thread. They produce, he argued, no irritation of the tissues, and consequently do not interfere with the process of union,

though introduced at intervals no greater than a quarter of
an inch. The introduction of small entomology pins, he
claimed, is attended with but little pain in comparison with
that produced by the passage of a needle and thread; and,
by the use of the pins, the edges of a wound can be ap-
proximated in the nicest possible manner by means of the
thread, as used in ordinary harelip operations; so that union
by the first intention is more sure to follow than in case of
any simple, interrupted. or even quilled sutures. He added.
" The advantages of this dressing are particularly manifest
when applied to the face and head, obviating the necessity
of adhesive plaster and similar appliances, and obtaining the
most perfect approximation without special fear of erysipelas,
unseemly cicatrices, or, in scalp wounds, the sacrifice of hair.
For my own part," he said, " I am in the habit of using this
dressing for every operation where it is important or desirable to obtain union by first intention, such as amputations
of limbs, tumors, etc.: in fact, wherever the thread-suture is
applicable, the pin is equally so. In consequence of its non-
irritating character, I am in the habit of applying it where I
should deem it imprudent to insert a thread." After treating
fully of the benefits to be derived, both surgically and in matter of cost, and giving a minute description of the method of
using the pin, he concluded his article by saying, " After one
year's constant experience with the pins, I should be loath to
resume the use of the old suture."

With that peculiar idiosyncrasy that actuated a portion of
the Albany profession at that time, — a desire to find a flaw in
the works or practice of Dr. Swinburne, — they cried. " Now
we have him !'" and one of the number, ashamed or afraid to
disclose his individuality, rushed into print with the idiom
peculiar to them, and, under the cognomen of " Subscriber,"
said, " the communication was at least five years behind the
times." The editor, after publishing "Subscriber's " comments, in a few lines at the end disposed of the criticism by
saying, in substance, that, prior to Dr. Swinburne's article,
there had been no articles published in which the use of the
entomology pins was recommended as a universal substitute

for all kinds of sutures, and then dropped the subject on the principle, *ex nihilo nihil fit* ("nothing comes of nothing").

In the large practice of Swinburne's Dispensary in Albany, no other dressing is used in these wards than pins, where thousands upon thousands have been used; and the doctor has never seen any of the evil results of lockjaw, erysipelas, or other unfavorable results; and, indeed, he has never, in all his extensive practice, had but three cases of lockjaw, and these were the result of dampness and cold in the homes of the patients.

Brief and concise papers of valuable importance to the profession, on other subjects pertaining to medical jurisprudence besides surgery, have been from time to time contributed; among them, treatises on cholera. small-pox, and yellow-fever, and papers on short and displaced femur, the cause of retarded labor, cases of rupture of the uterus, and on errors of diagnosis in cases of pregnancy. On the last thesis he said, "Do not take the opinions of any one of the profession, nor of every person in it, or you will be constantly deceived; do not interfere with a doubtful case of pregnancy, especially where the patient's health is not impaired by the cessation of menstruation."

In 1859 he read a paper before the New-York State Medical Society on the treatment of fractures of the femur by simple extension, ignoring splints and bandages, and related the histories of twenty-five cases, which, in his hands, had resulted better, with more rapid recoveries, and more comfort to the patient, than he had been able to attain by any other means. In 1861 he presented another, in which he advanced the idea that the same method could be applied to the treatment of fractures of all the long bones with equal success; and also that splints and bandages *per se* were useless, and in many instances worse than useless, if not absolutely injurious, except they are used as media by which the muscles are kept on a stretch, and even then should not be so used as to compress the soft tissues, or retard circulation. These papers attracted universal attention among the profession, and were, in addition to being published in the annual report of the society, republished in the New-York "American Medical Times " and the Philadelphia " Medical and Surgical Reporter."   These articles, giving a treatment not commonly known to traditional surgery, aroused the slumbering Rip Van Winkles of the medical profession, who believed the doctrines were erroneous because they were not found in the books; and to their author was the same spirit manifested as to Galileo when he declared that the world, rather than the sun, revolved.   Among those to declare their unbelief in these articles, or the mode proposed for the treatment of fractures of the long bones by extension, was O. C. Gibbs, M.D.   In these papers, Dr. Swinburne claimed, by actual experience, that the practical surgeon required no appliances for the treatment of fractures of long bones except such as are extemporaneously made; and that the same can be said of the treatment of fractures occurring in, or in close proximity to, any joint, such as intracapsular fracture of the neck of the femur, Colle's fracture of the radius, those involving the elbow-joint, the surgical neck of the humerus, compound dislocation and fracture of the ankle-joint, compound fracture of the tibia and fibula, etc.; and that the same is true of diseased hip-joint, morbus coxarius, and also incipient knee-joint disease. "It has been said," said the doctor, "that *accident makes the man*," and then asked, " Would *accident* make the *man* if he had not the knowledge to take advantage of the circumstances?"   He added, "I can conceive how *accident* might give us wealth; but *accident* developing *wealth* or *social* position, and *accident* developing one's *mental* and *scientific resources*, are two things quite separate and distinct."

In treating of the use of splints and the necessity of extension, he said, " All that Nature requires for perfect union of bone is rest and a moderate degree of excited action, while all pressure by splints, bandages, etc., only impedes the process of reparation; and this pressure, in my opinion, is a prolific cause of non-union."

The true use of splints, he held, *should* be to keep the fractured ends of the bone in apposition by placing the muscles on the stretch, and thereby making them the true splints.

The experiments of Reid and others show that muscles are not susceptible of being stretched beyond their normal capacity; that, when so stretched, they are capable of bearing great lateral pressure without much deflection; and any attempt at undue lateral pressure results in rupture of the muscular substance.

"While Nature," said the doctor, "requires rest for bony union, she requires also perfect apposition for union without deformity. How is apposition to be effected?" he asked. "We start with the knowledge that a living muscle cannot be extended beyond its normal capacity, and that any attempt to go beyond this not only provokes resistance, but a tearing of the muscles. Take, for instance, a fractured thigh: extension on the extremity by a strong man will stretch the muscles to their normal length only, which fact can be shown by the most careful measurement, thus proving that the danger of too much extension is only imaginary. Assuming the position," he said, "that the extended muscles act as permanent adjusters of broken bones, and are in reality the only means by which the fracture is maintained in apposition, I ask, Of what use are all the mechanical appliances and apparatus called 'surgical splints,' if not to effect the above-named results? The splint, beyond this, possesses no practical worth: on the contrary, it is apt, by its too careful adjustment, to impede the reparative process by interfering with the proper circulation of the proper part. . . . Then we may say that in extension the living muscles and other investments of the bone are the true splints, and that there is but little exception to this principle being universally applicable. As for myself, I employ this treatment indiscriminately, and I only ask my professional brethren who have the opportunity to try it, to do the same, and I am sure they will be able and willing cheerfully to bear witness to its entire efficiency, as have my friends, Drs. Thom of Troy, McLean of the Marshall Infirmary, Troy, Whitbeck of West Troy, and Willard of Albany."

He then proceeded at length to demonstrate minutely the ground taken, that fractures of the thigh or leg can be treated effectively simply by a perineal belt, and extension from the foot, and asserted that the method challenges comparison with the results of the most complex machinery of splints and bandages, and proved his deductions from about thirteen years' experience in private practice in the treating of fractures to be correct, in that in over forty cases of fractures of the femur and tibia, by extension, in no instance was there a shortening of over half an inch (and this the result of. inattention), while in a large majority there was no shortening at all.   He claimed there were many objections to the proposed elastic extending and counter-extending bands with weights and pulleys : among these, that it admits of spasmodic contraction of the muscles; that it presumes all muscular tissues are equal in tone and strength, which he held was by no means the fact; and that, were there to be applied a trifle too much weight, the object would be defeated by absolute separation of the bone.

Up to the time that Dr. Swinburne presented this paper, we have failed to find in any of the medical journals any account of where any surgeon had assumed to use extension for any fractures except that of the thigh, and of no attempts to treat the thigh without some of the long splints and bandages.   And even now, with the experience that time has given, only the more advanced scientific men have adopted extension for all the long bones, and the dispensing of splints and bandages, except where plaster of Paris is used.   A few years afterwards, in according "honor to whom honor was due," Dr. Louis A. Sayre, professor of surgery in Bellevue Hospital, said, "Dr. Swinburne was the first to introduce the principle of extension and counter-extension in the treatment of fractures before the profession."

CHAPTER XII.

CONSERVATIVE SURGERY.

WITH many of the old practitioners in the science of the healing art, every attempt at progress in the philosophy of the profession, counter to what has been published in the books and accepted as established practice, is regarded as *reductio ad absurdum;* and every new induction or appliance is held as an *experimentum crusis.* But Dr. Swinburne believed the true physician and surgeon, while always availing himself of the best methods suggested by others, should always be watchful for even better methods, and, using his own practical observations, be enabled to discover in this age of progress some means that may tend better to the accomplishing of the ends aimed at, fully realizing that in this branch of science perfection had not yet been attained. In private and hospital practice he had seen and taken an active part in many steps in advance. But a new theatre of labor had opened, and war gave him a greater opportunity, and again he made use of the knowledge acquired.

That the experience of Dr. Swinburne in conservative surgery in his private practice and in hospitals, as well as in our Rebellion and in the Franco-Prussian war, was productive of good results, better than from any other method, was affirmed by Dr. S. D. Gross, professor of clinical surgery in Jefferson College, Pennsylvania, embodying this treatment in his surgical work; and in one of his lectures before the students, entitled " Now and Then, or Forty Years Ago and Now," he said, in giving the names of men who had made progress in surgery, "that the only progress made in the treatment of fractures during that time had been made by Dr. Swinburne and another." Less than forty years before Professor Gross made that statement, Benjamin Rush, M.D., professor of medicines and clinical fractures in the University of Pennsylvania, published a work in 1835, nearly ten years before Dr. Swinburne commenced the study of medicine. on the diseases of the mind, in which he said, "The objects of fear are of two kinds, — reasonable and unreasonable. The reasonable are fear of death and surgical operations." He said, "The fear of a surgical operation may be very much lessened by previous company and a large dose of opium. Its pain may be mitigated by the gradual application of the knife, and. in tedious operations, by short intermissions in the· use of it."

In an address before the Albany Medical College in 1874, Dr. Swinburne said, "It is well known that the majority of surgical cases which a young practitioner is called upon to attend are fractures and dislocations. The reduction of the latter has been made very simple; but, with respect to the treatment of the former, I propose to enter into a somewhat detailed history, especially in regard to the progress made in the application of principles. Looking back, we can easily recall with what dread and anxiety all kinds of fractures were once approached by the student of medicine. The danger of bad results, and, more especially, the complicated machinery deemed necessary to acomplish even passable results, were obstacles difficult for him to surmount."

The attention of the profession was more than commonly attracted to conservative surgery during our Rebellion; and in an article treating of surgery on the battle-field, the "Medical and Surgical Reporter" said editorially on Oct. 25, 1862. —

"The temptations to perform capital operations are sometimes very great, and particularly so to the young surgeon on the battle-field during a sanguinary engagement. Under these circumstances, conservative surgery offers its claims under great disadvantages. But a determined will may overcome many seeming impossibilities, and limbs, and life too, be saved by deliberation and care. Where there is a possibility that a limb may be saved, the patient should have the benefit of great deliberation before it is decided to remove it (a right conceded even a criminal). . . . We have been led into this train of thought partly by witnessing the results of the deliberation and forethought that characterized the management of the United-States Military Field Hospital at Savage Station, Va., while it was under the care of Dr. Swinburne of Albany, N.Y. His praise is on the lips of many of the wounded troops who were in that hospital, and who have since found their way to the hospitals in this city [Philadelphia]. We have seen limbs that were badly wounded, in which amputation seemed almost unavoidable, but which were saved in spite of all the disadvantageous circumstances that followed their dressing. A few days ago we met one man belonging to a New-York regiment, who had the upper portion of the humerus shattered by a minie-ball. How few surgeons on the battle-field would have thought of any thing but amputation in this case! Yet exsection of the humerus was performed [by Dr. Swinburne], several inches of bone removed, and dressing applied; and the man passed through all the ordeals mentioned above, and now has an arm that is useful for many purposes. He does not even ask his discharge from the army, but intends going home on a short furlough, and then entering the cavalry service, where he says he can manage his horse with the injured arm, and wield a sword with the sound one. How much better that than amputation at the shoulder-joint!"

In 1862 Dr. Swinburne presented another addition to medical and surgical literature in an able paper on resection of joints, and conservative surgery in place of amputation, where otherwise amputation would be considered necessary. This was published in the "Proceedings of the New-York State Medical Society" of 1863, and largely copied in the medical journals. The "American Medical Journal" of Nov. 4, 1863, said of it,—

"The section on resection of joints, and conservative surgery, is an able defence of exsections as opposed to amputations, and a judicious discrimination of the rules that should be observed in the selection of cases and performing the operation. We most heartily concur in the opinions put forward, and can only hope that they will be widely circulated in the army, where they must be productive of good results. The simple truth seems to be, that, in wounds of the upper extremities, amputations should rarely be performed. Nothing but life can compensate the loss of the arm. Without the overpowering weight of statistics which Dr. Swinburne brings to his aid, we should be prepared to accept his arguments as conclusive."

Of the same paper the "Medical and Surgical Reporter" of Feb. 13, 1863, said, —

"We commence in this number the publication of one of the most valuable and interesting papers we have ever given to our surgical readers. We refer to Dr. Swinburne's admirable report. The paper is of especial value to surgeons in the army and navy just at this time, and we would call the especial attention of our numerous readers in the public service to it."

In this paper Dr. Swinburne treated of resection of joints; removal of the shattered fragments of the shaft, and sawing off the rough ends of the same; amputation, when and where necessary in preference to resection or excision; the relative mortality of the two operations as performed on the upper extremities; the cause of so much distrust as to the practicability of exsections in the field; and held that the objections to exsections, partial or complete, on the field, are equally applicable to amputations, or any other severe operation, if not performed at the proper period. With reference to exsections of the upper extremities, he argued that there were no circumstances which weigh against this operation that could not with equal propriety be urged against amputations. In the former operation, in the first or primary stage, the mortality is less than from the second or congestive stage; so that, if either be performed in the congestive stage, the danger of gangrene is at best as great from the latter as the former. The same is true of either, if performed in the third or suppurative stage. He claimed that it was not true that exsection predisposes the system any more to an attack of tetanus than does amputation, nor does the performance of either of them exempt the wounded man from this fearful disease : in other words, amputation is as often followed by tetanus as exsection. "Some," he said, "object to this operation [exsection] because it requires so much time. Now, I contend, that, if we are good dissectors, it requires very little more time to excise a joint than to amputate. As instances of the rapidity with which these operations can be performed, *I exsected four shoulder-joints, and ligatured the bleeding vessels, in one hour.* I trust that this is as rapidly as any one can amputate at the shoulder-joint. In my own operations," he added, "I have the satisfaction of stating to the world that I only amputated two arms, and they were torn off by shells or solid cannon-shot."

He held, as a rule, that excision (in military surgery) should be confined to the upper extremities ; the shoulder and elbow being the principal parts upon which that operation should be practised, and never at the shaft. The treatment of compound and comminuted fractures of the thigh becomes a matter of serious consideration, since it involves many important points. "Excision of the shaft is evidently out of the question," he said, "since all die after the operation. The question then arises, Shall we amputate, or shall we treat such cases as ordinary compound fractures? I prefer the latter, and have from the first thought it the most reasonable treatment. The plan I propose is to treat the patient on a bed or stretcher ; extend the limb as near as possible to its normal length without giving too great pain ; retain it in that position by fastening to the foot of the bed or stretcher by means of adhesive plaster, as in ordinary compound fractures, as I have on various occasions illustrated ; make the counter-extension thereon by converting the bed or stretcher into an inclined plane by elevating the foot, against which the body impinges, fastened to the head of the bed or stretcher. To obviate inversion or eversion of the foot, place bags of sand on each side of the foot. There should be no bandage of the leg or thigh. If collection of matter should follow, free incision may become necessary to relieve constrictions, and to facilitate the discharge of such matter and spiculæ of bone. Irrigation, or the application of cloths wet in cold or warm water, depending on the season of the year, must be continued to the limb until inflammation has passed off."

W. van Steinburgh, M.D., surgeon to the Fifty-fifth New-York State Volunteers, in his report, said, "Out of twenty-one cases of compound and comminuted fractures of the thigh, taken indiscriminately, nineteen recovered with tolerably useful limbs. My plan of treatment has been by simple extension, as taught me by Dr. Swinburne." Of twelve amputations performed by Dr. Van Steinburgh, ten died; and, of thirteen excisions of the shaft, all but one resulted fatally.

In the fifth volume of "Holmes's System of Surgery," by various authors, Carston Holthouse, surgeon to the Westminster Hospital, in a treatise on injuries to the lower extremities, in the section on fractures of the femur, refers to the cases cited by Dr. Van Steinburgh, their treatment and results, and details the methods used. He fails, however, perhaps from professional jealousy, — a failing with many of the English as well as American surgeons, — to accord the credit of the practice so successfully adopted to Dr. Swinburne; notwithstanding, in the work from which he gleaned his information, Dr. Van Steinburgh was particular to say that the treatment, and mode of operation, were taught him by Dr. Swinburne. The information was taken by Holthouse from an article published by Dr. Swinburne, incorporating Dr. Van Steinburgh's original letter (see " Transactions Medical Society, State of New York," 1864).

In the "Report of the Transactions of the New-York State Medical Society," published in 1864, is another paper by Dr. Swinburne, on compound and comminuted gunshot fractures of the thigh, and the means for their transportation. He introduces a plate of a stretcher for counter-extension without splints. "To my mind," said the doctor, "a little ingenuity and common sense can overcome all obstacles. I have adopted this plan, and have given directions for the management of this kind of fracture (of the thigh) in private practice. I have now treated about fifty patients, using the bed ordinarily met with in practice, instead of the stretcher. I know of many others treated by this plan, and in none have

I known of an unfavorable result. In the aggregate, the patients have been able to use the limb at an earlier period than under any other mode of treatment, without any lateral distortion ; nor would there be any, even if there were short-enings of the bone, as the extension of the muscles would keep the bone in a straight line." In the report he gives a minute and comprehensive description of the plan and method proposed. On the conclusion of the reading of the paper, by a unanimous vote of the society, Dr. Swinburne was re-quested to take the manuscript, with the drawings, to the surgeon-general, that he might see the advisability of adopt-ing them in the medical service of the army, the society always manifesting a deep interest in the troops at the front.

The reading and publication of these papers by this young surgeon aroused the comments, favorable and severe, of the profession; the " Medical and Surgical Reporter " editorially saying, —

" It has been well said by a recent writer on fractures, that it is not in the discovery and multiplication of mechanical expedients that the surgeon of this day declares his superior-ity, so much as in the skilful and judicious employment of those already invented. In no department of surgery has the simplifying of the mechanical requirements been more advanced than in the treatment of fractures ; and now it is asserted, and we believe proven, by one of the most practical and ingenious surgeons of this country, that the only correct and philosophic treatment of these injuries is almost abso-lutely *without apparatus.* The article by Dr. Swinburne of Albany, on the treatment of fractures of the long bones, as published in this journal, or read before the Medical Society of the State of New York, has attracted the attention of surgeons to the subject, and induced a repetition of his method in numerous instances. Such a revolution as he therein pro-poses in the treatment of fractures, which would displace from use so many popular contrivances, and require in sur-geons the abandonment of so many preconceived notions, could hardly be accomplished in a short period. But time, which proveth all things, has been allowed; and practical and unprejudiced men now adduce their testimony in favor of the logic of the reformer, and attest their experience in corroboration of the results obtained by him. . . . Dr. Swinburne's own experience during thirteen years, in his method of treatment, has been large, and, as he states, invariably successful. The plan has now received many practical tests by surgeons throughout the country, who have decided in its favor. In this city [Philadelphia] it has the approbation of Dr. Gross, Dr. Agnew, and others."

The "American Medical Times," in its editorial correspondence, said, —

" In regard to Dr. Swinburne's paper on exclusive extension in the treatment of fractures, we would express our appreciation. It is a meritorious and highly practical essay, based upon ample observations. We presume its author would admit, that, in his own treatment of fractures, he actually does secure, either incidentally or designedly, some lateral support for the fractured limb. That point admitted, his views and his practice agree essentially with those of the best surgeons everywhere."

In his thesis, Dr. Swinburne did admit support in this, that the living muscles acted as, and afforded the true and only necessary, support, thus obviating the use of any artificial support.

To the practitioners gathered at the meeting of the society before which these papers were read, and whose practice had been *secundum artem*, this *novus homo*, appearing before them with such advanced scientific ideas, created a sensation, and aroused a prolonged controversy or discussion : some of the older maintaining a perfect silence, but urging younger members to a criticism couched in language more acrimonious than elegant, the sarcasm of one of these being evidenced in a communication to the "Medical Times" afterwards, under the signature of " F. F.," in which he said of Dr. Swinburne, —

" That *young* surgeon evidently possesses the proper inventive and mechanical tact for good surgery. It is too manifest, that, so long as conceit boasts itself against accurate knowledge and common experience, lawyers and their deformed clients will surely make game of the best surgeons."

The correspondent said, —

"The older and more experienced surgeons very kindly reviewed and criticised the peculiar hobby of the paper, and finally its author found it very difficult to defend his exclusive practice of simple extension."

The "older and more experienced" had crossed professional swords with "that young surgeon" once before, and felt, in this case, they were *hors de combat.* Dr. Bly of Rochester, in discussing what degree of extension or force may be borne without completely separating the fractured ends of a bone, gave his experience of the extensibility of muscular tissues as demonstrated by him on the muscles of a dead sheep, in which he found that the extension amounted to half an inch. This argument was answered by Dr. Swinburne, who demonstrated the absurdity of comparing *dead* with *living* muscles.

Dr. James Wood said, —

" I fear the doctor, in his zeal, has not remembered that the muscles leading from one bone to the other are not straight. They are inserted at different angles, hence the force they exert must be in a corresponding direction ; and the only safe way to remedy the deformity which is thus induced is by lateral appliances in the shape of splints, with extension and counter-extension. If a muscle be irritated, it will contract: hence the necessity of keeping it quiet, and applying evaporative lotions until the inflammatory swelling shall have subsided, before the splints are applied with extension and counter-extension. I do not think that the doctor, when he shall have practised this method for some years longer, will feel safe to leave his patient without some such lateral support."

In reply to Dr. Wood, Dr. Swinburne maintained that it was only requisite to draw out the limb to its normal extent, when the natural positions and relations would be restored, and all sources of irritation would be removed. The amount of extension must be in all cases regulated by the feelings of the patient. In regard to the different actions of the several muscles of the thigh, he maintained that when the limb was placed upon the bed, and extension made, all the living muscles were so placed that they acted directly on the long axis of the bone. If any lateral influence was claimed for the abductors, the direction of their forces was certainly altered by the position and action of the perineal pad.

Dr. Wood said that he had never treated a fracture of the *os brachii* (large bone of the arm) by extension.

Dr. Batchelder referred to a case of a fractured femur, which was made from three-fourths to an inch longer, by extension, than the sound limb. Dr. Swinburne answered, that it was a simple matter to avoid this, and that a proper comparison of the two limbs by measurement would have prevented such an occurrence.

It will not answer, claimed Dr. Wood, in refractory patients; yet Dr. Swinburne had shown that he had treated by extension and counter-extension, successfully, a patient having delirium tremens, which lasted several days.

During the discussion, the doctor was challenged by Dr. Wood to produce a living proof of the success of his method of treatment, and, without any loss of time, accepted the challenge, and brought three cases before the society, they being the only ones that could be summoned on such short notice. These were: —

John A. Pitcher, a young German, who fell in January, 1854, a distance of thirty feet, fracturing the femur at its middle, also the left tibia and fibula at their lower third. He was treated by extension by perineal belt and adhesive strips at the lower part of the thigh, just below the patella. strips being also applied to the lower part of the leg. No splints were used, and in less than six weeks the extension was discontinued. Seven weeks after the accident he was cured; and at the time he was presented to the society, seven years after, the limb was so perfect that a most skilful surgeon was unable to detect the broken leg or thigh.

Hon. John Evers sustained an oblique fracture of the femur at upper third by being thrown violently against the curbstone by a run-away horse. Extension, without splints, was continued for six weeks; and in ten weeks he was discharged well, with the limb less than half an inch short, while he himself declared there was no difference.

Richard Hathaway, forty-eight years of age, and weighing one hundred and eighty-five pounds, while engaged in raising a monument on July 20, 1859, had a derrick fall on him, and sustained a compound comminuted fracture, the bone ground, with great contusion of the femur at its upper third. He was treated by Dr. Swinburne by extension and counter-extension, without splints; and in four weeks the limb was firm, and in eight weeks he walked with crutches. When this man was presented before the society for examination, the best surgeons present could not say which had been the broken limb, and decided it was the other limb.

Among the number of cases cited was that of James Mc-Kenzie, which was peculiar. On Feb. 22, 1854, he was admitted into the hospital with a compound fracture of the left femur through its middle, and treated by extension and counter-extension by perineal belt and adhesive strips to the leg, without splints, by Dr. Swinburne. In consequence of the fact that the other thigh had been fractured previously, and was three-quarters of an inch short, the extension in this case was only made sufficient to accommodate the length of this leg to the other. In less than six weeks the extension was discontinued, and in less than ten weeks he was discharged with legs of equal length.

In addition to the cases presented for the examination of the society, and those cited, the redoubtable doctor, said a gentleman, who was present at the discussion, to the writer, offered to bet five thousand dollars that the methods presented by him were more successful than any other, the winner to donate the money to some eleemosynary institution. But there were none present with sufficient confidence in their systems to accept the wager, and they hedged by simply remarking that they were not in the betting-business. Five thousand dollars was too much for them to risk on a practice that has filled the land with deformities against a man and method where eager and anxious watching had failed to discover a failure.

In the forty cases of fractured thighs cited before the society, and treated by the method laid down by Dr. Swinburne, there were no eversions or inversions of the foot, and no dis-

tortions of the thigh, and in but one was there any visible
shortening. These cases were, with a couple of exceptions,
taken from his hospital and private practice. Some of the
fractures were oblique, some compound, some comminuted (in
one case four inches of the bone being crushed in fragments).
Two were cases where the thigh and leg were *both* fractured,
and in *all* the results were considered *perfect*. Twelve were
fractures within the capsular ligament, occurring in patients
most of them over sixty years of age, and all treated with
this method of extension, with results much better than could
be expected, and which it would have been vain to expect
under the usual treatment.

The discussion of these papers was not confined to those
present at the meeting of the society, but was continued for
some time afterwards in the medical journals by the profession. Over the *nom de plume* of "Splints," in a communication to the "Medical Times," in a garbled report of the
discussion, a writer said, —

"Dr. Swinburne's object in thus bringing up the subject of
extension in a new form before the profession is a laudable
one : he is desirous of simplifying the treatment of fractures ;
and, for the attempt which he has made to bring about that
end, he certainly deserves a great amount of credit. He,
however, has, I think, allowed his enthusiasm to lead him
into error in regard to the adaptation of his principle to practice ; which fact, being assumed, proves to my mind that the
principle is erroneous. His honest efforts to prove the opposite state of things only shows how skilfully he can ride his
' hobby.'

" Every good surgeon [he wrote] uses a splint for coaptation of a fractured bone. In relation to the subject of exclusive extension, I must be permitted to make one remark,
and that has relation to its use in fractures of the *os brachii*.
Dr. Swinburne must pardon me when I give it as my conviction that he is indeed a bold surgeon to advocate a plan of
treatment which is so universally acknowledged to result in
non-union. In reference to the good results obtained by
this practice as applied to this bone, I can only express my
astonishment."

The critic adopting this, to him, euphonic signature of
"Splints," under which to cover his individuality, was under-

stood to be none other than Dr. Shrady, then editor of the "Times," and the father of a *splint* that was said by its author to be the best ever conceived, but which has long since been abandoned.

These are specimens of what the "young surgeon" had to meet with in his attempt to improve the methods of treating fractures; but, as in his practice, he was equally successful in his arguments and theory, as time, "which proveth all things," has shown by the success that has attended him. Nor has the prognostication of Dr. Wood, that the doctor, after he shall have practised this method a few years, will change his views; but, on the other hand, he has been more firmly convinced by years of practice that he was right, and has lived to see his methods triumph.

In "The Medical Times" of April 20, 1881, Dr. Swinburne answers these incognito writers and critics, in which he says, —

"When he ('F. F.') said, upon the question having been raised as to what degree of extension or force may be borne without completely separating the fractured ends of the bone, 'Dr. Bly of Rochester related the results of his experiments on the leg of a *dead* sheep, and produced extension of the muscles to about one-half inch,' Dr. Bly should have fairly stated the difference between simple extension, on the one hand, and, on the other, of suspending weights until the integrity of the muscle was destroyed; also the difference of *dead* and *living* tissue. I expressly say that the extension obtained by a strong man upon a broken thigh will not elongate it beyond its normal condition, and also expressly deprecate the pulleys and uprights, as they paralyze and elongate the muscles, and thereby destroy their usefulness as splints."

In reply to "F. F.'s" assertion "that its author found it very difficult to defend his exclusive practice by simple extension," he said, —

"If good results in the treatment of a hundred fractures of the long bones, and also Dr. Thom's experience as reported from the Marshall Infirmary, is not a good *practical defence*, then I have found it difficult to defend the exclusive *practice* of my *hobby*. His quotation, that I resort to lateral support to the fractured limbs in particular cases, is untrue. I expressly said that, where a lateral splint is used, it is only a means by which the extension is made and perpetuated, and not for lateral support. In the thigh there is no lateral support used; and in the article on extension I said that the treatment adapted to the femur is applicable to any portion of the thigh or leg."

With reference to the remarks of Dr. James Wood, " F. F." said, —

" The remarks of Dr. Wood constituted the most interesting event of the first day's session. Close attention was given to his remarks, which seemed to satisfy the obvious desire of all classes of practitioners, who fear the misapplication of judicial inquiry and prosecution for the correction of faults in surgery."

To this Dr. Swinburne replied, —

" No one could be more pleased than I with the frank, honorable, gentlemanly, and masterly manner in which Dr. Wood discussed the merits and demerits of simple extension. Though I defended what I *knew* was the true principle of the treatment of fractures, I was, nevertheless, anxious to hear the views of James R. Wood. That I had great confidence in my mode of treatment, is proved when I proposed (in the discussion which occurred between Dr. Wood and myself) to treat alternate fractures in any hospital (by his method), with any surgeon, and I would stake my reputation upon the *results* by obtaining union in less time, and with better results, than could be obtained by the use of splints as commonly applied. As to the last clause, it surely does not apply in the present instance, as I have never been sued for malpractice, nor has there been any occasion even for the insinuation."

In reply to " Splints," whose almost entire correspondence he characterized an evident perversion of facts and statements, the doctor said, —

" As to the idea that ' he seeks to establish the absurd principle that muscles cannot be extended beyond their natural length,' I maintain that any attempt to extend a muscle beyond its normal capacity not only provokes resistance, but a tearing of its substance (I mean the *living*, but not the *dead* tissue). Take, for instance, a fractured thigh : extension on the extremity by a strong man (and not with weights and pulleys) will stretch the muscles to their normal length only; which fact can be shown by the most careful measurement, thus proving that the danger of too much extension is only imaginary."

He quotes from " Splints,"—

" I am not aware that Dr. Swinburne claims any originality in the matter; i.e., simple extension. He has, however, allowed his enthusiasm to lead him into error in regard to the adaptation of his principle to practice, which (being *assumed*) is convincing to my mind that the *principle* is erroneous: his *honest efforts* to prove the opposite state of things only show how skilfully he can ride his hobby."

To this the doctor replied, —

" With reference to the first portion of the quotation, the principle of extension is acknowledged by all good surgeons; while, with reference to his ' *enthusiasm leading him into error*,' I think it is a good *error* when the results are so perfect that it baffles a good surgeon to discover which of the two thighs had been broken, though the fracture was compound and comminuted, occurring in a man weighing one hundred and eighty-five pounds. What is true of this case is also true of *all* the others, and equally so of fractured tibia. As to the ' *adaptation* of his *principle to practice*,' instead of showing that the principle was wrong, *practice* only serves to make the *principle* more fully appreciated, and demonstrates to the world that it is not the *kind of splint*, but the *mode and manner* of the *application* of the *principle* involved."

One critic thought the doctrines then laid down were dangerous to teach the students; but the doctor, knowing his method was correct, was anxious that the profession, as well as the students, might be benefited by his over twenty years of experience, as he is now always ready to impart his knowledge, acquired after forty years' experience, to all who have in charge or are in training for the care of the sick and maimed; and not only a large number of the college students avail themselves of this privilege, and are constantly in attendance at his large clinics, eagerly watching and listening to the man who has made no failures, but frequently regular practitioners of

years' standing are among those who come to learn of him.
This paper, covering fifty pages of the Medical Society's report, also treats of fractures in or near the elbow-joint, with or
without dislocation, and of the treatment of fractures of the
clavicle by simple extension.

Dr. Swinburne's attention was first drawn to the subject
of treating fractures by extension, because of the many bad
results he had seen from oblique, compound, and comminuted
fractures of the leg; and, being astonished at the number, he
was led to investigate the cause, and examined specimens in
a number of museums containing collections of broken bones,
where he found all were more or less distorted, both laterally
and longitudinally, with shortened tibias. He believed this
was an age of progress, and that there were no results without
cause, and that it was an obligation science owed to the
people to discover the cause of these bad results. He knew
that the first paths over our vast Western country were made
by the buffalo, and then followed in by the Indian, but that
as civilization, with its compasses and engineering genius,
made its way through the country, the long-trodden paths of
primeval days, over rugged hills and mountains, were ignored,
and more feasible and rapid methods of transport brought
into use. In his chosen branch of science, he did not desire
to travel in the uncertain and crooked paths of tradition, nor
in the dog-carts of more modern science; but, like the traveller who takes the iron horse and easy coach over the steel
track of civilization, he was anxious for the most comfortable,
safe, and speedy cure of the maimed, leaving others, if they
so desired, to travel in the path of the buffalo or the Indian;
and for this reason he was satisfied extension would obviate
the dangers of lateral distortion, and, as far as the spasmodic
contraction of the muscles would permit, overcome longitudinal distortion.

This paper was also incorporated in Professor Gross's "Surgery," and had an unusually wide circulation in this country,
and was extensively copied from in Europe.

The cases presented and referred to in this chapter were at
the time typical cases, treated by means not hitherto em-

ployed, and resulting in success not anticipated in previous treatment. They were then considered surprising; but a still greater advance has been made by him in his treatment by simplifying the methods of extension, since that time, with results more surprising, as may be learned by a reference to the work in his dispensary.

This plan for the treatment of fractures of the femur or the other long bones, without splints or bandages, was unknown to the profession at the time the paper was presented by Dr. Swinburne in 1859; and, although it was followed to some extent in our Rebellion, its superiority was not definitely settled in military surgery, on account of the prejudices of the profession, until during the Franco-Prussian war, where it was in every instance in the American ambulance followed by Dr. Swinburne with successful results and good limbs. The profession had never, up to that time, recognized the necessity of extension for the approximation of bones other than the thigh; and this fact was so conceded at a meeting of the Academy of Medicine in New York, as may be seen by reference to the "Medical Times." Nor had they ever dispensed with splints or bandages.

After a lapse of over twenty-five years since the publication of the paper by Dr. Swinburne, it is shown and proved that the theories he then entertained were and are the nearest possible to the true ones; and it is also conceded — because of the unprecedented favorable results in his own practice, daily carried out, as well as by others who have adopted the system — that the principles then laid down, in 1859 and 1861, for the treatment of fractures of the long bones, — viz., that any fracture or fractures, of whatever nature or kind, occurring between the elbow and shoulder, or between the ankle-joint and pelvis, — can be successfully treated by the plan commenced by him in 1848, and which has — since its being given to the public, up to the present — been practised by him, as well as his friends and many of the advanced and intelligent practitioners in surgery. In military surgery this treatment of fractures of the thigh, or otherwise as followed in the American ambulance at Paris during the

Franco-German war in the winter of 1870 and 1871, was shown to be the superior and most successful, as attested to by the most eminent men of Europe, and quoted in another chapter.

Professor David P. Smith of Springfield, Mass., while visiting in Edinburgh, Scotland, wrote, —

" Fractures will be most successfully treated by those surgeons who are best acquainted with anatomy and physiology, and know by experience what a bruised and perhaps lacerated limb can bear."

As late as the latter part of 1861, the principle of extension and counter-extension in the treatment of fractures found no favor in Europe, Professor Syme of the Royal Infirmary, Edinburgh, maintaining stoutly that the benefits supposed to be gained from the use of extension was a mere delusion; for if extension was employed, he argued, the muscles were roused to resistance, and always overcame such force.

With a large majority of the profession, devotion to established principles is a religious duty, from which it is almost a miracle to have them change. They hold that their principles are right because they are traditional, and founded on facts, as taught them. They forget, or seem to, that in medical and surgical jurisprudence all the advance science has ever made in their or other callings was made by a few enthusiastic utilitarians in any age. In many instances, and indeed almost universally, correct and advanced principles have only been accepted in great emergencies as *dernier ressort.*

The principle of conservation as applied to the limbs was but little discussed during the first years of our war, except by Dr. John Swinburne and a few others, the principal idea being the discussion of the best means of amputation, the purpose being to change the treatment of fractures from the carpenter-shop to the butcher's table. As an instance of what some of the medical journals contained from their most prominent contributors, we extract from the letters of a surgeon in charge of Fairfax Seminary Hospital, published in 1863 : —

" The multitude of amputations below the knee which I have performed, seen, and watched the results of, have convinced me that none of the ordinary methods are the best possible in any surgery. . . . In my remarks I may have seemed to lay too much stress upon my favorite method of amputation below the knee. I say emphatically that the advantages which I claim my method alone furnishes must be obtained if recovery is expected to follow."

These were the sentiments of Dr. David P. Smith, who, in asking, " Shall amputation be performed in gunshot fracture of the femur from a conical leaden bullet ? " said, —

" From dissection of such injuries after they were removed by such amputation, I was, however, enabled very early to recognize the hopeless nature of such cases if left to themselves."

These statements were made in 1863, after two years' experience in the war, and were answered by John T. Hodgen, surgeon in charge of the St. Louis City General Hospital, who said, —

" Dr. Smith and myself have seen such cases under widely different circumstances, — he on the battle-field, and I in the hospital, after they had been removed thither hundreds of miles. There have been received at this hospital sixty-five cases of gunshot fractures of the *os femoris*. Of these, eighteen have died, four remain under treatment in a fair way to recovery, and forty-three have recovered, and left the hospital with good limbs. It will be observed that the percentage of mortality is less than twenty-eight, thus giving better results, so far as life is concerned, than amputation of the thigh would do, besides preserving useful limbs. The above statistics are startling to surgeons who have seen the terrible work done by the conical leaden bullet, and they will naturally cultivate a feeling of incredulity; but to my mind these recoveries are not so incredible as that sixty-five men thus wounded should have escaped mutilation at the hands of those humane, patriotic, and time-saving surgeons, who, ' by order ' or without it, flock to the battle-fields (some days after the fight), who swarm on transports, and who rush to hospitals to gratify a morbid thirst for capital surgical operations."

At a meeting of the United-States Army Medical and Surgical Society of Baltimore, held in February, 1863, the vice-president, Surgeon Z. E. Bliss, said, —

"The operation of exsection of the joint as a mode of treatment of gunshot fractures involving the shoulder, elbow, and hip joints, has not, as yet, been fully tested; but sufficient facts have been already obtained to prove that this operation often saves life, and preserves a serviceable limb."

That our humane and patriotic fellow-citizen, Dr. Swinburne, performed an active part in introducing conservative surgery into the army, and saving a host of lives and innumerable deformities among those who were gallantly defending the nation, may be drawn from a report of gunshot fractures read before the United-States Medical and Surgical Society of Maryland, and published in 1863. The paper was by Edmund G. Waters, M.D., acting assistant surgeon. He said, —

"On the 21st and 25th of July, 1862, between four and five hundred sick and wounded Union soldiers were received into the National Hospital, Baltimore. Most of the wounded had been shot in the seven-days' fight, and, being taken prisoners, were sent to Richmond. Among them was a number with fractured thighs; and a better opportunity has rarely been afforded to test the several modes of treatment in secondary cases, after this kind of injury, than these presented. The writer regrets that he is not able to give the exact number of amputations performed for this injury, but is able to state positively that only one patient recovered of the many who underwent the operation."

He then gives the history of fourteen other similar wounds treated conservatively, all of whom recovered. One of these was a fracture in the neck of the bone.

These wounds were all received in that portion of the field of battle where Dr. Swinburne was in charge, and where amputations were not practised, but where conservation was the rule. The success of the doctor had, no doubt, much to do with inciting these efforts to save. In these instances cited, here is ample food for reflection by the profession, as well as facts on which to predicate a safe practice, unless they desire to exemplify the truth of Key's assertion, that "amputation is the last resource of the surgeon, at once the shelter and confusion of the surgical art."

Even the best of surgeons seem slow to learn; and it was not until 1863 that De Witt C. Peters said, —

"The era of promiscuous surgery, both in military and civil life, has passed nearly, if not quite, into oblivion. In discussing the important subject of compound fractures of the thigh, too little stress has hitherto been paid by surgical writers to the saving of limbs. Following the teachings of Dupuytren, Baudens, Hennen, Guthrie, and a host of others, we are too ready to admit that amputation is our sole reliance. They would have us believe that the patients who save their limbs, forever remain martyrs to a miserable existence. Others inform us, amputation of the thigh is a dangerous expedient, and in their hands has resulted in the majority of cases fatally; yet they carefully avoid entering into any details of their manner of treating fractures. The wonder to my mind is, that their patients ever recovered when laboring under this species of injury. The indications are to place the parts in a natural position, keep them immovable, and dispense with snug bandages and splints."

This was coming pretty near up to Dr. Swinburne's principle of treating without any splints or bandages, but with extension and counter-extension. One of the best authorities in the army said that no attempt had ever succeeded, that he had heard of, during the war, to conserve a limb where a compound fracture of the thigh had occurred, where proper extension was not used.

Dr. Swinburne, in a paper read before the Albany-county Medical Society at its annual meeting in November, 1874, and published in the Sunday press, said, —

"As to the causes which have led to the changes of the methods in the treatment of fractures, they have been wrought principally in accordance with the scientific law of making the muscles the motive power. The knowledge of the principles of the muscles, and their importance in the management of fractures, came by experience in practice and in the dissecting-room. The uselessness and injurious effects of bandages were, at an early period, a matter of firm conviction with me. The results obtained by the old-fashioned appliances were any thing but satisfactory. The upper parts were compressed to such a degree that all the soft tissues became a conglomerate mass. Muscles, nerves, vessels, cellular tissue, and investing membranes adhered to the bone, and, in time, were consolidated there. Months might, and often did, elapse after the union of the bone, before the soft parts would return — if, indeed, they ever did return — to their normal condition. The state of the muscles, when maddened by the goring, pricking, and tearing of the fractured ends of the broken bone, is one too often observed to necessitate a more than passing mention. The muscles, you will recollect, are thereby thrown into a condition of clonic spasm, which, sooner or later, becomes the cause of more or less longitudinal and lateral distortion.

"The old practice was to overcome distortion chiefly by the appliance of splint and bandages: the modern practice is to extend the limb to its normal length, and to retain it in that position, with as little compression of the parts as possible. The results of the former method, even if favorable, which were rather less frequent than one could wish, were obtained by the complicated processes of the period; the difficulty of dressing, the recurring redressing, and the adjustment of the apparatus and bandages, being incalculable, to say nothing of the pain, suffering, and inconvenience caused to the patient. By the simple method at present in vogue, the most satisfactory results are obtained, with little pain, with no distortion, and with little or no immobility of the soft parts.

"Impressed by some such considerations, I was led, at an early period after graduating, to examine the subject immediately from the dead body; and this examination clearly demonstrated that some other, simpler, and more efficient method could be devised. Various experiments upon fractured limbs of the cadaver and living subjects satisfied me that there was a principle involved in their treatment, which, being turned to the full extension of all the parts involved, would return the limb to its normal length and condition. It could be kept in place by the application of sufficient counter-extending force, without the use of splints in any shape or manner. This theory was put in practice in 1848, and proved an entire success."

Experience has confirmed the doctor beyond all question, that the system he espoused nearly forty years ago is better than any before or since suggested ; and in his practice, both civil and military (in two wars), he has practised it always successfully, and with better results than could be attained with any other method. If the assertion of the "Medical Times," always a great stickler for established rules, made in 1863, — "that practical surgery is evidently, at the present time, thoroughly committed to conservation," — is proven true, thousands who never saw, and perhaps never heard of, Albany's great physician and surgeon, will have good cause for thankfulness that Dr. John Swinburne lived, and inaugurated a system whereby pain is eased on the sick-bed, and limbs that otherwise would have been destroyed were saved, and deformity avoided. This alone would have been a life of usefulness rarely surpassed.

CHAPTER XIII.

CHALLENGING THE CRITICS.

Willing to back his Method with Money. — Preaching False Doctrine. — More Light wanted. — A Poor Excuse. — A Sharp Arraignment.

THE revolution in surgery that the doctor was aiming to bring about for the good of humanity was not only opposed by the lesser lights, but by some who had arrogated to themselves leadership, and, assuming the place of authors, conceived themselves infallible in this great science. But to none of them would the doctor yield a point, or admit superior skill. Among those who criticised his practice and methods was Professor Frank H. Hamilton, the author of several works on surgery. In one of his works he took exception to Dr. Swinburne's system of extension, and was very positively challenged to make a trial, and test methods; but the professor, like Dr. Clarke, was afraid to practically test the skill of Dr. Swinburne, and declined to enter into a competition with one he knew was so aggressive and skilful. The correspondence passing between them demonstrates how slow professional men are, at times, to accept any new or advanced ideas. The professor taught one theory, and the doctor practised another; and the latter, believing results were always the powerful arguments, sought a friendly competition to arrive at the best methods, and to this end challenged the author. The correspondence of the doctor, and the replies, are given as a public matter, and are as follows : —

PROFESSOR FRANK H. HAMILTON.

My Dear Sir, — In the fourth edition of your work on fractures and dislocations, p. 412, you say, in speaking of fractures of the femur, "I cannot think it necessary to do more than allude to the practice of Jobert of Paris, and of

Swinburne of Albany, who, rejecting side or coaptation splints altogether, have relied upon extension as means of support, and retention in the case of fracture of the shaft of the femur."

Now, my dear doctor, I have since 1848 practised the plan you so incidentally mentioned for fracture of the thigh, and feel constrained to say that the results not only bear out the treatment, but the patients are far more comfortable, and deformity far less likely to occur, than when dressed in any other manner. Not only have I pressed upon the profession the plans for treatment of the thigh, but also those for treatment of the other long bones; viz., the arm, fore-arm, and leg. Therefore I propose for your consideration the following: that we each deposit with some third party from one thousand to five thousand dollars (the whole amount to go to some eleemosynary institution when the trial is decided), and you taking a given number of fractures of the long bones before mentioned (whether simple, compound, comminuted, or complicated with luxation or other injuries, makes no difference), and I taking a like number, yours to be treated after your methods, mine after mine; and if I do not get better results in a shorter space of time, with less pain to the patients, I am to be declared the loser; but, if I do gain such success, you to be the vanquished, and, as I said before, the treatment for fractures of the long bones, as advocated by me in several publications and in my lectures, to be advanced, and taught in the schools.

I make this proposition, doctor, for the following reasons: first, for the benefit of those who are to come after us, and to whom will fall the care of these same injuries; secondly, because, living as you do in the metropolis, ample facilities can be obtained for making such a trial; and, thirdly, because in all the works on fractures with which I am acquainted, more or less deformity of wrists, elbows, and fractures in other localities, are spoken of as the attendant evils of such accidents. The minor details we can arrange later, in case you see fit to accept my proposition, and also decide upon impartial judges.

Hoping I may shortly hear from you in regard to this matter, as I now am able to give the necessary time for such a trial,

I remain, my dear sir, yours very truly,

JOHN SWINBURNE.

NEW YORK, Jan. 7, 1879.

PROFESSOR JOHN SWINBURNE.

My Dear Sir,—Having become convinced, after careful observation, that side or coaptation splints are, in a majority of cases of fracture of the shafts of the long bones, essential to the attainment of the best results, I do not think it necessary or useful for me to enter into the friendly contest which you propose.

Very respectfully yours,

FRANK H. HAMILTON.

ALBANY, Jan. 20, 1879.

MY DEAR DOCTOR,—I regret exceedingly that you should have declined my proposition to test the comparative value of our respective plans for the treatment of fractures of the long bones.

Our methods differ radically, and the results claimed vary so widely as to require some explanation : otherwise but one conclusion remains, that one or the other of us must appear to be preaching false doctrine.

Inasmuch as I am desirous of testing my treatment on a large scale, where competent and impartial judges can decide upon the results of this compared with other methods, I ask if you, as the author of a work on fractures, and a teacher of students, will afford facilities for the trial of a plan which has worked so favorably in my own hands. Inasmuch, again, as it is conceded that more than one-half of the fractures of the elbow result unfavorably, and as you, in the fourth edition of your work on fractures and dislocations, report a large majority of Colles' fractures as imperfect results, it would seem as if some plan, simple and efficient, should be perfected at once, by which the profession would be enabled to obtain good results in all forms of fractures. I ask again if you and your friends are willing to join me in this essay, —an important step in the reformation already begun, and which is destined to revolutionize the whole treatment of fractures.

The work I began in 1848, in private practice, is now bearing fruit in the treatment of all forms of fracture of the femur; and so the methods of treating other forms of fractures will undergo a complete change at no distant time, despite any efforts to retard or hinder it.

The more intelligent portion of the community are demanding greater light on this subject. They are tired of, and disgusted with, the multiplicity of plans and apparatus for the treatment of fractures, and with the want of an orderly body of clear and simple principles to guide them. They can endure no longer this blind adherence to, and perpetuation of, the quasi-charlatanism which has entered so largely into the subject. The classes of the Albany Medical College have, by a unanimous resolution, asked me to give them a synopsis of the treatment of all forms of fracture of the long bones, which I shall soon undertake to do; but, before doing so, I should like to give you and other surgeons full opportunity of examining in person results as they occur under my treatment. If, therefore, you are disposed to afford me the opportunity, I will gladly avail myself of the privilege.

Yours respectfully, etc.,

JOHN SWINBURNE.

NEW YORK, Jan. 22, 1879.

MY DEAR DOCTOR, — I shall be glad to see your practice and its results whenever it may be convenient for you to show them to me; but, as I am alone responsible to my patients for their treatment, I cannot employ, or permit others to employ in their management, methods or forms of apparel which an extended experience and observation have convinced me are not the best. Your error is in supposing that I have not seen fractures treated by the methods you prefer, and that I have no experience as to their results.

Be assured, my dear doctor, I am as much interested as yourself in the improvement of this department of surgery, that I hope to avoid "charlatanry," and that I shall hail with delight any thing which brings with it conclusive or substantial evidence of its utility or superiority.

Yours very truly,

FRANK H. HAMILTON.

PROFESSOR SWINBURNE.

ALBANY, March 18, 1879.

PROFESSOR FRANK H. HAMILTON.

Dear Doctor, — Your note of the 22d inst. surprised me. It is impossible to show you my "practice and results" in the treatment of fractures, if you are unwilling to come to Albany; for I am debarred by you and your friends from the treatment of fractures in the New-York hospitals. The words of your note are, "I cannot employ, or permit others to employ in their management, methods or forms of apparel

which an extended experience and observation have convinced
me are not the best. Your error is in supposing that I have
not seen fractures treated by the methods you prefer, and
that I have no experience as to their results."

Now, I have serious doubts about your having seen fractures properly and scientifically treated after my plan, if, as
you say, the majority of the cases resulted badly. In February, 1861, I had the pleasure of showing many fractures of
the several long bones to Dr. Sayre and other New-York surgeons, and they pronounced them *perfect results*. All the
cases which I have had before my medical class this and past
winters, and all those of my colleague, have also been perfect
results. I am in possession of equally favorable reports
from other surgeons who follow this method.

To be more definite, let us take a *Colles' fracture*. In
your work on fractures and dislocations, published in 1860,
you report nearly seventy per cent of failures in the treatment
of these fractures. In the edition of 1871, over seventy per
cent of failures are reported. I claim by my method a much
better showing than this. To make my statement as concise
as possible, I have never had a bad result in the treatment
of a *Colles' fracture*, and have never seen a bad result where
my plan was properly applied. Indeed, I have offered a premium of five hundred dollars to any one who will produce a
bad result from any form of fracture treated by me.

In your work on the treatment of fractures, etc., you are
very frank in confessing to so many bad results, especially
while the major portion of the profession, including many
professors of surgery, are obtaining equally bad results,
without the grace and extenuation of confession. Taking
such confession as a criterion, why, I ask, do you not speak
out candidly, and warn the profession of the dangers attending certain classes of fracture by my plan of treatment?
The mistake you make is in supposing that I desire to attend
your private patients: on the contrary, I assume there is
plenty of material in the public institutions of New York
for a proper test of the efficacy of my plan of treatment.
Again: you assume my plan of treatment is productive of
bad results. If that is what you mean, I am prepared to
put up five thousand dollars, as previously proposed, as a
test of our comparative results, to compensate persons in
whom bad results may follow my treatment. In this compensation for bad results, to be judged upon the basis laid
down in your works, or those of other prominent surgeons, I
deem myself safe, after a complete perusal of your published

works and occasional writings on the treatment of fractures in private, public, and military surgery, and a consideration of your confessed results.

Yours respectfully,

JOHN SWINBURNE.

NEW YORK, March 20, 1879.

JOHN SWINBURNE, M.D.

My Dear Sir, — I had supposed that my last reply was sufficiently definite to have assured you that I was not disposed to accept any challenge, or to investigate your mode of treatment any further, except in my own way and at my own convenience.

I will only add, before dismissing this correspondence, that when you say in your letter, "In your work on fractures you are very frank in confessing to so many bad results," — "to seventy per cent of fractures," — you convey the idea that those results were "bad," or "failures," which were not recorded as absolutely perfect, and that I intend so to say.

If you will read my books again, or whatever else I have written upon this subject, you will see that this is not my meaning, and that my language has never been capable of such a construction. I speak of results as perfect or imperfect, but imperfect does not necessarily imply bad results, or failures. You have a right, if you choose, to call a result bad, or a failure, which is not in all respects perfect; but I do not. And this is not the fairness which one has a right to expect in a controversialist, where a matter of science is involved, when you say I confess to seventy per cent of bad results, or failures. And, further, it ought not to have escaped your notice — if you have read, as you say you have, all of my published writings, including my treatise on fractures, and especially the preface to my paper on deformities after fractures, published in the "Transactions of the American Medical Association" — that a majority of the cases referred to in the general summaries were not treated by me, although they had all been examined by me; my purpose being, as I have repeatedly stated, to furnish, as far as possible, a fair estimate of what were the usual or average results in the hands of respectable physicians and surgeons. They are not, therefore, *my* confessions.

Intending no personal disrespect to you, I wish to say that I do not think it will prove profitable to continue, and I have no time to devote to a further correspondence upon this subject.

Yours truly,

FRANK H. HAMILTON.

ALBANY, April —, 1879.

PROFESSOR FRANK H. HAMILTON.

My Dear Doctor, — I regret extremely that you, in your note of the 20th ult., decided on "dismissing this correspondence." because I am sure much good might come out of its continuance. I regret, also, that you should have decided not to investigate my mode of treatment of fractures any further, except in your own way and at your own convenience, because I am quite sure, if you did fully investigate it, your sense of fairness to the profession, and desire to obtain good results, would induce you to accept the true principle, and teach the same.

I am very thankful that you added, before "dismissing this correspondence," that "a majority of the cases referred to in the general summaries were not treated by me, although they had been examined by me." Now, my dear doctor, I did not say they were treated by any one, but only assumed they were not treated by my plan. My statement runs thus: "In your work on fractures and dislocations, published in 1860, you report nearly seventy per cent of failures in the treatment of these fractures. In the edition of 1871, over seventy per cent of failures are reported." In this I say nothing as to who attended them. But you say it was your purpose " to furnish, as far as possible, a fair estimate of what were the usual or average results in the hands of respectable physicians and surgeons. They are not, therefore, *my* confessions." It is presumable that both you, and the "respectable physicians and surgeons " mentioned, made the best results you could in each individual case. If not, why not?

In the above-mentioned note you complain of my saying that you confess to seventy per cent of bad results, or " failures.",

In this I may have spoken hastily. I hope to correct the statement by quoting your precise language. In your work on fractures and dislocations (ed. 1871), p. 281, you speak as follows of ninety-five fractures of the lower third of the radius : " Only twenty-six are positively known to have left no deformity, or stiffness about the joint." In this quotation no reference is made as to who was the surgeon, but the inference might be drawn that it was the work of "the author." I am pleased, therefore, to learn from your note that the cases were not yours, because you confess in the next line that "it is probable, however, that the number of perfect results might be somewhat extended." It is pleasant, I say, to hear this; but unfortunately, if we consult the two following pages (pp. 282, 283), the illusion and the pleasure are at once dispelled. Your statements are as follows: "If we confine our remarks to Colles' fractures, the deformity which has been observed most often consists in a projection of the lower end of the ulna inwards, and generally a little forwards. In a large majority of cases this is accompanied with a perceptible falling-off of the hand to the radial side, while in a few it is not. After this, in point of frequency, I have met with the backward inclination of the lower fragment. Robert Smith found this displacement almost constant in the cabinet specimens examined by him; and it is very probable that nearly all of the examples examined by myself would present more or less of the same deviation upon the naked bone."

Again: "The fingers are quite as often thus anchylosed, after this fracture, as the wrist-joint itself,—a circumstance which is wholly inexplicable on the doctrine that the anchylosis is due to an inflammation in the joints. Indeed, I have seen the fingers rigid after many months, when, having observed the case throughout myself, I was certain that no inflammatory action had ever reached them.

Again, quoting Dr. Mott, and coinciding with him, "Fractures of the radius within two inches of the wrist, where treated by the most eminent surgeons, are of very difficult management so as to avoid all deformity: indeed, more or less deformity may occur under the treatment of the most eminent surgeons; and more or less imperfection in the motion of the wrist or radius is very apt to follow for a longer or shorter time. Even when the fracture is well cured, an anterior prominence at the wrist, or near it, will sometimes result from swelling of the soft parts."

In sixty-six of the ninety-two cases of Colles' fracture, there was "perceptible deformity," or "stiffness about the joint," and only twenty-six had no "perceptible deformity." Is it fair, then, for you to complain of my calling these sixty-six or seventy per cent of Colles' fractures "bad results," or "failures," simply because they were not treated by you, but were the "confessions" of other "respectable physicians and surgeons"?

I judge, however, that you have treated *some* cases of Colles' fractures: for I find on p. 290 (ed. 1871) a cut of " the author's splint," which seems to be a pistol splint, for the inside of the arm, and a plain straight deal splint for the dorsal portion of the arm, with accompanying directions for its use, and the dressings employed by " respectable physicians and surgeons ; " viz., compresses, bandages, etc. The advantages which the author claims for this splint are. " facility and cheapness of construction, accuracy of adaptation, neatness, permanency, and fitness to the ends proposed." And still the author does not claim that this apparatus in his hands, or in the hands of any one else, although it possesses all of these qualities, produces any better result than twenty-six out of ninety-two.

In speaking of the treatment of Colles' fractures, "the author" cautions the reader about the use of bandages, splints, etc., and goes so far as to assert, " I have no doubt that very many cases would come to a successful termination without their use, if only the hand and the arm were kept perfectly still in a suitable position until bony union was effected." In this belief I think we are quite agreed ; but may I ask, Does "the author's " plan accomplish this without injury to the soft parts? He does not tell us, but only adds that "during the first seven or ten days these cases demand the most assiduous attention, and we had much better dispense with the splints entirely than to retain them at the risk of increasing the inflammatory action."

Again on p. 292: " More than once, indeed, it has occurred that surgeons have been so intent on preserving fractures in their proper position, that the extreme constriction employed has actually caused destruction of the soft parts. A piece of advice which I have frequently given, and which I cannot too often repeat, is to avoid too much tightening of the apparatus for fractures during the first few days of its being worn; for the swelling which supervenes is always accompanied by considerable pain, and may be followed by gangrene." Then follows four pages of history of cases where gangrene supervenes on the use of bandages. With these facts before him, distinctly perceived and acknowledged, the author still persists in employing and recommending bandages, compresses, etc., instead of treating his fractures so that there should be no danger from compression, and gangrene from retarded circulation.

Since writing the above, I have received a letter from a lady of refinement and education, living in Auburn, N.Y., who some time in November, 1878, came to this city from near Philadelphia, and sent for me to redress her broken arm. I found that about three or four weeks previous she had fallen, and produced a Colles' fracture, which had been treated by a "respectable physician and surgeon," before coming here, with the pistol splint. On examination, I informed her that union had taken place perfectly; that the limb was strong, but that it was deformed and almost useless, and would remain so for life. I re-applied the bandages, as before, and told her that the deformity could not be removed except the bone be refractured and united, and that, aside from this, there was no necessity for surgical interference. She paid no regard to this advice, as will be seen from a note of hers, March 29, 1879, in reference to her present condition.

"Some four months have elapsed since I arrived here. You called upon me last November at the Delevan House in Albany, and bandaged my broken wrist. What you told me then about my broken bones I have found strictly true. I cannot shut my left hand: it is swollen on the back (silver-fork deformity), and the under part of my wrist near the little finger is also swollen. I am in poverty. I have suffered cold and hunger, and for medical services, since I came here." She adds, "If I had staid in Albany, and placed myself under your care professionally, I should have been well now."

I have no doubt that in this case I could have refractured, and restored the parts to their place. I have accomplished it in similar cases before. A lady in this city came to me with a Colles' fracture, having the following history: About thirteen years since, she fell, and sustained a Colles' fracture. It was treated by one of our most accomplished village surgeons with the usual pistol splint. Months passed before the wrist could be used at all; and from that time it continued deformed and measurably useless, until a few weeks ago, when she fell, and refractured the radius at about the same point (about one inch from the wrist-joint). This I treated by my plan. At the end of three weeks she had good use of the wrist; at the end of six weeks the wrist was as strong and useful as it was before the first fracture, and with no perceptible impediment to motion.

Authors concede that fractures of the elbow-joint are difficult to treat, and that a very large percentage result badly; or rather less than one-half are perfect after such fractures From my own plan, on the contrary, I know of no cases which have resulted badly, either in my own hands or in the hands of others. This consists in double extension, double counter-extension, and retention of the limb in its normal position; the restoring of circulation, thus avoiding inflammation; the effecting of apposition as much as possible, and retaining such apposition without constriction, thus avoiding excessive callus, or, rather, obtaining union as nearly as possible by the first intention, and thus escaping deformity.

The author's plan is in sharp contrast to this. He seeks to reduce the fracture, and retain it in position by the use of an apparatus which prevents a redisplacement only by excessive constriction, thereby risking gangrene; or, if not sufficiently tight, a redisplacement may result, and a perpetuation of the original deformity. In confirmation of this, I refer to the author's "elbow splint" (p. 252 of the work on fractures and dislocations, ed. 1871). I confess that with me it seems impossible to obtain good results with such an apparatus; for, if the bones are reduced in the first instance, I do not see how they can be held in position without excessive bandaging — unless, indeed, extension is made use of. It is bandaging, however, which the author recommends; but his recommendation is weakened by a concession of not the best results from this dangerous practice.

In proof of some of my statements, permit me to outline briefly a case which recently came under my observation, in which the patient was treated by one of my colleagues according to my plan. M. C., aged twenty-six, weight a hundred and sixty pounds, height five feet eleven inches, carpenter by trade, fractured his arm through the olecranon and coronoid fossae. His arm was dressed twelve hours after the accident: it was painful and much swollen. It was redressed only twice during the following three weeks. When the dressings were removed, union was firm: there was some thickening of the soft parts about the joint, but there was no pain on flexion, extension, or rotation. The flexion was perfect. Extension was made to within five degrees of a straight position. Apparatus was not again applied. The patient absented himself from his physician for three weeks; then he came before my clinic, stating that he had recommenced work at his trade four weeks after the accident. One week after the apparatus was removed, he had worked for a fortnight at his trade. At this time he found some soreness in the joint, and some spasms of the biceps from too violent exercise. The motion was as complete as at the expiration of the three weeks. By forced extension, the arm could be carried nearly straight to within not more than three degrees of perfect extension.

With regard to side or coaptation splints. In your note of January you say they "are, in a majority of cases of fractures of the shafts of the long bones, essential to the attainment of the best results," and urge that for this reason it is unnecessary to enter into a contest which designs to test any other method of treatment.

You may remember that in my first note to you I stated that, in the winter of 1848–49, I commenced the treatment of fractures of the thigh by permanent extension alone, and in 1859 I read before the Medical Society of this State, papers showing the results of my treatment, which were published in the "Transactions of the Medical Society" of that year. My work was begun in private practice, and before any hospital was organized in this city; and I, for this reason, neglected at the first to make notes. The results I speak of, however, were scrutinized by the skilled eyes of Professors Marsh and Armsby; and I could wish for no better evidence of their excellence than the inability of these able men to discover any bad cases or failures.

In your work on fractures and dislocations (ed. 1860, p. 404), in speaking of extension, you say, —

" If we consider the muscles alone as the cause of the displacement in the direction of the long axis of the shaft, the shortening of the limb, other things being equal, must be proportioned to the number and power of the muscles which draw upward the lower fragment. This will vary in different portions of the limb; but nowhere will this cause cease to operate, nor will its variations essentially change the prognosis.

"I have not intended to say that other causes do not operate occasionally in the production of shortening, but only that muscular contraction is the cause by which this result is chiefly determined, and that its power will be ordinarily the measure of the shortening."

In this passage you concede that the muscles are the main cause for the shortening of bone, or its longitudinal deformity, and still you cling tenaciously to the use of the long side and coaptation splint. You introduce (p. 414, ed. 1860) a cut of the treatment of fractures of the thigh by weight and pulley, side and coaptation splints, and state that this is the plan suggested by L. A. Dugas of Augusta, Ga. This was prior to the date at which Dr. Buck of New York commenced his treatment by weight and pulley. Nothing in your

work, however, is said or done toward simplification of the
treatment of fractures by means of extension alone.

This latter is the prime aim which I have ever had in view.
In 1861 I read a paper before the State Medical Society
(published in the " Transactions " of the same year), on the
treatment of fractures of *all the long bones by extension alone.*
It created a great deal of discussion at the time; but the
results shown were so satisfactory, that the treatment has
gradually and surely gained ground in the profession. I see,
on reference to your edition of 1871, that you have yourself
modified, if not changed, your views on this subject ; for I
find cuts (pp. 272, 238, 239, 487) representing fractures being
treated by extension, without side or coaptation splints. The
cut on p. 272 again carries out the principle I advanced in
1861 for treatment of all fractures of the fore-arm, except that
in the cut, extension is made with elastic bands, and the retention, therefore, is not so sure. It is a decided advance
upon the author's treatment of fractures of the fore-arm,
because it avoids compression, and longitudinal and lateral
distortion, and mortification. The principal objection to it is
its complexity. On p. 238 there are no side or coaptation
splints indicated as such. This principle is substantially the
one advocated by me in 1861. The cut on p. 239 shows
extension alone in its simplest form, and would, I doubt not,
effect good results, if it could be controlled night and day, so
as to avoid too much or too little extension. One can well
see that it might be open to the objections made against too
much extension in the arm, on the part of those who criticised
my paper on extension in 1861. Again : on p. 487 a cut is
given for the treatment of gunshot fractures of the thigh by
extension alone, without the side or coaptation splint, and, in
fact, without any of the appliances before adhered to, and
now advocated as necessary for good results. No mention is
made of my plan of treatment for gunshot fractures by extension without splints (" Transactions " of 1864) by impro-
vising a stretcher upon which soldiers could be treated on
the field of battle as well as in permanent hospitals. The
only difference was, that there was no hole in the canvas on
which the soldier was to lie, and the extension was to be permanent. By a vote of the society of the State, I was directed
to present a copy of the paper, and a cut of the plan, to the
surgeon-general of the United-States army. I complied in
March, 1864, and I have no doubt the plan given on p. 487
was taken from my paper (" Transactions," 1864).

I cannot help thinking that the time will come when you

will be induced to accept the plan of treatment of the long bones by extension and retention alone. On p. 407 you have really made a step towards it by giving an exact cut of the plan, given in your edition of 1860 as " Dugas's method," with the exception that the side-splint has sloughed off, and the coaptation dress alone is retained : p. 239 evinces a further advance. But still the plan for extension herein illustrated is defective : it is like a steam-boiler without a safety-valve, or a train of cars without brakes to regulate the motion of the cars.

Stated briefly, then, the difference between our treatment consists in this : you adhere to coaptation splints, bandages, etc., as necessary to good results ; whereas I claim, and am prepared to prove, that splints, bandages, etc., are entirely useless *per se*, even injurious, except only so far as through splints extension may be made to the normal length, and perpetuated. In view of the facts herein set forth, I ask in all fairness, Do not the public, and the honor of the profession, demand a full review of the methods now in use for the treatment of fractures, with a view to simplification and more perfect results ? Many men refuse to treat these injuries, as they know not what plan to follow ; and the fear of bad results only tends to make them more timid. The public cannot, nor can the physician, have always at hand a surgeon of experience in the treatment of fractures. And as the injured man must, of necessity, trust his limb to his doctor, he has a right to have the best result known to surgery, while the doctor must, in fear and trembling, lean upon the complicated measures laid down in the text-books, and consider himself wonderfully fortunate if a passable result is obtained, sufficient to save him from, mayhap, a ruinous lawsuit, and loss of professional standing.

I can only regret, my dear doctor, that you decline so absolutely to continue this correspondence. It was begun with the desire to simplify and advance the treatment of these classes of fracture ; and with that desire I wrote to you as an author, teacher, and authority for the profession on these injuries. May I hope you will reconsider your determination, and that I may shortly hear further from you.

I remain, my dear doctor,

Yours very truly,

JOHN SWINBURNE.

CHAPTER XIV.

MEDICAL JURISPRUDENCE.

THERE are few, if indeed any, physicians in this State who have been summoned to the witness-stand as a medical and scientific expert so often as Dr. John Swinburne, in cases at times involving the most difficult questions known to the profession, and in some instances where not only the liberty, but the lives, of persons depended on the solution of the scientific points involved. In these, neither persuasion, intimidation, social position, nor the opposition of many of the recognized lights in the medical profession, had any weight in preventing him from a fearless and conscientious discharge of that duty he felt he owed the living as well as the dead. He believed that in every instance of death, where the cause was an undecided question, it was a religious duty of science, to whose care the lives and health of the people were intrusted, to ferret it out; and that in so far as the profession failed to discover and reveal the causes of death, where enshrouded in mystery, so far the physician, as a scientist, was a failure; and that the physician who failed, when called upon, to make the proper investigations, and render an unbiassed, fearless, and honest verdict, was guilty of a criminal act, and recreant to his high and honorable calling. In many of the cases where he has been called as an expert, he had to encounter a bitter and stubborn opposition from most of the profession; in some of the most important cases having the influence and power of almost the entire profession against him. But a remarkable fact in connection with these investigations has been that circumstances, and the leading men of the profession, both in Europe and this country, demonstrated afterwards that he was correct. For years after graduating, most of his leisure time had been devoted to anatomical research in the dissection of dead bodies; so that, when first called as an expert, he was thoroughly conversant with the anatomy of man, and the nature and effects of mineral and vegetable poisons.

Less than a year after graduating, the young doctor was called to testify in an action for damages before Judge Ira Harris. A man, in passing through a store in Albany, had a box fall on him, injuring the bones of the neck. On the advice of the doctor, the man went to his home in another part of the State, and returned a year afterwards, when his head was so fixed, from the result of these injuries, that he could not turn it to one side or the other without turning the whole body. On the trial, the questions for the medical experts to decide were the injury to and the condition of the neck. On the stand the doctor held that the inflammation following the injury resulted in the seven bones leading from the atlas down to the vertebræ of the chest being anchylosed, and introduced half a dozen specimens analogous to this one to sustain the position assumed. As a result of his testimony in opposition to that of the experts for the defendants, the jury gave a verdict for the amount claimed as damages.

A half-decade in his early career as a physician and surgeon had scarcely passed, when he was suddenly brought prominently before the profession and the world in the trial of John Hendrickson, jun., for the murder of his wife, which was tried before Judge Marvin in the June (1853) term of the *oyer and terminer* in Albany. The trial lasted three weeks, resulting in the conviction, sentence to death, and final execution, of the prisoner.

Dr. Swinburne had then been in practice less than seven years when this trial took place, which was characterized by Attorney-Gen. Chatfield as a case of more importance than any that had ever occurred in this country, and of as great importance as any that has occurred in the civilized world.

"I do not mean," he said, "to say that one case of murder is any more important than another; but to all its surrounding circumstances, the mystery involved, the novel and stealthy instrument of death, the effect that the introduction of this means of securely murdering would have in increasing crime, the medical and chemical questions which have arisen, — I repeat, from all these reasons, it is one of greater importance than has ever occurred in this country."

On the 6th of March, 1853, Maria, the wife of John Hendrickson, was found dead in her bed in the town of Bethlehem, Albany County, by her husband, who occupied the bed with her, on his, as he alleged, being awakened by her crowding him. The following day Dr. Swinburne was called by the coroner, Dr. Thomas Smith, to view the body; and the succeeding day, in presence of the coroner and another physician, he held a *post-mortem* of the remains, and found: —

" Face and anterior portion of the body unusually pale, and apparently bloated, swollen, or puffed, — the face decidedly so, — and presenting an almost translucent and watery appearance, though very calm and composed, and no distortion. Eyes and mouth closed; teeth about one-quarter of an inch apart.

" On the inside of the lower lip, a little to one side of the median line, and down near the alveolar process, so that it could not have been injured by the teeth, was a distinct, true ecchymosis as large as a dime; and in this was a cut, of one-quarter of an inch in length, extending through the mucous membrane, and into the tissue beneath. Both were evidently produced at or near the time of death.

" On the posterior part of the body there was extensive suggillation nearly two-thirds of the way round, and extending from the hips to the head. The blood seemed to have all forsaken the anterior, and gravitated to the posterior portion, evidencing its great fluidity.

" *Post-mortem* rigidity and elasticity were remarkable. The entire voluntary system of muscles was so rigid and elastic as to prevent them from being relaxed. The jaws were firmly fixed. The arms and legs would fly back with great force when any attempt was made to flex, extend, or separate them. Upon dissection, the rigidity and elasticity were found to exist only in the muscular structure, and was not, in fact, simple cadaverous rigidity. The neck was so stiff, that, in attempting to bend it, the whole body would be lifted up. The lips were of a bluish white, and swollen.

"The tongue was extremely white, furred, swollen, and indented on the edges, as if by the teeth. The heart was healthy but empty, except a small clot in the right auricle; lungs healthy and normal (cavas contained about two ounces of dark fluid blood); liver healthy and normal, while the gall-bladder was not more than half full. Spleen, kidneys, and pancreas were healthy and normal. Womb was indurated and enlarged very much, about one inch adhering to the small intestine, while the os was ulcerated; internal cavity twice its normal caliber. The ovaries were enlarged to about twice their normal size, while one of them contained a clot of blood half an inch in diameter near its centre. The blood contained in the above-named organs had so far gravitated to the capillaries of the dependent portion of the body, that during the dissection the hands and instruments were scarcely soiled with blood; while the only blood in these organs was mostly in the cavas, and that in a fluid state.

"The dura mater was more than normally adherent to the skull; the arachnoid presented some opacity near the top of the skull: the brain was healthy, while upon its surface it was congested, or its veins were full of blood, slightly congested; the base and the spinal cord of the cervical vertebræ were normal and healthy. The peritoneal surface of the stomach and intestines was red and congested. The stomach was contracted to about two inches in diameter (one-third of its normal capacity), and thickened by this contraction to more than twice its normal condition. The mucous membrane was thrown, from the contraction of its muscular coat, into folds, and covered with bloody viscid mucus. This mucous coat was at least five to six inches in diameter; and from this some idea can be formed of its folding or corrugation. The duodenum and all the small intestines were contracted both ways, longitudinally and transversely: its inner coat was highly congested, folded upon itself, and covered with mucus mixed with blood. The jejunum was in a high state of congestion and contraction; its mucous coat covered, like the duodenum, with mucus strongly tinged with blood. The ilium was considerably congested and contracted, but a little less than the jejunum; the mucous coat, covered with viscid matter, and more highly tinged with blood. All these portions of the intestines were contracted to about one-half their normal diameter, while the corrugation was strongly marked.

The viscid matter had somewhat the appearance of chyle and chyme, while in none of them could there be found any thing resembling excrementitious or fecal matter. The cæcum was filled with thin, watery, fecal matter; and the walls in contact with it were considerably congested: in it were lemon, coriander, and other seeds in considerable quantity. The upper part of the colon contained thin and less watery fecal matter than the cæcum; nearer the rectum it became more solid; the lower part was quite dry and hard. The rectum contained fecal matter, dry and hard, as if from extreme costiveness. The bladder was quite healthy and empty, but contracted to about two inches in diameter, while its mucous coat was thrown into folds, and its muscular coat firm and rigid. Its mucous lining was full four inches in diameter."

The opinion drawn from these facts by Dr. Swinburne was, that the woman did not die a natural death, but that death was induced by the ingestion of poison; while, from the analogy of these *post-mortem* appearances to a great number of animals poisoned by aconite, he gave the opinion that this was the special agent employed.

Portions of the stomach and intestines were taken to Dr. James H. Salsbury for chemical testing and analysis, who, after testing for all the other poisons, tested for aconitine, and found it.

At the trial Dr. Swinburne was on the witness-stand upwards of two days, and Dr. Salsbury, the chemist, a day and a half, subject to a most skilful cross-examination; for on the breaking-down of their testimony depended the life of the prisoner. To rebut their testimony, and destroy the theory they set forward, that the woman died from the effect of poison, and that that poison was aconite, the defence introduced as expert witnesses, Dr. Barent P. Staats of Albany, who had practised thirty-five years; Dr. Lawrence Reid of Philadelphia, a professional chemist of thirty-five years; and Dr. Ebenezer Emmons of Albany, another chemist. It was a scientific contest between the old practitioners and those of the new school, Dr. Swinburne being only thirty-three years of age, and Dr. Salsbury, twenty-eight.

The counsel for the prisoner, in his argument, attempted

to ridicule the two young scientists, terming Swinburne a young Napoleon, and declaring both men without experience, when his witnesses had failed to overthrow their testimony.

During the trial the most intense interest was taken in the case by the public, and more particularly by the medical profession, many of the latter being in attendance in court during the examination of the experts; none of the resident members of the profession undertaking to place their views on the witness-stand in opposition to the two young men, except Drs. Staats and Emmons, although a number of them had positively declared that it was impossible to discover aconite, and that the doctor would fail to maintain his theory; one of these doubting Peters, at whose feet the doctor had sat to learn in his earlier professional training, asserting that the doctor was "going to make a fool of himself, and destroy his prospects for the future." During the examination of Dr. Swinburne and his associate, they gave the nature and results of the various kinds of poisons, and that of aconite in particular, as experimented with by them on cats and dogs, the symptoms and results being such as the *post-mortem* revealed in the case of Mrs. Hendrickson. It was the most difficult of poisons to trace its presence, to be established only by the marks it left behind and by taste. While Dr. Swinburne held that the cause of death was in the stomach, Dr. Staats held that the *post-mortem* indicated a disease of the brain rather than of the stomach; Dr. Emmons held that he experimented with aconite, and found it acted, not as an astringent, but rather created a swelling; while Dr. Reid, who had, as a professor of chemistry, declared the entire deductions of the two doctors for the prosecution erroneous, was compelled, under the cross-examination, to admit he had read no works on aconite, that he had never seen a case of poisoning from it, had never made experiments with it, and knew of no chemical test that would detect this vegetable poison. .

The moral evidence was all circumstantial, the scientific being positive; and on these the jury, after twenty-four hours' deliberation, returned a verdict of *guilty*. Judge Marvin, in pronouncing sentence, said, —

" You employed, for the purpose of accomplishing the deed, a deadly poison, — an active vegetable poison, peculiar in its character, and difficult of detection ; and I greatly fear that he who communicated to you the knowledge of poisoning by aconite, communicated to you also the difficulty of its detection. Relying upon this information, and confident that the instrument of your crime would be forever hidden from human eye, you committed the fearful deed. Empirics and quacks, though they may learn enough to do mischief, and even acquire the requisite knowledge to use as a medicine a deadly poison without always producing fatal results, often fail in acquiring the knowledge which enables men to avoid evil, and to know the force and power of the material which they use.

" I refer thus prominently to the opinion that there are poisons which cannot be detected, because I desire to impress, not only upon you, but upon all, the fact that as science advances — as it unfolds to the student the great storehouse of knowledge, and lets man penetrate into the very *arcana* of nature — that as it advances, step by step, it enables its votaries to detect the most subtle poisons, and to trace the very footsteps of crime. Chemists are enabled now, through the wonderful developments of science — and science detects your crime — to detect almost all poisons, whether vegetable or metallic ; to trace out cases of poisoning, no matter what may be the character of the poison administered, with almost unerring certainty. And it is as dangerous to attempt murder with the most subtle vegetable poison, and as certain to be detected, as if the murder were committed with the dirk or the stiletto. Your case may have its moral effect upon the community in this view of it. The community should understand that the crime of murder cannot be committed in this day of light, in any manner or by any means, without leaving the evidence of guilt ; and this evidence always points out unerringly the guilty individual."

Every effort known to the law was resorted to in this case to have the verdict set aside, but failed, both in the Supreme Court and Court of Appeals. These attempts failing, an effort was made for executive interposition, not, as District-Attorney Colvin said in a review of some of the medical witnesses, to save poor Hendrickson, but to save themselves. To their aid they brought Professor Alonzo Clark of New York, who thought Dr. Swinburne abused the confidence with which courts of justice so often compliment men of science, because, without having found the aconite in the blood, stomach, and tissues, he yet ventured to express the opinion that it had been present, — which Dr. Clark would not have done until after it had been found, although the marks were unmistakable that it had been there, — but admitted that *if the presence of aconite in the blood, stomach, and tissues were conceded, the post-mortem appearances would sustain such admission, — in other words, that the post-mortem appearances were just such as aconite would produce,* — and then said Mrs. Hendrickson's death was probably caused by urea, a disease generally conceded of long standing, preceded by stupor, and terminating in death after days of sickness. Several other " would-be " authorities were invoked, among them Drs. C. T. Jackson and A. A. Hayes, assayists to the State of Massachusetts, who condemned *in toto* the scientific processes resorted to by the witnesses for the prosecution.

T. G. Geoghegan, M.D., professor of forensic medicine, Royal College of Surgeons, Ireland, wrote of this case, —

" Having with much care considered the medical facts in their relative bearings, I have to state that they appear to me to establish clearly that the death of Mrs. Hendrickson was the result of the ingestion of poison, while they afford the strongest presumption that the special substance employed was aconite.

" The absence of any sign of disease, or cause of obstructed venous circulation in the adjacent organs, the empty state of the stomach, and the early performance of the autopsy, sufficiently attest that the appearances in the alimentary canal were not of a pseudo-morbid or cadaveric character.

" The foregoing considerations, in my judgment, clearly establish that *Mrs. Hendrickson's death was the result of the ingestion of a narcotic, acrid poison.*

" As respects the special substance employed, the analysis (when collated with the maximum duration of deceased's illness) shows that it was not of a mineral kind. Animal poison is obviously out of the question.

" It therefore but remains to consider what vegetable matters are capable of causing death in four hours; of leaving behind, in the stomach and small intestines, marked signs of mucous irritation; of producing, when applied to the tongue, an acrid taste, followed, after an interval of some minutes, by a sensation of numbness, and when administered, even under unfavorable conditions, to a cat, giving rise to choking efforts to swallow and vomit, muscular twitches, prostration, and well-marked stupor. I know of none but aconite, or its active principle, aconitine.

"The mode in which the case was investigated by the medical and legal authorities reflects much credit on both."

The trial of this cause was most ably conducted for the prisoner by Henry G. Wheaton and William J. Hadley; the effort of Mr. Wheaton being conceded a herculean intellectual and legal defence for his client, and it almost completely prostrated the able jurist. As he did but little professional work after this trial, it was considered that the effort then made was too great a physical strain, and more than nature could endure.

When an application was made to Gov. Seymour for a stay of the execution of the sentence of death, that official, always desirous of according justice to all, and exercising mercy where it was deemed deserving, asked Dr. Swinburne to write a letter in favor of the stay. To this the doctor replied, "However much I sympathize with the unfortunate man and his relatives, I cannot consistently write such a letter. It would be construed as my doubting the position I took on the trial, which I do not for a moment. You are governor of the State, and must exercise your own judgment in the matter. My testimony is before you and the world for criticism, and you must act without any influence from me." An incident which occurred in the executive chamber that evening convinced the governor of the prisoner's guilt, and caused him to refuse the application.

Years after this trial, Judge Marvin said, "At one time I had doubts of the matter; but these were all dispelled at the trial, and by subsequent events, and I was satisfied before the close that the charge was true and the prisoner guilty." The charge of the judge was an able and impartial one, in which every opportunity to throw a doubt in favor of the prisoner was availed. It was forcibly impressed on the jury that the prisoner was not to be held responsible because the expert witnesses for the defence failed to assign a cause for death, and that the prisoner was not called upon to account for the death.

The termination of this suit resulted in elevating the two young men to a very high position as medical scientists, and provoking natural professional jealousy.

In 1859, Dr. Swinburne, as an expert, made an announcement for which there was no precedent, and was met by one of the leading members of the profession in Albany with the exclamation, "Now we have you!" This case was reported in the "Medical and Surgical Reporter" in 1859. On the 26th of March of that year an attempt at abortion was made by a Mrs. Marston on a young woman at the house No. 40 Franklin Street, Albany, resulting in the death of the patient. On the following day Dr. Swinburne, in the presence of two physicians and two of his students, held a *post-mortem* examination of the body fourteen hours after death. He found the external of the body natural but very pallid. On cutting through the integuments into the cellular tissues, air was observed to issue from the divided veins in the form of a frothy fluid. On exposing the heart, its right cavities were found to be greatly distended with a spumous mixture of blood and air, and slight compression of the heart was seen to force out bubbles of air from the divided intercostal veins. A thorough examination showed that the jugulars, and the veins emptying into them, even to the small vessels of the brain, were all distended with air. On examining the membranes and their contents, the internal surface of the womb exhibited slight softening of the tissues, several abrasions (evidently not natural), a perforation communicating directly with the uterine sinuses about two inches from the cervix and in the right latero-posterior region: this opening communicated directly with the veins of the broad ligament, and thus with the ascending cava. The os and cervix were open to the extent of two lines, and filled with bloody mucus. The *post-mortem* appearances, and the description of the young woman's death, the doctor decided could not be accounted for on any other hypothesis than that of air in the veins. Death occurred while the instrument was in the uterus, and was immediate, for the woman mistook *death* for *syncope*.

The point of interest in the case was the manner in which the air was introduced. Several deaths had been reported from ingress of air into the large veins of the neck; and he held that even the subclavian was liable to the same thing under favoring circumstances, such as tension upon the vein from the subject's position during surgical operations, or by traction upon a tumor during excision, the vein being temporarily canalized. or prevented from collapsing. Under all the circumstances, he maintained, this canalization of a vein, or its conversion into a rigid tube, is the indispensable condition requisite for the intrusion of air. But this condition, he held, was inadmissible in the case of the uterine veins and ascending cava, from the nature of physical laws which govern the movements of the fluids in the body no less than in organic matter. Under all the circumstances, he was compelled to accept the presumption that the abortionist forcibly inflated the entire venous system by means of the catheter introduced into the uterus, perforating its parietes, and in contact with the lacerated vessels of that organ. The fact of forcible inflation was incapable of proof, there being no third person present at the time of death, and hence no witness. Absolute certainty was only to be arrived at upon the confession of the guilty woman herself.

This was another step in the development of science ; and, as its precedent was not in the books, it was necessarily considered erroneous, and an innovation not to be tolerated, coming as it did from a comparatively young physician ; and, as soon as one opponent raised his voice in opposition, there were a large number of others to follow in his wake, just as a drove of sheep would follow a leader over a precipice without stopping to look where they were going.

But again the young doctor's views and decisions were proven correct by the confession of the woman herself. She had been arrested, tried, convicted, sentenced, and imprisoned in less than four weeks. While in prison,. she made an

application for pardon to Gov. Morgan, maintaining innocence of the forcible inflation. On her application being
refused, she finally confessed to the governor's secretary, Lock-
wood L. Doty, that she was guilty ; and that she blew the air
in, hoping to get it between the membranes and the uterus, to
the end that it might effect abortion ; and that Dr. Swinburne
was correct. Thus another scientific victory was won by
him in the interests of virtue and the people.[1]

In 1862 he was again employed as an expert in the celebrated trial of the Rev. Henry Budge for the murder of his
wife, and again demonstrated that the hours of hardship
endured by him as a student, and his close application to
study after being admitted to practice, had not been in vain,
but developed a mind well stored with medical and anatomical lore. On the morning of Dec. 11, 1859, Priscilla, wife of
the Rev. Henry Budge of Lyons Falls, Lewis County, was
found dead in her bed, with her throat cut. The same day
a coroner's inquest was held, and a verdict of " death by
suicide " rendered. Afterwards whispers of domestic differences aroused suspicion that foul play had caused the death
of Mrs. Budge, and four months subsequently the body was
exhumed by order of the coroner ; and, at his solicitation,
Dr. Swinburne, assisted by Dr. Porter, held an autopsy. The
decision arrived at on this second inquest, from what was
revealed at the autopsy, and the evidence adduced before the
coroner, convinced the doctor that Mrs. Budge did not meet
her death by her own hands, and that the wound in her throat
was inflicted after death, or when nearly dead; and, on these
developments and deductions, Mr. Budge was held on a
charge of murder. The *post-mortem* revealed an extensive cut
from three and a half inches below the lobe of the left ear to
three and a quarter inches below the lobe of the right ear, four
and a half inches below the chin, the curved length of the
wound being five and one-half inches. The depth of the cut
was two inches, back to the vertebræ, cutting through the periosteum and into the osseous matter of the fifth vertebra, and

---

[1] Professor Dalton of New York said in his lectures that it was the only case
of this nature on record.

also shaving off a lateral portion of the transverse process of this vertebra. There was distinct ecchymosis of the tongue on either side, at points opposite the molar teeth. On the left side this covered a surface of one inch in length, and half an inch in a lateral direction. On the right, it was one and a half inches in length; on the upper and wider part, near the base, seven-eighths of an inch, diminishing towards the anterior portion, where it was one-half an inch, and extending through the mass of the tongue, and visible from either side, as was demonstrated by making incisions through its substance, and subsequently soaking it in water. The tip of the tongue was somewhat discolored, but not ecchymosed. The œsophagus, for the space of about two inches near and below the root of the tongue, was of abnormally red or maroon color. The right lung was congested, and engorged with blood, and apoplectic; pleuratic adhesion slight; otherwise healthy. The heart was entirely sound in every particular, while in the chest there was bloody serum in both cavities, — on the left side five ounces, and on the right eight ounces. The heart and large vessels were empty, while the capillaries of the extremities and dependent portion of the body were full of blood, and all the muscles retained their juicy and florid appearance. The right lung continued to discharge bloody serum, while the microscope distinctly revealed the presence of *diffused* and circumscribed apoplexy, as well as engorgement of the tissues. The left lung, when placed in a jar of fluid, presented a large amount of *débris* of broken-down blood in the dependent portion, while the fluid was very much discolored. There was no appearance of disease in the brain; and all the other organs were found healthy, and free from congestion.

Taking these results and the facts as elicited at the first coroner's inquest, — that the bedclothes were undisturbed and carefully tucked in at the foot, and she with her eyes and mouth closed as if asleep; the coverlids carefully turned down on the left side to about the breast, while on the right they were turned down about twelve inches farther; that there were no spurts or spatters of blood on the anterior part of the body, nightdress, or clothing below the cut, nor on the face and neck above the cut, except a slight stain on the under side of the chin, as if some bloody thing had been wiped against it; no blood-stains on the head-board, pillows, bedstead, clothes, walls, or otherwise, except about a quart-mug full in the feather-bed, forming a mass of bloody feathers, and a small amount on the pillow, — these circumstances were conclusive proof of themselves to satisfy the doctor that the woman had been murdered. This opinion was still further confirmed by the position in which the woman lay, — on her back, head resting on the pillow and inclined back, with only slight blood-stains on the right cheek and chin, as though something bloody had touched them, and no blood on the hands except on the fingers of the right hand, while there was none between the fingers.

The pregnant facts that the wound on the neck leaked from three to six ounces of fluid blood during its cleansing, so that it had to be stuffed with cotton batting, sewed up, compressed, and bandaged, to keep it from bleeding; and that it still continued to ooze blood through the side of the compress; and that four months afterwards, when the dissection was made, the cotton batting, when removed, was saturated with blood, and the parts under the neck also wet with blood, — were held by the doctor to be significant. The position of the body; the character of the cut; the almost bloodless condition of the surroundings; the entire absence of spurts and spatters of blood; the stains of blood from a bloody hand on the pillow and face, when her hands were not bloody, and a spot of blood ten or twelve inches in size on the sheet, and tucked under; the entire absence of a condition in the bed indicative of convulsions (a condition which always accompanies death by hemorrhage); the small amount of blood lost (not exceeding a quart); the condition of the lungs at the time of death; and other facts, as presented, — convinced the doctor that Mrs. Budge was dead, or nearly so, when her throat was cut, and that after death the cutting was done to cover up the crime of murder. The commencement of this cut, he held, was quite too abrupt for a wound made with the blunt point of a razor; that the extent and character of the tissue cut were quite too great for a delicate woman with one stroke of a razor to complete, and that, too, in a position where the muscular power is so materially impeded. He also held that the position of the blood-stains, and the direction taken by the blood, where it could flow only by gravity when leaving the body, taking into consideration the position of the head (particularly that of a female), rendered the idea of suicide to him quite preposterous, not to say ridiculous.

At the time of her death, as testified by witnesses, a razor was found lying under the arm, nearer the wrist than the elbow, two-thirds open; the blade uncovered, edge lying towards her. Two-thirds of the edge in length, and one-third in depth, or two-ninths of the razor-blade, was bloody. From the position in which the razor was found, and its nearly bloodless condition, Dr. Swinburne held that this was not the instrument with which the cutting was done. If it were, the cut being very extensive and involving the bone, the instrument would have been covered with blood, and its edge probably nicked.

At the second inquest Dr. Swinburne was on the witness-stand twenty-two consecutive hours; and at the conclusion of his testimony the verdict of the first inquest of "death by suicide" was reversed, and Budge committed on a charge of *murder*.

There were but three cases known to the profession, or recorded in the books, prior to this one, in English or American works, which had any bearing on this case; and in these three cases the evidence was suppressed for political and social considerations, all the parties being titled dignitaries in Great Britain. But, notwithstanding this absence of precedents, the repeated threats and intimidation made toward all parties who would dare to take part in the prosecution, and of the press if they published the proceedings, and the almost unanimous opposition of the profession, the doctor, still a comparatively young practitioner, held to his theory "that Mrs. Budge was murdered;" and the abuse heaped upon him was as powerless to deter him from the discharge of what he conceived to be his duty as would be an attempt to blow down the fortress of Gibraltar with a popgun.

After Budge's first commitment, he was taken before Judge Bacon at Utica on a writ of *habeas corpus*, and released on the ground that the second inquest was illegal. A month subsequent to this, his case was presented to the grand jury of Lewis County, eleven of whom were in favor of indicting. In September, 1860, his case was again presented to the grand jury of Lewis County, and an indictment of murder found against Budge. In 1861 he was tried before Judge Allen at Rome, Oneida County, when Dr. Swinburne was on the stand for several hours as the most prominent witness for the people, and was sustained by such eminent pathologists and scientists as Professors Valentine Mott of New York, and J. McNaughton of Albany, and others. During the examination, one of the witnesses (Professor Mott), who, in answer to a question by one of the counsel, said he was the only living student of Sir Astley Cooper, was interrupted by the judge while explaining in detail the action of the heart and lungs after the cutting of the pneumogastric nerves. Professor Mott testified that the only work he had ever read on the subject was Beck's, and that in that work it was laid down that instant death followed the cutting of the gastric nerve; and on this authority death was immediate, with perhaps one long respiration. On the professor making this statement, Mr. Conkling moved for the discharge of the prisoner; the judge holding that all the circumstances made out a strong case for judicial investigation, but that from time to time in the trial, qualifying circumstances had been proved, tending to show how the blood *might* have appeared as it did, how it *might* have got into the lungs without asphyxia. " It is not for me to say," he added, " that the case shall close: there are circumstances that might be forcibly urged to the jury; but it strikes me, that, as the case stands, it is only a balance of probabilities, in which it would be unsafe to convict; and, in view of the fact that these doubts have arisen, the prisoner is entitled to the benefit of them, and should be released." The case was then sent to the jury *pro forma*, and by direction of the judge the prisoner was acquitted.

The trial, as far as it proceeded, was a bitterly contested one, and made almost as prominent because of the array of counsel engaged as by the nature of the case. Among the most prominent of the scientific men to oppose the position of Dr. Swinburne was Professor Alonzo Clark, professor of pathology and practice of medicine in a prominent New-York college, and who boasted of three years' standing in Europe as a professor. This eminent gentleman subsequently presented a paper before the New-York Academy of Medicine on this case. Dr. Swinburne was present, by invitation of the members, to discuss the matter; but when his name was mentioned by Dr. Griscom, with the request that he be invited to participate in the discussion, objection was raised by Dr. Detmold, and discussion suppressed, a law of the academy requiring unanimous consent for a non-member to take part in debate. Years afterwards, Dr. Detmold, in explaining to Dr. Swinburne this act of professional discourtesy, said he did it at the instance of Professor Clark, and because he promised to do so.

When the case was so abruptly brought to a close, Dr. Mott, who had been interrupted, it was said, turning to Judge Allen, remarked *sotto voce*, "I would like to explain." — "It is too late now," said the judge. — " But I do not believe that poor woman ever killed herself," said the doctor. — " Neither do I," replied his honor.

The Rome " Sentinel," in commenting on the trial, said, —

" Those who heard the evidence in the Budge trial throughout, can easily see that the weak points of that case lay at the same spot. The village doctor, who was first called in to see the dead body of Mrs. Budge, did not seem to dream that a woman's head could be half cut off by anybody but herself. He actually did not suppose that the coroner would need him as a witness, much less that a judicial investigation might subsequently need his evidence. Instead of taking out his note-book, and carefully noting on the spot every atom of fact in regard to the spots of blood, the quantity, the position of the body, of the marks of blood, and every thing else which could throw a light upon the circumstance of the cutting, this doctor seems to have contented himself with poking cotton batting into the wound, and sewing it up."

As a sequel to this trial, the Rev. Henry Budge instituted an action for libel against the Hon. Caleb Lyon for slander, placing his damages at twenty thousand dollars. The complaint alleged the printing and circulating of the libel in which Lyon charged Budge in verse with the murder of his wife, criminal intercourse with other women, and other charges, which, the plaintiff alleged, held him up to ridicule, and injured his good name and character. In the trial of this case, the array of counsel was formidable, and consisted of the Hons. Messrs. Conkling, Kearnen, Doolittle, and Earle for the defendant, and the Hon. Judge Lyman Tremaine for the plaintiff. The only expert for the defendant was Dr. John Swinburne. In this case all the evidence in the murder trial was introduced, the only defence made by Lyon being justification as to the charge of murder, and nothing as to the other criminal charges. The trial occupied three weeks. Judge Mullen, in summoning up the case, charged the jury, among other things, that "the fact that if the defendant, at the time of publication, had reason, from the facts and circumstances existing at or before the publication, to believe the plaintiff was guilty of the acts charged, he would not be thereby relieved from liability for the damages which legitimately and naturally resulted from the publication, but it would relieve him from any liability which the existence of actual malice would justify, and require the jury to give. If the justification is proved, then the plaintiff is entitled to like damages for the injury sustained by reason of the other charges against him in the libel."

Notwithstanding this charge, and the legal acumen engaged in the prosecution of this libel suit, the jury gave the plaintiff a verdict of *one hundred dollars*, instead of twenty thousand dollars, as asked, — virtually, it seems, a verdict declaring him guilty of the charge, where justification was pleaded, and a sufficient sum to repair the damage to his character by the other charges, in which no defence was made. Among the expert witnesses for the Rev. Mr. Budge were Drs. Coventry, Hogeboom, and Thomas.

A significant incident in connection with these trials was

stated by a United-States senator, who said, "When the question of confirming Hon. Caleb Lyon to a territorial governorship was being considered, his confirmation was attempted to be defeated because of his connection with these trials as proving him unworthy the trust. The late Charles Sumner, a profound jurist and deep thinker, was in possession of a review of the case published by Dr. Swinburne, and from this review demonstrated the grounds taken by Mr. Lyon as honorable in every particular; and on his construction of the facts the appointment was confirmed."

In the "Proceedings of the Medical Society of the State of New-York, 1862," is a review of this interesting case, covering a hundred pages. In this review is given a synopsis of the evidence, both scientific and moral; the theory and arguments of Professor Clark and Dr. Swinburne, with a full account of the latter's views, and the grounds on which his deductions were made, and a reply to the theories of Professor Clark,[1] with a number of cuts showing how the cutting could be done by another than the unfortunate woman; as well as a report of fifteen cases of suicidal deaths by cutting carotid arteries, the opinions of leading scientists, and other interesting scientific matter.

Among the eminent men whose attention was drawn to this case, and who coincided with the views of Dr. Swinburne, were Alfred S. Taylor, M.D., professor of medical jurisprudence, Guy's Hospital, London, and author of "Taylor on Poisons" and "Taylor's Medical Jurisprudence;" T. G. Geoghegan, M.D., professor of medical jurisprudence, Royal College of Surgeons, Dublin, Ireland; Charles A. Lee, M.D., professor of medical jurisprudence, editor of Guy's "Forensic Medicine," etc.; S. D. Gross, M.D., professor of surgery, Jefferson Medical College, Philadelphia, and author of "Gross on Surgery;" S. Weir Mitchell, M.D., the celebrated scientist of Philadelphia; Alfred Stille, M.D., Philadelphia,

---

[1] In the review of this case Dr. Swinburne gives in full the paper read by Professor Clark before the Academy of Medicine, dividing it into sections, and answering the arguments as they are presented. He also gives in full the cases cited by Professor Clark.

author of Wharton and Stillé's work on medical jurisprudence; J. G. Wormley, Columbus, O., professor of microscopic
poisons. Because of the importance of this case, and the
prominent positions held by the writers, at the head of their
profession, their letters are given in full: —

CHEMICAL LABORATORY, GUY'S HOSPITAL,
June 30, 1860.

DEAR SIR, — I have great pleasure in sending you my
opinion of the case of Mrs. B. of G. Dr. Hendee left the
manuscripts and drawing at my house during my absence;
so that I had an opportunity of reading it, and writing out
my views, without having any communication with him. I
can perceive that it is a case of great importance. It somewhat resembles that of Lord William Russell, murdered by
Courvoisier in London in 1840, and the case which I have
reported under the name of Harrington, in my " Medical
Jurisprudence," 6th ed. (English), p. 281.

I am, dear sir, yours faithfully,

ALFRED S. TAYLOR.

DR. SWINBURNE.

[REPORT OF THE CASE OF MRS. B. OF G.]

I have read a report of the case of Mrs. B. of G., who
died Dec. 10, 1859. This report, with a drawing of position
of deceased in bed, has been furnished to me by Dr. J.
Swinburne of Albany.

From these documents it appears to me, —

1st, That the wound in the throat must have been inflicted
while the deceased was lying on her back; i.e., in the recumbent posture. There was no blood on the anterior part of
the neck below the cut, and there was no blood on the anterior part of the body or nightdress. Considering the blood-
vessels divided by the wound in the neck, the fore part of
the person and dress, if deceased were sitting up at the time
of its infliction, could not have escaped receiving a considerable amount of blood.

The description of the flow of blood being chiefly on each
side of the neck is in accordance with the view that the
wound was inflicted while deceased was on her back.

The head being deeply embedded in the pillow is also in
favor of this view, since, had deceased sat up at the time of
infliction, I do not believe that by any accidental fall such

an embedding of the head in the pillow could have taken place ; and, further, it is not conceivable that the head should have been thrown back as the result of an accidental fall.

2d, Taking the depth, extent, and direction of this wound in the neck, it is not such a wound as a person *could inflict on* himself or herself *while lying on the back in a recumbent posture.*

The large blood-vessels on the back side of the neck were divided, assuming that a suicide might have power, after dividing the carotids and jugulars on one side, to carry a razor through the trachea and œsophagus, as well as through the blood-vessels, on the other side.

I am decidedly of the opinion that there would not have been the power to shave off the left transverse process of the fifth cervical vertebra, or penetrate the osseous structure. In the recumbent posture, such an act would require the exercise of a great muscular force at a very great disadvantage in the position of the right arm for using the required force.

Assuming that the incision was made from left to right, the fifth vertebra must have been implicated in the incision *before* the weapon was carried to the right side at all ; and yet it is stated that on the right side of the neck there was a cut in the *skin* one-quarter of an inch farther than the tissues wounded.

This fact proves to my mind a deliberate withdrawal of the weapon, quite inconsistent with the fact that the blood-vessels on both sides of the neck had been divided, and the periosteum and osseous structure of the fifth cervical vertebra had been cut or penetrated.

3d, On the hypothesis of suicide, a wound of this extent and depth must have been inflicted with tremendous force and with great rapidity. There must have been a sudden and copious loss of blood from the divided blood-vessels of the two sides of the neck.

How came the right hand, only slightly bent, to be in a position by the side of the body, the weapon not grasped within it, but lying on the bed six or eight inches from the wrist? No muscular power would, in my judgment, have remained to enable the deceased to have placed her arm in this position after the infliction of such a wound in the recumbent posture ; and there is no conceivable accident by which it could have assumed this posture, unless the body had been interfered with before it was seen by the medical attendant. The weapon, on the view of suicide, should have been in the grasp of the hand, considering the enormous muscular power which must have been used in an act of cutting which involved the body of one of the vertebræ: if not in the grasp, the part by which the weapon was held should have been close to the palm.

The right hand presented only on the palmar surface a light streak of blood: the left hand is not described as having any blood upon it. Had the right hand of deceased inflicted such a wound as is described, the back of the hand, as well as probably a part of the palmar surface, would have been covered with blood. The presence of a light streak only on the second row of the phalanges of the palm is inexplicable on the presumption of suicide. The weapon must have been grasped and held firmly in the right hand: hence the palmar surface might have escaped, but the dorsal surface, in my opinion, *could not* escape, receiving some blood from the vessels divided on the left side, and subsequently from those divided on the right side.

The spot of blood twelve or fourteen inches in length, etc., on the bedclothes, and the spots on the pillow to the right, have no communication with the main source of hemorrhage: they must have been produced subsequently to the wound in the neck. There is no conceivable theory by which the deceased could have produced them, or that they could have resulted from any act on her part, on the supposition of suicide.

Taking the attitude of the body, the nature of the wound, and the medical circumstances in reference to the position of the stains of blood and the weapon, *I am of opinion that this wound was not inflicted by deceased on herself, but that it must have been inflicted by some other person.*

A case somewhat similar occurred to me some years since. The assassin, in this case, cut the throat of a woman while asleep. He cut off one of the cotton strings of her nightcap: this was found on the floor. The microscope showed fibres of cotton in the coagulated blood on the razor.

The head of deceased was pressed backward on the pillow, and it would appear as if the chin had been raised, or pulled upward, at the time of the act of cutting.

ALFRED S. TAYLOR,

*Professor of medical jurisprudence
and chemistry in Guy's Hospital.*

15 St. James Terrace, Regent's Park,
June 29, 1860.

[LETTER FROM PROFESSOR T. G. GEOGHEGAN.]

UPPER MARION ST., DUBLIN,
Sept. 10, 1860.

MY DEAR SIR, — I herewith apologize for having so long left your letter unanswered.

I have read your well-drawn report with great interest, and feel quite disposed to concur in the general conclusions you have drawn.

The autopsy was very well conducted. I find it impossible to understand how the division of the great vessels should not have discolored more of the adjacent surrounding surfaces with blood, unless by some such state of the circulation as you suggest, and which latter would explain the result.

The lungs also seem to have been congested, — a condition not to be expected in death from hemorrhage.

I infer, however, that what was found in the pleura was serum strongly imbued with blood, rather than pure blood, as I have never seen the latter except with a wound. Whilst .the bloody fluid is not unusual as the result of the process of putrefaction, especially under the influences of gases accumulated in the blood-vessels, and thus causing exudation; the absence, also, of more than slight stains of blood on the hand, — the division of the *transverse* process of the cervical *vertebræ*, and the condition of the *tongue*, are presumptive of *homicide*. My best wishes.

Yours very truly,

T. G. GEOGHEGAN.

DR. JOHN SWINBURNE, Albany, N.Y.

After transmitting to Dr. Geoghegan some tables embodying the results of experiments, he sends in reply the following able and comprehensive opinion : —

DUBLIN, Dec. 18, 1860.

DEAR DR. SWINBURNE, — I feel much obliged by your attention in sending me the report of the inquest in Mrs. Budge's case, and the valuable tables embodying the result of your experiments. Some time since, I wrote to you, giving you, I think, a sketch of my views of the matter. the date furnished by yourself.

I quite coincide with you as to the extreme improbability of suicide having been carried out in the present instance; and this for a variety of reasons, which you appear to have estimated very correctly.

I cannot conceive, in the first place, that had the division of the great vessels been the result of suicide, the circulation being ordinarily vigorous, the neighboring objects — as the head of the bed, and walls, bedclothes (i.e., pillows), and doubtless the deceased's face and upper part of the neck — could have escaped being copiously sprinkled with blood, and that part of these marks should have the dotted and interrupted character of an arterial jet; secondly, that the *lungs* should have been *exsanguined*, or nearly so, instead of *forming characters* which lead to the legitimate inference that they were *congested* at the time of *death*. The condition of the razor-blade, unstained by blood in a great part of its breadth, seems strongly also to militate against *self-murder*. I should have further expected that in case of suicide followed by rapid death, and where the extent and character of the injury would indicate a most determined effort, the weapon would have been found grasped in the hand, as it most usually is. Again : *suicide* by *cutting* the *throat* in the *recumbent* position is *most unusual*. Nor have I *ever seen* or *read* of a case of *suicide* where a portion of the *bone* was *sliced off*. The seat of the wound is unusual for a suicide, being commonly at one side more than the other, and generally above the *os hyoides*. These latter, however, are not decisive criteria. Lastly, the *injuries* of the *tongue* are very *significant*.

With best wishes, yours very truly,

T. G. GEOGHEGAN.

DR. J. SWINBURNE, Albany.

[LETTER FROM DR. CHARLES A. LEE.]

PEEKSKILL, Sept. 28, 1860.

DR. CHARLES H. PORTER.

My Dear Sir, — I am much obliged to you for the opportunity of reading your " report of the case of Mrs. B., who died under suspicious circumstances." I have carefully read it, and given it much consideration.

It is due to you to say that it is a most *ingenious, judicious,* and *satisfactory exposé* of the case.

The conclusions at which you arrive appear to me sound and irresistible, and entirely borne out by the facts. There is not a shadow of doubt in my mind that the *incision* was *inflicted after death,* and there is as little doubt that *death* resulted from *suffocation*.

The depth and extent of the wound argue a determination of purpose, and strength of wrist, possessed by very few suicides, especially females ; and I do not believe it possible that such an incision could have been inflicted by the deceased.

The *case*, in my judgment, could hardly be *strengthened* by any *collateral circumstances.*

If it should appear that the parties lived together unhappily, it would go far with a jury to corroborate your theory.

The supposition of suicide I should not suppose could be entertained at all by any person. But, even under such (*insanity*) circumstances, I should decidedly coincide with you in the opinions you have expressed in regard to the cause of death; for all the *facts* point *irresistibly* to the *agency* of *another hand.* I have nowhere read a more interesting case, or one which has been more ably or logically elucidated, where the reasoning throughout is so thoroughly based on science, and established principles of anatomy, physiology, and pathology.

I trust you will allow its publication in some of our medical journals, as it is too important to be lost to science.

Allow me to thank you again for your kindness in sending me your report of the case.

I am very truly yours, etc.,

CHAS. A. LEE.

[LETTER FROM DR. S. D. GROSS, PROFESSOR OF SURGERY.]

PHILADELPHIA, Jan. 31, 1862.

DEAR DOCTOR, — You ask me in regard to the probable manner of the death of Mrs. Budge, — whether, in my judgment, it was caused by her own act, or by the act of some one else. After a careful examination of the testimony submitted to me, I have unhesitatingly come to the conclusion that she was destroyed, not by her own hands, but by those of another person. My reasons for this conclusion are the following : —

1st, It is *impossible* for any person to *cut* the *large vessels* of the neck without being *inundated* with *blood.* If Mrs. Budge had been *alive* at the moment her *neck* was cut, the *blood* of the *carotid arteries* would have *spurted* about in *every* direction, soiling not only the *bed* and *body clothes,* but also the *floor,* and probably even the *wall* and *ceiling* of the apartment. I assume that *this* circumstance alone is amply sufficient to establish the fact that she had *ceased* to *breathe* when her *throat was cut.* As a surgeon, I cannot conceive of the possibility of such a frightful wound being inflicted without the occurrence of the most profuse hemorrhage, even if life had been destroyed in a few seconds; and the effects of this hemorrhage would unquestionably have exhibited themselves in the manner above indicated. Any one who has ever seen a chicken's head severed knows how long the blood continues to flow in a full stream from the carotid arteries.

2d, If Mrs. Budge had herself inflicted the *wound*, her *hand*, *face*, and *chest* would *necessarily* have been *covered* with *blood;* which, however, it appears, was not the case.

3d, From the fact that the woman was comparatively thin and feeble, I infer that she could not (even if we suppose she possessed most extraordinary will and determination) have wielded the *razor* with which the wound is said to have been inflicted, in such a manner and with such force as to shave off the left transverse process of the fifth cervical vertebra, or to divide all the structures in front of the neck, even down to the scalenus muscle. Such a wound as Mrs. Budge's is seldom inflicted by the most robust and courageous suicide.

4th, From the position of the *razor*, and from the almost entire absence of *blood* upon it, to say nothing of the *peculiar shape of the wound*, I cannot suppose that it *was* the *weapon* used to *kill Mrs. Budge*.

The above facts and considerations are quite sufficient for my purpose. I leave entirely out of the question all the minor points of the case. They establish most irrefragably, in my judgment, the conclusion that Mrs. Budge's *neck* was *not cut* until she had *ceased* to *breathe*, and consequently that she was *not* her own *murderer*.

How she was killed I will not pretend to affirm; but the probability suggests itself to my mind that the act was effected by *manual strangulation*, and that her *throat was cut immediately after*. This idea derives plausibility from some of the circumstances revealed during the dissection of the body.

I am, dear doctor, very truly and respectfully

Your friend and obedient servant,

S. D. GROSS.

Dr. John Swinburne.

PHILADELPHIA, Dec. 8, 1862.

John Swinburne, M.D.

Dear Sir, — I have received a copy of "A Review of the People against Rev. Henry Budge," for which I presume that

I am indebted to you. Its details have interested me very much, and they appear to me to sustain your conclusions. Will you permit me to call your attention to a point which does not seem to me to have attracted your notice? On p. 12 it is stated that "a razor was lying under the arm, *two-thirds open*." Would it have been possible for a suicide to inflict the wounds described in the evidence with a razor only two-thirds open? Or, supposing that those wounds were inflicted by the razor bent backwards as it is used in shaving, could it have been partially closed by a suicide who had inflicted the wounds described in the evidence? If these questions are answered in the negative, as I think they should be, Mrs. Budge was not a suicide.

I am, very respectfully, your obedient servant,

ALFRED STILLE.

COLUMBUS, O., Sept. 8, 1862.

DR. SWINBURNE.

My Dear Sir,— I am under many obligations for your kindness in·sending me your review of the Budge case. I have read it with very great interest, and fully concur in your opinion that it was not a case of suicide.

Very truly yours,

T. G. WORMLEY.

MY DEAR DOCTOR,— Some one, you I suppose, sent me your wonderful analysis of the Budge case. I read it with the utmost care, and think you have made out a clear case. As a physiologist, I can find no fault with your biological criticism, which appears to me to be just and well founded. Indeed, I am at a loss to understand how any one can or could take any view of the case but that which you have defended with a logic so convincing as to leave only room for expressions of admiration on the part of any one fitted to follow your argument.

You have added considerably to our knowledge of these cases; and thus much, at least, of good has come of it.

With many thanks, I am very truly yours,

S. WEIR MITCHELL.

1226 Walnut Street.

DR. SWINBURNE.

Nearly twenty years afterwards Budge is heard of in the West, where he was in the ministry, and a great favorite "with certain young ladies." Here he was recognized by a lady from Lowville, who disclosed the affair. Budge called a meeting of the church to explain the matter. "The explanation made the congregation believers in the crime," wrote a prominent physician, "and he was forthwith dismissed. From there he went to Buchanan, and then to Byron, O. Here," he writes, "comes in a sad picture. A Dr. Parsons and his wife were members of the church, and Budge went to visit them. He became more interested with a daughter than with her sick mother. At this point a rumor came that Budge had a wife in Canada. Dr. Parsons warned Budge never to enter his house again. Mrs. Parsons died, and Carrie, the daughter, became insane. They all believe that distraction in love caused this melancholy result." This moral evidence is a circumstance to strengthen the medical position taken by Dr. Swinburne.

The positions assumed in these three novel, unprecedented, and interesting cases, established him, in the judgment of the legal and advanced medical profession, as among the most reliable of medico-legal experts, and resulted in his frequent calls to the witness-stand. Among the other celebrated cases in which he was made prominent was one where the questions raised were entirely different from the cases cited.

On the 5th of June, 1878, in Northumberland, Saratoga County, Mrs. Jesse Billings was shot while sitting in front of her window, and instantly killed, the ball being fired from the outside, and passing through a pane of glass. She died instantly from the effects of the bullet. The bullet entered on the left side of the head, but did not pass entirely through the skull. On the right side a wound was found over the mastoid portion about two inches in length, undoubtedly, as the experts believed, made by a piece of bone cutting its way outwards. At the bottom of this wound, lodged in the upper surface of the petrous portion where it joins the squamous, lay the bullet. In its course, the ball had, in addition to passing through the glass, cut through the facia of the temporal muscles, the superficial facia, and the skin. As the result of the coroner's inquest, her husband, Jesse Billings, jun., was arrested, and held to await the action of the grand jury, by whom he was indicted. He was tried for the murder at the October (1878) term of the *oyer and terminer*, the trial resulting in a disagreement of the jury, the evidence being exclusively circumstantial and expert testimony. Not being fully satisfied with the autopsy first made, said an expert, in a pamphlet reviewing the case, the people's counsel had the body exhumed, and requested Dr. John Swinburne of Albany to make a further examination of the head. The cause for this act was the claim, on the part of the defence in the first trial, that *all* the lead fired at the murdered woman was found by the physicians holding the first autopsy, and the people wished to know whether more lead did not remain in the skull. Dr. Swinburne removed the head from the trunk, taking only the bones of the skull, sawing through the external angular processes and the anterior roots of the zygomatic arches. After maceration the skull was cleaned, careful search being made for any particles of lead (none, however, being found), and the broken bones wired together. The skull so prepared was put one side, and produced in evidence at the second trial, which took place in April, 1880. Two important points were raised; i.e., as to the foot-marks found leading from the house to an old unused well, and whether the shooting was done with an old Ballard carbine found in the well, and which three witnesses swore they believed belonged to Billings, and that they believed it was the same one that had been lying around his store, but which could not be found until the officers drew it from the well. The claim of the defence was, that the bullet was a smaller ball than a "44," and its full weight less than two hundred and twenty grains (about fifty-eight.grains); that in consequence the Ballard carbine could not have been the gun from which the shot was fired, for it not only called for a "44" ball, but would throw a bullet with such force that it necessarily must have gone entirely through the head; and that the weapon with which the wound was inflicted was a pistol.

One of the experts for the defence, Professor Jacob S.

Mosher of Albany, *did*, by actual measurement, fix the size of the ball. Dr. Mosher found what he considered to be, and swore to as, the "lands and grooves," and so distinctly that he could accurately measure them. Dr. Mosher did thus measure, and, when announcing the result, gave first of all the ball to be of 36 or 38 caliber, but, on his attention being called to errors in his calculations, corrected his statement, and admitted the ball was a "44." Although Dr. Mosher, later in the trial, again changed his mind as to size, still his own careful measurement of the "lands and grooves" he could so clearly point out, could only make the ball one that was able to fit and be fired from the Ballard gun.

Among the expert witnesses for the people was Dr. Swinburne, who was on the stand a portion of two days. In his testimony he contradicted the statement of Dr. Mosher, that the excess of loss to a ball in any instance, in firing, would be fifty-eight grains, and held that it would reach a hundred and fifteen grains. He demonstrated this by experiments in firing into a box of bones, and letting all the force be expended therein.

The defence produced a skull upon which an experiment had been tried, the Ballard carbine being the weapon used. The description of this experiment from the testimony as given by Dr. Mosher is, "With a gun which was furnished, and understood to be the Ballard gun, called by that name, a cartridge was fired through glass into a head, and the scalp and all the integuments as they were in life attached to the trunk, and containing the brain, care being taken to throw the ball as near as possible to the same place, on the left side, as in the Billings skull."

He testified, that, "after firing, the ball was preserved, and an examination made of the skull to see the kind of injury that the ball had made in passing through it. It had passed through both sides of the skull, and gone out of it, as a 44-caliber ball with an ordinary charge *always will*."

Upon cross-examination, measurements of the bullet-holes in the skull presented by Dr. Mosher, and in that of Mrs. Billings, were made. These measurements brought out the fact that the ball in the Billings skull entered its *full size lower, and nearer* the *meatus auditorius*, than the other: or, in other words, the Billings ball struck more squarely the petrous portion; Dr. Mosher's bullet going mainly through the mastoid portion, merely touching the petrous where its upper edge turns to join the squamous. By measurement, the amount of bone traversed by the two bullets was found to be two and three-eighths inches, scarcely touching the petrous portion in the Billings skull, and less than *one-half of an inch* in the other, or the skull presented by Dr. Mosher, and ploughing through the entire petrous portion of the temple on the one side, and through a portion on the other, thus accounting for the large loss in the ball.

Mr. Leet of the Union Metallic Cartridge Company testified to the shell taken from the carbine, and the ball taken from Mrs. Billings's head, as, in his opinion, being of the character referred to. Mr. Leet could not find upon the ball the "lands and grooves," or the marks of the rifling of the gun, but, from other characteristics, was positive the ball was a "44 long."

Mr. Hepburn of the Remington Rifle-Works at Ilion, N.Y., testified that he, also, believed the ball a "44." He could not find the lands and grooves; but the heel of the ball, and the lines and scratches upon it, showing a left-handed twist to the barrel from which it was fired, served, in his opinion, to draw the ball taken from Mrs. Billings's head into the Billings carbine, for this left-handed twist is peculiar to this make of rifles.

The experts for the defence testified that the ball from the carbine could not be the one with which the wound was made, as it was larger than the hole in the window. On this discrepancy, and that in the testimony as to the foot-marks, the prisoner was acquitted.

As an addition to this trial, George W. Jones, one of the witnesses for the defence, was convicted of perjury in the following March, in having sworn falsely in the trial of Jesse Billings, jun., for the murder of his wife.

Judge Westbrook, in charging the jury in the trial of John

Hughes for the murder of William J. Hadley, an attorney-at-law in Albany, tried at the March (1880) term of the *oyer and terminer*, said, —

"After receiving these injuries at the hands of the prisoner, which are not denied, and which the counsel for the defence, both in opening and closing, admit to have been inflicted, the deceased was attended by two eminent physicians of this city, Dr. Swinburne and another. I use the word 'eminent,' because I mean precisely what I say. No person who heard those two physicians upon the stand give their evidence, and who noted their intelligence and their knowledge of their profession, could fail to see they were men of eminence and mark in their profession and calling. They did for him, they say, all that was in their power to do. Mr. Hadley was much depressed. They gave him all the nourishment they could administer, in every form and shape; but he grew weaker and weaker, and on the twenty-first day of April departed this life. The body was examined after death by Dr. Swinburne, in the presence of some of his assistants. The *postmortem* revealed the fact that not only were those wounds upon his person, of which I have spoken, — the one upon the breast reaching backwards and downwards to the extent of some inches, and the one upon the arm going through and through the arm, — but the seventh rib was separated from the cartilage, and had dropped down. The eighth, ninth, and tenth ribs were also partially loosened, not, as the doctors say, by cutting, but by the force of the blow that had been given, or by the force of some blow upon the person of Mr. Hadley. I said by the force of the blow given, because there is no proof, so far as I can remember (and if I am wrong, your recollection will correct me), of any other blow having been given which could have produced that result. Abscesses had formed in the arm; and the muscles of the arm, in the language of the physicians, had 'rotted away.' There were also abscesses in the side, showing a most unhealthy condition of the system. Those doctors who were with him from the time of the occurrence down to the close of his life say to you unhesitatingly that those wounds were the cause of his death."

Hughes was convicted of murder in the second degree, and sentenced to imprisonment in Clinton State Prison for life.

Nearly twenty-five years ago a newsboy was passing down Maiden Lane, when he was struck by a wagon belonging to an express company; and afterwards his parents, through the law firm of Hill, Cagger, & Porter, brought an action for damages, claiming that the wheel had passed over and injured him. Several witnesses, employees of the company, swore to seeing the wheel pass over him. Dr. Swinburne as an expert, he having attended the boy, was placed on the stand, and testified that the wheel did not pass over him; that, so far as the witnesses were concerned, it was an optical delusion; that with a wagon weighing over six tons, the weight being equally proportioned, if one wheel passed over him as described, even if the wagon were in a state of inertia, the weight was sufficient to crush him in two, but where the wagon was in motion, as in this instance, the power would be increased, as in the case of a cannon-ball fired from a cannon. He held that, the planks being slippery, the boy was struck by the wheel and suddenly thrown around, and that the only damage sustained was the pain from a bruise on the side, and loss of time. On this testimony, the jury gave a verdict for nominal damages. For this testimony, Mr. Porter for a long time entertained unpleasant feelings to Dr. Swinburne, but subsequently was interested in a case where an inquisition was being held as to the cause of a death in East Albany, where his client was charged with murder. This case was where a man was struck by another, and, falling, was killed. The doctor testified that the fatal wound was caused by the man, in falling, hitting the axle of his head on the flange of a rail. After the discharge of the man, Mr. Porter said, "Doctor, I did not dare to ask you a question. You are right this time, and, in thinking over the other case, I am satisfied your conclusions were reasonable, and that you were right then."

In January, 1878, Asher B. Covill was tried before Judge Potter at Elizabethtown, Essex County, for the murder of his wife near Ticonderoga. At first he claimed that parties had forcibly entered his house, and killed his wife, but subsequently confessed that he murdered her, and that the blow was struck with a large wooden club. On the trial the question was raised as to insanity, and, at the suggestion of the judge, Dr. Swinburne was consulted. The case was laid clearly before the doctor, who knew nothing of the man nor his antecedents. From a description of the man's life and methods of living, remaining away from his wife for months at a time, the doctor said he was neither insane nor demented, as he never had a mind to lose, but that he was an idiot, more fitted for an asylum than a prison. The next day he visited the prisoner; and, in presence of the jailer, the man stated that he had been guilty of the unnatural acts on which the doctor had based his hypothesis. On the doctor's recommendation, the judge and counsel allowed him to withdraw his plea, and plead guilty to murder in the second degree, and he was sentenced to the Clinton State Prison for life. The man had been prominent in the church, and loud in his protestations of religion, and, because of this and the amiable disposition of his wife, the feeling against him was intense; and great indignation was expressed toward the doctor for his recommendation and interposition, the foreman and other members of the jury participating in this feeling. To all these the doctor merely replied, " You will thank me some day for saving you from committing an act you would afterwards regret." Here again he proved his superiority, as it was afterwards learned that some of the prisoner's relations had been insane, while others were idiots.

Dr. Swinburne has been an expert in all the most notable cases tried in this portion of the State, where questions arose which could only be decided by men versed in medical jurisprudence.

In no criminal proceedings where he has appeared as an expert has he ever charged or received a fee, holding, that, if his services were of value in ferreting out crime, it was a duty he, as a citizen, owed the State and society; while, on the other hand, if he appeared for an accused, he believed he was correct in his conclusion, and owed this duty to innocence. On no other considerations would he appear.

In 1870, he, with two lawyers, were appointed in New York as referees, to whom were submitted the case of Walsh against Sayre, which has become quite noted, and quoted in

the law-books. The case was an action for damages, in which
it was alleged the hip-joint of the plaintiff, from which secretions issued, had been opened by defendant, and a permanent
injury to plaintiff sustained. The case had been up two
or three times in the courts; but, owing to the intricate
question arising, which could only be intelligently settled by
a medical man of known ability, this reference was made.
Before the referees, two of the most prominent surgeons of
New York testified that twenty-four hours after the alleged
operation they found indications that positively demonstrated
that the secretions they then found came from the hip-joint.
Under the questioning of Dr. Swinburne, they admitted that
they had not examined the wound, either by probing or otherwise, except by putting the hand under the clothing. They
held in their testimony, that, because the secretion was adhesive and sticky, they were enabled to say conclusively that it
came from the hip-joint. Subsequently these two scientific
experts were compelled to admit that there were a number
of other secretions corresponding in test with this secretion,
and hence were forced to withdraw their first decision, and
confess it might arise from scrofula or some other cause,
and that even the blood or serum itself was as sticky as this
secretion. Notwithstanding the testimony of these men, the
hip-joint itself at the time of the trial, about three years afterwards, was found in a healthy condition; but the discharge
still continued from the alleged as well as other spontaneous
openings. In this action Mr. Edwin James, a former queen's
counsel and member of the British House of Parliament, was
counsel for the plaintiff, and Hon. Ira Shaffer for defendant.
Mr. James indignantly withdrew from the case because Dr.
Swinburne, as one of the referees, questioned the expert testimony for the plaintiff. The referees, in their decision, rendered in favor of Dr. Sayer, on the ground that the joint was
not opened. In this case Dr. Swinburne refused to charge
any fee for the time occupied in this suit, because it was a
case in which a poor family and one of the medical profession
were the parties litigant. Mr. James in this suit claimed
that the doctor had no right to question the deductions of the

experts, and was bound to accept their conclusions on the questions presented. The doctor maintained that, as a referee to decide the points in litigation, he had a right to know why the experts arrived at the conclusion they announced. He knew some of them were erroneous, and that, if there was union in the first intention, there could be no inflammation, and hence no discharges, within forty-eight hours. It was charged that, as soon as the cut was made, the flow commenced, and continued. The doctor maintained that, if the tissues cut were healthy, no flow would take place, and if there was secretion, it must have been caused by an abscess, or some other gathering.

In no instance has he ever appeared in court as a witness for the purpose of injuring the standing of his professional brethren, but only testifying to what he knew affecting the cases before him. An instance of his testimony in cases where professional men were sued for malpractice was cited to the writer a few days since by Mr. I. M. Lawson, a prominent attorney in the city of Albany. Mr. Lawson said, —

"I had a case recently, and had Dr. Swinburne as my witness, and he lost the case for me. A woman out in the country sustained a fracture, and was treated by a physician who made a bad job, resulting in a deformity, and loss of the use of the limb. The doctor demonstrated where the treatment was a failure, and why there was no excuse (scientifically) for the failure. When questioned by the other side, he said the physician was not responsible; that no man could be held responsible for what he did not know; that the physician had treated according to the teachings of the books and colleges; and that the colleges, and not the man, should be held responsible for the false doctrine they were teaching."

Mr. Lawson added, —

"I tried to convince the court and jury that physicians, like railroad companies, should be held responsible for all damages resulting, if they did not avail themselves of the most modern and best systems of protection to life and limb. It is surprising the success the doctor has met with. He is a remarkable man; and it is unaccountable why the profession are not compelled to accept his system, evidently so superior to the others."

The next important case in which Dr. Swinburne appeared as a medical expert was in the matter of Col. Walton Dwight, whose death occurred at Binghamton, Nov. 15, 1878. This gentleman was reported quite rich, his estate being mostly in short-term insurance policies, aggregating over two hundred and fifty thousand dollars. On the 18th Dr. Francis Delafield of New York, representing the Equitable Life-Assurance Company, made an autopsy of the remains in the presence of Dr. Swinburne and thirteen other physicians. He held that, as a result of this autopsy, there was no evidence of the action of any irritant poison, although the conditions of the stomach and intestines did not exclude the possibility of such poison existing; that there existed chronic inflammation of the stomach, but an absence of acute inflammation; that there was no evidence of the existence of malarial poisoning; that the immediate cause of death was paralysis of the heart; that there was no evidence of the existence of mineral poisoning; and that neither the medical history of the case, nor the autopsy, gave evidence of the existence of any but natural causes of death.

Dr. Swinburne was present by request, and acting for Professor Charles H. Porter, who represented the Union Mutual Life-Insurance Company of Maine. Dr. Swinburne held that the autopsy was too hurriedly made, and that, instead of a few hours, two days at least should have been taken in an important case like this, where the question probably was at stake as to whether it was murder, suicide, or natural death. In a case like this, he insisted, the people have a right to demand a most careful and perfect investigation. He held that the autopsy did not account for the death of the person on whose body it was made from natural causes, but, so far as it disclosed a point of death, he believed the person did not die of malarial fever, congestive chills, paralysis of the heart, nor any disease, but, on the contary, by unlawful means. At this inquest he called the attention of those present to an indentation running around the neck, in which all present concurred. The views of Dr. Swinburne were concurred in by Dr. B. F. Sherman of Ogdensburg, St. Lawrence County.

Because of these deductions of Dr. Swinburne, and a statement by W. F. Winship of Albany, — who believed Col. Dwight committed wilful suicide, and who deposed that, on visiting Col. Dwight before his death, he (Winship) had his suspicions aroused that Col. Dwight was committing suicide by slow poison, and that he so informed the colonel's wife, — the companies issuing the policies, with one exception, refused to settle, and demanded another autopsy and coroner's inquest, which commenced on April 23, 1879.

At the second inquest, Drs. Burr and Orton, who had attended Dwight during his illness, gave as their opinion from the autopsy and *post-mortem*, that death was from congestive chills resulting from malarial fever contracted while on a visit West.

Dr. Swinburne's deductions, noting the heavy indentation around the neck, and from the *post-mortem*, were, that the person on whom the autopsy was held died from asphyxia, and that asphyxia was induced by a cord or fillet around his neck, and thought the cord was drawn moderately around the neck. There are other forms, he held, of asphyxia, but this seems the most probable. In a state of stupidity from drunkenness or from opiates, a wet cloth over the mouth and nose would produce the same result, and about the same *post-mortem* conditions. The heavy indentation noted and described by Dr. Swinburne in the neck commenced just on the right side, about the point where the *os hyoides* is attached to the thyroid cartilage, and extending upwards and backwards around to the back of the neck at an angle of forty-five degrees; and it was an indentation that he could put his right thumb in, and was about that size as if made with a curtain cord.

At the second autopsy, and in the actions following in the Supreme Court, the doctor maintained that the coroner's report was not as originally made, and that, although the signatures were maintained, pages in which changes and suggestions were interlined were extracted, and others substituted without these interlinings. In the report of the first autopsy it was stated, —

"Dr. Swinburne notes a heavy indentation extending upwards and backwards from the *os hyoides* to right around back of neck, and on left side below the thyroid cartilage, running upwards and backwards at an angle of about forty-five degrees. Drs. Swinburne and Ayre think this is caused by the bending of the head and neck backwards."

This statement, the doctor insisted, was garbled; that he certainly never gave an opinion as to the cause; and, if that was put in afterwards, it was interlined or interlarded, and will be so found in the original copy; but, if it was done at all, it was done after reading. Dr. S. Burr, who kept the record, in explanation said Dr. Ayre first spoke of it (the opinion); and then he saw Dr. Ayre talking with Dr. Swinburne, who nodded his head; and then he (Burr) put in the opinion.

Among the peculiar indications found by Dr. Swinburne was, that, upon opening the chest, the lungs were found to be congested, inflated, and apoplectic; so much so, that they would not collapse when opened. These congestions were found to extend from the lungs up to the larynx and trachea, some of the parts more congested than others. Upon a careful examination, the windpipe, larynx, and trachea were found to be lined and filled with a thick, tenacious mucus, and the membranes reddened, congested, and full of mucus. Notwithstanding this condition of the lungs, trachea, and larynx, a witness, Charles A. Hull, a lawyer, who was watching with the deceased, swore that less than ten minutes before Dwight died, and he did not seem to manifest immediate danger, he said he had a new way of eating crackers, and, as he spoke, reached over and took one. This was a curious condition to reconcile in pathology, as it would be an impossibility for this mucus to gather in that time.

In answer to a question by the coroner, Dr. Swinburne said, —

"I don't believe a healthy person ever died of a chill. Mark what I say, I don't believe a person ever died in a congestive chill which was caught here or in Chicago, as you put it yesterday. I mean a healthy person. They may have complications of disease ; but take a healthy person, shown to be healthy, like Col. Dwight, both *ante mortem* and *post mortem*, as stated by a great many physicians, now pronounced healthy by the *post-mortem* by all — I say a person absolutely healthy like that never dies from ordinary ague chills such as you get from Chicago, because they have not had ague at Chicago for many years."

He held that if a man is specially ill, he has a pulse and heat different from what he would have if he were well. Aside from the times, he said that he had what they claimed as these chills. He was never sick, excepting that he had from time to time a sort of bilious vomiting; but that you may regard as not peculiar, when you take into consideration the fact that the *post-mortem* examination showed Dwight had chronic inflammation of the stomach. As physicians (the jury was composed of physicians), you know perfectly well what that means: no man gets chronic inflammation without he has first had acute inflammation, and no man gets acute inflammation unless he has taken some narcotic or narcotic acid. Inflammation of the stomach is not an idiopathic disease.

Dr. Benjamin F. Sherman of Ogdensburg agreed with Dr. Swinburne. He had been coroner of St. Lawrence County for a number of years, and believed Col. Dwight came to his death from asphyxia from a rope around his neck.

Dr. Elisha A. Bridges of Ogdensburg believed the person on whose body they held the examination came to his death from asphyxia, and that the cause was strangulation with a cord or rope around the neck.

The verdict in this second *post-mortem* inquest was death from inanition and congestive chills, upsetting completely Dr. Delafield's theory. The investigation and excitement attending this trial was intensified because of the nature of the will, in which, in addition to providing for his relatives and a number of individuals, bequests were made to the four churches of Binghamton for Sunday schools, to the press of that city for annual dinners, for the needy poor of the city, to the Binghamton Library Association, and to the fire department of Binghamton.

During the trial of the suit for the recovery of the policies, the theory that a man could commit suicide by hanging himself while lying in bed, as advanced by Dr. Swinburne, was ridiculed by many of the professional men, and declared an impossibility. Notwithstanding this opinion of these conceited medical *savants*, the coroner of Broome County, Dr. Johnson, afterwards had two cases of suicide by this method in the jail at Binghamton; the men tying the cord or sheet to the bedpost, and then pressing down in the bed.

In commenting on this case, the Albany " Press and Knickerbocker " said, —

" Drs. Burr and Orton, from the first *post-mortem*, concluded that Dwight died of malarial and congestive chills, but, from the two *post-mortem* examinations, they concluded there was no cause of natural death. . . . Dr. Delafield, in his report from notes of the first *post-mortem*, stated that Dwight did not die from malarial fever and congestive chills, but from paralysis or syncope of the heart. . . . It seems pertinent to ask just here, Could a man die of congestive chills from malarial fever, with a man sitting only a few feet distant, and yet that watcher not know that he was suffering from a chill until the sick man was discovered dying? The papers seem to suppose that, if a cord were used there in any manner for the purpose of hanging Col. Dwight, after he was dead he must have come to life, and taken the rope off and destroyed it. The theory of Dr. Swinburne is fast gaining ground as the correct one, that the gelsemium produced the congestive chills described in the case of Dwight."

In reference to the exhumation and *post-mortem*, the " New-York Herald's " correspondent said, —

" While the doctors were gazing uninterestedly at the corpse, Dr. Swinburne approached the head, and, pointing with his finger at the neck, said, ' I wish you to take notice of that indentation around the neck : it is very peculiar. You see here it is deep, and it runs at an angle of about forty-five degrees.' Dr. Burr ran his finger in the furrow, and said, ' Yes, there is an indentation, and it runs around to the back of the neck.' Dr. Bridges, one of the medical experts, wrote the following description : ' An indentation of the neck well marked; left side, beginning over hyoid bone, extending at angle of forty-five degrees to back of neck; right side, extending as continuation of this, a little lower down ; looks as though made by a clothes-line ; indentation one-eighth to one-quarter of an inch deep, and one-fourth to one-half an inch wide.'

" Dr. Swinburne said he desired a plaster cast of the neck. The coroner permitted this to be done, and an excellent representation of the furrow was obtained. The ' Herald ' representative inquired of several doctors present what was the theory of the men who brought about these proceedings. They replied that the evidence pointed to the fact that Col. Dwight either hanged himself or was strangled to death. They expect that the plaster cast, in connection with the facts adduced at the autopsy, will establish this. The 'indentation ' alluded to is very apparent, and looks as if it had been made with a rope. It seems strange that the fifteen doctors who made the autopsy should have paid so little attention to this, which is apparently of such vast importance now. Wax impressions of the teeth were taken, a portion of the spinal marrow removed, and the old wound in the left thigh explored. The body was then, in its terribly mutilated condition, returned to the casket. and the coroner adjourned the inquest.

" Dr. Swinburne said to a reporter, ' This inquest has only confirmed what I saw before at the autopsy. There was every evidence that the man died from asphyxia. His lungs were full of blood, and his heart was nearly empty. This fact shows that the air was shut off from the lungs before the man died ; and the heart, as in cases of suicidal hanging, continued its action, and pumped the lungs full. His doctors said that Dwight died of congestive chills. There is not a case recorded in which death has occurred from congestive chills in this latitude. Besides, the physicians reported on the day he died that his pulse was normal, and that no fever existed. Dr. Delafield gave it as his opinion that Dwight died of paralysis of the heart. The autopsy showed that the heart was nearly empty. If the heart had been paralyzed, it would have been normally full of blood. Instead of that, it contained but little fluid blood. My belief is, and this inquest will show, that Col. Dwight came to his death by asphyxia. If this inquest is fairly conducted, and the coroner permits a full inquiry, this fact will be demonstrated.' "

The case is still in litigation before the courts ; the legatees of Dwight simply proving death, and throwing the burden of proving cause on the insurance companies.

CHAPTER XV.

PRAISED AND SLANDERED.

A Brigadier-General and Baltimore Editor. — Driving the Surgeons with a Cocked Pistol. — Master of Surgery. — None More Worthy a Soldier's Gratitude. — What Senator McArthur knew. — Bloodiest Pictures in the Book. — Blood-stained Hands. — Base Libels and a Pseudo-Reformer.

In civil life Dr. Swinburne was as outspoken in condemning corruption in local, state, or national government as in military; and having the entire confidence of his fellow-citizens, they looked to him as the physician and surgeon who would cure their political ills, and apply the knife to the rottenness that was infecting the whole body politic, and rout out the disordered members. Of course, this invoked the hatred of his enemies, and involved the doctor in some lively controversies, in which he rose still higher in the minds of the people, and brought to his support many of his old comrades in the civil war, who were ready to defend him against his calumniators. From all parts of the State came letters praising the patriotic doctor.

John Meredith Read, formerly United-States consul-general to France and Algeria, and acting German consul-general, and for six years United-States minister to Greece, writes under date of March last (1885), to a friend, —

"Dear Sir, — You have referred to my services as consul-general of the United States, and acting German consul-general in France, during the Franco-German war, and particularly to the period when I was shut up in Paris during the siege and the commune.

"Among my most interesting recollections of the siege are those connected with the American ambulance, and especially with its distinguished head, Dr. John Swinburne, who in genius, common sense, executive talents, and the practical success of his theories, surpassed the greatest surgical lights assembled in the beleaguered capital. Dr. Swinburne at that time revolutionized surgery in France to such a degree, that the maimed and wounded French officers and soldiers invariably begged to be carried to him in preference to their own ambulances. The wounded German prisoners were equally outspoken. His unparalleled success in the treatment of the most difficult and dangerous cases inspired an unwavering faith in his judgment, while his uniform kindness implanted an affectionate respect in the hearts of the distressed.

"Dr. Swinburne's work in Paris placed him in the list of international benefactors."

Le Docteur W. S. Mosetig, *professeur de chirurgie agrégé à la faculté de Vienne (Autriche)*, and who was in charge, under Baron Larry, of the Austrian ambulance in Paris during the siege, wrote from Vienna to Dr. Swinburne, as the latter was about to leave Paris, —

"I thank you very much for your amiable letter, and for your kind promise of sending to me some photographs of several interesting cases of your ambulance in Paris. I will accept them with the greatest pleasure. As I do not know our consul in Milan, I beg you to send directly by the post the photographs, to the care of my address. I mentioned your model ambulance in my general report, and will especially write of your excellent surgery.

"I am sorry you are not passing Vienna. Be so kind as to accept, with my friendly compliments, my photograph as a token of mine, and as a remembrance of the good time we passed last winter in Paris.

"Excuse my bad writing, and be assured of my greatest esteem."

On a visit to the American ambulance, Professor Mustig wrote on the register, "We have the best ambulance in Paris, but yours is better than ours."

Before leaving Paris, Dr. Swinburne applied to J. Marion Sims for letters of introduction to some of the leading physicians and surgeons of England. Dr. Sims, who inaugurated the Woman's Hospital in New York, of whom the American profession may justly feel proud, had by his skill, and the practice of the same conservative surgery practised by Dr. Swinburne prior to the war, won a place among the highest

in his profession in Europe. He replied, " You require no
introductory letters in Europe, your fame is too well known:
all that is required is to announce your name, and you will
be gladly received." He, however, gave him letters, as requested, the substance of a few of which is appended. He
wrote, —

" To Sir Henry Thompson.

" This will introduce my friend, Dr. John Swinburne of
New York, late surgeon-in-chief of the American ambulance
at Paris, and one of our most distinguished surgeons. I hope
you will be able to show him something of your marvellous
operations."

" To Spencer Wells.

" This will introduce my friend, Dr. John Swinburne of
New York. No man in America stands higher as a surgeon.
He was in Paris during the siege as surgeon-in-chief of the
American ambulance, where he rendered, as you well know,
great service. I hope you will have something to show him
during his brief sojourn in London."

" To Barnard Holt.

" Allow me to introduce my friend, Dr. Swinburne of New
York, one of our most eminent surgeons, and lately surgeon-
in-chief of the American ambulance in Paris. I am sure it
will give you pleasure to show the doctor some of your
peculiar operations during his short stay in London."

" To Earnest Hart.

" Of course, you know all about my friend, Dr. Swinburne,
lately surgeon-in-chief of the American ambulance, and one
of the most distinguished surgeons in Paris. He will remain,
perhaps, a month in London. Let me beg you as a personal
favor to place the doctor in proper relations with such of our
brethren as he would like to meet."

Dr. Sims was the only other surgeon engaged in the war,
besides Dr. Swinburne, on whom the French Government
conferred the distinction of knight of the Legion of Honor.
In 1876, four years after Dr. Swinburne's return to Albany
from Europe, he had a controversy with the faculty of the
Albany Medical College because of his charging malpractice
in a case attended by one of the faculty, which resulted in

the abolishing of his chair in the re-organization. The report of this act reached Europe; and soon after he was invited, through Dr. Sims, to go to London and teach the surgeons of that scientific metropolis of the world how to treat injuries. Two colleges in New York tendered him chairs, and he was also invited to New York to treat fractures in St. Vincent's Hospital. The English surgeons in this instance were like the English judge, who, on hearing one of the bar before him cite the opinions of an American jurist, the late Charles Sumner, interrupted the counsellor to ask if that was the Mr. Sumner who had visited this country (England). On being answered in the affirmative, the judge added, "We will think none the less of the opinion because we have seen and know the man."

Without question, the highest compliment ever paid to the skill of any American surgeon, and to his ennobling characteristics as a man, is contained in a letter from Felix Agnus, late brigadier-general, and now editor of the "Baltimore American," written to a gentleman in Albany. He says, —

"It was the close of the day, June 27, 1862, and the second day of the seven-days' fight before Richmond. The fight had been hotly contested at Gaines's Mills with terrible effect to our arms. My regiment, the fifth New-York (Duryea Zouaves), as history shows, shared the brunt of the many charges and counter-charges. Near evening I was hit by a rebel sharp-shooter, the ball entering my right breast, ricochetting to the right shoulder, which it completely shattered. As a consequence, I was entirely disabled. Comrades carried me from the field to the hospital at Savage Station, where already the dead and dying were forming a large army. I was handled as tenderly as was possible under the circumstances, and placed in a tent with other officers of my regiment. The comrade to my left was dead, and the one to my right was slowly breathing his last. The terrible sight, together with the recollection of the fight, the recent death of so many valued friends, and the realization of my own almost mortal wound, made me feel that my end was near at hand. I was scarcely twenty-one, but had risen from the ranks to the position of lieutenant in a little more than a year. I was proud of my profession, and, with the feelings natural to a young officer in those stirring times, I felt that if I must die, I would hope to do so with my clothes on.

"While brooding over my situation, a young and inexperienced assistant surgeon came to examine my wound. He did so very carefully. He then asked if I had any friends to communicate with. I at once inferred that the case was hopeless. I dictated a letter to the dear ones at home, and then begged and pleaded that my arm should not be cut off, feeling sure that if it was done my life was lost. He disregarded my request. Other young students gathered around, and they all agreed that the case was too good a one to forego the operation. Weak as I was, the thought of my body being used to practise upon, moved me to desperation; and when they returned, with their instruments and assistants, to sever the much-valued arm, a pistol was pointed at them with the warning that they had better keep away if they valued their lives. I well remember with what haste they vacated the tent; for they saw that the hammer was cocked, and that I was terribly in earnest. I have never regretted my action, for it proved the saving of my life. I was at once reported to the medical director, who proved to be none other than your worthy and distinguished fellow-citizen, Dr. John Swinburne. He came to me in a kindly and cheerful manner, and assured me that no harm should be done. He examined my wound, and assured me that he could save my arm and my life. I could not mistrust his honest face, and I at once placed myself under his care. That night, by candle-light, one of the most skilful operations ever performed, up to that time, was successfully performed on me. Dr. Swinburne, after making a cross-like incision of from six to eight inches long, and after turning the flesh over, carefully sawed off my entire right-shoulder joint and about four inches of the right-arm bone, leaving nothing but the muscle. His prediction came true. I recovered, and to-day I feel that I owe my life and my arm, which is still sound and useful, to this master of surgery.

"From this time began my acquaintance with a man who not only showed his great eminence in a great profession, but whom I, as well as every other soldier who knew him, have held in the highest admiration for his many noble qualities of head and heart. During my convalescence of four months, I grew to know him well, and there is no one I ever met during the whole war whom I consider more worthy of a soldier's gratitude and esteem. He is every inch a man, and his work in the brave struggle of brave men for the preservation of the Union entitles him to every iota of credit and honor and heroism that soldiers win who carry the musket and wield the sabre.

"To show you the vigor and power of that same arm, I subscribe myself,

Yours very truly,

FELIX AGNUS,

Late Brigadier-General U.S.V.

The chirography of this letter is in an off-hand style; and if it were equalled by one-tenth the editorial writers of the press, it would bring joy, if not to the angels of heaven, to the newspaper printers in the upper floors of our daily newspaper-press establishments.

Of a case somewhat similar to this one quoted, the gentleman upon whom the operation was performed, in grateful remembrance, wrote several years afterwards to Dr. Swinburne from Batavia, N.Y., as follows: —

Dr. Swinburne, Albany, N.Y.

Dear Sir, — It has been many years since we met; and time, which makes so many changes, has perhaps driven me from your memory, but I have reason to remember you. I left the army in 1870, and entered the Medical College at Washington, and am now one of the knights of the scalpel, plying my vocation upon any miserable sinner who may favor me with a call. I am now visiting my good mother at this place, and shall remain until after the election, when I shall return to Washington. Should you still be residing in Albany, and would care to see one of your first "conservative surgical" patients, will do myself the honor to call on my way to New York, *en route* for Washington. I don't think you would know me, for ten years has made a great change. I think I would recognize both yourself and Mrs. Swinburne, notwithstanding our short acquaintance.

Very respectfully,

CHARLES F. RAND,

*Late Company K, Twelfth Regiment New-York Volunteers,
with a resection of head of humerus.*

Ex-Senator MacArthur of Rensselaer County, who was a brigade quartermaster during the war, and was at Savage Station at the time of the retreat, and who has watched with interest the course of Dr. Swinburne since that time, gave a very interesting history of the scenes he there witnessed, and also a cutting satire on the course pursued by some of the "stays-at-home," in an article published in the Troy "Budget," of which he is editor and proprietor, on April 6, 1884. The senator, in that article, said, under the head of "What we know of Mayor Swinburne," —

"When McClellan was fighting his men in front of Richmond, there was a call for volunteer surgeons from the North to assist the medical corps, which had been overworked night and day with attending the victims of Chickahominy fever and rebel bullets, and which corps was not sufficiently strong to minister to the needs of the local sick and wounded soldiers. During the night which closed over the last day's fight at Fair Oaks, the writer hereof, who was flat on his back with Chickahominy fever, received an order to have the wagons of the command under which he served loaded that night with ammunition, rations for the soldiers, and forage for the horses; to burn all the tents and other quartermaster's stores and property in his charge; and to take his wagon-train at once to the James River with all possible speed, and to there await further orders. With the bulk of the enemy in front, the dreaded Stonewall Jackson was menacing, on the north, McClellan's right flank. The writer hereof, not having eaten any thing for two or three days, finding it impossible to keep any thing on his stomach, in the early gray of the morning went over to the headquarters of the medical corps to see Dr. Swinburne, who had come at the call of his country as a volunteer surgeon while one of the Fair-Oaks battles was raging. Arriving at the plateau near the railroad-station, where the medical corps was stationed, the awful sight that met his eyes was one of the 'bloodiest pictures in the book' of battles ever beheld. There were one or two acres of ground covered with surgeons' tables, on which the surgeons had been operating all through the night on the wounded of the Union army who had been stricken down in the last and most destructive battle of the conflict of Fair Oaks, fought on the day previous, the result of which was disastrous to McClellan's army, and which led to his 'change of base,' and retreat to the James River. The canvas flies of wall-tents had been stretched over the operating-tables; but the sides and ends of the tables were open, with no barrier between them and the open air. The tables had been lighted with candles, lanterns, and torches, rudely improvised to light the bloody work which the surgeons had in hand. Many of these lights were still flickering in the early gray of that morning. The surgeons had been operating on the wounded all through that dreadful night. As fast as the wounded, who were constantly being brought in, left the hands of the surgeon, if they were not in imminent danger of soon dying, they were conveyed on stretchers to platform-cars near by, and went by railroad to the White House, on the Pamunkey River, thence to be conveyed to Washington hospitals. Such as could not be thus moved were put in hospital tents near by, and cared for as best they could be under the circumstances. All night long the surgeons were at work with the wounded on each of these one or two of the operating-tables, and all night long the trains of platform-cars were run to the White House with their freights of wounded and maimed soldiers. Many a poor fellow, minus an arm or a leg, was carried off by the wounded train during the night, among them Capt. Arts of the Second New-York Volunteers, with one leg off, and how many more Troy soldiers we don't know. On, about, and under the operating-tables that morning were legs and arms, amputated during the night, and bits of flesh, and ensanguined garments, pools of human blood being absorbed in the earth; and the tables were gory red with the life-streams from loyal wounded soldiers. The scene was ghastly, sickening, and horrid beyond description. That plateau had all the appearances of a vast human slaughter-house, where soldiers had been dismembered of their limbs, or cut up piecemeal, as if in a butcher's shop. When Dr. Swinburne was found, he was washing his blood-stained hands after an all-night's work at the surgeon's table. He gave the writer some medicine to keep him up until he could take the wagon-train to the James River,. spoke words of cheer and encouragement, and, as the Union army was to abandon Fair Oaks and retreat down the peninsula, he said he proposed not to desert the wounded who remained there, and had not been carried to the White House, but to stay, to be taken prisoner by the Rebels, and to do whatever he could to minister to the wants and needs of the wounded. He said this would be at great sacrifice to his private interests at home, but that he could not bear to hand these poor wounded Union soldiers to the 'tender mercies' and care of Rebel surgeons, with no friendly person left to minister to their wants in the dreadful circumstances under which the ill fortunes of war had placed them. And he did stay by them, was taken prisoner, was conveyed with the wounded to Richmond, and never deserted or abandoned them until every man of them was provided for, with as comfortable ease and medical and hospital attendance as could possibly be obtained, under the circumstances, from the Rebel authorities. If we remember rightly, he was assigned as the surgeon having the chief charge of these wounded Union prisoners. Whether he was allowed to return through the Union lines when his mission was accomplished, or whether he was held as a prisoner until exchanged, we have forgotten. For all these patriotic services, Dr. Swinburne never received, if he ever received any pay, any thing like professional compensation. At most, he could have received only the meagre compensation of an army surgeon, and we doubt if he ever got that.

"Dr. Swinburne is now the Republican and people's candidate for mayor of Albany. He was elected in 1882, but was counted out in favor of Nolan. At the time, all the decenter portion of Albany was greatly indignant over the Nolan swindle. Lawyer Hale addressed public meetings, and mouthed indignant sentiments against the gross frauds by which Swinburne was cheated out of his office of mayor. According to the 'Express,' he and others 'were profuse in their tender services to bring about a correction of the abuses of which they, and good citizens generally, complained. One lawyer (Hale) now presents a bill of nearly $4,000, which he asks the doctor to pay. Another modestly requests the doctor to hand him over $1,500.' The 'Express' says, —

"'It is a pretty hard thing to ask a man to pay out in lawyers' fees and costs, in an action brought to preserve his own and the people's rights, pretty nearly double the sum he receives for salary for the full term of the office when it is finally awarded to him by the courts. It must require "cheek," to say the least, for a lawyer who engages in a case of this nature from alleged patriotic motives, to send in a bill for his "services" amounting to more than a year's salary of the office finally awarded to the plaintiff.'

"Hale got judgment for his $4,000 fees; but, as Swinburne's finances are not in a flourishing condition, he couldn't pay. Now just on the eve of the election, Hale has from time to time been annoying and pulling up Swinburne on supplementary proceeding, with the 'Argus' on hand to take notes and publish every thing that could be construed into a meanness or humiliation against Swinburne. The 'Argus,' with the facilities thus afforded by Hale, has gathered hints by which it is enabled to taunt Swinburne with being 'an arrant debt-dodger,' and as a man who 'would jump into the assigned carriage, crack the pawned whip, and start up the hypothecated horses, to go through the same performances elsewhere.' If there ever has been any thing meaner, viler, or more despicable, done in a political canvass than the parts being enacted by Lawyer Hale, who claims to be a Republican, and by the 'Argus,' we have never heard of it. A pool of $40,000, of which the Democratic candidate for mayor is said to furnish $8,000, is reported to have been raised to beat Swinburne. While during the war the patriotic Matthew Hale remained vigorously at home in Essex County, Dr. Swinburne was volunteering, and taking chances of losing his life, as we have shown above, and he wasn't charging $4,000 for 'volunteer' services either. The careers of the two men are in striking contrast; and their different records since the war are in equally striking contrast. Dr. Swinburne has been maintaining, at his own expense, a medical dispensary at a great cost, where all the poor who were unable to pay were furnished with medical treatment and medicines without cost. During all this time Lawyer Hale's principal benevolent and patriotic endeavors appear to have been in the direction of piling up $4,000 fee-bills against clients. Quite a difference!

"Every soldier voter, every patriotic citizen, and every lover of fair play, in Albany, it seems to us, ought to support, under the above circumstances, Dr. Swinburne for mayor, for patriotic reasons as well as to rebuke those who taunt a public benefactor with his poverty."

At the time Dr. Swinburne tendered his services to Gov. Morgan as a volunteer surgeon, and received his commission, he was possessed of considerable property, and, through a large growing and lucrative practice, was on the road to a fortune. In relinquishing these comforts and inviting prospects, he understood the dangers that were to surround him; that he was not going as a pleasure-seeker, but into the jaws of death; and to provide against any unnecessary litigation or disputes before a surrogate or in a court of equity, in case of his death, he transferred all his property, unembarrassed by any financial claims, to his wife, and children of tender age. Recently, however, the "Albany Argus," a paper that persisted in declaring the unholy war a failure when the doctor was at the front, charged that the property was transferred to avoid the payment of claims against him, — a most disgraceful libel, and without any foundation, the only real or imaginary financial claim of any description against him being the one now under trial. This is made by a *pseudo-reformer*, Matthew Hale, a lawyer who sues to recover $4,000 counsel-fees for services in a *quo warranto* action of John Swinburne against Michael Nolan for the office of mayor of the city of Albany, to which the doctor was elected in 1882, but out of which he was defrauded. The plaintiff lawyer, at the time, was a very loud and apparently enthusiastic Republican reformer, and advocate of good government, and very vehement and positive in denouncing the political ring that ruled Albany, and was afterwards an unsuccessful candidate for Supreme-Court justice. At the last election he was a Democratic reformer, working with the ring he had so denounced as corrupt. Witnesses swear he was a volunteer lawyer in the case; and certain it is he received no retaining-fee as counsel, and did make a speech at an indignation meeting, outstripping all the others present in his protestations of the sacrifices he was ready to make to right this terrible wrong, punish fraud, protect the purity of the ballot-box, and vindicate the rights of the people. After having failed for nearly three-quarters of the term in having the case brought to trial, another lawyer, the late Henry Smith, succeeded in accomplishing in less than one month what Hale failed to do in a year and a half, but for which services the latter demanded $4,000, — a larger sum than the salary received by Dr. Swinburne as mayor. On this is based the only charge the enemies of good government were able to advance against this loyal citizen in the last congressional campaign.

While Dr. Swinburne was health-officer of the port of New York, his arrangements somewhat interfered with the *exclusive* privileges of the " New-York Herald " in gathering ship news; for which that journal became very indignant, and, besides resorting to rather questionable means to injure the health-officer, published some scurrilous articles on his administration. These schemes the doctor soon discovered and frustrated; and the " Herald's " venom was expended in vain on the doctor, and re-acted on that journal. An article in the " Rochester Democrat," under date of Aug. 20, 1868, referring to this controversy, said, —

" Amid the various signs which we have of ' hanging the " Herald," ' we occasionally see something in its management which looks like hanging itself. One of these things is its attack on John Swinburne, health-officer of this port. Before the ' Herald ' began its attack, it would have done well to take a look at its antagonist. Dr. Swinburne has a well-knit frame, muscular, and full of strength and vitality: he is a small Hercules, with a pleasant countenance, but one so full of purpose and determination that its slightest frown reveals the unconquerable will. We read this in Swinburne when we first saw him, many years ago, and time has only strengthened our conviction. He came to Albany a young physician from St. Lawrence County, without friends or patronage, but full of determination. In due time he was called to examine a case of sudden death. A woman who went to bed well was found dead in bed the next morning. Before retiring she had eaten a supper; but the next morning her bowels were empty. The bedroom was found freshly mopped, and the bed in decent order. Her husband, who slept with her, said she died in the night, and he could throw no light on the subject; while his parents, at whose house the couple were living, were equally unable to afford information. John Swinburne immediately saw through the mystery. The woman had been poisoned during the night by her husband, and the parents were in some degree cognizant of it; for the cleansing of the room after the effect of the poison was over proved this. The husband was arrested; and, with that peculiar fatality which attends guilt, he replied, when he learned that a *post-mortem* examination was to be held, ' They will find no arsenic there.' The stomach was empty, but Swinburne found traces of aconite. On his testimony the man was indicted, and on his testimony he was hanged. A fierce effort was made by the defence to break down Swinburne's professional character. He was cross-examined in the most bewildering manner, and medical testimony was brought to bear against him; but the lawyers had to learn a new lesson of calm determination as they saw John Swinburne ride through the storm. It was a conflict in which his reputation, as well as the cause of justice, were at stake; and he triumphed. Such was the famous Hendrickson case; and, now that it is past, no one has ever uttered a doubt of the guilt of

John Hendrickson.   Had he been matched against any other surgeon, he might have escaped; but in Swinburne's hands his doom was sealed.   Hendrickson was a desperate character, and had determined to get rid of a wife whom he had abused, and whom he hated.   He resolved on poison, and selected one with which the medical faculty is not generally familiar. This was aconite.   The trial was marked by a wide range of false swearing on the part of the prisoner's friends, who were important witnesses, inasmuch as the woman died in their house.   But justice penetrated the mystery : the murderer was hanged, and Swinburne was looked on as a new power in the medical world.

"A similar case occurred subsequently in St. Lawrence County.   A brutal husband, who had been long notorious for his abuse of his wife, finished his crime by murdering her in a manner more ingenious even than by poison.   He choked the woman to death, and then placed her in bed and cut her throat, giving out that she had committed suicide.   This theory was accepted by a coroner's jury ; but, suspicion being aroused, the theory was upset by Swinburne, who demonstrated its impossibility in the clearest manner.

"During the war, Dr. Swinburne left his practice, and volunteered to visit Richmond in order to attend to the sick prisoners from the Federal armies, — a service in which several other distinguished surgeons bore part."

The most appropriate conclusion, we believe, with which to close this chapter, is to copy an editorial article from the "Medical and Surgical Reporter" of August, 1862, as follows : —

"It will be remembered that Dr. John Swinburne of Albany, who had gone to the peninsula on special service, was one of the surgeons who, in the retreat of our army from before Richmond, remained with our wounded.   He was on duty; in charge, we believe, of the field hospital at Savage Station.   A great many of the wounded, who were captured by the insurgents, and who were exchanged or paroled, have been sent to the hospitals in this city [Philadelphia]. They uniformly speak of Dr. Swinburne, and of the other surgeons, in terms of the greatest admiration and respect for their noble and disinterested devotion to their welfare.   In an especial manner they have commended Dr. Swinburne for his *conservative* surgery.   One man exultingly showed us an arm, which he declared would soon be as good as ever, and said, 'If it had not been for Dr. Swinburne, I would have lost that arm, and yet it has been saved in spite of Richmond prisons.' Another told of the doctor's indignation when he found that a limb, on which he was going to perform the operation of resection to save it, had been amputated by a zealous subordinate, while he was attending to pressing duties elsewhere. It would be well for our soldiers if Dr. Swinburne's conservative ideas were more prevalent among our army surgeons."

CHAPTER XVI.

THE FIGHTING DOCTOR.

THE assertion of the politicians when speaking of the fitness of men eminent in the professions for political positions, with whom they do not agree politically, — that they are excellent surgeons, physicians, or theologians, but because of their education and training are not adapted to manage State affairs, — is no more applicable to those two than it would be to the profession of the law or to journalism. While Dr. Swinburne was mayor of the city of Albany, he exhibited a greater knowledge of the necessities of the people, and a degree of executive ability far superior to many of his predecessors. On this question, the "American Medical Times" has an article that answers fully this objection. It says, —

"The medical profession is, for the most part, committed to the belief that its duties are limited to the healing of the sick. If a physician directs special attention to any other subject, he is regarded as departing from his legitimate duties, and in a certain degree abandoning his profession. A known devotion to any branch of the physical sciences or to literature is most damaging; but if he engage, however remotely, in any secular business, he is at once 'read out' of the profession. We lately heard Professor Simpson of Edinburgh pronounced 'lost to the profession' by a half-score of medical gentlemen because he had addressed his class of medical students on their religious interests. But on no subject is there such a unanimous opinion in the profession as that a medical man is lost if he gives his attention to political questions. Medical and political science are regarded as so

240

entirely incompatible, that the pursuit of one is thought to disqualify for the pursuit of the other.

"We believe, however, that a just code of medical ethics would comprehend a much wider field of duties than is generally understood. It should measure the competency of physicians on all questions which concern humanity. Man is the object of all our study: all his interests are within our scope; every thing that can ameliorate his moral as well as physical condition falls within our domain. Consequently medicine is one of the tributaries of social science or general politics. Times are long passed when we were confounded with barbers and servants, and when army surgeons or physicians were considered little above the mercenaries employed à la suite of armies. Remnants of the humiliation of science in barbarous times can still be traced in the ordinances of European armies. But science is now fast dispelling those clouds, taking a high and most influential position in society and in the State. The question which we wish to urge is, Shall that influence be extended at all times, and under all circumstances, for the advancement of man's social and political as well as physical welfare?

"Virchow, the most distinguished representative of our profession, the leading medical mind of Europe, is a member of the Prussian Chamber of Deputies. He accepted unhesitatingly an election by the people, and is the leader of the liberal party. He has not forsaken his profession, but is as much absorbed as ever in his histological investigations. The medical sciences have not lost an ardent cultivator, while the cause of popular liberty and of human rights has gained an earnest advocate. Nélaton, the distinguished French surgeon, was recently offered a nomination for a seat in the French Parliament by the working-classes, but he declined the honor. He alleges in justification of his conduct that he was only a surgeon, and could not on that account have legislative abilities.

"No liberal mind can doubt which of these two medical gentlemen has done his duty, and accepted all the high trusts which have been committed to his care, whether as a citizen or a medical man. Virchow is adding new lustre to a fame which is already world-wide and of dazzling brilliancy. His name will be recorded high on the roll of those legislators who have advanced the civil and political interests of the people. Nélaton has failed to prove himself endowed with those great qualities of heart which distinguished Virchow. In declining the proffered appointment of the people, he al-

lied himself with the aristocracy, which ignore the claims of
the laboring classes.

" We rejoice in the example which Virchow has placed
before the profession of Europe, and trust its influence will
be felt in the United States.   Here, where a republican form
of government renders even the humblest talent useful, and
gives it a proper weight in the social and political scale,
medical men should accept official positions of trust.   We
cannot too often repeat the instructions of Rush: ' In modern times and in free governments, they (physicians) should
disdain an ignoble silence upon public subjects.'   The American Revolution has rescued physics from its former slavish
rank in society.   For the honor of our profession, it should
be recorded that some of the most intelligent and useful
characters, both in the cabinet and in the field, during the
late war, have been physicians."

It was after the return of Nélaton to Paris from Italy,
whither he had gone to attend to the wound of Garibaldi,
that the working-men of Paris tendered him the nomination
as a member of the Chamber of Deputies, which he declined
on the ground that he had no taste for politics.   They supposed he was in full sympathy with the people in every effort
to better their condition.   Actuated by the same motives, the
people of the city of Albany, groaning under the oppressive
taxation and the misrule of a corrupt and heartless ring, saw
in the great surgeon the patriotic and fearless citizen, who
had in every instance proved his devotion to the masses in
his aims for good government in professional and political
administration, — the man to lead the hosts against the heartless and intrenched enemy.   In 1882 they tendered him, as
the only man able to lead them to victory, the nomination
for mayor of the city of Albany.   He had no taste for politics; but, on the persistent pleading of the people that he
would be their leader out of the dark land of political corruption in which they were held, he accepted for their sake,
in the interest of good government, and entered into the contest with a zeal that won for him the title of " The Fighting
Doctor," — an honorable distinction he has honorably borne
out, not as a ring pugilist, but as a fearless denunciator of
fraud and corruption.   The election resulted in a triumph for

the people, and the choice of their candidate, overcoming the
majorities given the Democratic candidate of 4,376 in 1878,
and 4,693 in 1880. The ring, however, were up to their old
tricks, counted out the doctor, and gave his opponent, Nolan,
118 majority; but the doctor, having espoused the cause of
the people, determined they should have their rights. A
number of gentlemen of the legal profession, and others, volunteered to give their time and efforts to righting the wrong,
and punishing the fraud perpetrators. Among the legal gentlemen were N. C. Moak, James W. Bentley, W. F. Beutler,
the late Hon. Henry Smith, Andrew S. Draper, Fitch J.
Swinburne, Hamilton Harris, and Matthew Hale; the latter,
with other gentlemen, at a public indignation meeting immediately after the election, making speeches denouncing the
fraud, Mr. Hale offering the following preamble and resolutions, which were unanimously adopted : —

Whereas It is charged that an organized and desperate
effort was made at yesterday's election in this city to defeat
the will of the people by fraudulent and criminal practices,
including illegal voting, bribery, ballot-box stuffing, obstruct-
ing lawful voters, excluding witnesses from the polls, false
canvassing, and falsely certifying results; and

Whereas It is further charged that by such fraudulent
and criminal practices Michael N. Nolan, who was defeated,
was falsely made to appear to have a majority over John
Swinburne, who was lawfully elected, by a large majority of
the legal votes cast at said election, to the office of mayor of
the city of Albany: it is

Resolved (1) That the fraudulent and criminal practices
so charged, and all the persons guilty of the same, and all
persons who have instigated, connived at, excused, or justified
the perpetrators of such offences, deserve and should receive
the detestation and denunciation of every good citizen, of
whatever party, and the severest punishment provided for
them by law;

(2) That to permit such crimes to go unpunished, and the
person or persons in whose interests they have been committed to retain unmolested the offices to which they have
not been elected, but to which they have, by the aid of such
frauds and felony, been falsely declared to be entitled, would
be to renounce popular sovereignty, and to submit to a despot-

ism all the more galling because it is irresponsible, and assumes the mask of democracy;

(3) That such charges should be thoroughly investigated in appropriate criminal and civil proceedings, to be instituted and prosecuted for the purpose, to the end that the legally expressed will of the people may be ascertained and enforced, and that the guilty, whether high or low in position, may be punished;

(4) That we pledge ourselves, so far as our means and circumstances may permit, to contribute our time, our energies, and our money. to carry out the spirit of these resolutions, to defeat the apparent conspiracy against the ballot-box, to vindicate the will of the people, and to punish those guilty of the offences charged, which are the greatest possible crimes against a free government.

The resolutions were the sentiments of the people of Albany, represented in the ten thousand gathered at the indignation meeting. The esteem of the masses, and the confidence in which the doctor was held at that time, were no sudden outgrowth, but had taken root years before, and became more deep and intense as the years rolled on. In 1872, Ex-Speaker Callicott, editor of the "Albany Times," had this complimentary notice of the doctor and his abilities: —

" Dr. John Swinburne was born in Denmark, Lewis County. N.Y., in 1821. His father was a large farmer and merchant, and highly respected in that county. His star of progress began in the cold winds of envy and detraction, and wild storms of opposition hedged his pathway. But Dr. Swinburne was a man who grew the faster by opposition. The famous Hendrickson trial brought out Dr. Swinburne in a single-handed fight with the medical profession. The opposition was long and persistent, but he won at last; and with success came fame and fortune. Then came the Budge trial and its famous points of medical jurisprudence, in which he measured swords with the great 'medical head-lights' of the country, and came off victor.

" From this time Dr. Swinburne has been recognized as a medical genius, a bold and skilful surgeon, and a profound thinker, marking out new paths which are now followed by the foremost men of the profession.

" His administration at quarantine was a grand triumph over

all opposition, and placed him among the greatest organizers and managers that had ever controlled sanitary affairs in this country.

"In 1870 he was at the head of the American Ambulance Corps at the siege of Paris, and received the cross of the Legion of Honor for bravery and skill. This was the first time any American ever received such a compliment.

"Dr. Swinburne has shown a great executive ability, as well as scientific skill. His associations with several large enterprises in this city, and in the Far West, reveal the immense activity of the man, and show that he is a man for the people, alive to all their interests.

"In surgical and medical jurisprudence he has introduced important changes, and made discoveries which have now become practical all over the world. As a leader, he has shown intense activity, and a ready perception of men and events, united with a clear comprehension of the exact requirements of the times."

Mr. Callicott is recognized by all who know him as not only one of the ablest, but fairest, editorial writers and journalistic managers in the State, and true to the principles of his party (Democratic). During the last campaign, while giving a loyal support to his ticket, and having one of the very best men in the party on that ticket for Congress, he seemed, like the mass of his fellow-citizens, to have grown in appreciation of the doctor's "great executive abilities," and had not a syllable to utter against the Republican nominee for Congress, — Dr. John Swinburne. It was but natural that the Republican organs should contain many flattering panegyrics of their candidate, Dr. Swinburne, which are made the more important because of this commendation from an opposite political editor, of whom the "Express," always a firm Republican paper, said, —

"Mr. Callicott is unquestionably the most accomplished Democratic editor in this section of the State. He is also very cautious and conservative, and does not make assertions without understanding the subject thoroughly."

In 1880, when the connection of the doctor with the Albany College terminated, the news went over the land; and several applications were made to him to accept a professor's chair in other cities and institutions of learning, one of them being from London, Eng. He was seriously considering one of these invitations, and had about determined to accept, when the citizens of Albany, learning this fact, became fearful they were to lose the man they had known nearly forty years, and, bestirring themselves to avert such a "misfortune to the community," presented him with the following petition, which was published in the " Albany Journal " of July 22, 1880 : —

To Dr. John Swinburne.

Dear Sir, — Learning that you are considering proposals to engage in the practice and teaching of your profession elsewhere, the undersigned urge you not to accept such proposals, but to remain here.

We assure you that, whatever impressions you may have received on the subject, the people of Albany know and appreciate your great skill, and the generous use you have made of it to heal, without charge, thousands who could not pay for such service; that your fellow-citizens are proud of your just fame, and of the credit it reflects on our city, and would deplore your departure as a loss to the profession and a misfortune to the community.

Hoping that this expression of our feelings may lead you to remain with us, we are

Sincerely yours,

Matthew Hale, Erastus Corning, Joseph H. Ramsey, Hamilton Harris, Edmund L. Judson, Lyman J. Lloyd, Barclay Jermain, A. M. Brumaghim, Albert Wing, H. S. Van Santford, Eli Perry, Adam Van Allen, W. Dey Ermand, Charles S. Many, Robert C. Blackall, John H. Trowbridge, John Clemishire, Jacob Messenger, Thomas P. Rudd, E. Countryman, L. M. Van Santvoord, Benjamin Payn, Wm. G. Weed, W. S. Hevenor, A. C. Judson, D. Cady Herrick, Edward J. Boughton, John S. Dickerman, Geo. Dawson, James T. Story, Edwy L. Taylor, Jas. A. Houck, W. Frothingham, Daniel Casey, Thomas H. Ferris, Walter McEwen, Charles D. Rathbone, Sylvanus H. Sweet, Peter Kinnear, William Doyle, E. D. Ronan, Andrew J. Colvin, Geo. A. Birch, J. W. Mattice, R. R. Thompson, George H. Treadwell, William S. Paddock, Johnston & Reilly, A. S. Draper, John E. Page, Isaac W. Vrooman, Alden Chester, John C. Feltman, J. S. Robbins, J. McCann, H. C. Birch, Abram

Van Vechten, Edward J. Meegan, H. Dorr, J. R. Benton, S. G. Rice, H. McBride, John W. Van Valkenburgh, R. M. Griffin, Robert Scott, Lansing Hotaling, Thomas D. Coleman, William H. Haskell, William Thornton, Galen R. Hitt, John H. Farrell, D. L. La Monte, H. P. Prime, Henry T. Bradt, Robert Strain, John Pladwell, William H. Low, Franklin W. Miller, Jonathan Tenney, Isban Hess, George W. Coonley, Charles E. Burgess, Walter S. Brown, John T. Gorman, Peter Snyder, Theodore D. Smith, jun., William Casey, Thomas P. Lynch, Frederick Andes, Richard B. Rock, William A. Donahoe, J. Van Wormer & Co., Jacob H. Ten Eyck, Ignatius Wiley, George Weber, Richard Bortle, A. B. Pratt, George Downing, Frederick U. Bressler, John W. McNamara, and two thousand others.

To this petition the doctor replied, —

GENTLEMEN, — In reply to your kind and friendly letter requesting me not to leave Albany, or abandon my work here, I have to say it is true that I am considering propositions for the teaching and practice of my profession elsewhere. It is but fair to state the reasons therefor. On my return to this city in 1871, after an absence of seven years, I was warmly welcomed by the profession; and sought to show the great advance that could be made in surgery by the use of conservative modes, preferring to do this in the place where my professional career began : in other words, having long known that it was but rarely needful to cut off an injured limb, that the maimed member could almost always be saved; and feeling that to despoil, deform, or to perpetuate deformity in any patient, however poor, of a limb which could by reasonable means be saved, was wrong, and not in accord with the object of our profession, — I undertook to prove, on a scale large enough to obtain conclusive results, that this harm could be avoided. I can only say my efforts have been misunderstood. It is needless to refer to the various differences which have arisen between myself and other members of the profession, by which the conclusion to seek broader fields and more liberal minds have been forced upon me. The public know, and can judge for themselves. My work has not been done in the dark, and I leave it to the verdict that time may bestow. I should, in justification to myself, add, that, at the request of some of the profession, I entered upon my work without a desire to obtain a lucrative practice. What has been done, has been done for the poor, without charge to them, but necessarily entailing large expense upon myself. But that very fact alone has been used against me ; and notwithstanding results obtained by my methods of treatment, of which I may rightly be proud, my course has been misrepresented, and every endeavor made to retard the work. For these reasons, therefore, I have considered the oft-repeated request to go elsewhere.

Allow me to assure you, gentlemen, of my highest regard for you personally, and, adding my thanks for your letter, to sign myself,

Yours very truly,
JOHN SWINBURNE.

This petition, signed by the leading men of every profession and industry in Albany, prevailed with the doctor ; and among the names of those still living are found his truest and warmest supporters, the only exception among them known to express different views from those then entertained being the first to appear on the petition, Matthew Hale. This opposition, it is believed by a large portion of the people, was induced by the appointment of the late Hon. Henry Smith. a lawyer in whom the doctor recognized integrity and ability, as corporation counsel, instead of appointing Mr. Hale.

To decide the questions, whether the purity of the ballot-box should be maintained, the rights of the people vindicated, and fraud punished, criminal proceedings were commenced in the courts the next day, and followed by a civil proceeding in *quo warranto.* to determine by what authority the "counted-in" mayor held the office. In these proceedings it was generally believed the lawyers in the case were acting *pro bono publico ;* and from the declarations of Mr. Hale, both in public and private, his strong denunciations of the corrupt ring that ruled the city, his protestations as an honorable citizen in favor of good government, and the sending of the fraud perpetrators to prison, he was especially considered a reformer working for the object he professed to have so dear at heart, when he pledged himself, publicly, " to contribute our time, money, and energies, to defeat the apparent conspiracy against the ballot-box, to vindicate the will of the people, and to punish those guilty of the offences charged, which are the greatest possible crimes against a free government." When Mr. Hale made this declaration, and that to submit to the frauds " would be to renounce popular sovereignty, and to submit to a despotism all the more galling because it is irresponsible, and assumes the mask of Democracy," it was thought he was speaking as a citizen prompted by patriotism, and not as a lawyer agitating for a lawsuit in which he was to have a four-thousand-dollar fee from a client who was contesting an election in the interests of the people, and not for selfish ends. Yet the sequel to his action, then, — Mr. Hale's becoming a reformer at the last general election, deserting the party with whom he had worked, or pretended to, for good government; and the overthrowing of the corrupt ring which ruled Albany; and affiliating politically with the very ring whom he declared " deserve and should receive the detestation and denunciation of every good citizen of whatever party, and the severest punishment provided for them by law," — naturally leads to the conclusion that his patriotic and political professions were all " bumbcomb." The special reference to this action, as a part of the doctor's first political contest, is made because of the false charges growing out of it, which were handled and published as reports of the trial in the organ of the ring, — the mouthpiece of Mr. Hale's new political associates, — in an attempt to defame the name of Albany's most popular, honored, and philanthropic citizen.

The history of this action of Hale against Swinburne, as we understand it (and we have generally attended the courts officially, and as one interested in the result, because of the doctor's position as a representative of the people), in brief is this. On the morning after election, a consultation was held between several of the lawyers and the doctor, one of the gentlemen terming it a " council of war." It was decided to institute criminal proceedings, to ferret out the frauds, and procure evidence for a *quo warranto* action. Before the recorder the criminal proceedings were carried out, and hundreds of voters, who had been summoned, examined; these proceedings occupying several months. Besides this a thor-

ough canvass of the city had been made. These were all
preliminary, and necessary to obtain the facts on which to
base the *quo warranto* action. All this work was carried
out under the direction of Messrs. Bentley, Beutler, and
Fitch J. Swinburne, and were voluntary acts by these gentlemen, none of whom looked for any compensation from the
doctor, and were working in the interests of the people;
Mr. Hale only appearing once or twice in these proceedings.
When the facts were all accumulated to prove the fraud,
the only apparent labor during the entire litigation. an action
quo warranto was commenced, Mr. Hale assuming the leading part, it being understood among the other counsel that
the papers were to be served at Hale's office, simply as a
matter of convenience. After nearly two-thirds of the term
had expired, in which the opposing counsel were able, by
motions and technicalities, to postpone the trial from time
to time, the late Hon. Henry Smith appeared in court; and,
when another attempt was made to delay, he succeeded in
doing at one session of the court what Mr. Hale failed in
having accomplished in the many months, — that of having
the action set for trial on a definite day. Before that day
arrived, the incumbent, Michael Nolan, seemingly to avoid a
penalty, resigned. The action went by default; and, under
the direction of the Court, the verdict of a jury was taken,
awarding the office to Dr. John Swinburne.

It may be pertinent, here, to add, that the doctor and
others were led to doubt the sincerity of Mr. Hale in the
matter; as he had written, April 27, 1863, a few days before
the action was to be heard in court, in substance, that he
was going out of the city, and that the doctor must have
some one else prepare the case, as he could not get ready.
This, after many months in which he claims to have been engaged in the suit, looked, to be mild in expression, "funny
practice."

On assuming the office of mayor of Albany, the doctor
appointed the Hon. Henry Smith, long the leader of the
Albany bar, corporation counsel. Soon afterwards Mr.
Hale presented the doctor with a bill of four thousand dol-

lars, for alleged legal services in this contest; and in the Supreme Court obtained, without trial, a judgment for that amount, the judge deciding that the answer of the doctor was frivolous.

The next point with Hale was to recover the amount; but he failed to find any property, the doctor having, when he entered the army during the Rebellion, transferred his property to his wife, and children of tender years. Supplementary proceedings were commenced, the doctor placed on the stand, and subjected to insult and abuse by Mr. Hale, who, only four years before, said of the doctor, in a public document, "The people of Albany know and appreciate your great skill, and the generous use you have made of it, to heal, without charge, thousands who could not pay for such service." What a burlesque is presented in Hale asking four thousand dollars for alleged services to right a great outrage perpetrated on the public, from a man who healed, " without charge, thousands who could not pay for such service." All the dirt and vilification, and attempts to make the doctor appear dishonest, that could be construed out of this testimony in supplementary proceedings, was dished up in the " Argus," the ring organ.

Dr. Swinburne pays his debts, and liquidates all just claims against him; but denying any pecuniary obligations, direct or implied, to Hale, he determined to resist what he claimed "extortion." On an appeal to the general term, the decision, that " the answer of Dr. Swinburne was frivolous, was overruled," and the judgment and supplementary proceedings set aside. When the case again came into court, Mr. Hale moved for a reference, alleging that his claim set forth several separate and distinct retainers; that the investigation would involve a long account, and consume much time. On his affidavit and motion, the case was given to three referees. It is, as the case has progressed and facts have been developed. and by the utterances of Mr. Hale himself, becoming a settled conviction in the minds of many, that Mr. Hale knew he had no just claim against Dr. Swinburne, and that he was afraid of a trial in open court before a jury, asserting as his reason

that the doctor hoped to get on the jury, if tried in open court,
"a sprinkling of his patients and political heelers," as the people were termed by Hale.

Before the referees, Mr. Hale has offered proof of but one
retainer, and that the doctor squarely denies. It is admitted
that there was no money then paid; and according to Hale,
and the testimony of the other gentlemen present, nothing
was said about remuneration; the entire consultation being as
to how they should proceed, and what steps should be taken.
No witness has been able to place a value on any separate
service, except Mr. Hale himself, who values the drawing of
an offer of reward for the conviction of the perpetrators of the
frauds at fifty dollars. He could not, or would not, place a
definite value on any other particular or separate service, and
all the witnesses he placed on the stand were equally incapable
of placing any value on any separate service; but, on hypo-
thetical questions propounded by Mr. Hale, they estimated his
services, if they were as he stated, worth four thousand dollars. Two of the lawyers summoned by Hale, who were
counsel for Ex-Mayor Nolan, testified there were no questions of law involved in the *quo warranto* action, as these had
all been settled: the question was simply one of fact, to be
determined by proof of votes. Another thought, according
to Mr. Hale's statement, that his services in the proceedings
were worth four thousand dollars: yet it is understood this
very lawyer thought fifty dollars was ample compensation for
Dr. Swinburne's professional skill and services in attending
his (the lawyer's) son, who had been thrown from a carriage,
and sustained a fracture of the leg; the doctor saving the
limb, and perhaps the life, of the injured young man, as
believed by the family. But then, the difference in the value
of the service of these men of different professions was, that
one was successful in as short a time as possible, while the
other was unsuccessful. The doctor, on oath, denied having
retained Mr. Hale, or that he was to be in any way responsible to him, and never had any intimation that Mr. Hale hoped
to get a fee from him until the case had been in litigation
about a year, when, through one of the other counsel in the

case, Hale sent word to the doctor that he thought he ought to have a thousand dollars. The doctor then declined to pay any money; but Mr. Hale did not withdraw from the suit. It was understood that the money requisite in the action was to be raised by subscription; and some funds had been raised in that manner, Mr. Hale at one time early in the litigation drawing from the treasurer of the Citizens' Committee two hundred dollars. That this was to be the method of raising money is further proven by the fact that a subscription list was drawn by Mr. Hale for that purpose, with the name of his firm second on the list for two hundred and fifty dollars. When Mr. Hale took the prominent part he did, it is said that he understood there were then two thousand dollars in the hands of the Citizens' Committee for this very purpose. The other counsel named, when asked if they had any bills against the doctor, with one exception replied, "No, we have no bills against the doctor." Mr. Moak, a leading Democratic attorney, cordially took a part in counselling, and was always ready to discharge any duty that he might be called to perform in the action, adding that, while he was Democratic in politics, he believed in good government and the protection of the purity of the ballot-box. His interests in the matter were, like all the others excepting Mr. Hale, for the rights of the people. It was no party movement, and was supported by able men of both parties. In his charge against Dr. Swinburne, Matthew Hale has but few sympathizers. After his attempt to injure the doctor, the public rendered two verdicts at the polls, — one defeating Mr. Hale for judge of the Supreme Court; and the other, by electing Dr. Swinburne to Congress by a majority no other man in the country could command, changing the popular vote by over seven thousand. The people believe the doctor is as truthful and firm as he is tender and aggressive. And here it is pertinent to ask a simple question; i.e., If Mr. Hale, in making his application for a reference, swore to the truth as to separate retainers, and could before the referees make no account or swear to but one retainer, did he swear to facts on both occasions? The two statements are contradictory; and, until they are satisfactorily explained, there will exist an impression that there is still need of reformation. A credible and un-impeached witness, a lawyer by profession, testified that Mr. Hale did say, that if Dr. Swinburne had consulted him before appointing Mr. Smith, this suit might never have been com-menced.

The only excuse or explanation we deem necessary in placing this matter here, is to illustrate how shrewdly some men can cover up their real designs, and by a smiling coun-tenance deceive the most penetrating; how men anxious to become popular, and see their names in print, are confounded with their own utterances; how the loudest advocates of reform are not at all times to be believed; how rapidly a defeated aspirant for office can change his political creed, and go into full fellowship with the men he had denounced as fraudulent and corrupt, without their changing or improv-ing morally; and how easy it is for the new convert to find only honest jurors among his new associates, where there are no "patients or political heelers," and to expose the "true inwardness" of the only grounds on which the doctor's ene-mies could draw any thing to say against him in the last campaign, and to indicate how hard it is for a friend of the people to obtain a fair chance to have justice and a public vindication in the courts in a public matter, instead of hav-ing the question relegated to the almost absolute secrecy of a referee's room. The case is still in litigation, and the doctor is fighting for an open trial.

In the issue of May 16, 1884, the "Morning Express" said of this action of Hale against Swinburne, —

"The people of Albany will doubtless remember that, in the charter election of two years ago, Dr. Swinburne was elected to the office of mayor; but by means of a corrupt cabal was prevented from at once assuming the reins of city government. A number of patriotic citizens immediately enlisted in his cause, and proffered their time, their means, and their talents to enable him to secure the office to which he was honestly elected. First and foremost among the num-ber was the Hon. Matthew Hale, and none could excel him in his zeal in the cause of righteousness. The case, however, dragged slowly along; and, for fourteen long months, Dr. Swinburne was knocking in vain at the door of the temple of justice. Finally Hon. Henry Smith was taken into the case, and the blind goddess at once smiled more benignly upon the applicants for justice. The suit was brought to a successful culmination, and ere long the 'Fighting Doctor' was duly installed in office. In due time he appointed his faithful advocate to the best office in his gift. Almost simultaneously with that appointment, a suit was inaugurated by the Hon. Matthew Hale against the doctor for services rendered in the mayoralty proceedings. The value set upon these services were such as to cause most of the people to believe that we had again returned to the golden days of Aladdin. The doctor, of course, demurred paying for 'patriotic' services; and returned an answer to the complaint, setting forth the fact, already familiar to all. that the services of Mr. Hale, as well as other gentlemen, were taken up in the interest of law and order, and were of course gratuitous in their nature. Judge Westbrook granted an order of judgment in favor of Mr. Hale. upon the ground that the answer was frivolous; and also denied a stay of proceedings pending an appeal. The public will remember that Dr. Swinburne was then hauled up before a referee, upon an order of supplementary proceedings, *immediately before election*, and subjected to the grossest sort of an examination, all of which was thoroughly ventilated in certain daily papers of an opposite political faith, with elaborate embellishments added thereto. The examination failed to reveal that Dr. Swinburne was worth four thousand dollars, the sum demanded for the services rendered. Then an order was obtained to bring up Mrs. Swinburne upon supplementary proceedings, the subpœna designating May 29 as the first day for such examination. In the mean time the Hon. Henry Smith appealed the case to the general term, now sitting at Binghamton; and that tribunal, upon Wednesday last, handed down an opinion reversing the order of Judge Westbrook, and denying the motion of Mr. Hale for the relief demanded. This, of course, supports the position assumed by Mr. Smith; and admits that the answer set forth by him to Mr. Hale's complaint was, in legal parlance, 'good.' All further proceedings of a tantalizing nature, of course, will be dropped, and the case tried upon its merits at the next circuit; and it will then be determined whether or not 'patriotic' services are worth the princely sum of four thousand dollars."

Nearly a year after this article was published in the "Express," the case being still in the courts, the Hon. Ira Shafer of New York having been substituted as counsel for Dr. Swinburne, in place of Henry Smith, deceased, the "Citizen" of April 11, had this to say of the controversy, —

"The irrepressible conflict between the people's friend and genuine reformer, Dr. John Swinburne, and the pseudo-reformer, Matthew Hale, still continues; and the end is not yet. With the merits of this case the public are familiar, and need no repetition, further than to remind them that it was Hale who was so loud in his protestations that justice should be done the people, when the fraudulent ring of this city counted out their candidate for mayor, and counted in Michael Nolan. They remember the indignant countenance of Hale as he faced the thousands assembled at the indignation meeting at the old Capitol, and the emphasis with which he read the resolutions declaring it was the duty of the people to give their time and money to right the great wrong, and bring to justice the abettors and perpetrators of the fraud. Not one man in that audience, we venture to assert, ever dreamed, at that time, that Hale was then playing the lawyer under the garb of a patriot, and deceiving the multitude before him. Yet, if he is to be believed, that was just what he was doing; as he recently, in this action to recover four thousand dollars for the services rendered in the suit that followed, testified that he was retained the morning before the speech was made. The case, the people remember, has had many turns in the legal mill, and has been before referees. Mr. Ira Shafer, counsel for Dr. Swinburne, desires, in the interest of his client, that the case should be taken from the referees, and tried in open court, where the public gaze may be upon the proceedings; feeling, as he says, that no jury would be found to render a verdict in favor of Hale, any more than they would think of awarding four thousand dollars to John Hancock for his patriotic act in signing the Declaration of Independence.

"Mr. Hale, afraid, it appears, of public exposure, and that a just public verdict might be rendered, resists this attempt; and, when last the motion to take it from the referees was argued, the addition to the Albany bar demonstrated his ability to abuse his best friends, who had placed so much confidence in him as to vote to elevate him to the Supreme Bench. Some of whom now think it was the interposition of a wise Providence that caused their votes and labor to be in vain. When Mr. Hale asserted that the object of the doctor in having the motion made to take the case from the referees and tried in open court was that he hoped to have on the jury ‘a sprinkling of his patients and political heelers,’ and thus prevent justice, he insulted not only the worthy poor, but a large majority of the voters of this country, who, despite the opposition of Mr. Hale and his associates, and the libellous, scandalous, and defaming stories they circulated about the doctor, gave a public verdict of over three thousand in favor of the doctor at the polls. In the Democratic party are thousands of true and honest men; but when Mr. Hale insinuates that in his new political affiliations alone are to be found honest jurymen, he implies something that is false, and deserving of contempt.

“When he charged the doctor with dishonesty, perjury, and fraud, he made a charge that the people of Albany County know is false. No man charged perjury but him; yet if it is true that Mr. Hale, in making a motion for a reference, swore that there were several retainers, and before the referees could only swear to one account, did he swear to the truth on both occasions? With these contradictions as a matter of record, to put it mildly, does it not come with questionable grace from Mr. Hale to insinuate that the doctor is dishonest, or lacking in integrity and truth? The sympathy, not only of the public but of a very large portion of the bar, is with the doctor.

“The real animus of the suit, it appeared to us, was developed before the referees, when a credible witness testified that Hale said that if the doctor had consulted him before appointing Henry Smith corporation counsel, the suit might never have been commenced. If that is the real cause of Mr. Hale’s fight with the doctor, he should not feel so bad; as he has a number of companions in disappointed hopes of office.

“Really, what an absurd spectacle is presented in this suit! While the men who did the work, and the best counsellors in the case, such as Messrs. N. C. Moak, the late Henry Smith, James F. Bentley, W. F. Beutler, and others engaged in the suit, had no claims to make against the doctor, Mr. Hale, the loudest protestant, asked four thousand dollars for an action won by others, where he failed for fourteen months.

“Will Mr. Hale publicly answer one simple question in this suit? ‘If he expected the doctor to pay the bills, why did he continue in the suit when he said he thought the doctor ought to give him one thousand dollars, which was refused; why did he draw up a petition to raise funds to pay the expenses, heading it with his own firm's name; and why did he send to the treasurer of the Citizens' Committee, Mr. Fort, and draw two hundred dollars for disbursement, instead of sending to the doctor?'"

In disposing for the present of this controversy, an article first published in the "Albany Express," in April, 1884, and republished in another paper, under the title of "Matthew Hale, *alias* Dugald Dalgetty," places the matter so fairly before the public, that it is, we consider, deserving of preservation, that the comparison between these two men may not be forgotten, and is as follows: —

"Two years ago, at the charter election held in this city, Michael N. Nolan and John Swinburne were opposing candidates for the office of mayor. Nolan was the nominee of the Democratic party, while it can hardly be said that Swinburne was the nominee of any party.

"Nolan, as well as the leaders generally of the Democratic party, scorned and laughed heartily at the idea of Swinburne's candidacy. But Swinburne was elected, undoubtedly, by an honest vote of thousands. Yet he was counted out. That this result was accomplished by frauds upon the ballot-box, in every conceivable shape, was freely admitted, and finally abundantly proved; and so fully proved, that Nolan's grip upon the office, after he had clung to it for two-thirds of the term, was wrenched from him. The outrage he had perpetrated upon the people was ended by ignominious resignation; and Swinburne, the rightfully elected, was accorded the place.

"'Bribery,' 'forgery,' 'perjury,' were the terms hurled at the villains who had perpetrated this great crime against the ballot-box. Every honest man was in a state of indignant denunciation, and was unselfish enough to be willing to contribute something towards punishing the villains, and helping Swinburne in the fight, not so much his own, as that of a defrauded people. Chief among these unselfish, patriotic citizens, as was supposed at the time, was Matthew Hale, attorney and counsellor-at-law, a recent annex to the profession, in Albany, from Essex County. Matthew Hale should not forget the conspicuous position he occupied in this preliminary fight of patriotic denunciation. He was in the midst of it from the start, and in the hottest. In all his many speeches on the occasion, at the Capitol park and elsewhere, his was the voice most outspoken against the stupendous frauds by which Nolan was counted into the mayoralty chair. He it was who, at the Capitol park, on the very next night after the election, counselled that the fight was not Swinburne's but the people's; that the battle was not so much for Swinburne as it was to secure and uphold the purity of the franchise.

"'The truth is,' said Hale, 'a crime has been committed against the life of our government. The moment the people sacrifice the principle of an honest ballot, they become slaves, — worse than Russian slaves: they become the slaves of money, which buys men to any crime. That crime was illustrated yesterday. When you said you would have Dr. Swinburne for mayor, it was claimed by conspirators that you should not. Will you submit to it? Let us see that it is stopped. Let each of us, as far as in him lies, work for the result.' 'We will not be dictated to,' exclaimed Hale, in excited, stentorious tones, 'by force and fraud.' Not a word in all this that Hale himself would not go into the patriotic fight except for money. He was then playing the *rôle* of a high-toned patriot; and his own soul seemed to throb with unselfish zeal, which he strove to infuse into the hearts of others. But a change came over the spirit of his patriotic impulses. He was not now, and had not been, battling for justice and a pure ballot. He was now, and had been, fighting for pay, and for pay only. He was become a Dugald Dalgetty; and, Dugald-Dalgetty-like, he would not fight except for pay. And he that would pay most might have his services, and all the fires of his patriotic soul.

"In frankness, Hale should have informed Dr. Swinburne that he had gone back on the patriotic impulses, speeches, and promises, before he went into the fight. The doctor was confiding enough to believe in them; and supposed they were made in sincerity, and from disinterested motives, and not for reward, or expectation of reward of any character, except that reward which springs from the approbation of an exalted conscience.

"Nolan decamped from the ill-obtained office; Swinburne was installed into it; Peckham resigned the office of corporation counsel; Smith was appointed to succeed him by Mayor Swinburne; and Hale soon thereafter commenced edging Dr. Swinburne for pay for services, and finally sued him for four thousand dollars. Who is credulous enough to believe that Matthew Hale would ever have commenced that action had he received the appointment of corporation counsel?

"Well, Hale obtained his judgment because, it seems, Dr. Swinburne did not interpose a sufficient defence. The true defence for the doctor to have interposed was Hale's public speeches and promises.

"They would have established the defence that Hale's services were gratuitous, and publicly offered as such by him in the presence of assembled thousands of witnesses. Hale — discomfited and mad that execution on his judgment for gratuitous services was not collected, had the same returned unsatisfied: and the charter election approaching, and Swinburne likely to be a candidate again for mayor — took supplementary proceedings against him to drive him to payment, by a system of bull-ragging as ungentlemanly as it has been insultingly conducted; and, if that did not answer, then to force the doctor from the field as a candidate for mayor; or, if he persisted in running, then to defeat him, unless he submitted to pay the extortionate demands of Hale.

"But Swinburne was unscared and rebellious; and, as he stood in the way of Democratic success in the mayoralty contest, the 'Argus' and its reporters have been harnessed in to help Hale in his legal conflict with Swinburne, and defeat him in election. And so the 'Argus' has taken up the work of malignity; and for weeks has been engaged in publishing Hale's interviews and Hale's letters in the matter, proclaiming the dishonesty of Swinburne, and the purity, magnanimity, and disinterestedness of Matthew Hale. When has the testimony of a party in supplementary proceedings been taken by a reporter, and his every word, and nod, and smile, and unrest under insulting and provoking questions, before been given to the public through the columns of the 'Argus'? And how studious and persistent have Hale and the 'Argus' been to have Swinburne's examination forced upon the people before election takes place.

"Matthew Hale has been fortunate in finding in the 'Argus' a coadjutor willing and anxious to spread abroad his venom and his malignity against John Swinburne. The working twain may accomplish the doctor's political death; but they will fail to deprive him of the hushed blessings which daily go forth from thousands of wretched poor whom he has benefited, to whom he has ministered with marvellous skill as physician and surgeon without compensation: these neither Matthew Hale nor the 'Argus' can filch from him. And of one thing Matthew Hale may rest assured, that, as Dr. Swinburne promised his services should be gratuitous to these wretched unfortunates, he will not forfeit his word and his honor by charging them four thousand dollars for such services, or any other sum whatever."

Under date of April 5, 1884, a paper published in Albany had this to say of the man who has been and is still vainly trying to injure the reputation of Dr. Swinburne:—

"Hon. Matthew Hale having, on the old Capitol steps, offered his time, energies, and money to right the wrongs of the people in the charter election of 1882, sued for his services in the sum of four thousand dollars, about ten times their value. This seemed a strange thing, but recent developments show that this thing is chronic with Hale. He (Hale) is president of the board of trustees of the First Presbyterian Church. When securing funds to erect their new church on Willett Street, Mr. Hale liberally subscribed a thousand dollars. In payment therefor, it is said, he handed in a receipted bill for 'legal services' for the same amount.

"This information comes from those connected with that church, who also state that the 'legal services' rendered by Hale would have been amply paid for by twenty-five dollars, and that it was fair to suppose that the president of the board of trustees would not make an exorbitant charge. But Church and State are, alike, free plunder to some of the high-toned legal lights."

CHAPTER XVII.

A PLUCKY LEADER.

Unearthing Corruption. — Renominated for Mayor. — Why nominated, and why he accepted. — Defamed and defended. — Remarkable Incident in Politics. — Victorious, and again counted out. — Return from the West. — A Magnificent Reception.

DURING the period that the "Fighting Doctor" was contending in the courts for the mayoralty, developments were made which exhibited the most corrupt and disgraceful state of affairs ever brought to light in the city of Albany: it being clearly demonstrated that nearly three hundred repeaters were used, some of them voting from five to twenty times at the election. It was also brought out that these miserable wretches were the hirelings of corruptionists, most of whom held official positions at the time; and many of them are still in office, some in very high positions. Indictments were found against inspectors, growing out of the investigation; but these have never been prosecuted, and the guilty tamperers with the ballot-box, and fraudulent manipulators of returns, are at liberty to persue their rascally vocations, and repeat their crimes. It was not the doctor's duty to bring these men to justice, nor to prosecute and send to prison, where they ligitimately belonged, the leaders who hired, encouraged, and abetted these fraudulent voters and inspectors. Evidence sufficient was ready to convict them; but these officials, instead of living on prison-fare, are faring sumptuously on public pap, while the superintendent of the penitentiary, and the contractors who employ cheap convict-labor, are becoming rich on the work of dishonest men, to the injury of honest labor. The success of the doctor in fighting the corruptionists, and because of the reform he had inaugurated in the civil government. and the general shaking-up he gave the departments, induced the citizens, in 1884, to re-nominate him for mayor, notwithstanding the fact that the criminals who worked the frauds at the former election were still in power, and would use even more desperate efforts than before. To oppose the doctor, the Democratic ring must have a candidate who would come down heavy for the corruption fund, and satisfy the "better element" of the party. The "better element" did not mean the honest voters, but that class who believed in caste, and disdained any man who was poor, or sympathized with the poor.

A very natural question with many at that time, even in the city of Albany, was, "How did Dr. Swinburne become persuaded to accept a renomination for mayor, after being cheated out of his election, compelled to undergo the vexation and expense of a litigation for fourteen months to recover the office to which he was elected, as well as being subjected to the abuse of Hale, in whom he placed so much confidence, and who was among the very loudest of his supporters?" The best way to answer this question is by copying an editorial article from the "Press and Knickerbocker" (Independent Democrat) of April 7, 1884. The article is headed, "Swinburne's Nomination," and says, —

"With some it has been an enigma how Dr. Swinburne, after all the annoyance he has been subjected to, consented to make another canvass for the mayoralty. We confess ourselves to have been among the number thus situated, and took the pains to inquire into the matter. We know him to be at the head of a public hospital and dispensary, in charge of a staff of surgeons and physicians, which is constantly thronged with patients of the poorer class, seeking relief without the means of paying for it; we know him to have a large private practice; and we know his tastes and inclinations were not of a political nature. We therefore took it upon ourselves to inquire into the causes, and found that an appeal had been made to him by leading property-owners and merchants, representing over twenty million dollars' worth of property subjected to taxation, entreating him to take the field. Such an appeal, everybody must admit, it would be hard for any man to resist. It was something more than a compliment: it went straight to the man's heart. These gentlemen knew Dr. Swinburne to be a humanitarian throughout; and they believed if he would listen to the appeals of the maimed, the sick, and the dying, he would not turn a deaf ear to the appeals of the tax-payers of this ring-accursed city. They knew he had the ability, the courage, and the indomitable will to grasp with and throttle the hydra-headed serpent which has the city treasury enfolded in its coils. Hence, in their despair, they turned to him; and he consented to be their candidate. Dr. Swinburne is a man of great executive ability, of immense brain-power. In his profession he has no superior organizer. Fortunately for the interests of the city, he has his free hospital and dispensary organized so fully and systematically that he is able to give all necessary attention to the duties of mayor. He has been an active, hard worker all his life. For month after month he has worked from fifteen to eighteen hours per day; and, in thousands of instances, he has worked constantly, without the respite of half an hour's sleep, for three days."

The nomination by the Citizens' Association was promptly indorsed by the Republicans; and the struggle opened with honesty and fair work on one side, while corruption, intrigue, lying, and deceit were the weapons used on the other. The "Argus," true to its policy to oppose every man, whether Republican, Democrat, or Citizen, who was not an "Argus" (or ring) Democrat, opened its flood-gates of filth, basing all its abuse on the statements of Hale, and a physician who was opposed to the doctor professionally, and asserting the doctor never did any thing for humanity. This was the only paper that would stoop so low as to abuse the doctor personally. This opposition was met by the other papers; the "Evening Journal," in an article, saying, —

"What our esteemed contemporary, the 'Argus,' expects to gain by deriding, vilifying, and insulting Mayor Swinburne is not easy to understand. There is neither logic nor argument in making faces and calling names. No reasonable person will be moved to change his vote by such tactics. The 'Argus' may think that its course of action will lead the public mind away from contemplation of important features of the municipal election, but it is mistaken. Mayor Swinburne represents the element that fearlessly antagonized, and finally drove from power, the old and utterly disreputable element that had become a stench in the nostrils of all decent citizens. Who would have the old *régime* restored? Do we want another Nolan dynasty? Where was the ' Argus ' in the fight made under the leadership of Mayor Swinburne for a free vote, a fair count, municipal reform, and the ousting of the city's plunderers? It was against Mayor Swinburne and it is against him now. Where were the people in that memorable conflict? They were with Mayor Swinburne, and against the ' Argus.' That is their position today, and it is impregnable."

" The Citizen," the independent organ of the Citizens' Association, said of him, —

" Generous John Swinburne. No pen of ours need describe him, for he is too well known by our citizens to need description. Bold, fearless, a lion in combat, and as gentle as a lamb in his compassionate tenderness for the afflicted, he is the noblest type of manhood that ever ventured into the arena of politics. Those who have seen him simply attending to his professional duties, and, like the ministering angel, scattering on all sides the magic of his great healing art, have no adequate idea of the hero who has devoted his time and his invaluable services to an attempt to ameliorate the condition of his fellow-citizens. He has been eminently successful in his treatment of the physical ailments of the people; and we are sure that, under the penetration of his lancet, the moral condition of the people will be much improved.

" But he is not suffered to pursue his way in peace. The bloodhounds of calumny and slander have been let loose upon his track; and a few machine sheets, aided by a few scalawag lawyers, seek to poison the public mind against him. But who can defame the name of John Swinburne? Who can slander his great reputation as a philanthropist? Not a handful of disappointed lawyers! Not a hundred unscrupulous editors! The name of Dr. Swinburne is engraven on the hearts of the people; and despite the clamor of ring tools, tricksters, and the backbiting of liars, the genial, modest, generous, and valiant reformer will be again placed triumphantly in the executive chair of the city, amid the utmost enthusiasm of all good citizens.

" There may be some persons who will be influenced by what Matthew Hale said about Dr. Swinburne through the columns of a paper called the ' Argus,' — a Democratic organ which seems to think more of party fealty than it does of honest men or good government. That is the only paper in the city which would lend its columns to an abuse of Mayor Swinburne, and it does it on political grounds; while Hale's is a personal matter, which he seeks to make public, thinking it will injure Dr. Swinburne in his candidacy for mayor. Matthew Hale told Dr. Swinburne in the spring of 1883, just before the doctor started on a trip to Kansas, that he thought the best way to raise the money to defray the expense of the mayoralty litigation was by subscription; and he accordingly drew up one, which was signed by Hale & Bulkley and C. P. Williams for two hundred and fifty dollars each, and said to Dr. Swinburne, 'I will have enough raised before your return to pay all expenses.' Does that look as if Hale intended to look to the doctor for the money? What has become of that paper, or how much money was raised, is not known. More than that, a perfectly reliable gentleman says that Hale told him that if Mayor Swinburne had appointed him (Hale) corporation counsel he would not have made any charges for his services. So it seems that the depth of Hale's earnestness was measured by an office; and, because he did not get it, he is found now on the side of the very parties who caused Dr. Swinburne to be defrauded out of his election. Away with such consistency. It's a sham; and Mr. Hale will fall — in the eyes of the community — into the pit he is trying to dig for Mayor Swinburne. Mr. Hale has something to say about Mayor Swinburne hiding behind his wife. Who did Mr. Hale hide behind when the Hon. Henry Smith was defending him in a breach-of-promise suit? Perhaps Mr. Lightbody could throw some light on the subject. Why did Mayor Swinburne convey his property to his wife? Because, when the war of 1861 broke out, he felt it his duty to go into the field to relieve the sick and wounded patriots — many of them from this city — who were enduring every hardship to save our country; and before he left he made the conveyance to his wife, so that if he should never return she would be provided for. Why, Dr. Swinburne has done more for suffering humanity in one day than Matthew Hale has done in all his life. Then for him, in a sneering manner, to assert that Dr. Swinburne made the said conveyance to get rid of paying his honest debts, is not only contemptible, but false. The sale of Hale's property was like Billings's boots and Billings's gun. The whole matter means persecution, and at a time when they think it will injure the mayor. But in this they will find themselves mistaken; for, the more they persecute

him, the louder are the masses in his praise. The people
know Dr. Swinburne; and whatever disappointed office-
seekers and Democratic-ring henchmen may say derogatory
of him, falls flat to the ground.

"One thing more we desire to call the attention of the
public to, which shows plainly that Mayor Swinburne is wil-
fully and maliciously persecuted; and that is the publication
at this time of the proceedings of a court instituted to inquire into the private and personal matters of an individual.

"In conclusion, and in order that the people may see for
themselves how the patriotism of Matthew Hale oozed out in
the short space of fourteen months, we lay before them the
following resolution, which was offered, among others, by him
while making a speech at the grand indignation meeting
held at the old Capitol the night after the last mayoralty
election : —

"'*Resolved*, That we pledge ourselves, so far as our means and circumstances may permit, to contribute of our time, of our energies, and our
money, to carry out the spirit of this meeting, to defeat the apparent conspiracy against the ballot-box, to vindicate the will of the people, and to
punish those guilty of the offences charged, which are the grossest possible crimes against a free government.'

"We will leave it to our readers to judge how Mr. Hale
lived up to the spirit of the above resolution, and as to how
much of his time, his energies, and his money he contributed
to further the cause of honest elections and good government."

The attacks of the "Argus," that Mayor Swinburne had
never done any thing for humanity, is answered in the
"Press and Knickerbocker" in these words : —

"In the editorial page of the 'Argus' is a statement to the
effect that John Swinburne had done nothing for humanity.
Was it nothing he did, when, during the War of the Rebellion, he, time and again, of his own accord and at his own
expense, hurried away to the scenes of suffering and death to
relieve the wounded of our New-York companies; passing
through the lines, allowing himself to be made a prisoner of
war by the rebels, if haply he might save the lives of our
brothers, fathers, and sons? Was it nothing, when, on such
occasions, he used to go, and, on his own shoulders, carry
provisions for miles to feed the wounded prisoners? Will
the fourteen thousand poor and unfortunate who are annually cared for at his dispensary on Eagle Street say that he
has done nothing for humanity?

"Let the poor man and the laboring man, when he goes to the polls to-morrow, ask himself this question, 'If accident or disease were to befall my family to-day, to whom would I go for aid, to the silk-stocking, purse-proud Banks, or to the large-hearted man, the people's friend, JOHN SWINBURNE?' and vote accordingly.

"The 'Argus' evidently begins to think 'the better element' will not save the ring, and that, too, after putting on such a bold front; for who ever heard of such a thing before as the leading Democratic daily issuing an extra campaign sheet in a simple charter election, when they have every thing their own way, and a Democratic majority of fifteen hundred at least to back them? We like it; and would willingly pay for an extra edition of the 'Argus' on Monday, because it makes votes for Swinburne. We would like the 'Argus' to attack Mayor Swinburne's official acts, if it dare. It has avoided doing that, and devoted itself to personal attacks; and they have re-acted upon itself disastrously.

"But this election is not on a question of politics: it is one of good government. It is quite the common remark of some of those who to-day arrogate to themselves the title of 'blue-bloods' to say, 'We want one of our own set for mayor.' But the people — the laborer, the merchant, the artisan, and the poor man — will see to it that we have one of the people for that office, not an aristocrat."

It was a remarkable incident in political contests in Albany, that only one paper published in the city had any thing to say against the nomination of Dr. Swinburne; a hearty and cordial support being given him by the two Republican journals, by the "Press" (Independent Democrat) and the "Post" (Independent), besides the organ of the Citizens' Association, "The Citizen," while the "Times," an honorable Democratic sheet, was silent.

The "Evening Journal" (Republican) said, —

"The renomination of Dr. John Swinburne for mayor was assured from the day when, after long, vexatious, and obstructive delay, he was given the office by the courts, which he had fairly won at the polls months before. Indeed, so evidently just and proper was this course recognized to be, that at no time have the names of any contestants for the honor and responsibility of the position been mentioned. Even in the unfortunate, and we believe unnecessary, differences which have arisen in the party, there is complete and emphatic accord that Dr. Swinburne deserves and must receive the votes of all Republicans.

"But the votes of Republicans will not be enough to secure an election. They do not accurately measure the extent of the support to which Mayor Swinburne is entitled. His canvass this year rests on higher grounds than partisanship, and appeals to a larger constituency than a party. It may fairly be questioned at any time whether the broad lines on which men divide in National and State politics form the basis of a legitimate division of sentiment on questions relating simply to honest and economical municipal administration. Certainly they have no place in the election to be held in this city a week from to-morrow. Only two questions are to be answered at the polls on that day: first, whether the claim in political equity of John Swinburne to a full term as mayor shall be allowed, and, second, whether the certainty of a ruggedly honest local administration shall be sacrificed to the possibility of a return of the corrupt and extravagant government of the old Democratic ring.

"No fair-minded man can deny the right of Dr. Swinburne to a re-election. For fourteen months he was kept out of the office to which he was chosen. For more than half his term a usurper filled his place. The wrong was finally set right, but less than one-half the stolen goods were returned. The time for full restitution has now come. The morality of the issue, however, is but one aspect of it. For more than a year Dr. Swinburne carried on an untiring warfare — at what detriment to himself none but himself can accurately estimate — to secure to the citizens of Albany rights of which they had been forcibly robbed. Others had attempted the same fight; but they had become disheartened and dismayed at the vicious power arrayed against them, and had succumbed in failure. When it seemed that the people of Albany were never again to have their votes counted as they were cast, the unflagging pugnacity of this man, almost single handed and alone, won back for them this primal right of citizenship. It is not in gratitude simply for these exertions that Mayor Swinburne asks the suffrages of the citizens of Albany, which he has almost literally given them. It is further in the belief that by their ingratitude now they will not say to others, should the same emergency again arise, 'we are indifferent to your labor, and careless to our interests which you seek to protect.'

"Even were there no such commanding principles of right

and wrong involved in this election, the good government of the city requires the re-election of the present mayor. During his brief administration, every interest of the city has been carefully guarded. Expenses have been reduced, officials have been forced to the performance of long-neglected duties, order and economy have been established in all departments of the city's service."

The "Express" of April 8, said, —

"True to its character and traditions, the 'Argus,' which called on the Grand Army of the Republic to disband. and asserted that its prominent membership comprised 'loud, brawling men, who went to the war to escape their characters, or because there was money in it,' now attacks a man who was captured a prisoner of war before he would desert the soldiers wounded on the battlefield, the living among whom now wear the badge of that organization. That man was Dr. John Swinburne."

The "Express" (Republican) thus indorsed the nomination : —

"For a long time past it has been apparent that the Republican City Convention would indorse the nomination of Dr. John Swinburne for mayor, as made by the Independent Citizens' Convention. There was, indeed, no other candidate for the office on the Republican side. Delegates and others remembered the proceedings of the convention two years ago, when a 'straight' Republican ticket was placed in the field, and the gentleman at the head of it declined to go into the race. They remembered the plucky fight made by Dr. Swinburne against corrupt ring-rule, and the victory he won, without the use of money. They further remember the gallant fight he made against the inspectors, who sought to deprive the people of their just rights by counting him out, and against the man who for several months took advantage of the false count. The people admire pluck: they can forgive a man for wanting in some other qualities, if he has the courage to stand up and fight for his own and their rights. "So it was a foregone conclusion that Dr. Swinburne would be nominated by the Republicans. He had earned the distinction. All factions into which the party in this city is unfortunately divided were agreed that he should be the candidate. For fourteen months kept out of the office to which he was elected by the people, by an iniquitous combination, it seemed to most right-minded people only fair and just that he should be elected for another term; and the expectation is that he will be by a majority of sufficient proportions to deter dishonest inspectors from making another attempt to count him out.

"Dr. Swinburne's administration of the office of mayor has not, in all things, been to our liking. But it has been a great improvement upon that of his predecessors, and has been thoroughly bold and courageous. Let the 'Fighting Doctor' have the chances which will be afforded by another term. The people have good reason to know that he means to be their friend, not only in the matter of endeavoring to heal such of them as are sick and afflicted, but also in affairs of municipal taxation and expenditure. We know it is alleged that some Republicans will refuse to vote for the doctor. Probably the allegation is true. It was so two years ago; but he was elected nevertheless. But mark this, for every Republican vote the doctor loses he will receive ten from the other side. The citizens, irrespective of party, are very much in earnest in this matter."

These two articles from the many published in these papers recognized as the organs of the two wings of the Republican party in Albany, the city of political contentions, differences, and jealousies, clearly demonstrate the unanimity of feeling that existed on all sides toward this non-factional Republican and thorough representative of the people. A support such as these gave is made more significant because of the silence of one Democratic paper, and the hearty support given him by another Democratic journal having the largest circulation of any paper published in Albany.

The renomination of Mayor Swinburne was recognized, not only by the respectable Press of the city, as a wise and advanced step in reform and good government, but by the Press of other sections having an interest in seeing fraud and political dishonesty driven out of the civic government of the capital city. Among these was the "Troy Evening Times," which, after watching the administration of Mayor Swinburne, said, in its issue of March 31, —

"The Republicans of Albany have nominated Dr. Swinburne for the office of mayor. He deserves this indorsement.

He was the only citizen who apparently had the courage and determination to fight the corrupt Nolan-ring government. He won the struggle only after a long and costly controversy before the courts, and to-day the city of Albany is enjoying the fruits of his victory in a better government than it had had for many years before. The chances seem to favor Dr. Swinburne; as his election would best subserve the public interest, and give the people a government wholly freed from ring-rule or grossly partisan administration."

In answering the only attacks that the opponents of Dr. Swinburne could make against him, which were all groundless and of a personal nature, the "Express," in an article published April 5, 1884, under the head of "The Tactics against Dr. Swinburne," said.—

"In the history of local politics in this city and county it would be difficult to recall a more cowardly or dastardly attack upon the character of a political opponent who happens to be a candidate for office than has been made by the enemies of Dr. Swinburne, the Republican candidate for mayor. The columns of the 'Argus' are daily filled with personal abuse of a man whom that journal ought, in most things, to commend. Efforts are constantly made to show that the doctor does not pay his just debts ; but so far nothing in that direction has been proved, except that he has refused to pay the exorbitant bills of certain lawyers who pushed him into the mayoralty contest with Mr. Nolan, organized and addressed 'indignation' meetings over the gross frauds perpetrated at the municipal election of 1882, and were profuse in their tender of services to bring about a correction of the abuses of which they, and good citizens generally, complained of. One lawyer presents a bill of nearly four thousand dollars, which he asks the doctor to pay. Another modestly requests the doctor to hand him over fifteen hundred dollars. There are plenty of working-people in the city, skilled and competent workingmen at that, who would be glad of an opportunity to work three years for the compensation which one of these lawyers demands of Dr. Swinburne for the few days' time he devoted to the suit brought to vindicate the right of the people to select their magistrates, and to seat them when elected.

"It is a pretty hard thing to ask a man to pay out in lawyers' fees and costs, in an action brought to preserve his own and the people's rights, pretty nearly double the sum he receives for salary for the full term of the office when it is finally awarded to him by the courts. It must require 'cheek,' to say the least, for a lawyer who engages in a case of this nature, from alleged patriotic motives, to send in a bill for his 'services,' amounting to more than a year's salary of the office finally awarded to the plaintiff. In the other contested mayoralty cases in Albany, — those between Quackenbush and Perry and Judson and Thacher, — the entire expenses of the litigation were borne by the city. This time, although the courts have decided that Dr. Swinburne was fairly elected to the office, he is asked to put his hand into his pocket and pay all the expenses, including the exorbitant lawyers' fees. It is not true, as we understand the facts, that Dr. Swinburne does not pay his 'just debts.' He pays his grocer and his butcher, the dry-goods merchant, the tailor, the coal dealer. His *just* debts he does pay: there are some which he considers to be of a different nature, which he declines to liquidate. Not every voter in Albany blames him for pursuing that course.

"It is undoubtedly true that Dr. Swinburne is not as rich a man as the Hon. A. Bleecker Banks. He cannot afford to live in as grand style as that gentleman does. Probably he cannot afford to contribute as liberally to the 'campaign fund' as his competitor can. Part of his modest residence is occupied as a dispensary, where the sick and the afflicted are treated, and without charge if they have not the means of paying. The rich and the poor are there treated alike. Only those pay who can afford it. Of course the doctor's enemies say that all this is done for effect. Suppose it is: it *is* done all the same, and the people reap the advantage. Those who are healed under his care or direction will not be likely to inquire very anxiously about the motive the doctor had in treating them.

"Yes, we suppose Mr. A. Bleecker Banks is much the richer of the two candidates for mayor. But we venture the assertion that in time and money and skill the doctor has contributed to the relief of suffering humanity tenfold as much as his opponent. To attempt to hold up such a man to public execration, to harass him with 'supplementary proceedings' because he refuses to be ground by grasping lawyers, and to daily fill the columns of a newspaper with coarse abuse of one who has done so much good as Dr. Swinburne, is neither manly nor courageous. Perhaps it is just as well for the doctor, for in the end it will re-act. The people are not fond of too much of that kind of opposition."

In this election the candidate opposed to Dr. Swinburne was a gentleman of great wealth and social position, president of a very large corporation, and of whom the Press said, when he was elected mayor in 1876, by a majority of fifteen hundred, "He is a young and rising citizen. He has proved thus far a very available candidate for the Democracy." The Democratic candidate had twice been elected to the State Senate, in 1869 and 1870, by large majorities; and hence the impression that he was an available candidate. He was considered, because of his wealth and social position, again, "a very available candidate." But notwithstanding these strong elements, and a reputed electioneering fund of forty thousand dollars to support the ticket, and all the Herculean efforts of his party, and the practice of their political tactics in counting the returns, it required up into the "wee sma' hours" of the morning to figure out an apparent majority against the doctor of two hundred and fifty.

The feeling in the city on the evening of the election was intense; and as messengers were seen hurrying too and from Democratic headquarters, and carriages with the leaders rapidly drove from one section of the city to the other, it was pretty generally believed the ring had been again honestly vanquished by the " Fighting Doctor," and that a forlorn hope was being fought under the darkness of night, and after the poles were closed, to save the ring from complete rout.

The announcement that the ring had succeeded did not surprise the people of Albany; and it was hoped another investigation would take place, and that justice should be done the people. In announcing the result the "Troy Times" said,—

" The Albany city-election yesterday resulted in the defeat of Dr. Swinburne, who had been renominated for mayor by the Republicans, and a victory for the entire Democratic ticket. This result was the *finale* of a memorable campaign, in which every device that desperation could invent was called into play. An enormous corruption fund was raised, and money flowed like water from the pockets of the politicians. For days the Democrats had poured out upon Dr. Swinburne a deluge of vilification and falsehoods such as few

candidates ever encountered, no lie being too monstrous for
assertion and circulation.   At the polls, yesterday, fraud was
freely employed to compass Swinburne's defeat.   To combat
against all these adverse influences called for Herculean
strength on the doctor's part; and, under the circumstances,
it is amazing that he should be defeated by less than three
hundred."

The " Express," in announcing the results of the election
and the count on the morning after, said, —

" Dr. John Swinburne, the Republican and Citizens' candidate for mayor, is alleged to have been defeated by the meagre
majority of two hundred and forty-one, in a poll of nearly
twenty thousand votes.   The doctor had no money to spend in
this election.   Such as he has made and saved has been freely
expended in the maintenance of a dispensary and hospital,
where the poor have been treated without fee or reward, and
only those of means asked to pay.   That is not a lucrative
sort of business, in one sense of the phrase; but in another
sense it pays.   Yesterday's vote shows it.   With a corruption
fund of fifty thousand dollars against him, — with the members of the State Committee, the chairman and one of the
secretaries of the County Committee, and certain prominent
Federal office-holders also against him, — the best showing the
opposition to Dr. Swinburne can make is given in the figures
printed above.
" Of course it was not an honest count.   Of course the courts
will be compelled to reverse the figures, as they were in the
contest between Swinburne and Nolan two years ago.   Frauds
upon the ballot-box, as against Dr. Swinburne, were undoubtedly committed yesterday in the eastern district of the sixth,
the eastern district of the seventh, in the eighth, in the
northern district of the ninth, and in the middle and eastern
districts of the sixteenth wards.   These frauds will be fer-
reted out, and this time by lawyers who will not charge
exorbitant fees for the performance of alleged ' patriotic ' service.   The people will see to it, this time, that the rights of
the majority are vindicated; and that repeaters, ballot-box
stuffers, and dishonest inspectors are not permitted to have
things entirely their own way.   The doctor has already given
evidence that he knows how to fight for his own and the people's rights.   He will be quite as ready to make a fight of
that kind to-morrow as he was two years ago.
" The city was flooded with Democratic money yesterday.

It was as free as water. There was none upon the other side. And yet, notwithstanding this lavish expenditure of Democratic funds, the inspectors are able to count out the doctor by only the bare majority named above. It was a wonderful fight that the workingmen made yesterday against the Democratic candidates and their corruption fund. Mr. Banks, surely, has no reason to feel proud over his alleged ' victory.' Nor have the Republicans and workingmen any reason to feel ashamed over the showing they made yesterday. If they had undertaken to buy the venal and corrupt, not even dishonest inspectors would have had the cheek to endeavor to count them out. But the ' buying ' business was left to the ' better element ' yesterday. A day of reckoning is coming, gentlemen. Corruption funds will not always tell. Honest citizens are learning their rights, and, knowing them, will dare maintain them. Political rings and political corruption-funds must go."

To accomplish the results claimed by the ring, the most desperate efforts were resorted to during the election, as well as in counting the votes: Republican watchers were brutally beaten at the polls; old men were assaulted, while others were prevented from reaching the polls and depositing their ballots; and open bribery was carried on all day, — the price paid for votes in some wards being as high as eight dollars a vote.

The " Journal," in commenting on the returns, asserted there had been, unquestionably, fraud and violence practised during the election, and wondered if A. B. Banks would dare to take the office under the circumstances, asserting there was evidence sufficient to establish fraud, in the mind of any fair man, at the returns. The total vote cast at that election was 19,914, an excess of 1,854 over 1882, which was proven to have been greatly increased by fraudulent votes. This increase the " Journal " claimed was not possible in the growth of the city population in that time.

On account of the serious illness of Dr. Swinburne, resulting from overwork and blood-poisoning while performing an operation, he was unable physically to contest the seat to which he was elected, but which was accorded to his opponent, and went West to recuperate his health. A few days before his return to the city it was learned that he was on his way home; and the Citizens' Association, under President William Manson, decided to extend to him a reception on his arrival. This was, at its inception, intended to be confined to the association; but no sooner was the announcement made than it assumed a popular movement, in which the almost entire community expressed a desire to take part. Not the least prominent among those desiring to participate were many who, although having voted against the doctor, believed he had been a second time defrauded, and were willing to so testify. A large number of his political opponents, who always vote the party-ticket, also desired to unite in their personal appreciation of the doctor as a philanthropist and citizen, and in expressing their satisfaction at his returning health and vigor. On the evening of his return, July 24, 1884, although but a few days had elapsed from the time it was known he was to arrive, Albany was the the scene of one blaze of enthusiasm, such as it has never before or since accorded any man, whether public or private citizen. From the depot, along the route of march to his residence, the streets were packed with a solid mass of humanity; while the sound of a cheering multitude made the hills around echo, and the heavens were made brilliant with a grand pyrotechnic display. The arrangements, in which several of the Republican clubs and thousands of citizens participated, were under the direction of President William Manson and a committee of the Independent Citizens' Association. In the demonstration a number of physicians of the city and from the surrounding country took an active part. Of this reception, the "Express" (Republican) said, —

"Our ex-mayor, John Swinburne, was the recipient of an ovation last evening, at the hands of his fellow-citizens and admirers, that was not only a pronounced indorsement of his official career, but a personal compliment, carrying with it the evidence of the high regard in which he is held by a very large constituency. The reception was conceived and carried out under the direction of the Independent Citizens' Association. The line was formed at half-past seven P.M., and moved to the Union Depot.

" An immense throng of citizens surrounded the depot ; and, as Dr. Swinburne entered his carriage, he was greeted with tumultuous cheers and a blaze of pyrotechnics. The carriage of the ex-mayor was placed between the ranks of the Citizens' Association, and the line of march taken up as follows : Broadway to Hudson Avenue, to Green, to State, to South Pearl, to Hudson Avenue, to Eagle. Along the entire march the doctor was vociferously applauded. The residence of the ex-mayor was brilliantly illuminated, and the trees beautifully festooned with Chinese lanterns. The roadway and sidewalks, for at least a block on each side, were packed with a dense mass of people. After a brief space Dr. Swinburne appeared upon the balcony, accompanied by John T. McDonough, Esq.; and several minutes elapsed before the latter gentleman could make his introductory speech, so prolonged was the welcoming and the hearty cheers. Mr. McDonough, in a brief speech, stated the cause of the demonstration, alluded to the sterling qualities of Dr. Swinburne as an official, a philanthropist, and a citizen, and on the part of the citizens of Albany welcomed him to his home. The doctor responded in a few words, in his characteristic way, and expressed his gratitude for honors shown him. With three hearty cheers for Mayor Swinburne the ovation ended, and the line was dismissed. The demonstration, as a whole, was unique in its way, and one that cannot fail to be always held by the recipient in grateful remembrance."

The " Press and Knickerbocker " (Independent Democrat) said of the demonstration, —

" Ex-Mayor John Swinburne returned from his Western farm at Silver Lake, Shawnee County, Kan., at eight o'clock last evening, having been absent from the city since May 8.

" For the past few days the Citizens' Association had been arranging for a proper reception of the distinguished gentleman. It was found, however, that the public were desirous of cordially co-operating with the movement ; and the ovation of last night was a grand recognition of the many acts which have endeared Dr. Swinburne to the hearts of the people.

" Public notice was given that citizens would assemble in front of the headquarters at No. 44 North Pearl Street, promptly at half-past seven o'clock. It was but a few moments after six o'clock when the first gentleman entered the room, and an hour later the apartment was thronged. Citizens gathered on the walks, and the large crowd was augmented by the appearance of Maj. Kenealey with the Albany City Band of twenty pieces. Upon arrival at the Grant Club quarters, the band gave a selection; and, as the melody was heard, the team and carriage of the doctor, in charge of faithful Phil. Albert. dashed around the corner to the depot.

"Lines were then formed, and the procession marched to the depot, where an immense throng was found clustered about the street and approaches. As the train rolled into the depot, and the doctor stepped upon the platform, a score of hands were outstretched, and ringing cheers from the multitude greeted his appearance. There was also a brilliant pyrotechnic display.

"Throughout the entire march there was a very general burning of colored fires, coupled with a profuse display of bunting and the discharge of rockets and candles. The insurance patrol are deserving of very great praise for the artistic combination of colors displayed. Double lines of lanterns arched the street, and the house of the patrol was dotted with the bright lights from many a highly colored shade. Colored fires illumined the scene, and a profuse discharge of Roman candles proved that the protectives were the best of friends with the ex-mayor, and heartily pleased to thus publicly display their feelings.

"As the head of the procession filed into Eagle Street from Hudson Avenue, the street fronting the residence of the doctor was found to be densely packed with people.

"The vast assembly waited but a moment for the greeting between husband and wife, and then shouted for 'Swinburne,' who appeared on the balcony, followed by Mr. J. T. McDonough, who delivered the

ADDRESS OF WELCOME.

"'LADIES AND GENTLEMEN, — We are here to-night to extend a cordial welcome to our honored and distinguished townsman, Dr. John Swinburne.

"'A few months ago, borne down by the cares of office, the excitement of an unparalleled political campaign, and the overwork of his profession, he sought repose and rest in the seclusion of the Far West. He had scarcely departed when his political opponents rejoicingly reported the news about the city that he had gone to stay. They labored under the delusion that rest meant retirement. The doctor never retires in the face of a foe, and so we have the pleasure of greeting him again to-night, and seeing him hale and hearty and courageous as of old.

"The great respect, the warm affection, we have for him, is evidenced by the vast numbers assembled here to do him honor. And well may we be proud of him, — proud of his marvellous skill, proud of his great and powerful achievements, and proud of his well-earned reputation.

"'In peace and in war, at the bedside of the sick and suffering, at home and abroad, as well as in the camp of the soldier and on the battle-field, he has devoted his time and energies and strength to healing the sick, relieving the sufferings of the wounded, and consoling the afflicted.

"'His professional life has been as a benediction to tens of thousands of his fellow-men; and so large have been his charities, so generous have been his offerings to the people, that, not satisfied with devoting his own services to them, he has gone further, and given up to a free dispensary the better part of his own home. Who could do more? Nor has he been less distinguished in public and official life. Through fraud and corruption, and the law's delay, he was unjustly deprived of more than half of the term of office to which he was elected by the people of this city. And yet, during the short time he acted as our chief magistrate, without professing to be a reformer, or pretending to be better than his neighbors, he brought about many valuable reforms, and gave us an honest municipal government.

"'By superhuman efforts, if not by forbidden means, he was deprived of a second term.

"'But neither malicious slander nor malicious prosecution, neither corrupt practices at the polls nor doubtful decisions of courts, have deprived him of the thousands of warm friends who will rejoice at his return to-night, and in whose behalf I now extend him a hearty welcome home.'

"After an appropriate selection by the band, Dr. Swinburne said. —

"'FELLOW-CITIZENS AND FRIENDS, — I do not feel strong enough at this time to say much. I feel it impossible to thank you for the honor you have conferred in this welcome home after my absence. I am not foolish enough to believe that this is for me alone. It is in favor of good government. I intend to remain with you as a citizen. I was thrown into politics by reason of my work. You know what the result was. The ring deprived us of our privileges. Since my absence I have received hundreds of letters asking what was to be done, what steps I proposed to take. To these I made no response, but I will answer them and answer you now. As a citizen, I am prepared to take hold, and to most heartily help you to right a wrong If you, the people, wish good government, I am ready to go with you. Two years ago they counted me out by three thousand votes. They did the same thing last year, aided by their corruption fund of forty thousand dollars. I think Gen. Butler hit the nail on the head when he said, " The time for discussion has passed : the time for action has come." With him I believe that the time for action has come. I hope we will meet together, and continue our great work. Gentlemen, I am with you in every movement; and, when my health is fully restored, I trust that we may combine together in the interest of good government. Gentlemen, good-night.'

" Following the speeches the crowd quietly dispersed, and the doctor passed the remainder of the evening with a few intimate friends."

The "Citizen" (Independent) thus described the reception : —

" After a prolonged absence from the city, Ex-Mayor John Swinburne returned on Thursday evening last, and was the recipient of an ovation seldom, if ever, accorded to a private citizen of Albany. It was a purely spontaneous gathering of his friends and fellow-citizens, who sought in this manner to testify their appreciation of his worth, and their gratitude to the man who was twice cheated out of the office to which he was fairly elected by the honest votes of the people, by methods which, for downright audaciousness, are without a parallel in the history of the country. His reception was not the result of any cut-and-dried arrangements, but was as unexpected by our citizens generally as it was by Dr. Swinburne, who was utterly taken by surprise at the enthusiastic reception which he received. The arrangements for the demonstration, which it may be said were impromptu, were under the auspices of a committee of the Independent Citizens' Association; and well and faithfully did they perform the duty assigned them, considering the short space of time at their disposal. As early as half-past seven o'clock the clubs which were to participate assembled on North Pearl Street, and together with thousands of well-known citizens proceeded to the Union Depot; and, when the train bearing the champion of the people's rights rolled in, shouts and applause rent the air. The route of march being taken up, the enthusiasm all along the line was spontaneous and tremendous. Handkerchiefs were waved by fair hands at all the windows, and fireworks were almost continuously displayed from one end of the route to the other.

" Dr. Swinburne returns to us much improved in health and appearance, having almost totally recovered from the fit of sickness with which he was prostrated last spring. He comes back to his much-loved city, fresh and with all his old-time vigor, ready and willing to carry on the conflict against rings and corruption, now, as of yore; and if the demonstration of Thursday evening may be taken as a criterion, he is sure to

find ready allies in the people of Albany to push to completion the good work which he has undertaken to perform.
Let us hope and trust that he will long be spared to our citizens, and that he will shortly witness the downfall of the
ring-masters and their henchmen, who plotted and planned to
rob him of his hard-earned victories."

CHAPTER XVIII.

A Believer in the Republican Platform. — Received with Deafening Cheers. — Why Nominated for Congress. — What the Independent Press said. — All Factions united. — As Incorruptible as Independent. — A Brilliant Victory and Disgusted Democrat.

BELIEVING thoroughly in the principles of the Republican party as enunciated in the platform of the Chicago convention of last year, Dr. John Swinburne believed it his duty to take an active part in the triumph of these principles, and the election of the men the convention had chosen as representing them. He felt it a duty every citizen owed the state and nation to labor for the best form of government, and for the party representing the best interests of the American people at large, and the protection of American industries, and promptly declared his allegiance and active sympathy, which meant aggressive work. No other course was expected from him, as all his labors in times of peace and war had been honestly directed to the perpetuity of republican principles, and for the good of the people at large. On his return from the West, the marshalling of campaign clubs had commenced, and the people were preparing for the bloodless but important battle of the ballot. In no part of the State was a more intense feeling growing than in the capital city, the residence of the Democratic candidate for President, Gov. Cleveland, and the home of the leader of that party, the present secretary of the treasury. In this county, with a Democratic majority of over three thousand, and all the advantages to be derived from the State offices (except one department) being in the hands of the opposition, the Republicans of the district realized they had a hard struggle before them to even hold their own in the conflict, but determined to make the best fight possible, and wisely looked around for the best man to open the campaign and unite the discordant elements. There was no question as to who that man should be; and, when the first grand rally was decided on, the " Fighting Doctor " was invited to preside. On the evening of Aug. 6 the meeting was held, and addressed by Hon. J. C. Burrows of Michigan and Ex-Gov. W. M. Stone of Iowa. Of that meeting the " Express " said, —

" As Ex-Mayor Swinburne, who had been selected as the presiding officer, came upon the stage, the immense crowd which filled every available inch of space sent up a deafening cheer which shook the building, the doctor bowing his acknowledgments. The programme at first arranged was for both Hon. J. C. Burrows and Ex-Gov. W. M. Stone to speak in the hall; but the great mass of people who could find no accommodation within the walls of Music Hall, and had assembled outside, clamored so loudly, that Mr. Stone consented to address them, and left the hall for the street. After Sullivan's Tenth Regiment Band, which had secured places in the gallery, had played " Hail, Columbia ! " and the " Red, White, and Blue," Mr. Burlingame called the meeting to order, and said, —

" ' We are met this evening for the purpose, not only of ratifying the nominations of the Republican National Convention for President and Vice-President, but also to give expression to some of the many reasons why those nominees should receive the cordial support of the people : in short, to give expression to some of the many reasons why the party that has been in charge of the affairs of the nation for the last four and twenty years, and within that time has written into our national history the grandest achievements of modern times, should be still further trusted and continued; in other words, why the principle that is invoked for civil-service reform, in behalf of individuals who serve the government faithfully, should have the broadest and most complete fulfilment in continuing in power the party that has done all things well. It affords me great pleasure, upon this occasion, to present to you, as your presiding officer, a gentleman well known to you all, — one who has labored in our midst for his fellow-man, and who in his political duties knows only the people's interests. He comes to us to-night, not as a partisan, but as an independent citizen, who with us believes that the true interests of the American people will be best promoted by the election of James G. Blaine for President, and John A. Logan for Vice-President, of the United States. I present to you the Hon. John Swinburne.'

" The applause and cheers greeting the ex-mayor was continued for some minutes, and at its conclusion the doctor
said, —

"'FELLOW-CITIZENS AND FRIENDS, — For this cordial and enthusiastic
greeting I have no words to express my feelings. I thank you for the
honor you have done me in calling upon me to preside over this large
gathering of our citizens. During my absence in the Far West I have
seen an earnest and enthusiastic uprising of the people in favor of the
election to the management of our government of those who favor protection to our industries against foreign competition, and the protection alike
of all citizens of the United States, wherever born, while in the performance of any lawful duty. I am glad, upon my return, to find a like spirit
manifested here ; and, while I shall leave to other and more eloquent
tongues the defence of principles and the advocacy of candidates, I congratulate you upon the auspicious signs indicating the election of Blaine
and Logan, and the continuance of good government through an honest
expression of the people's wishes, unembarrassed by repeaters here or
shotguns elsewhere. Again thanking you for your confidence, I await
your further pleasure.' "

The " Evening Journal," in speaking of this meeting at
Music Hall, said, —

" Notably was the reception of Mayor John Swinburne
when he made his appearance upon the stage to preside. A
storm of applause swept through the vast auditorium, and
lasted several minutes. Such a tribute to a citizen was
remarkable."

In their former struggles, the citizens remembered how
their efforts for good government in local affairs had been
frustrated by fraud at the ballot-box, and determined to place
their chosen leader in the field, to represent them in national
affairs ; and hoped the presence of the United-States marshalls at the polls would secure a fair vote and count. They
remembered that when they, in 1882, placed Dr. John Swinburne in nomination for mayor, the Republican City Convention, after some hesitation, declined to name a candidate, but
recommended Dr. Swinburne for indorsement. They remembered the fraudulent count, the litigation that followed, and
the final success. When the ring counted in their candidate,
and he assumed the office of mayor, the new city charter, passed
but a short time previously, provided that the various offices to

be filled by the mayor should be so filled within two months
after the commencement of his term of office. Mayor Nolan
entered upon the duties of the office which had been awarded
him by the canvassing-board on the first Tuesday of May,
1882, and proceeded to nominate or appoint the city officers
and heads of the several departments from among his personal and political friends. When, therefore, in the latter
part of June, 1883, Dr. Swinburne assumed the duties of
mayor, he found all the departments filled with those who
had no sympathy with him, or with his economical methods,
and a board of aldermen unwilling to co-operate with him in
his efforts for municipal improvements and the curtailing of
expenditures; the carrying-out of which had been his motive
in accepting the nomination to the office of mayor. During
his brief term, with the zealous and efficient aid of his chosen
counsel to the corporation, the Hon. Henry Smith, Dr. Swinburne was enabled to do much toward a curtailment of the
city expenses and the correction of abuses heretofore existing.
He caused a thorough investigation of the affairs of the poor-
department; and, satisfied that these had not been managed
either in the interest of the city or the deserving poor, he suspended from office the superintendent thereof, and stated his
reason to the commission of aldermen provided by the charter, who failed to sustain his action, evidently more in the
interests of their party than of the public good.

One of the abuses long prevalent in the city government
was the establishment of the grades of streets by piecemeal,
and because of the demands of officials or residents in accordance with their ideas at various times. The result of this
course was an uneven and irregular grade of the street within
short distances; and the mechanic who had by his industry
purchased a lot beyond the paved portion on any of the
streets, and built thereon his humble home, conforming his
building to the grade of the street below him, would not un-
frequently find that when the grade was fixed for his block,
his house was either stilted many feet above the street level,
or his first floor was depressed far below it, thus destroying
the beauty and comfort of his home, and forcing upon him a

considerable expense. Dr. Swinburne at once took measures to correct this abuse. He caused grades to be made and established for all new streets for their entire length, so that all those who might build beyond the graded and paved portions might know just where their street-grade would be when improvements where made: he caused, also, complete maps to be made of the sewers and drains of the city, showing their location, size, dip, and of what material constructed. This was a step in the direction of improvement in the system of drainage of the city, followed by earnest, but ineffectual, efforts to secure the co-operation of the city fathers in a plan suggested by him for constructing large main drains in the principal arterial streets, sufficiently ample to carry off the surface waters from the large amount of water-shed west of Eagle Street, during the season of heavy rainfalls; this being desirable, not only for sanitary reasons, but because the large damages so frequently adjudged against the city for overflows consequent upon inadequate sewers, would thus be saved. Since the retirement of Dr. Swinburne, his plans have to some extent been adopted, and a portion of these main sewers have been ordered. Much attention was given by Mayor Swinburne to the question of an ample supply of pure and wholesome water; but here, again, political, professional, and personal jealousies prevented the accomplishment of his wishes, and, in direct opposition to his views, a bill was passed by the Legislature giving to the effete-water board power to expend four hundred thousand dollars for increasing the supply of river-water. So objectionable has this plan appeared to the citizens of Albany, that, in a year after its adoption, aldermen and people were crying with one voice for some relief; and a bill was introduced this year authorizing an expenditure of ten thousand dollars to ascertain if some other plan may not be secured. Well would it have been if the suggestions of Mayor Swinburne had been adopted: that new life be infused into the water-board, that they be empowered to seek other supplies than that from the river, and that all plans adopted by them should first secure the approval of the Common Council before having binding effect.

It fell to the lot of Mayor Swinburne but once to have control over the tax levy; but it will be remembered by all Albanians how wisely he acted upon that occasion, vetoing or reducing extravagant appropriations for parks and other purposes, so that even the Common Council sustained his action, and the tax budget was reduced by twenty-five thousand dollars by his action. This budget, although levied for the support of the city for fourteen months, was nearly sixty thousand dollars less than the one levied for the subsequent year for but twelve months.

Dr. Swinburne held the office of mayor but little over ten months, terminating May 6, 1884. He had, however, so impressed upon the city officers the importance of an economical administration, that the tax levy to provide means for the city expenses from August, 1883, to Dec. 31, 1884, a period of sixteen months, was at the rate of sixty-three thousand dollars per month; while that for the twelve subsequent months was at the rate of seventy-nine thousand dollars per month. It was unfortunate for the citizens and tax-payers that he was not given the certificate of re-election for a full term, to which many believed he was justly entitled by the voice of the people.

The administration of Mayor Swinburne, brief as it was, showed his great power in the management of public affairs; and these, with other considerations, induced the Citizens' Association to nominate him, by acclamation, for Congress.

The "Citizen," in announcing the nomination of Dr. John Swinburne for Congress by the Independent Citizens' Association, said, —

" The convention of the Citizens' Association, held in this city on Wednesday, the 24th inst., was very successful, both in the harmony which prevailed and in the results of its deliberations. Of course, ere this paper has reached the reader the action of that convention has been spread broadcast over the county.

" The nomination by acclamation of Dr. John Swinburne for member of Congress was a moral and political necessity. In his person is represented the reforms inaugurated by the people; and his ceaseless combat against the rings and

machines which have controlled municipal affairs has made
him a notable figure in the politics of the county. While
in the ranks of the Citizens' Association can be found numbers of citizens fully competent to fill any office in the gift of
the people, yet it was pre-eminently proper that the tried and
trusty champion of the people's battles should again put on
his armor, and enter the lists against the contingent of the ring.
What need is there of words of praise of Mayor Swinburne?
What honest heart in this whole county does not thrill at
the mention of his name? Praise of him and of his deeds
would be superfluous. The nomination was indeed a well-
deserved recognition of the invaluable services he has rendered
to the people. No political machine, no cut-and-dried bargain,
no scheme of trickery, secured that nomination. It was a
natural and spontaneous movement of the people. The man
who has devoted the best years of his life to the aid of his
fellow-creatures could not be, and is not, forgotten by them.
Base, indeed, would be the ingratitude of the community
were the name and merits of Dr. Swinburne, even for a
moment, overlooked. His nomination at this time is significant, and shows that the same aggressive policy of the people's
party is to be adopted. With Mayor Swinburne as a candidate, no other policy is possible. The *cliques* and gangs, and
political machines of all kinds and classes, must take note
that they will have to sustain the same vigorous attacks made
by him in previous campaigns.

"This time that portion of the county lying outside of the
city will be heard from. The farming classes, and the residents
of West Troy and Cohoes, will, for the first time, have an
opportunity to display their sentiments by heartily sustaining
the popular candidate. His name is powerful in those places.
His record is as well known to them as to us; and, unless all
signs of the times are fearfully deceptive, his vote outside of
the city will be unparalleled. We congratulate the Citizens'
Association on the wisdom of their nomination. The man
who almost alone in the city government attacked the ring,
and protected the treasury, will do ample justice to the people
at Washington. Reforms instituted here will be carried into
the national councils.

"With half an effort our next Congressman will be John
Swinburne; and, with a united and systematic support, the
election returns will scarcely show that his opponent is in
the race. Let the people see to it that their own candidate
is borne into a seat in the House of Representatives by an
overwhelming majority."

The "Press and Knickerbocker," also Independent, indorsed the nomination in this manner:—

"The county convention held by the Citizens' Association, Wednesday, acquitted itself handsomely. It made most excellent nominations, and set an example to the other like conventions, yet to be held, worthy of emulation. The 'Press and Knickerbocker' asks for nothing more than the nomination of such men. believing that the voters will exercise a discriminating judgment. and, despite party lines, elect the right men. In selecting Dr. Swinburne for Congressman, we think we voice the sentiment of the people of this district when we say he is the right man for the place. Firm and inflexible in integrity, with a reputation for honesty sc high that professional lobbyists will be unable to overreach him, he would, if elected. fill with credit the place once filled by such men as Daniel D. Barnard, from this district."

In taking these quotations from Independent journals, we desire to add that they were not what was known during the last campaign as Independents in bolting the Republican nominations. and had no affiliation with the then so-called Independents.

In presenting the name of Dr. Swinburne to the Republican Convention for indorsement as the nominee for Congress, Mr. Clifford D. Gregory said, —

"I rise to exercise a high and valued privilege of nominating a candidate for member of Congress from this district, who, by the pure motives which have actuated him in his private life, and the sound and humane principles which have controlled him in his public career, appeals directly and powerfully to the popular heart. I desire to present to your consideration the people's choice, and defrauded mayor, Dr. John Swinburne. With marked ability and unflagging zeal he has presided over this municipality. During his brief term of office he devised many salutary measures of reform, which proved of great economic and sanitary value to the people. One of the most important is the improvement in the system of sewerage. Mayor Swinburne also caused to be established a uniform grade for streets and buildings in the western portion of the city; and, thanks to his administration, a map is now contained in the office of the Common Council, to which all changes in the grades of streets must conform. The absence of such a system has heretofore proved disastrous to property owners in many parts of the city.

"During Swinburne's term of ten months, the expenses of the city parks were reduced several thousand dollars. This was due simply to the rigid application of rules of economy. Did not the parks look as beautiful, and was not the pleasure afforded by them just as great? A competent and reliable Democratic authority has affirmed that never in the history of Albany has there been so great economy and care displayed in the administration of the city as during the too short period that Swinburne directed its affairs."

Notwithstanding the dissensions in the Republican party, both wings recognized the necessity of a strong candidate; and that to overcome the large Democratic majority, the heavy corruption-fund used in the district, and the popularity of the Democratic candidate, they must have as their nominee a gentleman of tried integrity, whose character was above reproach, and who had the confidence of the masses. Under these circumstances, and the necessities of the times, all factional differences were put aside, and by acclamation the "Fighting Doctor" was made the standard-bearer of the party for the nineteenth district, and the political fight opened in earnest, only one paper in the city having any thing to say against him. During this campaign, as well as the preceding canvass for the mayoralty, it was pretty well understood that the very intimate relations existing between the editor of that journal and a certain doctor, with whom Dr. Swinburne had crossed professional swords in previous years, had much to do with the attacks on the Republican nominee; while, in the local department, the abuse in that paper was generally supposed to be actuated because of the relationship existing between the local editor and a physician whom Dr. Swinburne had professionally silenced.

Not only was he supported heartily by all the Republican and Independent papers in the district, but by the Republican and Independent papers in the neighboring counties. The "Troy Budget," edited by Ex-Senator MacArthur said, —

"Dr. Swinburne of Albany, the 'Fighting Doctor' as he has been not inappropriately termed, is the unanimous choice of the Republicans of the Albany district for Congress; having been nominated by the conventions of both wings of the party there. The doctor has a wonderful popularity in the city of Albany, and the presence of United-States officers at the ensuing election will prevent any repetition of the fraud which resulted last spring in hoisting Mr. Banks into the mayor's chair. Although a Democratic district, there is so much dissatisfaction with the machine tactics practised by Mr. Manning's heelers, and Dr. Swinburne has such a large personal following, that, with the Republicans thoroughly aroused and united, there appears to be no good reason why the Republican candidate should not be elected. His labors for reform, his great and unpaid exertions in the cause of humanity, his services to his country in the field, the fact that it is on record in the courts that he was once counted out for mayor, and the strong probability that he was cheated out of that office a second time, — all give him a strong hold on popular sympathy, and inspire strong hopes of his election."

The "Troy Evening Standard," the independent organ of the workingman, in an article on the nomination of Dr. Swinburne, said, —

"The doctor has positive ideas; and these are not hidden under a bushel, but are almost as well known as his acts of charity and deeds of philanthropy. His nomination came from the people, because he was of the people. His whole life has been one of continuous study of how to better humanity. In the practice of his profession, his patients have been all classes, from the sumptuous home to the lowly hovel; and so widespread has become his renown, that, on his recent return from the West, his reception by the masses was an ovation such as was never before tendered any man in the city of Albany. The claims of Dr. Swinburne to an election to Congress are greater than those that could be advanced by any other man in the district. Coming to this part of the State, he opened his free dispensary in the city of Albany seven years ago, where the sick, wounded, and disabled have been cheerfully treated, to the number of over sixty-five thousand, besides over thirty thousand poor who did not desire to have their names on the register; and there is not a street in the city where his carriage has not been seen

hastening to the call of the suffering, with the same alacrity
to the poorest dweller in the southern part of the city as to
Ten Broeck Street. A man of quick observation and sympathetic nature, he discerned the corruption of the city
government, and the way the people were oppressed, and
reluctantly consented to run for mayor. The popular vote,
twice electing him to the office, demonstrated how the
poorer elements recognized in him a friend, whom neither
bribes nor threats could induce them to desert. Again the
people have called him to come up higher in affairs of State,
and have nominated him for Congress. Can there be a possible doubt as to the duty of workingmen in deciding
whether they shall vote for him, opposed as he is and has
been by every corrupt political ring in the district, or for
his opponent? The great issue before the voters is protection to American industry or free trade to foreign pauper
labor. On this issue Dr. Swinburne is a pronounced protec-
tionist, who believes not only in a revenue, but a tariff that
will protect the American manufacturer and laborer. He
does not believe in a tariff for revenue only; but that, if a
large surplus over the incidental expenses of government
should accrue from a protective policy, it can and should be
employed in public works and improvements that would give
work to the unemployed in times of distress, and thus elevate
the dependent, rather than degrade them by poverty or pauperism. All matters of public policy the doctor is thoroughly
conversant with; and, not being an office-seeker, his views are
not twisted to suit the caprice of partisanship, but are formed
for the best interests of the nation at large. Liberal in views,
sound in judgment, honest in his transactions and intentions,
patriotic in his motives, and charitable to such an extent that
he is hated by the penurious, Dr. Swinburne should be
elected. He deserves the votes of all fair-minded men. As
he was faithful in the discharge of the duties imposed upon
him by the electors of Albany, so will he be faithful in the
enlarged sphere of national law-making usefulness."

Of the nomination, the "Press and Knickerbocker" said, —

"Dr. John Swinburne has accepted the nomination for
member of Congress by both the Republicans and the Citizens' Association. His letters of acceptance are brief and to
the point. Every voter in this congressional district must
know that Dr. Swinburne would make a faithful representative. He fully understands that the people of the country
have not been faithfully and truly represented in the House

of Representatives, and that they have become dissatisfied and restless."

The Albany "Morning Express" (Republican), in commenting on this extract from the "Press and Knickerbocker," said, —

" This is an unbiassed opinion of Dr. Swinburne's qualifications from an independent standpoint. It is also a correct view of the action of the Democratic majority in the last House of Representatives, in making a party issue of the attempt to inaugurate the free-trade policy by the passage of the Morrison twenty-per-cent reduction bill. Four-fifths of the Democrats in Congress voted for that bill. Nothing is surer than that the complete control of the legislative and executive departments of the government by the Democrats will insure the passage of that or a similar measure. This threat to break down our manufacturing interests has already operated disastrously. Capital has been frightened from investment in that class of industries, mills have been closed, and operatives have been thrown out of employment.

"The Democratic majority in the House refused to pass a bill to put our seacoast cities in a condition of defence; because they were so determined that there should be no need for a surplus in the treasury, beyond the ordinary expenses of the government, and consequently no necessity for a protective tariff, that they are willing to leave Boston, New York, Philadelphia, New Orleans, and San Francisco at the mercy of any first-class hostile power, to be battered down by their modern armaments while lying safely beyond the reach of our ancient guns.

"Dr. Swinburne does not belong to that class of statesmen. He believes in the policy of protecting the wages of labor from foreign competition. He believes in the wisdom of putting the country in such condition of defence as to place us at least beyond the contempt of foreign powers, in case of their refusal to redress wrongs inflicted on our citizens abroad, or their attempt to interfere with the rights of independent States on this continent. He has given evidence of his loyalty by his services and sacrifices in the war for the Union; and of his desire for good government by his civil services as chief magistrate of this city. He has endeared himself to the poor and the suffering by his gratuitous professional services. His popularity has twice broken down the Democratic majority of Albany, though cheated out of his office a part of one term and all of another by Democratic frauds in the count. He cannot be thus cheated this time, under the Federal election-laws; and an earnest and united effort by the opponents of the Democratic ring-rule in Albany will insure his election by a decisive majority. Every tax-payer and rent-payer who feels that he has been swindled by the corrupt ring now in control will help to crush it by voting for John Swinburne."

It was well understood throughout the State that there were local differences in the Republican party in Albany. which threatened, as they had often done before, to result in the defeat of the candidates. Of these differences the "Express" said, on Oct. 6, —

"The nomination of Dr. Swinburne for Congress by the Republican Convention, on Saturday, will undoubtedly be indorsed by the convention to be held under the auspices of the other committee. So that, although the Republicans of Albany are divided on a question of organization, they will not be divided on a question of nomination.

"Dr. Swinburne is both a professional man and a working man. The people of Albany know him in both capacities. He is eminent as a physician, but he is equally eminent as a friend of the poor. There is where his phenomenal strength lies. The poor are grateful to him for his unnumbered and unrewarded professional services. He is also a many-sided man, in his adaptability for usefulness in politics as well as in professional life. He has great executive capacity. Albany never had a better mayor. His honesty was not of that negative character that permitted others to do the stealing. Obstinately honest himself, he enforced honesty on his subordinates. He stopped the leaks in the city treasury wherever his power reached, and saved the money of the people more guardedly than if it had been his own. He made enemies, for this reason, among the profligates and spendthrifts; but the people became his friends. They will stand by him now. His popularity has broken down the Democratic majority in this city on two occasions, and he will do it again. The citizens of Albany, and the farmers of Albany County, want just this kind of sturdy economist at Washington. With proper effort his election is assured."

And on the 11th the "Express" again said, —

"By acclamation, and by unanimous vote, the 'Fighting Doctor' was yesterday nominated as the Republican candidate for Representative in Congress from this, the nineteenth. district of our State. We had supposed the convention would show that great good sense. The doctor is able, and has shown wonderful popularity in this city, where he has been twice elected mayor, and once accorded the office, notwithstanding the frauds perpetrated by Democratic inspectors, with the expectation of keeping him out. This year, as we remarked yesterday, Federal inspectors will have something to say about the vote cast for Dr. Swinburne for a member of Congress. That business will not be left entirely to the Manning machine inspectors. Every man's vote will be properly counted and properly placed. There will be no foolishness this time. Let Republicans vote as they expressed themselves yesterday, and Dr. Swinburne's election will be assured. The direct choice of two conventions, opposed to the machine and to the machine rule, why should he not be elected?

   .   .   .   .

" That the 'Fighting Doctor' has lost none of the popularity which he has displayed in so marvellous a degree in his two contests for the mayoralty of the city is most evident. Go into the strongest Democratic wards of the city, and you will hear his praises most loudly sounded. Dishonest inspectors of elections, and the money so freely expended by Democratic candidates, prevented the doctor from receiving the certificate of election as mayor last spring; but this fall the election for member of Congress will be conducted under Federal laws. United-States supervisors and marshalls will be at their posts in each election-district, and an honest count will be insured. There will be no fooling with the returns *this* time. There are hundreds of Democratic voters in this city who can be neither coaxed nor bribed to vote against Dr. Swinburne. He has helped them and their friends in distress, and they are too honest and manly to forget the fact. And this time their votes will be properly counted and scored. The Democratic inspectors of election will not have things entirely their own way in this city next month.

   .   .   .   .

" On the 4th of November next the people of Albany will decide whether or not they desire a continuance of ring-rule. With the 'Fighting Doctor' at the head of the county ticket, it will, indeed, be a strange thing if victory will not perch upon our standard. To accomplish this result, it is necessary, of course, that our brethren should work in harmony, marching upon the enemy's rank with an aggressive, unbroken column. That this end will be attained we have no doubt; and, the battle entered upon under these favorable auspices, we feel confident of victory. Honest, fearless, manly John Swinburne will lead the way."

The nomination again of the doctor was hailed by the people as an omen of coming victory and triumph of right, so far as the county of Albany was concerned; and, although the majority to be overcome seemed to anxious people almost impossible of accomplishing, yet the name of the never vanquished Dr. John Swinburne infused a new hope, and inspired a new life, that once more Albany would do her duty to the nation, as it did in the great struggle of years before. It was a repetition of the feeling of April, 1861, when men doubted how New York would stand in the Rebellion. The nomination of the doctor settled the question for the populace of Albany, as did the appearance of the first regiment in New York on its way to Washington for New York. On that occasion, as the regiment emerged from the Astor House with bayonets gleaming in the spring-day sun, and the column moved to the tune of " Yankee Doodle," a slight murmur of applause was heard, like the whispers of a gentle zephyr, which, in a few moments, had grown to a deafening cheer from the thousands that lined the streets, silencing all other sounds, and driving away all the clouds of doubt which had hung over the possible action of New York in the coming conflict. At the first announcement that the " Fighting Doctor " was in the field, there was a ripple of approval, and the questions were asked, "Is it possible for him to win? How near can he come to victory?" In a short time the rippling stream became a rushing torrent, carrying every thing before it; and, wherever the doctor made his appearance in a public gathering, a spontaneous burst of enthusiasm greeted him, leaving no sound to be heard for a time but its own reverberation. An instance of this popular feeling of hope and confidence was shown at a mass meeting in the Hudson-avenue tent on the evening of Oct. 24, when the Hon. Alexander Sullivan, the brilliant Irish orator, was addressing a multitude on the issues of the campaign. The Swinburne

Guards had escorted their eloquent countryman to the tent where he was to deliver his address, and then returned for their " boss," as they called the doctor. On arriving at the tent, a cheer rent the air, such as the speaker said he never heard before, and wondered how it escaped without ripping the tent into threads. The cause of this outburst perplexed him for a time, as he had never before seen the doctor.

In speaking of that meeting and the doctor's appearance on the platform, the " Express," on the following morning said, —

" The banker, the broker, the lawyer, and the merchant mingled with the sturdy sons of toil, and all seemed delighted with the incisive aphorisms and unanswerable arguments of the talented and eloquent young leader. We said there were no interruptions. In that respect we slightly erred. There was an outbreak during Mr. Sullivan's address, but it was not a Democratic one. It occurred after the meeting had progressed somewhat, when Dr. Swinburne, puffing from overhaste and exertion, had emerged from the side-wings, and taken a seat in the front of the stage. When his genial, kindly face was recognized, the whole audience rose *en masse*, and a roar which would have drowned that of a hurricane greeted the war-horse. This, however, was only an episode of the meeting ; and, barring that, every thing was conducted in the most orderly fashion."

The interruption consisted of three times three cheers and a tiger for the doctor.

In the issue of Oct. 29, under the head of " A Man to be elected," the " Evening Journal " editorially said, —

" That high sense of fair play which dwells deep down in the heart of every American citizen should elect Dr. John Swinburne to Congress. Twice he has been a candidate for mayor of Albany. Once he was counted out, and the courts were compelled to give him his due. The second time his competitor was seated by a bare majority, and grave doubts exist to this day if he had any majority at all.

" The brave man — in fact, the only man — for the emergency, in overthrowing local misrule, was Dr. John Swinburne. His active mind, his intelligent judgment, and his brave heart led the fight, and conducted it to a successful termination. It is not too much to say that it was a public calamity that he was not seated for a second term. Had he been mayor of Albany, no political organizations of either side would have dared to occupy and to destroy public property. Dr. Swinburne would not have been the partisan that Mayor Banks has proved himself to be. Nor would he have sneered at tax-payers, and snapped his fingers in their faces. Nor would he have promised to right a wrong, and failed to keep his promise. No trifler with the public, no subservient instrument of any politician, or ring of politicians, is Dr. Swinburne. He is as incorruptible as he is independent.

"If Republicans will do their duty faithfully and earnestly, Dr. Swinburne will be elected. His following embraces many men who do not belong to the Republican party, many of whom will throw a Blaine with a Swinburne ticket."

On Nov. 3 the "Press and Knickerbocker" (Indiana) said, —

"The voters in this congressional district can make no mistake by voting for Dr. John Swinburne to represent them in the next Congress. He is a man of the highest integrity. No swindling lobbyist can tamper with him, or swerve him from a faithful discharge of his duties. He is sound on the tariff and the great labor question. All his life he has been the friend of the poor, and has given the best years of his life in service for the amelioration of their condition. He understands fully the wants and the needs of the industrials of the country. His sympathies have always been with the people, as against political rings. He has never been a candidate of theirs for any public office, for the reason that they knew they could not control his action. He is one of the most brainy men ever nominated for that office from any district in this State, and would wield an immense power in Congress. One sentence from him on any public question would have more weight than columns of sophistry from political demagogues. And he would always vote right. In short, he is just the man to send to Congress at this time, when men of integrity and ability are so much needed in that body."

The campaign was one of the most bitter ever contested in the county of Albany. Men holding positions in the State departments, under Democratic officials, were under a system of espionage, where their loyalty was in any degree questioned. Intimidation was resorted to, threats indirectly made, and every effort devised to rob men of their manhood, and reduce them to political slavery.   Albany was the home of the Democratic leader, Mr. Manning, who had made Gov. Cleveland the nominee of his party for President.   Gov. Cleveland, it was ordered, must have the regular majority increased at any sacrifice.   Coming into the capital city with a majority in Albany County in 1882 of 9,432, and having resided there up to the time of election, with all the influence that his patronage was supposed to secure, the Democratic leaders would figure no majority lower than 5,000, and boasted it would be 10,000.   For Congress the Democratic nominee was a gentleman with a popularity second to no man in the party in the county of Albany; and so confident were the leaders of the party, that they were willing, the evening before election, to wager odds on his election by a handsome majority.

But the elements of reform were at work in the county; and, by scores and hundreds, men who had always voted with the ring were leaving the party and coming over into the Republican ranks, while hundreds of others, who would vote the head of the Democratic ticket, were determined to and did vote for Dr. John Swinburne for Congress.   In one of the strongest wards in the city, the third, was organized the "Swinburne Guards," composed of independent Irishmen, who had always been in the Democratic ranks; and they were seen in every Republican parade, and presented as fine an appearance as any in line, and were proud of the stand they had taken for principles.   No other man in the Republican party could have wielded such an influence as did Dr. John Swinburne in that campaign.   His name was a magnet that drew men wherever it was pronounced; and the very appearance of his carriage was often the signal for cheers from men and boys, while from the home of the lowly, and the heart of the humblest laborer, came an honest "God bless John Swinburne."

With a united Democratic party aided by free-trade Republicans, and an immense electioneering fund, the victory of Dr. John Swinburne and the Republican ticket on that November day was an eventful page in the history of political contests in Albany County.

The results of the day were the reducing of Gov. Cleveland's majority from 9,432 in 1882 down to 647 in 1884; 1,059 less than Hancock's majority in 1880. The majorities in 1883 for comptroller, of 3,534; for Senator, 3,173; for justice of Supreme Court, 2,939; and for county clerk, 3,162, — were all wiped out, and the Republican county treasurer and coroner elected. The majority given Dr. Swinburne's opponent when the latter ran for Congress in 1882 was 6,393; but this time the people's friend was in the field, and the "Fighting Doctor" saw his system of extension and counter-extension illustrated by the pulling down at one end of the 6,393, and adding at the other 2,504, as his majority for Congress, — a majority his friends expect to see doubled this fall for him for governor.

As the news came in to a prominent Democratic resort, where a number of leaders were anxiously awaiting the returns, and the final footings showed all the towns for Swinburne, and that every ward in West Troy and Cohoes had gone for the doctor, one of the most prominent politicians cried out, in almost tones of anguish, "My God, can that be so? Well, Swinburne can be elected to any office; and we might as well throw up the sponge on him now."

After the battle, the Republicans of Albany, while regretting that the head of the ticket was not elected, were more than delighted with their success in the county; and they pointed with just pride to their standard-bearer and leader, and felt if one or two other districts had had such a leader, around whom all true citizens could have rallied, the whole ticket would have triumphed.

The "Express," on Nov. 20, said, —

"What is enthusiasm? It can be explained without a dictionary by the masses who assembled last evening to pay their respects to Dr. John Swinburne, the Congressman-elect from this district. It was a spontaneous exhibition of the people for the worth of one who has done more for the needy poor than any other; who for years has occupied a position of trust among us. Defrauded of the suffrages of a free people, his vote taken from him, and after a sturdy fight installed into an office it was sought to take from him, running again for the office of mayor, defrauded by the use of thousands of dollars, the city officials against him, the work of dishonest inspectors throwing him from a position he was honestly elected to, yet still he stood to the fore; and, while not maintained by others who looked for personal aggrandizement and political favors, he always remained the ' friend of the people.'

" Knowing this, these people have made him their representative in the next (forty-eighth) Congress from this district; and last evening a reception was tendered in his honor by those who stood by him through the heat of a campaign, wherein it was the hope and the speech of henchmen that ' Dan Manning would carry Albany County for Cleveland.' It was carried, we admit, by a plurality of 647 for Cleveland; while Dr. Swinburne went through with a majority of 2,500.

" It was not of his seeking that the reception was tendered him last evening. It was the work of friends. The Capital City Blaine and Logan Club, under a pledge made to the Jacksonians, a Cleveland and Hendricks campaign club, agreed to act as escort in case the standard-bearer of their party was elected, and it was understood they would fulfil their promise last evening; but, owing to the inclemency of the weather, it was agreed by both commands to postpone the parade until next Tuesday evening. It was the intention of the ' Capital Citys,' after fulfilling the pledge, to serenade the ' Fighting Doctor,' County Treasurer-elect Battersby, and Lansing Hotaling, the elected Assemblyman from the second district; and this they will carry out.

" At eight o'clock citizens generally began paying their respects to the Congressman-elect, they being received without formality in the parlors on the second floor."

On Nov. 5 the " Evening Journal " said, —

" Search the returns, by counties, of every State from Maine to California, and not a single one will show so positive, so unexpected, and so decisive a gain as that of Albany.

" There are many reasons why Republicans to-day should rejoice; but there is no matter, we believe, for heartier congratulation than the election of Dr. John Swinburne to Congress. It was a magnificent tribute to the man, unprecedented in the political history of this county, — a demonstration that Dr. Swinburne enjoys the confidence of the people of Albany County in a larger measure than has any other man. He will take with him to Washington the same conscientious regard for the interests of the people, and scrupulous zeal in their behalf, which characterized his administration of the affairs of this city."

CHAPTER XIX.

SWINBURNE'S DISPENSARY.

Establishing a Free Dispensary. — Opposed to Deforming the Poor. — A Conscientious Instructor. — Showing up Malpractice. — War among the Doctors. — A High-handed Proceeding. — Esteemed by Students. — A Committee's Investigations. — A Name that gave Tone.

REVOLUTIONS are never backwards, whether in political or scientific economy; and these are, as a general rule, set in motion because of mismanagement by those in authority, protested against by some advanced mind, who, in behalf of humanity, demands a reform in one, and a deeper application to study and the laws of nature in the other. In the rupture beween the doctor and the professors of the Albany Medical College, and the establishment of the dispensary in Albany by Dr. Swinburne, the public at large have become better acquainted with the cause of deformities, — results which they have learned were, in a great degree, due to bad surgical treatment. As the public, ignorant of medical ethics, have had the light thrown to them by one so eminent and learned as Dr. Swinburne, they have been better able to understand these matters; and, in answer to their unmistakable demands, many of the profession have been compelled to attain a better knowledge of medicine and surgery, although but comparatively few in the vicinity of Albany have made any perceptible advance, while a great many remain, professionally, where they were when they received the "sheepskin" from their Alma Mater which entitled them by the laws of the State of New York to practise medicine and hang out the "M.D." This, of course, only applies to those physicians who believe the colleges and tradition teach the only gospel to which they owe allegiance. Deformities and poor results have decreased largely; but this is owing to the fact that very many of the unfortunate maimed, instead of calling in every professing surgeon, insist on their treatment coming from the dispensary, and those who practise the systems there laid down.

The first incentive to establish the dispensary arose from the doctor's earnest desire to save the maimed poor from mutilation and deformity; and to have accomplished this revolution without opposition and sacrifice would have been phenomenal, and a consummation unprecedented in the history of the world since the first and greatest sacrifice for the human race was made on Calvary by the Great Physician and Maker of all mankind; as it appears to be ordained that all efforts to raise men, or to ameliorate the condition of humanity, are only to be attained by sacrifices. The history of the founding of the dispensary, and its work since that time, are peculiar, and a part of the history of Albany.

Dr. Swinburne's connection with the Albany Medical College, as physician to the almshouse, and as consulting surgeon to St. Peter's and the City hospitals, brought to his notice many instances of deformity, where he believed different treatment would have been productive of better results; and he determined, no matter what factions or professional opposition might be aroused, to insist on a more enlightened and advanced system of treating the injured, that the poor, and even pauperism, might, in the name of humanity, be protected from deformity, and a higher order of surgery, with better results and more definite learning, be reached; leaving out the practice of traditional surgery, so that the best results in accordance with scientific laws might be accomplished. Occupying the chair of professor of fractures and clinical surgery in the Albany Medical College, he felt the double responsibility devolving upon him,—that of the treatment of the people in the future by those who were looking up to him as a teacher, and the duty he owed the students to place before them true surgery, and not malpractice or quackery. This double duty he performed faithfully; and most of his associate professors, instead of gladly availing themselves of his knowledge, preferred he should close his eyes to their apparent ignorance, and be silent to the injuries their practice had inflicted, and not attempt to educate the students in any line not in accord with the teachings they had advanced. To illustrate the evil results of radical, hasty, and ignorant traditional surgery, he did not seek subjects in some foreign clime or among the books; for there was a very numerous class of these from whom to choose in Albany, who had been treated in the hospitals, institutions professionally under the direct supervision of the college. In citing these cases, he drew attention to some treated by members of the faculty, according to a report of the Common Council, without giving the surgeons' names. One of these cases, against which he warned the students not to pursue a similar treatment, was that of a young man, William Lawton, a brakeman on the New York Central Railroad, who had had both legs crushed under a train. He was taken to the hospital, made unconscious with ether, and, against his protest, the right leg amputated above the knee; Dr. Vandeveer, according to Lawton's statement before the committee, declaring he was sure to die of the injuries, and that the leg might as well come off; Drs. Vandeveer, Ward, and Mosher performing the operation. They sought also to cut off the other leg, but were prevented by Lawton's brother. For seven months he remained in the hospital under the treatment of Drs. Ward and Mosher; they, with Dr. Vandeveer, declaring the other leg must come off as soon as he became strong enough to bear the operation, Dr. Vandeveer declaring the leg would be of no use. Meanwhile the foot became clubbed, and the toes also so clubbed that, if he ever walked at all, he would have had to do so on their knuckles, being able to put no other part to the ground. After a useless pasteboard case had been put around the limb with some oakum, nothing was done for it by the surgeons. After six or seven months he was discharged from the hospital; though, besides these bad results of the treatment, his leg was bent backward at the broken place, the bones having failed to grow together and overlapped each other. Though Dr. Swinburne was consulting surgeon to the hospital, the case was never brought to his notice while Lawton was therein. When called to see him at his home about a month after his discharge, unhealed, from the hospital, Dr. Swinburne said that there was no need to cut the leg off. He cut the tendons attached to Lawton's foot, bent the foot around to its proper place, kept it there, drew the leg out to its full length, so that the bones fitted together again instead of overlapping, and kept the limb thus extended till the broken ends rejoined and the tendons grew together; all this having to be done to remedy the deformity which had grown up in the hospital, under the surgeons' eyes. When Lawton appeared before the committee, the leg seemed, and he said it was, in good condition; while the crutches on which he came bore mournful evidence of the treatment he had received before Dr. Swinburne saw him. Another case was that of John Dolan, a cartman, who was thrown from his cart by a railroad train, and his right leg broken in three places, one break being near the hip. He was treated by Dr. Vandeveer, who for some time failed to discover the break near the hip. Some time after he pronounced Dolan well enough to leave his bed, and took off the dressing; but the leg thereupon swelled up terribly. About three months later he took the dressings off again; but, as soon as Dolan tried to move, the break at the hip showed itself. The knee was stiff; and the foot was turned out sidewise, so that Dolan could not turn it into the proper position. When Dr. Swinburne was called to see him, he found that the bones had not been joined; that the dressings had been removed, and all efforts to heal abandoned, that the muscles had become hopelessly shortened, and that they had drawn up the foot so that Dolan's leg was six inches shorter than the other. Dr. Swinburne advised that the leg be drawn out, and fastened till the shortening was lessened, and till the broken bones united. The leg was thus made but two inches and a half short. Despite all Dr. Swinburne could do, Dolan is a cripple for life,—stiff in the joints, and has a permanent bad swelling near his hip.

For this service Dr. Vandeveer charged two hundred dollars; and collected this sum without Dolan's knowledge, before Dolan was able to go out, from the railroad company, who were to pay Dolan damages. For warning the students against repeating similar errors Dr. Swinburne was removed: so said the report to the Common Council.

Because of these and other instances in which he differed with the faculty, in insisting on proper treatment of patients in the hospital, and a better system of surgery, the chair to which he was appointed in 1876, as professor of fractures, dislocations, and clinical surgery, was abolished. The college was an institution in which the public were interested, and how was this act accomplished? It was a star-chamber arrangement. At eleven o'clock at night, a majority of the faculty, — having previously agreed among themselves to pass a resolution recommending the trustees of the college to abolish the chair of surgery occupied by Dr. Swinburne, — by a pre-arranged agreement with a majority of the trustees, met, and decided to abolish the chair; and the next day at eleven o'clock the trustees did so.

On Professor Swinburne appearing at the amphitheatre of the college, where he was in the habit of delivering his lectures, and where a large number of students were congregated and awaiting to get in, he found the doors locked against him; and was informed such action was taken by order of the board of trustees. Deprived of the privilege of holding his clinics there, he went to the hospital to hold them, where he found many cases of deformity, some of them congenital, but a much larger number the direct results of bad surgery; and he was then more than ever convinced that the people were too much and too badly doctored by incompetency, and of the necessity of a more enlightened and conservative surgery. But because he was unyielding in his conviction of right and duty, in his determination to save the poor from mutilation, and to educate the students in a better practical and scientific surgery, he was again frustrated by a collusion between the college faculty and the governors of the hospital, and he retired. At that time the hospitals were receiving a large number of patients: and, although professing to be charitable institutions, they were only pseudo-charitable, and not so in fact; as all the poor patients were paid for by the city, while the paying patients were pouring mints of money into the pockets of the doctors.

Finding, on account of his connection with the hospitals, that their business was running behind, and they losing their surgery, these zealous professionals entered into another combination with the city authorities, by which they hoped to have the doctor's skill and labor withdrawn from the poor. But, as usual, their schemes came to naught; and Dr. Swinburne, holding to his motto, "Labor omnia vincit," was more determined than ever to carry out his humane purposes. He, during all this time, sought no conflict with the profession which had solicited him on his return from the Franco-Prussian war, knowing his humane and generous impulses, not to inaugurate any system of relief that would interfere with their professional practice pecuniarily; they promising to adopt the most modern and enlightened system of conservative surgery as practised by him, and to consult with him in all important matters.

Although this was the first conflict between Dr. Swinburne and the college faculty that became a public matter, it was not, in reality, the first. Many years before, when he was a very young man, so skilful was he that he was made demonstrator of anatomy in the college, a position he held for three years. Having, then, settled and positive views as to the branch of the profession it was his duty to present to the students, a difference arose between him and the faculty; and he retired from the chair. He then fitted up a private dissecting-room, and conducted a private school of anatomy, having an attendance of students that outrivalled that of the college class of anatomy.

In 1878 and 1879 the students of the college, strongly impressed with the value of his instruction, passed resolutions, asking the publication of his lectures, in book form, to guide them in their practice. The last resolution, Jan. 15, 1879, reads thus : —

"That we respectfully and earnestly request Professor Swinburne to publish his work on the 'Treatment of Fractures and Dislocations,' for the benefit of those who have listened with much interest to his lectures upon the subject: and we, judging from the wonderful results we have witnessed at his hands, deem the principles as defined by him the true ones, and the appliances used to carry them out the most consistent, simple, and best that can be adopted."

The action of the trustees of the college in abolishing the chair may have enabled them to carry out what schemes they had in view; but that they had no sympathy from those most interested, — the students, — is evident by the following article, published in the " Albany Argus," under the head of " Handsome Recognition of Respect ": —

" It will be remembered that, at a recent meeting of the faculty of the Albany Medical College, a resolution was adopted declaring the chair of fractures, dislocations, and clinical surgery abolished; the terms of the resolution requiring that the action on the part of the faculty should be ratified by the board of trustees. In accordance therewith the trustees held a meeting, before which the action of the faculty, as above stated, came up; and the resolution was ratified by a vote of eighteen to four. The chair in question was held by Professor John Swinburne; and it is said that more or less comment has been made, not only including the students, but also members of the board of trustees as well.

" The students attending the college, desiring to give expression as to the existing relations between Professor Swinburne and themselves, and desiring also to return thanks for the much valued service rendered them by their professor while occupying the chair of surgery, held a meeting on Wednesday afternoon, on which occasion Mr. Griffin of New York acted as president, and Mr. Spencer of Massachusetts as secretary. The president stated the nature of the meeting; and, on motion, a committee was appointed to draft resolutions suitable to the occasion, and expressive of regret at the loss they had sustained by the abolishment of the chair of fractures, dislocations, and clinical surgery.

" The following is a copy of the resolutions alluded to, which met the hearty approval of the students, and which were unanimously adopted: —

" ' *Whereas* The chair of fractures and dislocations and clinical surgery has been set aside by the recent action of the board of trustees of the Albany Medical College, of which institution we are students, which action removes from the faculty Professor John Swinburne, whose pro-

found erudition in the science of surgery, and universally gentlemanly
bearing towards the students, has endeared him to us; therefore be it

"' *Resolved*, That we deeply regret the severing of his connection with
the college, of the faculty of which he was to us a desirable and valued
member;

"' *Resolved*, That through the action of the trustees we are compelled to
sustain the loss of much valuable instruction on the subject of fractures,
and other branches of clinical surgery;

"' *Resolved*, That a copy of these resolutions be presented to Dr.
Swinburne.'

"The lectures on fractures, dislocations, and clinical surgery,
by Professor Swinburne, have been held Friday afternoons;
and it is said large numbers of the students have availed
themselves of the opportunity to be present on those days.
The action of the faculty and the board of trustees having
been made public, it was a question whether or not, under the
circumstances, Dr. Swinburne would deliver his usual lecture
on Friday afternoon. But it is said that on the appearance
of the professor at the usual hour designated he was received
with rounds of applause, and the students generally expressed
themselves as being deeply grateful for the many courtesies
and valued services rendered. It was probably the last lecture that Professor Swinburne will deliver, as it was learned
that he was denied the privilege of holding his usual Saturday clinic yesterday; and, in commenting on the subject, the
students have expressed themselves as noted in the resolutions above."

The matter had become public talk, and caused considerable newspaper comment. The city of Albany was a member
of the corporation of the college, the mayor and recorder
being *ex-officio* members; and on Feb. 2, 1880, the Common
Council, a large majority being Democrats, appointed Thomas
B. Franklin, Edwin V. Kirtland, and M. J. Gorman a committee on the affairs of the Albany Medical College, and the
removal of Dr. John Swinburne. The committee, after a
prolonged investigation, submitted their report, in which they
said, —

"Dr. John Swinburne is one of the most eminent citizens
of Albany, a man in whose fame every Albanian is entitled
to take a just and generous pride. For the four years'
instruction given by him in the college, he has received no
compensation.

"He is now conducting a practice of about a hundred and

twenty patients daily; about a hundred of whom are treated at his office, or in an adjoining dispensary built by him for the purpose last fall. He holds a surgical clinic every Saturday morning, where are treated weekly from twenty to forty patients. These clinics, during the last session of the college, were attended by thirty or forty of its students. From twenty to thirty young men are entered as students in his office, and learn the art of surgery by practice under his direction. Since the first of October last, about two thousand cases have been treated in his practice, without a single failure to heal; a result almost, if not quite, unparalleled in the history of the surgical art. What is perhaps more remarkable still, this immense scientific result has been achieved almost wholly at Dr. Swinburne's own cost. Possessed of means that place him beyond the need of working for his bread, instead of retiring from practice, he continues it with singular energy; instead of seeking practice among the rich, he has repeatedly refused it when offered, and has long and freely given his services in nine-tenths of the cases he has treated, often refusing fees from poor patients when tendered. Leaving to less fortunate brethren the remunerative practice, he has contented himself with dispensing one of the noblest of charities, the use of great professional skill, to aid a mass of sufferers unable to pay for it. Even this, however, has not availed to save him from envy. Some members of his profession, instead of admiring and emulating his generosity, have complained of it as tending to prevent them from getting fees from some of the poor persons whom he has healed without charge.

"He is now consulting surgeon to two hospitals — St. Peter's and the Child's; and, though not a homœopath, surgeon-in-chief to the Homœopathic.

"Things were in this condition, when, on re-assembling after the holiday recess in January last, the students of the college were amazed by the news that Dr. Swinburne had been 'legislated out of office,' — that his chair was abolished; and that they would not be allowed to complete the course of instruction by him, for which they had entered and paid. The public were startled by the news that one of the foremost of their number had been suddenly expelled from a faculty, — his membership wherein was a matter of proper civic pride and of city benefit, — and that the arrangement for the special instruction of the coming physicians of Albany in a most important branch had ceased."

After describing the manner in which the abolishing of the chair was effected, the committee said, —

"Such in brief is the history of this extraordinary transaction. The city's representatives in the board of trustees, the mayor and recorder, were kept in utter ignorance of the project until it was carried through; and they severely condemned it when they learned of it. The mayor states that had he known of it the resolution would probably not have passed, and that he deems its passage an outrage. The president of the board, Hon. Amasa J. Parker, strongly disapproved the act, and voted against it. The dean of the faculty, Dr. Thomas Hun, knowing that the act was to be done, refrained from presiding at the faculty meeting, absented himself thence, and avoided all connection with the matter. The secretary of the trustees, Mr. George Dexter, expressed regret at the abolition of the chair, and said if he had to vote on the subject again he should oppose it. Hon. Bradford R. Wood, formerly United-States minister to Denmark, one of the most prominent and respected citizens of Albany, opposed the resolution in the board, and testifies that it was sprung on him without notice, and that he disapproves the entire action. Hon. Joseph H. Ramsey, president of the Albany and Susquehanna Railroad, formerly State Senator from Albany County, testifies that he considers the action unjust, and a grave injury to the interests of the college. President Potter of Union University was not present at the meeting of the board, and seems to have known naught of the affair. Mr. Clarence Rathbone also opposed the abolition.

"The majority of the trustees who voted for the abolition almost unanimously confess that they did so in ignorance of the facts of the case, and in deference to the wishes of the faculty. They say that, as laymen, they did not deem themselves competent to decide physicians' disagreements; and that, being informed that there was a want of harmony in the faculty, they thought it a hopeless task to sift the matter, and preferred to dispose of it by letting the member of the faculty go who could not agree with his colleagues. But herein they plainly failed in their duty. As the legal corporation and rulers of the college, they should have ascertained the nature and cause of that 'want of harmony' among the faculty,— which your committee have found by no means impossible to do,—and should have seen that the interests of the college and of the public were protected, and no injustice done. The custom of the majority ruling has very positive bounds. A majority has no more right to commit injustice than a minority. Your committee are aware that this view — that the man who cannot agree with his colleagues should go out — obtains in other institutions and places ; but it cannot be too severely condemned. It is a product of laziness, cowardice, and carelessness, and often breeds gross wrong. Under its practical working a man may know, or be the victim of, a great injustice ; and if he will not silently acquiesce or suffer, but dares resist or complain, the appointing power, because he " cannot agree with " those who misconduct, displaces the innocent and retains the misdoers. This puts a penalty on innocence and a premium on wrong. Men who act on such a view as this deserve to be despised. Nor does it seem to have occurred to either trustees or faculty that if any one was to leave the college it should have been those who failed, instead of him who had succeeded where they failed.

" The reason ascertained by your committee for the faculty's recommending that Dr. Swinburne be legislated out of place, — that he showed his classes failures made by his colleagues, — assumes that he was bound to conceal the shortcomings of his colleagues and brother physicians ; but this assumption cannot be tolerated an instant. It is a gross violation of that right of free speech which is dear to every American freeman, and which no man worthy the name of freeman will ever yield. Besides, every man must stand or fall on the record he makes : no man has a right to demand that others shall help him to hide his misdeeds; and, to these plain rules of fairness and common sense, physicians are not exceptions.

" But the matter is far more important in another way. The demand that one physician shall aid to cover up the shortcomings of another, aims to keep the incompetent physician employed in treating patients who employ him under a mistaken belief in his skill, and to enable him thus to realize an income he does not deserve. If this is successful, it results in placing the competent and studious physician at a disadvantage, by compelling concealment of his superiority over his less competent brother, and thus defrauding him of repute, practice, and revenue, which are justly his, for the benefit of him who is not entitled thereto.

" Since it became known that he had ceased to be connected with the Albany Medical College, two colleges in New York have offered him chairs. He has also received invitations to treat fractures at St. Vincent Hospital ; and has been invited by Dr. J. Marion Sims to go to London, and teach the surgeons of that scientific metropolis of the world how to heal such injuries. Thus the fruit of his removal has been to expose Albany to the risk of the total loss of his skill. He informs your committee that he does not wish to be re-instated in the college.

" It is stated by some of the trustees that the board were informed by Dr. Vanderpoel and others that the faculty stood ready to resign in a body unless Dr. Swinburne was ousted; but every member of the faculty — a majority — whom the committee have been able to examine flatly denies having taken any such position. Your committee, however, are unable to perceive that had the faculty taken this stand, or been believed to do so, it would justify the hasty action of the majority of the trustees. The latter are supposed to be men competent to act intelligently and justly, and not to be liable to intimidation. Besides, the facts ascertained regarding Drs. Vanderpoel, Vandeveer, Ward, Mosher, Bigelow, and Hailes, by no means indicate that had they resigned the interests of the college would have materially suffered.

" Regarding the ' want of harmony' which many witnesses, by evident preconcert, alleged as the cause for abolishing the chair of clinical surgery, Dr. Swinburne testifies that, though experience had given him bad impressions of some of the faculty, he had no ill will toward any of them, and was astonished at their course ; and it does not appear that he ever tried to keep or put any of them out of the college.

" The utter flimsiness of the reason assigned for depriving the college of its most illustrious instructor suggests the existence of other reasons, and these are not hard to find. The abolished chair has been divided between the two men whose failures Dr. Swinburne felt obliged to warn the students against repeating ; and it may be expected that those men will instruct future students, and be resorted to by future graduates as consulting surgeons, with consequences to the patients which, in view of those failures, may be imagined.

" Dr. S. Oakley Vanderpoel — who as temporary presiding-officer of the faculty, and as a member of the trustees took part in the removal of Dr. Swinburne, and who seems to entertain strong objections to investigations — was, during Gov. Fenton's administration, twice a candidate for the post of surgeon-general, which he had held under Gov. Morgan. Dr. Swinburne, being consulted by the governor on the subject, advised against the appointment. When, on the re-organization of the present college faculty in 1876, it was proposed to make Health-officer Vanderpoel dean, and Deputy Health-officer Mosher registrar, Dr. Swinburne strongly opposed this, and defeated Vanderpoel's election, deeming him unfit. The services courageously rendered by Dr. Swinburne in these matters were such as to entitle him to Dr. Vanderpoel's life-long remembrance. Indeed, Dr. Swinburne seems to be afflicted with an unfortunate propensity, which Lord Chester-field would have regretted and condemned, — a propensity for speaking the truth; and this habit appears to have peculiarly endeared him to others besides Dr. Vanderpoel.

"Besides the reasons already referred to, Dr. Jacob S. Mosher, now registrar of the faculty, who, as well as Dr. Vanderpoel, has placed himself in practical contempt of the authority of the Common Council, by refusing to answer questions about this subject, was, as deputy health-officer under Dr. Vanderpoel, necessarily privy to many of the latter's transactions; and, in the first investigation of his superior's acts, he received one or two severe touches from Dr. Swinburne. For instance, Dr. Mosher swore before the Senate Finance Committee that the running-expenses of the quarantine steamer 'Fletcher,' in 1872, were about five hundred dollars a month : Dr. Swinburne put in evidence the fact that the expenses were just about twice what Dr. Mosher swore they were. The latter, as executive officer of quarantine, swore that the 'Fletcher' was needed to carry the sick, and that he had seen there hundred cases of cholera on her in one year : Dr. Swinburne showed that during the whole of Mosher's administration to that time there were by official report only fifty-two cases of cholera. He also suggested that the Senate Committee inquire whether the deaths of a number of convalescent patients on Swinburne Island was due to Dr. Mosher's introducing a small-pox patient among them. It is true that Dr. Swinburne did none of these things till Dr. Mosher had joined with Vanderpoel in misrepresenting him to the committee. When Dr. Mosher was made registrar, Dr. Swinburne spoke and voted against it, saying he considered him unfit to take charge of the funds. Favors like these are apt to be long remembered. It was Dr. Mosher who pre-arranged the meeting of the trustees at which Dr. Swinburne was removed from the college; and it was Dr. Vanderpoel who, besides falsely informing the trustees that the faculty would all resign unless this abolition took place, also informed the trustees that there was no need of Dr. Swinburne's services.

"Dr. William Hailes, jun., who voted for the resolution to displace Dr. Swinburne, was disquieted by Dr. Swinburne's showing to his class the dislocated shoulder of Mrs. Ann Ballard, which Dr. Hailes, though not a surgeon, had tried to treat, and, after carrying the patient through a month's terribly painful treatment, had wholly failed to replace. Dr. John M. Bigelow, who voted for the same resolution, was annoyed by Dr. Swinburne's showing the students the case of Miss

Reilly, whose limbs, under six months of Dr. Bigelow's treatment, became so deformed that she could not move ; and whom Dr. Bigelow gave up as sure to die of the rheumatism which deformed her, but whom Dr. Swinburne cured.   Dr. Samuel B. Ward, who seconded the resolution looking to Dr. Swinburne's removal, was displeased by that gentleman's comments on his reading a paper before the County Medical Society, and publishing it in 'The American Journal of Obstetrics,' wherein he stated, as facts, things of a very doubtful sort.   He was also disturbed by Dr. Swinburne's healing many patients whom he had treated without success.

" Mr. Robert H. Pruyn, who aided in the board of trustees to abolish Dr. Swinburne's chair, and whose refunds of large sums to the Japanese government in a way not precisely voluntary are matters of notoriety, was far from pleased by Dr. Swinburne's expressing the belief that he shared Vanderpoel's quarantine profits, and observing concerning him that 'it was fortunate for Japan that she was anchored.'   Mr. H. H. Martin was not exactly gratified at Dr. Swinburne's strictures as an expert on a scheme to supply the city with water, with which scheme Dr. Martin was connected.

" But the financial affairs of the college afford another reason for the desire to get rid of Dr. Swinburne.   The latter testifies that the income of the college has never been properly stated, or accounted for, since he entered the faculty in 1876. Professor Balch, chairman of the finance committee of the faculty, testifies that, except in one year, he has never been able to get a sight of the books of account.   The mayor and recorder, and nearly every one of the trustees, state that they know naught of the financial state of the institution beyond the debt secured by mortgage ; and few of them really know aught of that.   One gentleman had to be convinced before he could testify that he was a member of the board : he did not know, nor at first believe, that he was.   Very few of the faculty, not even the dean, knew, or could intelligently state, the financial condition of the concern.   The registrar, Dr. Jacob S. Mosher, into whose hands the money paid in by the students has gone. was unable when on the stand to state the annual income or expenditure of the college ; and, being desired to produce the books and accounts for the committee's information, committed an additional contempt by refusing to produce them ; giving as an excuse the extraordinary assertion that the finances of the college were a strictly private matter, and that even the trustees, the legal corporation of the college, had no right to examine into the finances of their own institution. Mr. George Dexter, treasurer of the trustees, states that he handles none of the funds, does not see the books, nor know the receipts or expenditures. The reports of the college to the regents of the State University, since the appointment of the present faculty in 1876, have failed to comply with the law since Jan. 31, 1877, having made no statement of the finances of the college."

Dr. Swinburne's withdrawal from the Albany Hospital was a necessary step, demanded by every consideration of professional pride, and the honest protection he felt bound to accord such of his private patients as were in that institution. The particulars of this quarrel are given in an article in the "Albany Morning Express," Nov. 13, 1878, in which that paper mentions Dr. Swinburne as one of the names which gave character, tone, and dignity to the institution. The "Express" said, —

"Yesterday was a day of quiet but intense excitement within the cold walls of the Albany Hospital. Dr. Swinburne, the consulting surgeon, did not put in an appearance. Dr. Russell, the house physician, was in the blues over a snubbing he had received from some of the doctors; and whispers were current that the splendid staff, comprising the leading physicians of the city, was about to dissolve, and that a row was imminent which would cast in the shade all previous quarrels of the doctors. We were aware that the board of governors had held secret sessions, and that the house physician had been on trial for some offence; but it was not until yesterday afternoon that we were enabled to get at the facts of the case, which we now present entire to the readers of the 'Express.'

"It now seems evident that there is to be a break in the ranks, and that some of the physicians will retire. Dr. S. A. Russell, the house physician, is a gentleman who is presumed to be a warm partisan of Dr. Vandeveer, and whom Dr. Swinburne, the consulting surgeon, evidently regards as inimical to his (Swinburne's) interests. Dr. Russell is charged with interfering with the patients of Dr. Swinburne, and has been so persistent in it that the consulting surgeon at last preferred formal charges against him. The case of the offending doctor has been acted upon by the board of governors, who have acquitted the gentleman with a slight reprimand, as will be seen by the following letter, which Mr. Sartell Prentice has forwarded to Dr. Swinburne: —

ALBANY, Nov. 9, 1878.

DR. JOHN SWINBURNE,
    Consulting Surgeon of the Albany Hospital.

Dear Sir, — At the meeting of the board of governors of the Albany Hospital last evening, after the retirement of the several members of the hospital staff, who had by visitation favored the board with their presence, the charges preferred by you against the house physician, Dr. S. A. Russell, were taken up for consideration.

After a general and free interchange of views, the following resolution. a copy of which I was instructed to convey to you, was unanimously adopted: —

Resolved, That this board, having heard the full charges against the house physician, together with his explanations of them, think that the charges should be dismissed; while at the same time they do not think that the house physician should attempt to retain private patients in the hospital, against the desire of the physician attending them. They believe, however, that the house physician acted in good faith, and for what he thought to be the best interests of the hospital, and therefore the charges are dismissed.

I remain very respectfully your obedient servant,

SARTELL PRENTICE, *Secretary*.

"The trouble, we believe, originated in this way. A Mr. Alexander Sheppard of Rondout visited Dr. Swinburne late last summer. He wished to be treated for some serious difficulty, and was advised by the doctor to remain in town, and enter the Albany Hospital. He agreed to do so, returned to Rondout to arrange his business affairs, and within a month came back, and, at the solicitation of Dr. Swinburne, entered the hospital. He was, it seems, not contented; for he left the institution, and removed to No. 9 Lancaster Street. It is said, and Sheppard verifies it by an affidavit, that there was a quarrel between Drs. Russell and Swinburne, after which Russell spoke against Swinburne, and endeavored to wean Sheppard from Swinburne; and that he (Russell) refused to treat Sheppard as Dr. Swinburne desired. In his affidavit Sheppard says that Dr. Swinburne, in company with Dr. Whitehorne, assistant house surgeon, called to see him on Saturday, Oct. 19, 1878, at about ten o'clock A.M., and before the clinic; — that the first words of Dr. Swinburne, upon entering, were, 'Well, old fellow, are you ready for an operation before the students?' — that deponent said, 'No, sir, I will not be operated upon in this hospital; I will go home and bring my wife here, and make some different arrangements; I will get private quarters, and have you operate upon me privately; I will not remain in this institution;' — that Dr. Swinburne thereupon remonstrated with deponent, saying that that would delay deponent another week, and urged deponent to remain in the hospital and go on with the operation that day, as this course would cost him nothing but his board, while the other would cost considerable money; — that Dr. Swinburne continually praised the said hospital, and urged deponent to remain there, but that deponent, notwithstanding such advice, utterly refused to remain in said institution, for reasons which deponent stands ready to make known to the board of governors of said hospital, if desired. Sheppard further says that he stands at all times ready to answer any inquiries which the board of governors of said hospital may think proper to make.

"Yesterday afternoon we sent a reporter to see Mr. Sheppard at his boarding-house, and he made the following statement. Mr. Sheppard is an intelligent man, and talked in the presence of his wife and child. He said he regarded the present management of the Albany Hospital very bad. 'I was there for two weeks, paying nine dollars per week for board; which was an exorbitant price, considering the poor accommodations and food which I had. In the treatment of my case it was necessary for me to use hot water. I made repeated requests that it be furnished me, but was at last obliged to get out of bed at night, and heat the water in an old coffee-pot over my lamp. Dr. Russell called upon me daily, making inquiries how I felt. I told him I was suffering with a severe pain in my head; but he did nothing to relieve it until I told him I would report his neglect to the managers of the hospital. This threat seemed to have the desired result, for he gave me something which eased the pain. During all this time I was attended by Dr. Swinburne. I feel very thankful to him for his care and attendance. My wife and myself are living for a trifle more here than was charged for my board at the hospital, besides having proper food. I will say, however, for the nurses of the institution, that they are excellent, kind, obliging, and well versed in all that pertains to their business. I found I was not getting along as fast as I should under this kind of treatment: so I left. After leaving, Dr. Swinburne performed an operation on me; and so successful was he, that I will recover. I know nothing as to how the other patients are cared for; but, if they receive the same kind of treatment which I did, I wonder that any of them ever get well. Dr. Russell was inattentive, and at times impertinent.'

"It seems that Sheppard is not the only one who complains; for, in the trial of Dr. Russell before the board of governors, the following affidavit from another patient was read: —

City and County of Albany, ss.

Bella E. Humphrey, being duly sworn, says that she resides at Salisbury, Herkimer County, N.Y. ; that she came to the Albany City Hospital on Saturday, the twenty-fourth day of August, 1878, for surgical treatment of the knee-joint; that deponent was treated by Dr. John Swinburne, whom deponent supposed was the regular attending surgeon of the hospital, and has continued under treatment by said Dr. Swinburne up to the present time; that about three weeks since, deponent's knee was operated upon by Dr. Swinburne before the class of students, and has upon several other occasions been before the class for classical instruction; that during the week following such operation, Dr. Russell, house surgeon of the hospital, came to the room of deponent, — which is No. 20, and is a private room, deponent being a private patient of Dr. Swinburne, — and said to deponent, "Bella, if Dr. Swinburne comes here after you to-day, don't you go;" that deponent said, " What do you mean, doctor?" that said Russell then said, " Dr. Swinburne and I had a flare-up this morning, and he is coming to take his patients away; " that deponent said to Dr. Russell that she did not mean to go anywhere else to board, but wanted to remain at the hospital, and under the care of Dr. Swinburne, until able to go home with safety; that said Russell said that thereafter deponent would be under the care of Dr. Ward or Dr. Vandeveer, and would receive as good treatment as heretofore. Deponent further says that Dr. Swinburne never advised deponent to leave the hospital, but has continually urged deponent to remain at the hospital until able to return home, and that the treatment by Dr. Swinburne has always been satisfactory to deponent.

BELLA HUMPHREY.

Sworn to before me this sixth day of November, 1878.

A. S. DRAPER,
Notary Public, Albany County.

"But the board of governors, after hearing this, and conversing with Drs. Ward and Vandeveer and others, retained Dr. Russell, whereupon we believe three members of the staff have retired from the institution, and much bad blood has been engendered throughout the profession generally.

" Yesterday evening a reporter of the ʻExpressʼ called at the hospital to see Dr. Russell, and get his statement in the premises. The doctor is a young man, polite, natty, and insinuating. He received the reporter graciously, and, upon being informed of the object of the visit, appeared anxious to make a full statement; but a second thought compelled him to ask to be excused for a moment, while he retired, probably ʻfor consultation.ʼ In a few minutes he returned, and asked the reporter to accompany him to the office of Rufus W. Peckham, as he evidently did not wish to speak without legal advice. The two then marched down State Street, and saw Mr. Peckham. The lordly gentleman advised ʻsilence for the present; ʼ and, evidently much against his inclination, Dr. Russell refrains from giving his version of the story."

The position of Dr. Swinburne before the public as a professional man, and the high reputation he had won before this nation during the Rebellion and in this State as a health-officer at quarantine, with the eminence attained by his skill in Europe, was of such an order as to forbid his quietly submitting to the interference of a house physician of the hospital, where, it was generally conceded, political and social favoritism were of more weight than professional ability. In this instance, as in every event of his life, his great incentive was the best possible care of all, without distinction of social standing, whose treatment was in any manner confided to his skill and care. Acting under these impulses, he opened the public dispensary, which has since proven such a boon to both rich and poor, and has become an indispensable blessing to the section of the State in which it is located. A brief outline of the work there done, and the systems practised, is given in the following chapter.

CHAPTER XX

SCIENCE DEVOTED TO HUMANITY.

An Unkept Promise. — What the Dispensary has done. — Great Advance in Science. — Treating Tens of Thousands. — Remarkable and Interesting Cases. — Helping Nature. — An Unequalled Man and Record.

On the establishing of the Swinburne Dispensary in the city of Albany, the entire sympathy of the public was with the doctor, and greeted the enterprise and philanthropic undertaking of the founder as one of more than ordinary significance. So strong was popular sentiment with the doctor at the time, that the men who held the political control of the city voluntarily promised the same pecuniary assistance to the dispensary that was extended by the city to other institutions recognized as charitable. The opening of the doors of the elegant residence on Eagle Street, for the treatment of the poor without money and without price, was hailed, as it has proven to be, as the philanthropic event of the age at the capital city; and none more readily saw the benefits the future were to enjoy from it than those in authority, who, then acting on the first or better impulses of their natures, promised the pecuniary assistance. The college faculty and the hospital governors were, however, opposed to the undertaking; some of them, it was reported at the time, going so far as to threaten that if Dr. Swinburne persevered in this course they would ruin him professionally, and drive him from the city. In undertaking to vanquish the man who had proven a Samaritan among them, in binding up the wounds of the afflicted and caring for them, and who purposed to continue that course, they forgot two very important considerations, — first, that the doctor was following the Christian example of one greater than they, who went about curing the sick, and healing the maimed, eighteen hundred years ago;

322

and, second, that the doctor's skill was such as to defy them, professionally, and his individual courage such as would brook no intimidation, and that every threat would but make him the more determined. Through this professional jealousy, and the influence brought to bear on the officials, the aid voluntarily offered was never extended; and even the committee's report, in which the professional controversy was recited in the last chapter, was quietly put out of sight. But the work went on in the dispensary, and tens of thousands have since realized its benefits at an individual expense to the founder of over five thousand dollars per year; and although one entire building has been exclusively devoted to this truly charitable work, with a portion of another, no aid has ever been asked or given, even to the extent that would buy the shoes worn out by the girl attending the door-bell, further than donations of old linen by private individuals. The city government, well aware of the good work being done, not only failed to abate any portion of the taxes, but, on the other hand, the property is assessed for a much larger sum than it would sell for.

Day and night the doors have been open for the treatment of all the diseases and accidents that man is heir to, with a competent staff of assistant surgeons, and physicians, and students always ready and anxious to serve the unfortunate; and it is safe to make the assertion that from the dispensary have gone forth to the world physicians and surgeons who, because of their training there, take a front rank professionally, are equal, and in most cases superior, to those coming from any other institution, where theory has the benefit of practical illustration and practice. It is also safe to make another assertion, that in no institution of medical or surgical training has the same advance been made in these sciences as in Swinburne's dispensary, or any thing approximating thereto, during the years of its existence. The large-brained head of the dispensary, Dr. Swinburne, brought to the institution knowledge gained in a wide field of science; and, having no professional jealousies to encounter from those practising under him, he has solved many problems, and made advances in treatment, known only to those coming directly under his tuition and direction. It is safe to go still further, and make another positive allegation; i.e., that in no institution in the State has a greater and more difficult variety of diseases and accidents been treated than in and from this dispensary, with results that cannot be surpassed, and it is doubtful if ever equalled.

The system of extension in the treatment of fractures without splints, given to the public and the profession years ago by Dr. Swinburne, has been strictly adhered to and followed out with unequalled success in the practice of the dispensary. During these eight years only two amputations have been performed, — one of the thigh, and one of the leg; and these were so badly crushed as to be beyond all possible hope of saving. During the last six years there have been no amputations, not even of a finger or toe, and no deaths resulting from the injuries treated by the doctor or his assistants, unless they were in cases necessarily fatal at the time they occurred.

In the dispensary every physician and student is trained to conservative surgery, and they become ardent believers in conservation, — a system the doctor has steadily adhered to all his professional life, amputations never being resorted to or sanctioned by him except in very rare cases, occurring in military or railroad practice: and in no instance has his practice resulted in gangrene; but, whenever the parts were dead, they were so treated that they sloughed off. Three legs have sloughed off near the knee, one hand, several feet, and a large number of fingers and parts of fingers, leaving better stumps than any surgeon could make by amputation; thus avoiding the second shock and hemorrhage, and the attending additional risk to life, besides giving less pain to the patients and allowing the wounds to heal more rapidly. In the treatment of fractures of the long bones, — thigh, leg, arm, and forearm, — the same conservative system which the doctor has taught and practised for over forty years is followed.

In the over seventy thousand cases (of which at least ten thousand have been accidents) treated by the doctor and his assistants, every form of disease, accident, and deformity the medical and surgical profession are called to treat, has been cared for in that institution; and in no instance in these tens of thousands has there been even an intimation of unskilful practice or bad results. In the treatment of fractures of the wrist (Colles'), of which there have been over three hundred, the system has been so successful as to defy experienced surgeons to locate the place of the explosion. By a method of operation and treatment devised by Dr. Swinburne (known only in the dispensary), hands that had been turned over and deformed by scrofula abscesses, burns, paralysis, and other causes, have been straightened into their natural positions without removing the scars, which have been made as soft and smooth as a glove; while old ulcers have been made to heal at the rate of from an eighth to a quarter of an inch daily. Extensive cicatrices, or scars, of the neck have been made to entirely disappear, and the tissues and skin to assume their normal condition.

In cases of necrosis, or death of the bone, the books teach, and the profession universally practise, the cutting-out of the dead bone. The conservative surgery of the dispensary entirely ignores this system; the doctor doing away with the use of the knife, and simply assisting nature to throw off the dead portions.

In no institution in the State, excepting perhaps in New-York City, has there been a larger practice in gynæcology in the treatment of diseases of women, and in the performance of the delicate and difficult operations connected therewith, than at the dispensary.

Among the corrections and operations constantly being performed at the dispensary are those for curvature of the spine; deformities, congenital or acquired, whether as the result of paralysis, disease, or bad treatment of an injury; single or double club, or "reel" foot; and the removal of tumors, cancers, and hare-lip.

In the treatment of wounds from toy pistols, the results have been equally as satisfactory and remarkable as in any other kind of accidents. These wounds received by those applying to the dispensary for treatment have reached as high as fifty as the result of one Fourth of July; and yet, while lockjaw has been reported in all parts of the State, resulting from these accidents, not a single case of lockjaw has set in among the large number treated at the dispensary.

The success attending the treatment of fractures of the leg, thigh, and long bones is due to Dr. Swinburne's system of treatment by extension, without splints or bandages, with results so perfect that no surgeon can tell the parts that were broken. In order to secure these results, generally, the doctor insists that the profession must abandon the traditional surgery of the books, and get rid of the splints and bandages, and keep the temperature of the injured parts up to blood-heat. This he insists is done by retaining and adding to the normal heat, and excluding the cold. The compression by plaster of Paris, splints, bandages, or other methods, he holds, constricts the limb, and does mischief because it arrests circulation, interferes with the nerve force and influence, and often produces gangrene or congestion, resulting in inflammation and absorption of poisonous matter, known as septic or pus poisoning, or irritation of the nerves or tetanus. All these sequels as a rule, he maintains, are the results of bad management, or the chilling of the parts injured before proper attention had been given, or before the injury was seen by the surgeon or after, providing proper circulation had not been restored. He holds that in whatever injury done to a limb or to a part of a limb, from which injury death to the part injured has taken place, in the stopping of circulation, and sloughed off, if the residue is properly treated, and restored to good circulation, less bad results will follow this treatment than if amputated, — a process which does not save from gangrene, lockjaw, or septus inflammation. In fact, he holds that not an instance of these has occurred where the restoration and maintenance of proper temperature had been kept up from the beginning. Out of the thousands and tens of thousands of accidents treated by the doctor and in the dispensary, but three cases of lockjaw, or tetanus, have occurred; and only one of these was seen at an early period, or before the mischief was done.

To demonstrate the efficacy of conservative surgery as practised in the Swinburne Dispensary, where there have been no bad results, and by the doctor outside, a few traumatic and other cases are given, each being typical of a class treated and entered on the register of the dispensary.

Eugene Masterson, a young man twenty-one years old, living at No. 24 Clinton Street, Albany, and employed as a brakeman on the Delaware and Hudson Canal Company's Railroad, was run over in April, 1883, by an engine weighing eight tons, and his limb crushed to atoms half-way to the knee-joint, including the foot. His first words after being picked up were, "Take me to Swinburne's." In this case, had amputation been resorted to, it would have been difficult to find a point near the knee at which to amputate; the tissues were so badly bruised, that the doctor would have been obliged to go up to the middle of the thigh. The condition of the injured man was such, no re-action having taken place, amputation would be sure to result in death. In view of these facts, and his indifference as to whether he lived or died, circulation was restored and kept up, and in one week the injured part of the limb sloughed off between the living and dead part. In four weeks all the the loose bone was thrown off the lower end of the stump; and in twelve weeks the wound was healed, with a better stump than any surgeon, not even excepting Dr. Swinburne himself, could make.

Among the first accidents in the building of the new Capitol at Albany was that occurring to a strong, robust young man, named Brown, in charge of a gang of men in the construction department, who fell backwards from a staging to the ground, a distance of about twenty-five feet, striking on his head and shoulders, breaking one of the dorsal vertebræ, and filling his chest with blood, as demonstrated by the aspirator and by percussion, producing paralysis of the lower extremities. Dr. Swinburne, who was summoned on an examination, saw that it was quite evident there was an inequality in the spine and vertebræ, showing a distortion. With the assistance of four strong men, one at each shoulder and leg, in extending the patient, who was laid on his stomach, by

manipulation the doctor succeeded in getting the spine back
into its place. By restoring circulation none of the blood in
the chest, or otherwise, was allowed to devitalize, or clot, but
was absorbed with the gradual restoration of motion and sen-
sibility in the lower extremities. This treatment was carried
out on a water-bed, to avoid sloughing from undue pressure at
any point; and in a few weeks the man was well and walking
about, and in four months was back at work, and continued
in good health for several years, up to his death about one
year ago.

Thomas McAvoy, a young man living at No. 64 Franklin
Street, Albany, was also an employé in the construction of
the new Capitol. A stone weighing between seven and eight
tons fell from the derrick, and in falling caught McAvoy's
leg and foot, crushing them into the ground, so that he could
not be removed from under the stone without cutting off the
leg. The derrick was adjusted to the stone, the man released
and taken to his home. When Dr. Swinburne examined the
man he found the leg and foot a shapeless mass. They were
moulded into position, congestion and inflammation avoided,
the bones rapidly uniting; and in twelve weeks he was walking with a good leg and foot, the only evil result being a
slightly enlarged ankle-joint; and this is now scarcely perceptible.

Dr. Swinburne is opposed, under any circumstances, to
amputation for any injury to, or dislocation of, the ankle-joint.
One especial case, where, under the treatment of ninety-nine
out of every hundred other institutions or physicians, under
the circumstances, amputation would have been resorted to,
is noted in the records of the dispensary. An unfortunate
woman, while intoxicated, dislocated her ankle-joint, and sustained a compound fracture. In this condition she lay on
the street during an entire cold October night. When the
doctor first saw her, the limb was terribly swollen, and phle-
betis, or inflammation of the veins, had set in, extending up
to the pelvis; and the appearances were that the inflammation
would extend up to the heart, and result in death. By restoring circulation the inflammation subsided; and the reduc-

tion of the ankle being effected, by holding it in position without compression, the woman recovered, with no perceptible injury or deformity of the limb.

Henry Fitzgerald of Rexford's Flatts, near Schenectady, fell from a high bridge on to the ice, and crushed his ankle-joint. The physician who was called to attend him declared it was necessary to amputate. To this Fitzgerald strongly objected, and insisted that Dr. Swinburne be sent for and consulted. When the doctor, with one of his assistants, arrived, the man was found to be in such an extremely nervous condition, that, had amputation been attempted, the operation would have proved fatal; and besides there was danger of blood-poisoning. Through Dr. Swinburne's treatment, conservative surgery triumphed, and the man recovered with a good ankle.

Mr. Schemerhorn, a driver for an Albany brewery, was thrown from a carriage, and an explosion took place at the ankle-joint, which was dislocated, and the fibula fractured. He was treated from the dispensary, and in a short time was well; and he declared he would not take the world for that ankle.

Timothy Sullivan, a heavy, robust member of the Albany police-force, while jumping at a picnic, dislocated and fractured the ankle-joint, driving the tibia down into the ground. Three hours afterwards he was seen by Dr. Swinburne, who, after cleaning the dirt off the protruding bones, united the parts, and succeeded in getting restoration by the first intention. In twelve weeks Sullivan was out and well, and ready for duty.

On June 25, 1881, John Erringer, a workman employed in the construction of the post-office building in Albany, fell a distance of thirty-seven feet, striking on both feet. In the right ankle the tibia was fractured at the middle third, with a dislocation of the fibula and tibia in the lower extremities, with a fracture of the astragalus, which was dislocated from the smaller tissue and bones. In the left there was a dislocation of the lower extremities of the tibia and fibula, and also of the tarsal bones, the foot turned inward at a right angle to the leg. The lower ends of the tibia and fibula were crushed. Of necessity the wounds were very painful. Through restoration no undue inflammation set in ; and, by manipulation and moulding, the bones were restored by Dr. Swinburne as near as possible to their normal condition, and on Nov. 15 he was discharged well. Both feet have been restored almost as good as they were before the accident. A similar case occurred to a man named Young, a workman on the Capitol, who fell a distance of thirty-five feet, and was treated by Dr. Swinburne with the same favorable results.

A man by the name of Lynch, employed as a porter in a large printing-house in Albany, was caught under some machinery and his leg crushed. At his request he was taken to a hospital, where he remained some months. Several unsuccessful attempts were made to unite the broken bones. He was then removed to his home, by his employers, and placed under the treatment of Dr. Swinburne ; and in a few weeks his limb was cured, and he was able to walk without a crutch.

Frank Miller, a newsboy on the Delaware and Hudson Canal Company's Railroad, had his head and face crushed between cars. So severe was the wound that he bled from the eyes and ears, one eye being partly knocked out of the socket. Circulation was restored by Dr. Swinburne, and kept up, and the boy recovered ; and he was afterwards a brakeman on the same road.

John Healy, brother of a physician, sustained a compound fracture of the skull, in front of the left parietal bone. The wound was about three and a quarter by one and a quarter inches, the dura mater being injured. Two fragments were removed, the wound trepanned, and the boy recovered.

Alfred Cornell of Oneonta, had his jaw become deformed by an abscess, and twisted around to one side of his head. Dr. Swinburne removed part of the jaw and bone which had been destroyed by mortification, and cut around so as to place it in its normal position, and allowed it to fill with granulation and bony tissue. The deformity was so far remedied that he has since presented a good appearance, and has been married. A surgeon of large practice, who was present at the operation, declared it was the most difficult and skilful piece of surgery he ever witnessed.

A peculiar case of injury to the hand was that of a man whose fingers of one hand, excepting the little finger, were cut off with a cleaver. He was treated at the dispensary, and the next season laid two hundred and fifty thousand bricks with the injured hand.

On the 4th of August, 1883, William P. Greene of Berlin, Albany County, over fifty-seven years of age, dislocated his shoulder; and four months afterwards came to the dispensary to be relieved. He was put to bed, treated by Dr. Swinburne's system of extension, and in two weeks sent home with a good arm.

M. D. Breene, a gentleman well known in Albany, residing at No. 183 Greene Street, while riding on the cars, his arm resting on the car window, was struck by an open door of a passing freight-car, and all the bones of the elbow crushed into fragments and practically cut off; the only parts left to keep the arm together being the front tissues and a piece of flesh. By the doctor's system of extension the broken bones were united and the arm saved.

Patrick Kelley, a young man, a railroad employé, had his whole hand completely crushed between car bumpers, and applied to the dispensary for treatment. As usual, there was no thought of using the knife or of amputating. The treatment of that institution was followed, and the hand naturally sloughed off at the wrist.

Martin Consandine, of Clinton Heights, Rensselaer County, was struck by a railroad engine, and the top of the scalp of his head lifted off so as to expose the brain substance. Under Dr. Swinburne's treatment he has recovered, although the intellect is somewhat injured.

John Moore, nearly sixty years of age, living at No. 129 Phillip Street, and employed in an Albany coal and wood yard, met with an accident by which several of his ribs were fractured, and crushed into the lungs, producing a marked emphysema from head to foot. The case was a very difficult one to treat, requiring nearly fifty visits from the dispensary

before he was fully recovered. It was recognized as an ex
ceedingly interesting case professionally.

John Simmons of Blue Mountain Lake, Hamilton County,
had his foot frozen, and about a month afterwards applied to
Dr. Swinburne for treatment. Other physicians who had
examined the foot declared it would have to be cut off, and
he came to Dr. Swinburne to arrange for the operation. The
doctor declined to perform the operation, and subjected the
man to the treatment pursued at the dispensary. The toes
were all blackened, and in time sloughed off; and soon afterwards he returned home with a good foot.

A gentleman residing near Palatine Bridge, while in
church, was attacked with a great pain in the lower extremities, from the foot up. He was removed to his home, and
a physician summoned. Three days afterwards Dr. Swinburne was called to see him. On his arriving with one of
his assistants, and examining the man, no circulation could
be discovered in one leg or thigh; and in the other only the
slightest pulsation could be discovered in the artery at the
groin. The limbs were cold and seemingly lifeless, the man
suffering from an embolism; a blood-clot having been crowded
down into the pelvis arteries, cutting off circulation. The
man anxiously inquired where amputation was to take place;
and the doctor quaintly remarked, if amputation were to
take place at all, he would suggest that it be performed just
behind the ears. Circulation was restored through the small,
or capillary, vessels in one limb; and in a few days complete restoration was secured. In the other, circulation was
more difficult of accomplishing, and the limb sloughed off
just above the ankle-joint.

In the work of Dr. Swinburne and the dispensary many
interesting cases occcur, not only because of the nature of
the wounds, but the circumstances surrounding those treated.
One of these was that of Michael Devine, residing at No. 42
Arch Street, Albany, who, while in New-York City, met
with an accident, in which the ankle was crushed, and the
foot turned completely out of a line with the body. He was
taken to a hospital in that city, where the surgeons declared

the foot must be amputated. Devine would submit to no such operation until he had seen Dr. Swinburne, and returned to Albany. The doctor, on examining the ankle, declared amputation was not necessary, and demonstrated the superiority of conservative surgery, as a science, over the traditional surgery of the New-York hospital, by removing a large piece of the dislocated and broken bone, and bringing back to its natural shape and saving the foot. Afterwards Devine's wife, who was employed in one of the large shoe factories in Albany, had her arm crushed in a half-inch space in the elevator. She was taken to one of the Albany hospitals, where, according to her statement, amputation in her case, as in that of her husband, was recommended; but, like her husband, she would not submit until Dr. Swinburne said so. She was brought under his treatment, saved from mutilation and from being maimed for life; and through conservative surgery has a good arm, which she has found very useful ever since. Subsequently, Devine's mother fell and dislocated her shoulder. A physician, who was called in, was unable to effect a reduction, and another physician was about to be sent for, when Devine entered, and said, " Never mind, we want no more humbugging: I will run up to Swinburne's, and get somebody.who can do that right." He did so, and the injury was repaired.

Another interesting case, in its history, was that of Robert Ibbertson of No. 52 Canal Street, a slate-roofer, who, at various times within three years, had broken his left thigh, right wrist, and both bones of the right leg, besides sustaining a terrible scalp-wound; yet, so perfect was the cure in each case that the limbs are all as good as before they were broken, and only a very careful examination would reveal the fact that he had ever received any of these injuries. At the time that Robert broke his wrist, his father, also a slate-roofer, fell with him from a staging, while at work near Syracuse, and broke his neck, surviving the accident nearly one week. The value of these limbs, which by improper treatment might have been permanently crippled, is incalculable to this young man, upon whom the support of a large family has thus devolved.

These cases, taken from the records of the dispensary, and the history of which has been learned from the assistants and the parties injured, are but a moiety of the cases treated and on the record, and are given for the benefit of the public, that they may know the nature of the work done at the dispensary by Dr. Swinburne and his assistants, and that they may realize the benefits of a humane and truly scientific method of treatment in what is known as surgical practice. If the profession desire to learn more of this work, with the modes of treatment, we have the assurance of the assistants that they will gladly aid in the work; and we feel satisfied that the doctor, whose only aim in life is to help others, will cheerfully give all the particulars necessary on his return from the West, where he has recently been taking rest and recreation.

Since the opening of Swinburne's dispensary in 1879, up to the close of last year, there have been 824 fractures treated, besides the re-breaking of and re-setting of 34 Colles', or fractures of the wrist, which had been ill-treated by others, resulting in deformity. Of these fractures, 47 have been of the femur, or thigh, — 43 simple and 4 compound; 4 simple and 2 compound patella, and 12 Potts'; elbow-joint, 26 simple and 4 compound; clavicle or collar-bone, 92; of the tibia, 78 simple and 7 compound; of the fibula, 51 simple and 5 compound; of the nose, 11 simple and 1 compound; of the humerus, 88; of the hand and ribs, 49 simple and 2 compound; Colles', or fractures of the wrist, 301; and of other fractures, 46. Ninety-three dislocations, unaccompanied by fractures, were reduced. Of these, 55 were of the shoulder, 25 of the arm, 8 simple and 1 double of the jaw, 3 of the legs, and 2 of the knee-joint. In the surgical operations, 61 cases of simple, and 19 cases of double, club-feet have been treated; 72 Tendo Achilles or heel-cord, and 9 other tendons, cut to re-form deformities; and 128 cancers removed; in addition to 51 large operations.

For the year 1885, up to April 28, there had been treated 2,258 cases, of which 76 were fractures and dislocations, 275 other accidents. 286 operations, and 391 other surgical operations. The total number of surgical cases was 1,028, and medical 1,232.

The applicants at the dispensary for bodily relief are not confined to the residents of New-York State, but come from all portions of the country, particularly from Vermont, Massachusetts, Connecticut, and Pennsylvania. The writer of this has himself seen in the dispensary a young man from New Orleans, who was being treated for deformity, and who presented, when he arrived, a most deplorable sight, being twisted and deformed to such a degree that scarcely any portion of his body was in its natural condition. To many surgeons and others the remedy of these deformities seemed a physical impossibility, and beyond all human skill. Yet a few months demonstrated that it is within the scope of science, combined with a perfect knowledge of the anatomy of man and the methods to be pursued, to prove that few cases of deformity are incurable.

On the records are the names of patients from Illinois, Nebraska, and other Western States, even from the golden shores of the Pacific, who have come to the doctor for treatment. Nor is his fame confined to this nation, but it reaches through out Canada and out on to the ocean. A newspaper reporter tells of a woman who came to the dispensary with a child in her arms, whose lower limbs were deformed, and who said she had but recently arrived from England. When asked by Dr. Swinburne why she did not have the child treated in one of the hospitals of London, she replied that she had been to the hospitals there, and the doctors told her they could do nothing for the child; that, on the passage over, a lady had told her of Dr. Swinburne, "and I have come to see you." The doctor, after hearing the woman, said, " I guess they did not want to trouble themselves because you were poor; but, never mind, I will make the little one all right," and named a time when she was to present it for an operation, which was afterwards performed, and the child made to assume a natural position, although the deformity was serious and congenital.

A few days before writing this we were shown by one of

the assistants a sample letter of the kind he was receiving during the doctor's absence. It was from a member of a large manufacturing firm in Connecticut, in which the writer described the pain and sensation arising from some unaccountable affection of his leg. The gentleman gave the opinions and recommendations of several physicians he had consulted, and whose disagreements in the matter induced him to believe the case was serious; and hence he wrote Dr. Swinburne to inquire, if he were to come to Albany, if the doctor would treat him. The case, said the assistant, by the contents of the letter, is a serious idiopathic one; but doubtless, on the return of the doctor, he will decide what is the matter, and what is to be done.

Every aim of the doctor in life has been and is to benefit the sick and needy, and to economize the expenses of the afflicted. To accomplish this *desideratum*, he believes an observance of the laws of nature are the best remedies. Prescriptions are not written at the dispensary, merely for the sake of writing them; but, in most cases, such articles as are found in every household are recommended, and, where necessary to use medicines, the simplest, cheapest, and most efficient remedies are prescribed, thus virtually "throwing physic to the dogs." As a substitute for the costly oil-silk, he has introduced oil-cotton, which will wear four times as long as the silk, and costs only a few cents per yard.

In this dispensary, where thousands and tens of thousands of the poor have been cared for, and where every manner of operation has been performed, from the minor to the most delicate and difficult in surgery, it has been demonstrated that amputation is necessary only in the most rare emergencies; that, in a very large majority of the cases where it is resorted to, it is not only not necessary, but actually cruel, inhuman, and barbarous; and that where the knife has heretofore been used by the profession, and too largely practised now, with fatal results, conservative surgery has accomplished, and is accomplishing, much more favorable results than any other system practised.

The record of this dispensary is remarkable; and there are

but few institutions in this country where more patients have been treated in the same period of time, and probably in none have so many accidents occurring on railroads been attended, and in none have the results been so successful. Among the railroad accidents, six have been to the legs, eight to the feet, thirty-two to the hands, and forty to the arms. The results have been remarkable and unequalled in the treatment of these, and have almost revolutionized surgery in this section in treating railroad cases. Among no class of men is the name of Dr. Swinburne held in higher esteem than among those who are constantly subjected to the dangers of railroad life, not even among the poor of Albany, who almost reverence him for his skill, and the many noble qualities of his generous heart, which have caused him to do so much for them.

So widespread has become the fame of the Swinburne Dispensary, and the eminent skill and benevolence of its founder and head, that from every part of the State the unfortunate, rich and poor, have come to him to be treated; and, in many instances, the private resources of the doctor and his staff have paid the board of poor and needy patients while in the city under treatment. One instance was that of a poor patient who had walked all the distance from New York to have an injured wrist treated, which prevented him from earning a living for his family and himself.

The work of Dr. Swinburne and his staff has not been confined to the walls of the dispensary. The calls of any of the physicians of the dispensary for medical attendance, outside of the doctor's private practice, is as great as that of any physician in Albany; and no hour is too late, or weather too severe, to deter them from promptly responding to calls for help. The doctor, whose carriage may be seen daily in front of the homes of the rich and the poor, is a worker himself, and full of human kindness; and no cruel, lazy, or negligent physician or student can remain in the Swinburne Dispensary, where no charges are made for treatment, these being left to the patient's own voluntary impulses, and where, in no instance, are fees received from the really poor.

The cases cited, the methods of treatment pursued, and the results accomplished, as well as the extent of country over which the doctor's healing skill and the blessings of the dispensary have reached, are given as indices of the work of this truly humane institution, where the very poorest are treated with the same care and tenderness as are those upon whom fortune has smiled, and where the poor Lazarus has his sores and wounds dressed and bound by the same methods as does the rich man.

A branch of the dispensary has been established in Troy, and placed in charge of one of the doctor's trusted and efficient assistants. Here, where nearly four thousand cases have been treated during the year, the doctor himself attends once a week, and holds a clinic, examining cases and performing operations.

Such is the work of this eminent physician and surgeon, and tender-hearted humanitarian; and, for these impulses of benevolence, he holds a place in the hearts of the poor, which binds them to him by that sacred cord of love and gratitude no power on earth can sever. In him they see a friend in affliction, with a heart in full sympathy with them, and for whom no sacrifice is too great for him to make. Truly blessed is this work of Dr. John Swinburne, — the philanthropic act of the age; and long after the bricks of the building have crumbled, and the structure gone to ruin, will his name be remembered as one who lived to make the world better, and left an example, for other generations to follow, in the exercise of the virtues that ennoble the human race, and bring men and women up to the high position which their Creator ordained they should occupy.

CHAPTER XXI.

BEHOLD THE MAN.

Self-made. — Incidents in Early Boyhood. — A Muscular Teacher. — Hard Life of a Student. — Entering College and Leading. — Brief Sketch of a Remarkable Professional Life. — The Friend of the Poor, and an Enemy of Corruption.

THE brief story of this eminently typical American's life, as detailed in the preceding chapters, stamp Dr. Swinburne as one having scarcely a peer, and few superiors, in this land, so prolific of self-made and remarkable men. Like others of humble origin, he has illustrated the possibilities that are open to courage, industry, and an indomitable will to rise from the surroundings and difficulties always attending the poor, and to attain to eminence. His battle in life, from early boyhood to fame, has been a continuous round of heroic struggles and victorious achievements. Born at Black River, Lewis County, N.Y., on May 30, 1820, he possessed in early boyhood all the qualities, virtues, and robustness which have enabled so many of the natives of New-York State, on entering the arena of public and professional life, to surmount the obstacles always meeting those of humble birth, and to become successful in their contests with others. Of all the successful achievements won by the rugged sons of the North, there are none of which the northern section of the State of New York may feel more justly proud than those achieved by this native of Lewis County.

The death of his father left John Swinburne, at a very tender age, without the strong paternal assistance which would aid him in the conflicts that were to meet him in boyhood, and confront him through his minority up to the age of maturity. His parents were natives of Connecticut, his father descending from a long line of Irish ancestors. From his father he inherited a quick sense of humor, and a ready response to every appeal of suffering and want, which, combined with the hopeful and spiritual temperament of his mother, have proved a richer heritage than silver or gold. Endowed with brilliant intellectual faculties and superb physical gifts, he has made the alleviation of suffering humanity the governing-principle and study of his life. The grateful testimony of thousands of "the maimed, the halt, and the blind" who have received aid at his hands is abundant evidence of his success.

His earlier or preliminary education was obtained in the public schools of Lewis County, and in the academies of Denmark, Lowville, and Fairfield; although he had but few opportunities of obtaining more than the first rudiments before he was twenty-one years of age, having been compelled, up to that age, to assist his widowed mother in providing for the other bereaved children. His first real victory in his battle of life was during his attendance at the academy. At that time he was a strong, vigorous boy verging on manhood, and uncommonly agile and quick of motion, — a physical condition which he has preserved, in a large degree, up to the present time, and which has enabled him to continue an active life, to endure hardships, and to perform arduous labors that would have physically broken down most of men. This physical condition and preservation he attributes largely to his observance of the laws of nature, and his habits. His whole life has been one of abstemiousness, and almost absolute abstinence from the use of liquors or tobacco in any form. For this virtue he claims little credit to himself, as it was a forced necessity; because, in his earlier life, he could not afford the luxury of a cigar, and hence formed no taste for smoking: and, although liking the taste of liquors, he has been restrained from using any, because they did not like him; and he never could drink even beer without its making him sick.

While studying at the academy at Denmark, he was asked to take charge of a school for a season in St. Lawrence County. The school was considered the hardest to manage in the county; the seven teachers who in succession had preceded him, and attempted to manage the school, having been driven out by the pupils. The same fate was expected to befall young Swinburne, but he was equal to the emergency. Upon arriving at that hamlet, the committee informed him that they would delay his examination with regard to his qualities as an instructor until he had demonstrated whether or not he possessed the power to control the scholars. A number of the pupils were older, heavier, and stronger than the young teacher, but were lacking in his quickness of motion; and on the first attempt to mutinize, and use him as they had used his predecessors, they discovered that they had, in their new instructor, one to deal with who was more than a match for the best of them, and were promptly taught an example in evolution that laid them on their backs in quick order. He conquered quickly his bellicose and mischievous scholars; and won from them, at first obedience, and then respect. Afterwards, on suggesting to the committee that he was prepared to be examined, they informed him that that course was not necessary; that they had decided to retain him, being fully satisfied that any man who could suppress insubordination in that school must necessarily be a competent teacher. He remained there until the close of the term for which he had been engaged, when he left; his departure being regretted by the people and scholars alike, who believed his like they would never look on again. He was then offered a school in Denmark, which he declined, and came to Albany.

Years before arriving at the age of manhood, and when there were no prospects of his ever being able to obtain the requisite education, except such as he would, under adverse circumstances, be compelled to struggle to attain for himself, he had decided on the practice of medicine and surgery as the profession he would study and practise; and for a year before arriving in Albany, at the age of twenty-one, he had devoted much time to the reading of medical works and the study of anatomy. On his entering the Albany Medical College, from which he graduated in 1846, he was accredited further advanced in a knowledge of therapeutics than many of the students who had been there for two or three years, and was conceded superior in anatomy to students who had attended that institution four years.

During his college and student terms, young Swinburne's life was one of continuous hard work, study, deprivation, and self-denial; he being compelled, from necessity, to sleep on the floor or tables, and often living on an outlay of seventy-five cents per week. For the truth of this statement a lady now living in Albany offers to vouch; and she further asserts that, when a girl, she has often watched from a back window the young student as he washed his own linen. It was these hard knocks from the fickle Goddess of Fortune, while John Swinburne was travelling the rugged path of his early years, which so well fitted him for the many battles he has since fought and won. The hardships he endured, combined with a naturally tender heart, have enabled him to more fully understand the perplexities and struggles of poverty, and conduced to bring his after-life of usefulness into such close relationship and sympathy with the poor and suffering. As the dark, heavy clouds filled with the roar of heaven's artillery, and rent asunder by the crashing and purifying lightning, pass away, bathing the hillsides in a new verdure, giving to the flowers a brighter hue and more fragrant perfume, putting into the throats of nature's plumed and beautiful warblers a more cheerful song, purifying the atmosphere, and infusing new vigor into all life, so it was with the early life of John Swinburne. When the clouds of adversity that had so long hung over him were dispelled, and the trials that test men were overcome, he came forth the grander and nobler because of the trying ordeal through which he had passed; and in 1847, one year after graduating, he was appointed by the faculty of the Albany Medical College, demonstrator of anatomy in that institution; a position which he held for three years, since which time his civil and military career, as a physician and surgeon, stand without a precedent.

His extraordinary success as a practitioner, and his rare executive ability, have earned for him various positions of responsibility and trust. In 1851 he was appointed almshouse physician: ship-fever was then raging; and, after successfully treating over eight hundred cases, he was himself stricken with the disease. In 1861 he was appointed chief medical officer of the staff of Gen. John A. Rathbone, at the Recruiting Depot in Albany. During a space of three months, only twelve deaths occurred from among 1,470 patients under his care, being less than a half of one per cent of the whole number. On April 12 of the succeeding year, he received an appointment from Gov. Morgan as auxiliary volunteer surgeon, and went to the front. His first step was to establish the hospital at White-House Landing. On June 12, 1862, he was commissioned by Gov. Morgan as medical superintendent of the New-York troops. To render this office more effective, he was indorsed and commissioned by the government as acting assistant-surgeon, United-States Army, — the only honor of the kind ever bestowed upon a volunteer surgeon. By order of Gen. McClellan he was placed in charge of Savage Station, where he made immediate preparations for the relief of the sick and wounded. During the engagements in that section his entire time was spent in the operating-room : his meals were hurriedly dispatched in presence of the wounded and dying, and no thought given to rest or sleep. On the 29th of June, when Porter retreated from Savage Station, Dr. Swinburne voluntarily remained a prisoner with 4,000 sick and wounded men, too weak to be removed. His tenderness and heroism in their behalf won for him the utmost admiration and courtesy from the Confederate officers, who permitted him to pass through their lines on his visits to the hospitals, at all hours, without molestation. For these services he never asked or received any pecuniary compensation from the state or nation.

During his service in the army, he designed a stretcher for the conveyance of wounded men on the field, and for the treatment of fractures by extension, an illustration and description of which is given in a previous chapter. On request of the State Medical Society, he submitted the design to the head of the medical department of the army, that it might be used in the service ; but, from want of knowledge in the proper authorities, it was rejected. Its adoption, afterwards, by the English and French governments have proved it to be of great value.

In 1863 he was elected permanent member of the medical society of New-York State, and has since successively filled the positions of professor of fractures and dislocations and clinical surgery in Albany Medical College, president of the Albany County Medical Society, surgeon-in-chief of the Homœopathic and Children's hospitals (since their foundation), and consulting surgeon at the Albany and St. Peter's hospitals.

In 1864 he was appointed by Gov. Seymour, health-officer of the port of New York, the nomination being unanimously confirmed by the Senate. For the ensuing six years his life was one of incessant activity. In order to more successfully combat the ravages of yellow-fever, ship-fever, cholera, and small-pox while at quarantine, he planned and had constructed two artificial islands in the lower bay, the first of the kind ever built, thereby making the harbor the best and most effective quarantine in the world. He was removed from this position by Boss Tweed, who had no affiliation with men of Dr. Swinburne's stamp. In appreciation for, and recognition of, his meritorious services, one of the islands was, by legislative act, named Swinburne Hospital Island.

At the beginning of the war between France and Germany, while travelling with his son in Europe, he received an invitation from Minister Washburne, America's representative to the French Government, to come to Paris, and assume charge of the American ambulance at that place. With his usual ready response to humanity's call, he arrived in Paris, Sept. 16, and remained on duty during the siege. His services there were but a repetition of his untiring devotion to the heroic wounded in our late war. The "Press" of Paris, and the leading journals of England, eulogized his unparalleled success in military surgery and hygiene; and he was made the recipient of the highest honors. The Knights' Legion of Honor, and the Red Cross of Geneva, are included among the ninety decorations that have at various times been conferred upon him. His sympathy and unwearied exertion in behalf of the suffering gave him great popularity among all classes; and Consul-Gen. Reed declared that he had created the most profound impression upon the public of any man in Paris. His practice of conservative surgery was at that time almost an innovation upon the prevalent custom of amputation. In all cases the mutilated member or limb was given the fullest benefit of the doubt; the salvation of the body being, with him, a vital clause in his professional creed. His system speedily commended itself to the leading surgeons of Europe, who to-day follow almost exclusively his method of practice.

A number of years after this professional victory in that foreign nation, an enterprising showman was exhibiting through this country a panorama of the Siege of Paris. In one of his audiences in Chicago was a man suffering from an injury to the leg, of long standing, and for which he could get no relief among the professional men of that city. When the lecturer, in his description of the panorama, arrived at that point where the hospitals were presented, he exhibited, as most prominent, that of the American ambulance, and its head, Dr. John Swinburne, who stood, with sleeves rolled up and arms covered with blood. The lecturer devoted about twenty minutes to a description of the ambulance and the eminent and conceded skilful surgeon. The suffering man listened attentively, as one to whom a great and vital message was being delivered; and, seeing in it relief for him, decided then and there to return to Albany, where he had resided many years before, believing this eminent and skilled surgeon could relieve him. The decision was carried out, and the long-sought relief at last secured.

During his professional life in Albany, he enjoyed, in the years that he would accept it, a larger practice in obstetrics than any other three physicians combined, attending as high as a hundred and fifty cases in one year, and performing almost all the surgical operations of females in the city for years.

In the treatment of the diseases of the eye, as an oculist, he was, and is, without a superior. When this branch of the profession was made a specialty by others, he largely relinquished the practice, sending almost all of these cases applying to him for treatment to those who had become specialists; he refusing to treat but very few outside of the really poor.

Dr. Swinburne has contributed many valuable and able articles to the literature of scientific surgery ; and has clearly and practically demonstrated that compound fractures of the thigh, from gunshot wounds, can be as successfully treated as any other form of fracture of the thigh. As a medical expert he is widely known, having on many occasions assumed and maintained independent opinions on the diagnosis and treatment of diseases, in contravention to the generally accepted theories of the profession. In the heat of controversy he has at times been unjustly assailed, but his opponents have as often been silenced or convinced by the force of facts too plainly demonstrated in the able hands of Dr. Swinburne.

From the beginning of his professional life, his humanity and benevolence naturally drew to him the poor who could not pay, and to whom no other avenues were open, unless they applied to the city or county as paupers, which many of them would not do, preferring rather to suffer pain and sickness to such humiliation. These virtues also brought him a very large practice from among the mechanics and industrial classes, who did not seek charity, but felt unable to pay the exorbitant charges too often exacted. His reputation as the friend of the poor, added to his acknowledged skill and ability, gave him also a very large and more remunerative practice among the wealthier clasess; and hence his patients were among all classes, who equally appreciated his qualities. In June, 1876, the late Charles J. Folger, who became physically exhausted in the discharge of his duties as a judge of the Court of Appeals, and was treated by Dr. Swinburne, wrote him, " Since I had the pleasure and profit of calling upon you in your professional capacity last winter, I have been very much out of the city. I returned in May. I have called at your house several times, but you were not at home."

His success as a practitioner is only eclipsed by his unexampled philanthropic spirit, which has always been attuned to the mute appeals of distress and want. He believes, in his large-heartedness, that no home is too lowly for him to visit, and no surroundings or circumstances strong enough to prevent him from answering the call of a suffering fellow-being. As an instance, we cite the case of a man at one time prominent as an oarsman, and residing in a village near Albany, who had been attacked with disease. He was the father of a large family of small children, and had worked hard to support them by driving a pedler's wagon, after he had become too emaciated and exhausted to work at his trade as a stove-mounter. He had been attended by an Albany physician as long as he had money. As the disease progressed, he became too weak to follow even the occupation of pedler; and the horse and wagon were sold, and the money expended. The physician had no more interest in the case; and, from that time up to the man's death, he was treated from the Swinburne Dispensary, and visits made as regularly as if he were as rich as the wealthiest. This story was told us at the sick man's bedside a short time before his death.

Perhaps the crowning act of his professional career was the establishment, in 1879, of the dispensary in Albany for the treatment of every form of disease and accident.

Notwithstanding the large amount of work he is doing in the carrying on of the dispensary, and attending to his large private practice, his advice and counsel are being constantly sought by his professional brethren in other parts of the State, as well as in the city of Albany and vicinity. Indeed, one of his assistants declares that if the doctor were to give up every other practice, and attend only the consultations to which he is invited, he would be like a presiding elder of the Methodist Church, — constantly on the move, and seldom at home. Whenever it is possible with him, he either attends, or writes his opinions, in all cases where his skill is called into requisition, without waiting to inquire to what peculiar or particular school of medicine the parties inviting him may belong. He thinks only of suffering humanity and the victims of disease and pain, and never hesitates to inquire whether the old or new or any other school will approve his action, however lightly he may hold in estimation certain methods of treatment. He holds that greater than all professional ethics is the divine injunction "to love thy neighbor as thyself," and to do unto others as he would have them do unto him.

So generally acknowledged is his skill as a physician and surgeon, that even those of his profession who condemn his great benevolence, and envy his success, are compelled to admit his superior scientific abilities. Said a physician from a village in another county recently, "There is not a physician in Albany I can call to consult in a critical case I have. In their anxiety to gain reputations in surgery, they are almost entirely neglecting medicines. They all want to be Swinburnes, but will not succeed either as physicians or surgeons." Another said to the writer, in presence of another physician, that if he had done what Dr. Swinburne had done for science, and had his renown, he would be satisfied with the good he had done, and would kick any man to the capital who would undertake to write his life, as they were doing Swinburne's, believing it was only done for political purposes. This physician, who himself seeks notoriety, and desires to be prominent, it is said on good authority, has frequently called on the doctor for advice, and has taken to himself the credit of performing operations where the generous and unselfish surgeon stood by, and directed every movement as it was made in the operation. The would-be kicking doctor, who is in close fellowship with the political ring whom the doctor has so often vanquished, was pertinently informed there would be no occasion for his kicking, as there was no material to write about in his case such as in that of Dr. Swinburne.

The smiles which Fortune have bestowed upon Dr. Swinburne have been widely radiated upon those who are slighted by the erratic dame. His estimate of wealth is in exact proportion to the amount of good which may be conferred by it upon humanity; and his fine turnout is none too good to be placed at the service of his patients. His large, generous heart and kindly disposition symbolize the flag of his country, and is broad enough to take within it all the oppressed, suffering, and unfortunate of every nation. His pleasant countenance in the sick-room is a greater solace than many of the antidotes administered, while his cheerful smile and social deportment among men radiate a light and cheerfulness that dispel all gloom, and reflect an ease and humor wherever he appears. In himself, he is the true embodiment of that democracy which knows no aristocracy except that of worth or merit.

An ardent lover of justice, and a firm believer in the sovereignty of the people, he proved himself equal to maintain their rights in the contest over the mayoralty vote of Albany in 1882, when Nolan was fraudulently declared to be elected by a majority of 188 votes.

During his entire career, both military and civil, in the discharge of duties professionally, or as a private citizen, or in the administration of public trusts, Dr. Swinburne has maintained that errors winked at always grow upon us; and that it is therefore the duty of every citizen who loves his country, at all times fearlessly to call attention to manifest imperfections and mismanagement or wilful misconduct in the administration of any branch of the government, without regard to whose interests or feelings may be affected by the exposure. He is a stanch adherent to the doctrine that the people should rule, and that, when they do in fact, we will have as a nation attained the *ne plus ultra* that good government will be secured, and the object of a free republic attained. He holds that if the idea once obtains an abiding hold that citizens must wink at or pass silently over demonstrated derelictions, or even indiscretions, in the government or its officials, simply because they are the derelictions or indiscretions of the government or its officers, we surrender at once the right of the people, who are the masters, to hold their servants in office to an accountability for their stewardship. He insists that an honest administration of the government of the state or nation never can be weakened, but, on the contrary, will be strengthened, by a frank exhibition of its defects; and that that public official who is unwilling to have his attention or that of his sovereigns called to errors in his administration is a dishonest man, and will always be an unsafe and unreliable servant of the people.

Some idea of his popularity, and the estimation in which he is held by the voters of the Nineteenth Congressional District, may be formed from the fact that his strength on the Republican ticket reduced Cleveland's majority in Albany County of 9,819 for Governor in 1882, to 626 for President in 1884. He was elected to the Forty-ninth Congress by 2,504 majority, and this in face of the well-known popularity of his opponent, — a revolution of public sentiment within two years that resulted in a change of over 7,000 votes.

Such is a brief sketch of this typical American, so eminent as a physician and surgeon, esteemed by the business-men of his county because of his integrity, honored by the soldiers as their friend, and loved by the poor as their benefactor. Possessing all the firmness, excutive ability, and integrity requisite in the honest and faithful discharge of any public trust, his friends and fellow-citizens believe he would make one of the best governors the State of New York has ever had, and for that office are desirous of seeing him secure the nomination of his party, believing that, if nominated, he will be elected by a greater majority than any other man in the State can command.